SACRIFICE OF SEPTIMUS
PART TWO

BY

STEPHANIE HUDSON

Sacrifice of the Septimus - Part 2
The Afterlife Saga #9
Copyright © 2020 Stephanie Hudson
Published by Hudson Indie Ink
www.hudsonindieink.com

This book is licensed for your personal enjoyment only.
This book may not be re-sold or given away to other people. If you would like to share this book with another person, please purchase an additional copy for each recipient. If you're reading this book and did not purchase it, or it wasn't purchased for your use only, then please return to your favourite book retailer and purchase your own copy. Thank you for respecting the hard work of this author.
All rights reserved.
This is a work of fiction. Names, characters, places, brands, media, and incidents are either the product of the authors imagination or are used fictitiously. The author acknowledges the trademark status and trademark owners of various products referred to in this work of fiction, which have been used without permission. The publication/use of these trademarks is not authorised, associated with, or sponsored by the trademark owners.
Sacrifice of the Septimus - Part 2/Stephanie Hudson – 2nd ed.
ISBN-13 - 978-1-913769-26-0

Dedication

I dedicate this book to my wonderful husband Blake Hudson. When we met it was a journey I faced like no other but it just proves that sometimes love is worth the sacrifice and following your heart is what truly matters, for it will guide you through the storms that life sometimes puts your way…

"You are my Anchor'

Time is a path we weave ourselves through,
Pushing against the waves as stormy winds blew,
The haters, the sinners and all bitterness in between,
Is never enough to crush us, from all there is to be seen.

The love that we can reach with fingers entwined,
Across the waters of life, like ships travelling blind,
But discovery is vast and never far away,
For those who are brave enough to sail into the fray.

So hold out for hope or hold out for the day,
That your love comes looking for you, waiting at the bay,
You stand there alone, waiting with baited breath,
For something to take with you into life and into death.

A memory of one heart, so connected with your soul,
Fusing together two lives and making you whole,
For a life lived without love, is no life lived at all,
And waiting for you on the other side is nothing but the fall.

Cast into darkness with no light to guide,
You through the empty abyss, love lets you decide,
If you travel alone or with a hand held to your heart,
Knowing one day that the two of you must part.

But hoping that through time, you will soon find,
That sweet voice calling to you in the depths of your mind,
For he has found you again, in this life and the next,
Burning his promise against the sands of time and ancient text.

For love conquers all and will stand tall through the test,
It doesn't lie down for others or ever needs the rest,
For love is power and power is gained,
Through the invisible connection, with souls forever chained.

'I will always love you'

xx

WARNING

This book contains explicit sexual content, some graphic language and a highly addictive Alpha Male.

This book has been written by a UK Author with a mad sense of humour. Which means the following story contains a mixture of Northern English slang, dialect, regional colloquialisms and other quirky spellings that have been intentionally included to make the story and dialogue more realistic for modern-day characters.

Please note that for your convenience language translations have been added to optimise the readers enjoyment throughout the story.

Also meaning…

No Googling is required ;)

Also, please remember that this part of a 12 book saga, which means you are in for a long and rocky ride. So, put the kettle on, brew a cup, grab a stash of snacks and enjoy!

Thanks for reading x

PROLOGUE

BEHIND THE BLADE

PREVIOUSLY IN PERSIA...

Once more I found myself awakening but at least this time I had exchanged sand for silk. I opened my eyes feeling the sudden pain at the side of my head as soon as I tried to move it too quickly. I would like to believe all this had been a dream and as before I would find Draven by my side. But from the new smell of a distant land and the pain I was now suffering, I knew that no amount of wishing would make it so. This was when I needed to get my thoughts in order of what had just happened. I thought back and remembered waking in the sand, getting up and then searching for...

"Sophia, Pip and Ari?" I asked in a raspy voice that spoke of my time without water. This was when I moved despite the pain, sitting up and holding myself steady when I rocked to the side.

"I need to find them," I said realising this was the next

mission that lay ahead of me, and finding three people, who might have been separated, in an ancient city I didn't know was going to be like finding a four leaf clover growing in the desert.

I looked around the room, trying to get my bearings on where I was this time. The main thing I noticed was that the room I had been put in wasn't one I recognised from my dreams, so at least could I breathe easier knowing that it didn't belong to a king. It wasn't a large room but it was still decorated comfortably and I had to wonder if this was Ranka's room.

"Ranka." I remembered everything now, the attack and the pain of being struck down. Putting a hand to my ribs, I hissed in pain as I could feel the tender tissue that was no doubt bruised and I had to wonder why I hadn't healed yet? I still held Draven's essence inside of me, knowing from experience that it lasted quite some time even after we had parted. But then again I had travelled back in time, so maybe that's why it hadn't worked…could this also be why I no longer had my powers?

One by one it felt like every advantage I once held had been stripped away leaving me more vulnerable than ever before. I didn't know what I was going to do but I knew waiting here wasn't going to help my situation right now and even if it could, what about the others?

At this point I didn't even know if they had made it through and if they had, what if they had been attacked like me. The thought made me fist the silk cushions underneath me as that worrying thought gripped my heart and wouldn't let go. Well at least I wasn't as alone as I first thought, now having Ranka who was obviously helping me in all this. And speaking of Ranka, I decided it was time I made an attempt to find her.

I looked around the room for any obvious exits and found the only door across one corner. The rest of the room consisted of little more than a cushioned bed, a large wooden chest and numerous bows hung on the walls. I had to say that her weapon choice certainly suited the attire I had last seen her in, and if she hadn't seemed like a bit of a loner, I could have quite easily pictured her with a band of merry men, stealing from the rich and giving to the poor.

Getting up was a challenge and one I attempted a few times before getting it right. I must have taken quite a blow for it to still be causing me problems. I wasn't one for normally getting headaches and if I'd have known none of Draven's essence would have followed me this far then I would have at least slipped a packet of aspirin in my jean's pocket. Actually scrap that because knowing me I would need a whole first aid kit and a course of antibiotics to get me through even two weeks of being here. I mean I had only been in the past for a few hours and already I had lost my friends, been brutally attacked and witnessed six people killed by someone who was undoubtedly in love with my husband. At this point I was afraid to ask if it could get much worse.

I looked down at myself and shook my head.

"We didn't plan this very well," I said to myself and lucky for me no one else was listening. I referred to the fact that I had thought it a great idea to drop into the past nearly two thousand years before my own life and about one thousand and eight hundred and sixty years or so before jeans were even invented. This wasn't one of my finer ideas that was for sure. This had me thinking that if Pip had made it through at least she would be easy to spot considering she had green hair. Saying that, even in my own time, she was easy to spot if not for her hair then certainly for her crazy outfits.

I looked around to see if there was anything useful I could use to conceal the obvious 'time traveller' style I was wearing and thankfully found a cloak of some sorts. It was a rich green colour, which wasn't surprising given this must have been a favourite of Ranka's.

"I hope you don't mind." I said out loud as I spread it out over my shoulders, happy that it hid most of my twenty first century get up. I raised the hood and knew I couldn't put it off any longer...I had to venture into this new world.

I lifted the iron latch and opened the door slowly praying there was no one on the other side keeping guard. Thankfully the hallway was empty and I slipped out of the door, shutting it quietly behind me. I lifted up the hood to hide my face and walked slowly along the hall, hoping not to bump into someone.

For a start I wasn't sure that I would be able to understand them, not knowing if the drink Ranka had given me would only work when speaking to her. If this was the case then that would make chatting Draven up incredibly difficult, especially considering I wasn't exactly a seductress when it came to acting cool or luring people in with my sexy body language. Now if there had been a prize for face planting, snorting and tripping over when trying to get dressed, then I would have nailed it.

The sandstone arches I walked past showed me a view of another world and I could easily believe I was in Egypt, half expecting to see the pyramids through the next arch along. I still hadn't passed a soul and was more than grateful for that but I knew it couldn't last, not when I heard what could have been the cause for such isolation. The sound of exotic singing combined with drums, lured me closer and led me through the passageways as if I was transfixed on the authentic sounds of ancient Persia.

It led me through an elaborate scalloped arch that was painted gold with tiny red flowers. I walked through, pulling my hood down concealing me further from the many people I now saw. I must have walked into some kind of banquet or celebration of sorts because the room below the balcony I now stood on was full of people. It was a sea of vibrant colours of embroidered silks, gold threads and jewels from distant lands that reached the far corners of the globe.

The hall itself was lined with pearl white pillars that were cut from the finest marble, carved into giant vase shapes. The balcony I stood on surrounded three sides of the room and was highly decorated with the same arched scalloped design underneath as it was above where I stood. Lush Persian carpets covered the stone floors on different levels and mosaic patterned walls matched the fountain in the centre of the room where half-naked dancers shook their hips. There looked to be hundreds of people all sat around the edges of the room, drinking from decorated chalices and eating fruits from large serving dishes made of gold.

The music continued to play and there were plenty of exotic beauties to entertain the people. I also took note of all the guards that stood along the walls, all dressed in white and heavily armed. It was as incredible to witness as it was terrifying. I felt like an intruder and I couldn't stop my hands from shaking because of it.

"You can do this Keira, just keep your eyes on that exit." I whispered to myself as I spotted my goal and that was getting out of here as quickly as possible before I got myself into trouble yet again. At the end of the room were two castle sized doors which thankfully were open and if I could just make it through the mass of people then I knew I would be safer out there than in here. I couldn't see what lay beneath me as the part I stood on jutted out further than the rest but if it was who I thought it was, then I wasn't ready for him to see me yet. No, first I needed Sophia, Pip and Ari to help me then if that failed and it turned out they weren't here then I would come back to the palace I was obviously in and find Ranka.

So with this in mind I followed the balcony round and

through another arch before coming across a staircase down to the main floor. I quickly found myself with my back against the wall as a man and woman ran laughing up the stairs, obviously lovers in haste to be reunited once more. They paid no attention to me and just as I stepped down into the lower level some kind of flute and a tambourine started to play, giving the next song a quicker pace so the dancers could shake their hips to a faster rhythm. I thought this would be the perfect opportunity to make my escape as all eyes were on them, so I walked quickly, stepping around all the servants and guests scattered everywhere. Some were sat and others stood around in groups chatting and laughing. Some smoked great long pipes and passed these along to their fellow men…and this was when the next lot of trouble began.

I was trying not to look at the front, I really was but because I knew he would be there I lost the battle with my mind to my heart. Just one look would be enough and it was just this one look where it all went wrong. For there he now sat, as magnificent and glorious as I knew he would be and just as terrifying as I knew he could be.

"My husband." The uttered whisper escaped before I could control it. And for that small second in time he looked up and found me, frozen in the mass of people all moving around me. He sat upon a mighty throne of gold and there above his head was a cruder symbol of my birthmark, carved from stone. But these were the only details I could absorb as the man himself was a stronger harsher version of Draven, who held a raw beauty I was scared to look at for too long. So I tore my hooded face from his and turned so quickly that I ended up pushing into someone by accident.

"I am sorry it was an…"

"Little fool, you dare to push a Royal Satrap!" The man said, enraged that I had spilt his drink, grabbing me by the throat and squeezing hard. I struggled to breathe for a second and just before I passed out he let go. I gasped for air and if I'd hoped not to draw attention to myself then I had certainly failed. The music had stopped and a small crowd had gathered to watch the unfolding drama.

Meanwhile my anger was getting the better of me and when he slapped my face and said,

"Now be gone with you, you ugly little whore!" I officially lost it.

"Hey dickhead, you forgot something." I said patting him on the shoulder and when he turned back around to face me and said,

"What!" I let my fist fly the way Draven had taught me and punched him square in the nose. The gasps of horror around me and the silence that followed could have cut the room in half. Everyone took quick steps away from me and it took me a moment too late to realise it wasn't from me, it was from their King. I spun round and everything seemed to happen in slow motion. Draven was no longer seated at his throne but instead was walking straight towards me as his subjects parted for him, falling to their knees and lowering their bodies to the ground.

I didn't know what to do, whether to run or to follow them to the ground and join in worshipping him. The look on his face told me to run but the speed in which he reached me gave me no time to do either and in that moment I knew this had all been a mistake. This man didn't love me. This man didn't adore me or be willing to risk his life for me. For this man, this Draven...

Didn't know me.

So if you could choose how you would die which would it be? Would it be a quiet and peaceful death surrounded by those who love you, whereby you simply slipped into an everlasting slumber? Or would you go out basking in a blaze of glory and forging your name in history for all of those who love you to remember?

Or…

Would it be by the hand of the man you loved. Would it be by the blade he quickly held against your throat. Because this was no longer a fairy tale of love and honour.

That story had come to an end.

And what if you *couldn't* change that ending? What if it was the person you never thought possible who held control of it all in the palm of his hand? The one you would have risked everything you ever cared about to prove time wrong. What if the knife that was threatened against your throat was being held by a hand you knew…by a hand belonging to a man you loved?

No, when I thought about my own death I never saw what faced me now. If I could have been ruler of my own fate then my death would have been in sacrifice to save the other half of my soul. It would have been so that the man I loved would live because of my death. So many times before I felt myself die without actually leaving this earth and every time I spoke the name of who I lived for the most.

But now… well now I spoke his name to save my life. Because he held my life in his hands and as the blade dug deeper into my fragile flesh, one already bruised and beaten, I knew the horrifying truth…

Love couldn't save me now. It was all for nothing. My sacrifice wasn't my happy ending it was my lost beginning. I could see that now as clearly as I could see my fear reflected in the cold metal that collected my tears. So did I see myself dying of a broken heart and soul along with a broken body…no, that was never supposed to be my sacrifice. That wasn't written in the fates or seen by any God, which could only mean one thing…

I wasn't *his* Chosen One after all.

So as the tears started to fall for a new reason other than fear, I looked into the deep dark eyes of the man I loved and pleaded for my life…one…last…time,

"Please Arsaces, King of Kings…

"Don't kill me."

CHAPTER ONE

MISTAKES

Visions of your own death can make a person cower in fear or want to stand tall and face the end with brave dignity. But what of the middle ground? What if you shook with fear and cried tears of hurt, but also straightened your back and held your head high, just so that the man you loved could see the pain he inflicted not only upon your body but also upon your *soul*. What if you wanted him to look deep into your eyes just as the knife he held to your throat took your life and have him remember just how deep the blade actually went.

But what if it was all for nothing because in actual fact the man in front of you didn't even know who you were? What then? Would you beg for a love that you had to convince someone to feel? It's strange how many questions can riddle your brain in the seconds before your death and in reality what a waste of time it really was.

So I wasn't *his* Chosen One after all and even though tears wouldn't help me now, they came anyway. I looked into the deep dark eyes of the man I loved and asked him to spare my life, a life he didn't yet know would change his…

Forever.

"Please Arsaces, King of Kings…*Don't kill me.*" In that moment time really did stand still for me and I couldn't tell if it was on my side or not. Nothing moved around us and once more in my life it was as if we were the only two people in the room. His hand didn't move one centimetre, meaning neither did the blade move away from my tender flesh but his other hand raised up so slowly, I would have laughed thinking it was because he didn't want to startle me…obviously though I swallowed the insane urge to do so.

I held my breath the closer his other hand got to my face, too scared to move from fear of this seemingly gentle gesture turning into the opposite and lashing out against me. Thankfully for me it remained as I hoped as he gently pushed back the hood that was keeping me concealed from him. I wished in that moment for nothing more than to find the man I loved staring back at me but his eyes held only curiosity and nothing more. It was heart-breaking and I swallowed hard, momentarily forgetting about the blade. He watched the motion, eyes focussed on my neck and I let myself hope for mercy when he pulled the blade back ever so slightly. Surely if the man holding the blade to your throat was concerned about cutting you as you swallowed heavily, then did that mean I had something to hope for?

I was surprised that he hadn't yet spoken but simply continued to stare as if we didn't have over a hundred people all watching us. No, instead he gripped my chin and moved my face up and down, then from side to side as if examining every inch, all the time keeping the blade there as if ready to strike out at any minute.

"What is your name, girl?" Finally, he spoke and I couldn't

help but jump a little hearing his voice for the first time as it scared me. It was like my Draven but then again it wasn't. Almost as if his voice seemed older, which was of course the opposite to what it should have been considering I was currently thousands of years in the past. But the deeper rasp and harshness to his voice sounded as though it came from many more years of being a ruler than the Draven I was used to.

I watched as a pair of lips framed by a black beard tilted up in a slight smirk and it was as if he was amused that he had frightened me. It was only when he raised one eyebrow that I knew he was still waiting for his answer…one I didn't have for him.

"What does it matter what a scurrying rat is called as it sneaks through the alley, it is a rodent that needs to be punished!" The man who I had bumped into shouted as his rage bubbled over. For the first time since holding me hostage Draven's eyes left mine and looked over my head to the angry man. Now if I thought the look he had given me was harsh then it had nothing on the cold calculating look he was now giving to this man, who I guessed would also soon know what it feels like to have a blade against his throat.

"Correct me if I am wrong, for it rarely happens, but have I been sitting in your throne all these years, for I was under the impression you were a loyal Satrap serving the King of Kings… is this not so?" Draven said with confidence and it was as striking as it was mocking, but all the while still managing to maintain his commanding tone. I didn't actually know how he accomplished it to be honest but either way, it was something to behold.

The rest of the room also seemed to hold their breath, waiting to see how this would play out just as I was. However, the man in question blustered around with his words trying for an answer, but in the end he couldn't keep his King waiting any longer.

"You are...are not...wro... wrong my King."

"No, as I said, I rarely am. But just to be sure, once more correct me but last I checked, your name was Narseh...*not Arsaces!*" Draven roared these last two words, driving his dangerous point home. The man suddenly dropped to his knees like the rest of the room and cowed beneath him without Draven having to move a threatening muscle towards him.

"Yes my King, forgive my insolence," he pleaded, with his face to the floor and I half wondered if it would've been better had I done the same when begging for my own life.

"And do you wish for such insolence to go solely unpunished?" Draven asked of him and the man nodded his head frantically stating a definite 'yes', still keeping his eyes to the floor. It was obvious to me that he feared his king's wrath enough to want to beg not to receive it.

"And are you yourself willing to extend the same forgiveness to an act against you that was equally as insolent as the disrespect you showed your King?" Hearing this I sucked in a sharp breath and once more, he moved his blade slightly further back to allow for my movements and in doing so saving my skin from being sliced.

"I do, my King," he quickly said raising his eyes to Draven's for the first time and knowing that the only way to save his own skin was to also save mine.

"Then perhaps I am in a forgiving mood, as are you, Narseh." Draven said and as soon as he was obviously finished with the man his eyes looked back to mine. Then as quickly as he had put it there he removed the blade from my neck and I could finally breathe freely for the first time in a small eternity.

"You may all rise," he commanded the room before looking to me and then nodding to the man named Narseh behind me.

At first I had no clue what he was trying to tell me or wanted me to do, so with the weapon now once more tucked safely away in its sheath, I braved to ask,

"Umm…I'm sorry my Lord, but I don't know what you want me to do?" I whispered leaning forward a little and feeling braver than before. It quickly became apparent that this was something else I had done that amused him as that handsome smirk was back before he leaned his head down to my short height and whispered back,

"Time to apologise, my little damaged lamb." The sound of his velvet sweet voice was enough to make me remember that this was *my Draven* I was speaking to, even if he himself didn't know it yet. It was enough to ignite that tiny spark of hope within me and fan the flames of my reasons for being here. So my response was my most natural yet as I couldn't help but bite my bottom lip as I always did when hearing that seductive tone in his voice. His eyes quickly became captivated by the sight and it was only when I finally let his actual words sink in that I broke the spell for both of us.

"Oh right, yes, yes…of course…uh Nar…uh…"

"Narseh." Draven whispered behind me as I had turned to face the man who had been the cause of this whole fiasco. He was trying to help me say his name and I quickly repeated it before I forgot once more how to say it.

"Narseh, I am sorry for my actions, please forgive me." I said in a rush and trying to ignore the look of utter disdain that he was giving me in return. I had, of course, felt like adding 'but if you weren't such a dick to me then I would never have tried to break your nose', but thought better of it.

"All is forgiven," he said through gritted teeth and then quickly added,

"Now if you will allow me to take my leave my King, I believe my taste for the festivities is somewhat bitter now." I looked back to Draven who nodded without saying another word and did so without even looking at him. Perhaps because he was too busy looking at me which in turn was making me blush a healthy rose colour.

"Now as I trust I will not be interrupted again you can answer my first question," he said and for a dumbstruck moment I had to think about what that question was.

"Your name, little lamb," he said reminding me softly. I almost asked why he kept calling me that but in the end decided to accept it as the unfortunate nickname he had obviously chosen to call me.

"I'm sorry but I can't remember." I blurted out thinking this was the best course of action. Although when he crossed his massive arms over his chest and raised a disbelieving eyebrow at me, I wasn't so sure.

"You can't remember your own name? Do I have that right?" he asked unconvinced. I nodded not trusting myself to speak.

"I am not satisfied with that answer. Guards take her to my chamber where she will be questioned further," he said motioning them forward with a simple hand gesture. In my mind I was in full blown panic mode as I had no idea what being 'questioned further' actually meant and suddenly explicit thoughts bombarded my mind of what happened in my dreams the last time I was in his bedchamber. I knew this thought shouldn't have bothered me as after all it was why I was here, but it was as if something was telling me not to do this. Almost as if the time wasn't right.

"I uh…well I am not sure…" I was just about to try and worm my way out of it when suddenly a voice spoke up for me and at that moment it was one I couldn't have been more thankful to hear.

"My Lord, forgive me for intruding."

"What is it, Ranka?" Draven said looking to the side over his shoulder at her as she approached from in between the people in her way. Once they saw who it was trying to pass through, the people quickly started to move out of her way, letting me know that they probably knew what she could do with a bow in her hand.

"I came to tell you that what she says is true." This obviously surprised him as much as it did me, thankfully though it was his reaction I witnessed not the other way around as he had turned fully to face Ranka, missing my mouth dropping open.

"Explain!" he ordered sternly after making a head gesture to his guards which obviously meant 'at ease' or something. And he did all this without unfolding his arms, easily showing his displeasure.

"I found her on my hunt, my Lord. She couldn't tell me her name or where she had come from before she lost consciousness." Draven looked back to me and raised a hand slowly to my face once more but this time, he gently ran the back of his fingers down my heated face, one that still burned from being hit by the bastard who had attacked me in the desert.

"And this?" he asked in a hard tone of displeasure. In that moment I had to force myself to hold his gaze because all I wanted to do was look away, feeling ashamed of what he must now see when he looked at me. Now I knew why he had called me 'damaged' earlier.

"I found her being attacked by men of the West. They were about to take her unwillingly before she fought back the best she could," Ranka said and for a small moment Draven looked over me as if surprised that someone of my size would try and fight back. Was that a small glimmer of respect I saw in his eyes?

"And what of them now?"

"They answered for their crimes, my Lord," Ranka replied bowing her head.

"Good, see that their heads are mounted at the gates for all to see what happens to those who commit crimes against our people on my lands." Ranka nodded again in respect and said,

"My Lord," as a way of answer. Meanwhile I shivered at the thought of such a brutal statement being made, thinking, 'well I definitely wasn't in Kansas anymore'.

"So you believe our little lamb here can't remember who she is?" Draven asked Ranka but still looking at me and again making me blush because of it. Jesus, but was there a time in history where Draven wasn't this intimidating?! Maybe in the 60's when everyone was smoking weed and all about the flower power. But even then, I couldn't picture Draven at the time wearing bell bottom trousers and loud shirts with big pointed collars. If anything, the thought was just funny. Thankfully for me in that moment the next sentence from Ranka was sobering enough not to laugh at the thought of Draven as a hippy.

"She received a few heavy blows from her attacker my Lord, which if the Elder theories are true, may account for her memory loss." Thank the Gods for Ranka, that's all I could say right then…well, obviously not out loud.

"So I can see," Draven said, once more taking my chin in between his finger and thumb and turning my head to the side to get a better sight of my injuries.

"Your personal thoughts?" Draven asked and I couldn't help but dart my eyes sideways looking to see if we still had an audience like before. I was amazed to find that everyone seemed to be purposely looking anywhere but at their King and, sampling his temper for myself, I couldn't say that I blamed them.

"I think that it is possible she may have been a slave transported here to sell for the pleasure house when the attack occurred." I had to stop myself from wrinkling up my nose in disgust at the thought of being both a slave and being forced into prostitution.

"Were there other victims?" he asked, continuing on the conversation as if I wasn't even there, but I guessed in this time most women were seen and not heard. Well he will most certainly be in for a shock when he gets to the 21st century, that was for damn sure!

"No, my Lord," Ranka said honestly.

"Then the question remains, has our little lamb here run from her flock or is she merely lost from them?" This question was one I think was directed at me as he was staring straight at me when he said it. I decided the best course of action was to remain on the lost memory path as it seemed to be working for me so far.

"I don't remember." It was only when he raised a questioning brow at me and then quickly to Ranka that I realised my mistake. Thankfully she came through again for me and mouthed the words 'My King' giving me the prompt I needed.

*"Oh, right...*My King." Okay so it wasn't my best performance but it was obviously keeping him amused, which was far better than angry. I got the impression that if in that moment Ranka could have gotten away with smacking her forehead in frustration then she would have.

"I doubt she has ever been granted the honour of such an occasion as to address a King, my Lord." Ranka said, trying to make excuses for me.

"I don't know what I find more curious Ranka, this pale uncultured creature before me or the fact that you wish to defend and protect her," Draven said obviously pulling her up on what must seem to him unusual behaviour.

"I saved her life by taking the life of others, I merely do not wish for it to be done in vain, my Lord." Oh but this was a great answer and I could tell that it was also enough to satisfy Draven's curiosity. He was about to answer her when a quiet gentle voice interrupted.

"My King?" A servant said who approached Draven with their head bowed and kept to the floor in deepest respect.

"What is it?" Draven demanded in a harsh tone as if he did not appreciate being disturbed at this time.

"My King, Stateira wishes to know if you request her presence in your chamber tonight?" As soon as she had finished this sentence my heart plummeted and if I thought the fear of death had been bad, then it was nothing to having the hand of the man you loved unknowingly tear out your heart, forget about slitting your throat.

Draven's eyes hardened for a few seconds and it was the first time I noticed that I hadn't yet seen the flash of purple that was so often to be seen when Draven's emotions came into play. He obviously thought of me the same as any other human and hid that side of him because of it. The thought was more than a little depressing.

"Very well then, I entrust her future into your care and leave it in your hands as to what is to become of her," he said to Ranka, as if only now making up his mind because of this sudden disturbance. He turned his back on me and I couldn't help but let my eyes drop to the floor to hide my misery.

"As for you…" then his voice startled me as I was sure he had left already but instead he came back over to face me and leaned in until we were merely inches apart. I held my breath and in that moment his grin told me that he knew how his presence affected me.

"…I suggest you try and stay out of trouble little lamb, for Ranka might not be around to save you next time." I wasn't sure if this was said out of concern or as a threat but either way my reaction was the same...I shivered and not because I was cold. He looked at me a second longer, silently capturing my gaze and then he turned his back to me once more, allowing me to breathe freely again.

"Oh and Ranka, she doesn't leave the palace... *understand?*" he said as he was passing her, stopping long enough to issue the command.

"Yes, my Lord," she answered lowering her head to her king just as the servant had. It made me realise just how shit I was at all this ancient tradition and royal culture crap, so it was no wonder I could finally let my shoulders drop once he had walked away. I couldn't remember the last time I had been so tense being this close to Draven as years ago it would have a been a regular occurrence. Which had me wondering if this wasn't part of our destiny? Was it written somewhere that no matter what time in history we found ourselves in that we were destined to meet in these intense ways, ways that seemed powerful enough to carve our very existence into the Earth itself.

Or maybe deep down I was always going to be intimidated by Draven and that was what would always attract me to him. Which made me wonder, what was it about me that drew *him* in?

"Come with me." Ranka's stern voice brought me out of my thoughts and plunged me straight into new, darker ones.

"Who is Stateira?" I asked knowing that I wouldn't forget that name, not considering I now had something to call my new heartbreak.

"Not here!" Ranka hissed as she grabbed my arm and dragged me back the way I had come. I ignored the looks and gossiping whispers I received from everyone we passed as it was obvious they were probably wondering why their King

hadn't killed me. To be honest I was half wondering that myself.

"Are you trying to get yourself killed again?!" Ranka shouted once we had finally made it back to the room I had woken in.

"Obviously not...Gods I am melting." I said before wrestling with the material I had taken from her room, only hoping I didn't smell as bad as I thought I did.

"You never should have left this room," she said scorning me again.

"Yeah, I kind of get that now."

"Good," she snapped back as if losing her patience and I was starting to think that I preferred the Ranka from my time.

"Look, it's great that you saved me out in the desert and had my back down there..."

"Had your back? I didn't touch your back," she said, making it clear that I was going to have to use some common sense in this time, because they were about two thousand years behind with the lingo I was used to.

"No I didn't mean...oh never mind, look I am just saying thanks for getting me out of trouble back there with Drav...I mean the King but I have to go." It didn't take me long to interpret her rapid head shaking and eyes of disbelief to know I was screwed.

"That is not possible."

"Why?" I asked folding my arms across my chest and adding,

"Because the King said so?"

"Precisely for that reason," she said crossing her own arms over her chest.

"But how would he even know? He made it perfectly clear to me that I am in your hands and he cares little for what happens to me." I told her trying to keep the hurt of that statement from my voice. One look told me I wasn't fooling anyone, especially not myself.

"You do not know the King as I do." Okay so that statement hurt. I wanted to beg to differ and say, 'Uh, well I am actually his wife, so I think I win that round' but instead I remained quiet because the painful truth was that she was right...*I didn't know this Draven at all.*

"So what, when he says he will leave it in your hands as to what is to become of me, he means what exactly...?" I asked sarcastically.

"He means protect you and don't let you out of my sight," she said shocking me.

"What?!"

"You do not yet understand our ways and even though I know not of your time, I do know mine...*very well,*" she said emphasizing this last part so that I would hopefully understand.

"Alright, point made. So tell me, what exactly did he mean?" I couldn't help but ask feeling once again that spark of hope ignite. I suppose it wasn't all that surprising that I would naturally seek out the attention from any version of Draven, no matter what time period he was from.

"Being King means keeping your enemies close but in doing so you put those you care for at risk." I couldn't help but snort out a humourless laugh before saying,

"Well if you would have turned up about three minutes before then you would be singing a very different tune."

"I do not sing," Ranka stated in a serious voice making me want to groan out loud.

"What I mean is, he didn't look as if he cared when he was holding a blade to my throat," I said trying to make my point. She walked straight up to me and grabbed my head back roughly so she could examine my neck.

"Alright Miss Grabby, you can let go now...Jeez, talk about

heavy handed much," I muttered to myself after pulling myself free from her manhandling.

"I do not see a mark," she told me frowning and I automatically put a hand to my neck as if remembering how the blade felt there.

"And your point?"

"If he wanted to harm you he would have done so." At this point I was close to giving her a salute and thanking my very own Miss Captain Obvious. My look must have said it all, which I was glad, as I was getting tired of asking her to state what she clearly thought was the obvious.

"I was there watching it all and what I saw was my King being the ruler he is respected for. You struck one of his Satrap and this offense is punishable by death. By acting the way he did, he not only preserved his authority and respect, but he did it in a way where he could also save your life." The Keira part of me really wanted to ask what a Satrap was but thankfully the logical part of me shone through and instead I thought more about what she was telling me.

"So you're saying that he was never going to kill me?" I asked needing to be perfectly clear.

"You are his Chosen One, are you not?" I looked away as she asked me this question and walked over to her bed before dumping myself onto it and releasing a big sigh. I didn't know how to answer that anymore. Half of me wanted to stand up and say, yes I am his Chosen One and always will be. But the unsure, insecure part of me was scared to say yes, especially when faced with a Draven I didn't even know whether he was trying to kill me or not. No, it didn't exactly look good for me right now.

"I am out of my depth here…do you understand what I am saying?"

"The King is different in your time?" she asked and I couldn't help my response,

"Yeah," I said on a laugh and then reiterated my answer,

"He is very different."

"Ah I understand…he frightens you?" she said coming to sit next to me on her bed and I gathered this was the only way in which she knew how to give comfort.

"He does," I admitted feeling both shameful and relieved that at least I had someone to talk to. But as helpful and as lifesaving as Ranka had been, I knew it wasn't enough to get me through this. I needed to find my friends wherever they may be and get this done before our time here ran out.

"Which is why I need to find my friends. They came on this journey with me not knowing what would happen to them but they took that leap of faith with me and I can't repay that loyalty by ignoring what could have happened to them." I told her and felt a shred of hope when she started looking thoughtfully towards the door as though thinking about what their next course of action should be.

"I am not promising that I will be able to find them and if I try then it will only be when you are in his harem getting ready to be with the King."

"Uh…I will be what now?" I said letting my mouth drop at the thought on hearing the dreaded word 'Harem'.

"Why else is it you think the King doesn't want you to leave the palace?" Ranka asked me with the slightest hint of a smile touching her lips.

"Uh…to protect me?" I said in that hopeful tone only reserved for times like this. Ranka shook her head and this time smiled before she dropped the final bombshell on me using just one word beginning with C…

"To be his Concubine."

CHAPTER TWO

THE VERY LAST PLACE

"So let me get this straight, the King has a harem full of concubines?" I asked knowing I would most likely end up choking on the answer.

"Yes of course, as many have before he became King…why does this bother you, this doesn't happen in your time?" Ranka asked genuinely interested.

"No, most certainly not!" I said crossing my arms and making Ranka smirk at my behaviour.

"I see things must be very strange for you in this time… yes?" On hearing her ask me this I let my shoulders slump and sighed.

"They are strange and I am scared because I think I am in way over my head," I said looking sideways to her and one look told me she didn't understand the term.

"I don't know if I can do what I was sent here to do," I said explaining what I meant and she nodded letting me know she now understood.

"And I gather that the King doesn't know that I am his

Chosen One then?" I asked in a deflated tone as I already knew the answer.

"I think if he did you would already be in his bed," Ranka said bluntly. I thought about that and quickly realised how hurt I felt to know that Draven and I were in this world together and in his eyes I was just like the rest...*I wasn't special to him.*

I quickly swiped at the tears that were falling and rubbed them away on my jeans.

"Although I do not understand why he doesn't know," she pondered and I did the same.

"He thinks I am just like any other human," I said looking at my lap, this time seeing the tears fall on the denim.

"But you know that you are not."

"Yes, but that means nothing if he doesn't know it too. I think if I am honest I expected him to take one look at me and just know that I'm the one destined for him," I said opening up to the one I once thought would have been the last person I would have confessed to.

"A journey worth taking is never an easy journey to take," Ranka said patting my leg in comfort. I took a deep breath, straightened my back and said,

"You're right. I am not going to accomplish anything just sat here feeling sorry for myself." I stood up and turned back around to face Ranka and asked,

"Right, so what's our plan?"

"Our plan?" she said repeating what I said with a clear look of confusion across her face.

"Okay, so I guess that means we don't yet have a plan."

"The only plan is for me to do as my King asks of me and that will shortly be escorting you to his harem," she said making me wince at the thought of it.

"We don't know that and besides, he was the one who told

you that it was left up to you what becomes of me." Ranka started shaking her head and quickly informed me,

"That's maybe what he said but not what he was saying." I cocked my head to the side and gave her a 'please explain' look.

"What he said in a crowded room was for the benefit of prying eyes and ears seeking tall royal tales to tell." So that explained why he was quite happy letting our meeting play out surrounded by a banquet hall full of people.

"So he doesn't want people knowing he has a new girl all ready and waiting next in line for his bed!" I snapped getting angry at the thought. Of course this was when she delivered the next big blow and what would most likely be a huge flaw in my time travelling plan.

"The King doesn't bed humans, but this you must already know."

"Oh shit," I said and almost laughed when Ranka took a step away from me as if worried I had literally soiled myself.

"We use the word to express ourselves," I told her and the relief was clear to see as she regained her position beside me once more, obviously now knowing it was safe to do so.

I couldn't believe how I could have forgotten that. I mean, on one hand it was great news for me, knowing that he had a room full of beauties at his beck and call, only to know they never actually received that call. But this got me thinking...how did he get away with that exactly, did they all just think he was secretly gay?

"So how does it all work exactly, I mean they must wonder why none of them ever get picked for a romp in the sack with their King?"

"Sex," I said after getting used to what her frown was telling me.

"Many of them get picked and very frequently in fact." My

response to this was to actually growl and to storm around the room like a teenager.

"What?!"

"I think you need to calm yourself, it is not as you think."

"Oh no, how so? Because from what you just told me my husband has a harem of beauties keeping him busy every night!" I knew I was being irrational but that didn't mean I was going to be adult enough to forgo the extreme jealousy that was burning in my veins.

"Well in this time he is King of Persia and you are not his Queen, so you have little say in the matter."

"Gee thanks, rub it in why don't you," I muttered ignoring her when she rolled her eyes at me.

"So how does it work then? I mean, he's not allowed to touch them so…"

"He can touch them, that is not forbidden, only entering them is." Why, when I kept praying that this would get better, did it only seem to be getting worse! I stopped my angry pacing and swapped it for hopeless dumbstruck silence.

"Please try and remember the world you now live in. He doesn't know who you are to him and he still not only has needs as a man, but also has a reputation as a King of our time to uphold. It is a man's world and women are here to serve them, it has always been the way of the human world, a world the King is very much a part of," she said softly trying to get me to see sense and as much as I hated to admit it, it was working. I knew what she was saying was true and I couldn't just stroll into this world and think the way I always have done.

Equal rights were thousands of years away from seeing the light of day and Draven was simply acting as a King was expected to act. I couldn't exactly blame him for that and I needed to get over my hang up with it pretty quickly if I was going to get what I had come here to do in the first place. Which begged the question, if he didn't know who I was then how would I ever get him to break the rules and sleep with a human?

"At least tell me that he isn't married." I forced myself to ask, bracing myself for the answer.

"He is not." I could tell that even Ranka was happy to be able to tell me the first bit of good news I had heard.

"Oh thank the Gods!" I said letting myself crumble to the floor in relief.

"You truly love him don't you?" she surprised me by asking and I raised my head from my knees to look at her.

"What do you think?" I said letting my flowing tears answer her question.

"Then, as long as it does not cause harm to my King, I will vow to help you in any way that I am able."

"Thank you, Ranka." And I was truly thankful for her right now for I didn't know where I would have ended up if she hadn't found me. The thought was chilling and one I was more than happy to shake off, sending it away to the forgotten mountain part of my mind.

"Okay, so there is one more thing I need to know," I said once again wiping away the Draven tears.

"Ask it of me."

"How did you even know about me?" But even as I asked the question the answer came to me and we both said her name at the same time...

"Pythia."

"Pythia...of course." Ranka's eyes widened hearing the same name coming from my lips along with her own.

"You know of the Oracle of Delphi?"

"Who do you think sent me on this quest?" I told her and suddenly Ranka was on her knees bowing to me as if I'd just told her I was now her Goddess and she should be worshipping me.

"Uhhh Ranka...what are you doing?" I asked hoping she would get up off the floor any second now. But then there was a knock on the door before someone barged in and I panicked not knowing what to do. I dropped to the floor and pretended to be looking for something, hoping that whoever just entered would think that this was what Ranka was doing also.

"Ranka, the King sent me."

"Ah ha, here it is!" I shouted pretending to pick something up and giving Ranka a look of urgency, telling her that we still had a role to play here. Thankfully she took the hint and got to her feet, a lot swifter than I did I might say. Well in my defence I was still injured.

"Is this the slave girl?" The large round woman asked and jingled when she moved thanks to having half her arms covered in bangles. Ranka placed herself between me and the scary woman, making the woman's beady eyes bulge.

"This is the Chosen..." I coughed reminding her not to slip up and she paused looking back at me before carrying on,

"...Chosen girl to be the King's new concubine." Ranka corrected and the big woman rolled her eyes and went to go around Ranka to get to me when Ranka stopped her. Her hand shot out and gripped onto the woman's arm and I could see the pressure she applied, one that made the woman wince.

"She is a favourite of the King's and he has expressed to me the importance of her safety Parmida, so I suggest you do not let him down and displease him, for he put her in my care for a reason." Now this definitely got her attention. Those little eyes stayed wide this time as she took in the sight of me.

"I understand," she said in a way that I didn't doubt it for a second as I think everyone under Draven's rule knew what it meant to piss him off.

"Now let me see what I have to work with," she said once Ranka deemed it safe for her to pass. I had to admit, it was quite nice having someone to stand up for you when the occasion asked for it.

"But her hair?" the woman said confusing me. Okay so I knew I must have been a mess but was it really that bad? I raised a hand up and one feel of the knotted mess pretty much answered that question for me. Ranka gave a little shake of her head and the woman moved swiftly on to the next question.

"What is your name, girl?" She snapped out the question obviously thinking that Ranka's warning only went as far as keeping my body safe and ready for a night with the King, but she obviously didn't give a shit about my mind.

"She doesn't remember who she is so the King has decided to name her when he sees fit. Until then he calls her his Little Lamb." Oh great, thanks Ranka, just what I wanted, to take that animal nickname with me for the rest of this bonkers trip!

"Very well. I see she has injuries, are these just on her face or extended to the body as well, as the healing time will only add to the year." I screwed up my face in confusion. What was this woman talking about? Ranka must have recognised what I was thinking because she said,

"Getting a concubine ready for the King usually takes a year in preparation." I almost choked on my own tongue hearing this.

"A year!?" I shouted at which I received a dirty look from Miss Persian Piggy who stood next to me, snorting her disbelief, from what I could only assume was my behaviour, but screw that! A bloody year getting ready to see Draven, jeez what was I going to be doing, re-growing new skin after they scrubbed me raw!

"Allow time for her to heal but nothing else, Parmida," Ranka said ignoring my outburst. The woman she called

Parmida puffed up her red blotchy face as if she would soon run out of air and pass out.

"That is not possible! What of skin conditions or fungi, they take six months to heal!?" After hearing this it was my turn to look flabbergasted.

"Little Lamb, do you have any skin problems or fungi growing?" Ranka turned to me and asked. I choked on a snorted laugh and said,

"No! No I most certainly do not!" Then I folded my arms letting them both know how insulted I was by the idea.

"Well, that is something at least," the woman scoffed.

"I mean what I say odalik, the King will not wait for this one." Ranka's last warning was enough to make the woman take this seriously and I could only hope that it meant I wouldn't be 'beautified' for long.

"Good, I will escort you both down," Ranka said.

"That won't be necessary, I can take it..." Ranka's hand came up telling Parmida with one motion to stop talking, clearly making Ranka the one in charge here.

"*I* deem it necessary, as did the King when he declared *me* her protector and as you know, I do not ever fail in doing my King's will." I don't know how the woman took Ranka's words of warning but at a guess, I would say as seriously as a heart attack considering how much she had suddenly paled.

"Very well," Parmida forced herself to say and quickly moved to the door. Ranka looked back to me for a moment and then around the room as if looking for something. Then she found the garment I had discarded as soon as I had entered the room and walked over to pick it back up.

"You'd better put this back on." I frowned but refrained from telling her it was like being dressed for an Arctic expedition when in Florida, because for one Florida didn't even exist yet and wouldn't for quite some time and second, I very much doubted Ranka had ever seen snow in the desert! So in the end I did what I was told and pulled up the hood like a Jedi before following her out of the room.

We walked through long hallways with scalloped arches and down painted tiled steps until reaching the lower levels of the Palace. The woman named Parmida seemed to be leading us deep below the foundations of the palace until soon it was an endless row of pillar after pillar, reminding me of the Duomo cathedral in Milan. I couldn't help but smile thinking back to being on its rooftop with Draven's arms around me as we gazed at the beautiful city around us. Of course, just one look at the narrow stone walkways that were raised above the underground lake and the surrounding crystal blue water that looked as if it had been filtered it was so clean and I knew it was like nothing I had ever seen before.

"This place is incredible," I muttered as I took a moment to turn and look back at its architectural splendour.

"Come along little lamb, much work to be done!" Parmida said clicking her fingers over her head and Ranka and I exchanged the same look with each other. I don't know about her thoughts but mine were 'which one of us is going to slap her first?'.

In the end neither of us did such a thing but instead we continued to follow her along the marble walkway and to the huge double doors at the end which looked big enough to fit Ragnar carrying Sigurd on his shoulders through without needing to duck. The thought actually made me chuckle and the sound echoed through the massive space making me cover my mouth quickly.

"What? I giggle when I'm nervous," I told Ranka who shot me a disapproving look. Then I just shrugged my shoulders and continued on, wondering if we were going to get to the Emerald city before my Dorothy legs gave up on me. It was true that I wasn't looking forward to this but more a case of being anxious in getting it over with, which was good because when we finally arrived at the massive doors I was more than ready to walk through them.

Two guards opened the doors and the sight of pure opulence and beauty was everywhere to be seen and not just in the women.

"Come, come now!" Parmida shouted, clapping her hands as she walked in first and some of the girls who were lounging around hurried away from her. I took this as a sign that this woman most likely had a heavy hand when it came to preparing her girls, which didn't look good for me.

The next thing I knew servants wearing grey tunics hurried towards her and she quickly started barking orders at them. I decided to take this opportunity to check the place out, so I let my eyes wander around the room. In doing so I quickly established that there was a definite divide between the girls. On one side there were those who were definitely shy and timid and I wondered if these girls hadn't been here as long as the others. Because on the other side, lounging on luxurious cushions and relaxing by the side of the huge pool in the centre of the room were those who looked as though this was home to them.

The room was massive, which wasn't surprising given the height of the doors we had just walked through. It was split up on different levels, some with seating areas sunken into the ground but all of them surrounded the luxurious circular pool at the centre. Extravagant furnishings decorated the room along with painted panels on the walls depicting exotic views of distant lands. And positioned throughout all of this sensuous setting were half naked beauties from all around the world. I could see every ethnicity I could think of and I had to wonder where they had all come from.

"What do you mean he doesn't wish to see me?" Suddenly a shrieking voice cut through the peaceful room and what quickly followed was the sound of a large gold dish hitting the stone floor after some angry brunette had slapped one of the servants across the face.

"You must be wrong, go and ask again!" she shouted down at the poor girl who was now picking up the scattered fruit.

"Yes, Stateira," she said bowing her head over and over. I hated bullies with a vengeance and as a result was fighting with myself not to go over there and see how she liked being smacked to the floor.

"Idiot! I am surrounded by idiots!" she started ranting to one of the other girls next to her who looked as though she had a bad case of fangirl going on. She obviously had a thing for bitches, clearly.

"And what do we have here, another crow to squawk at the King, in hopes that he will notice her?" she said looking over at me laughing and I wanted to walk over there and start pecking her eyes out, showing just how crow like I could be!

"And what do we have over there, another power bitch wannabe Queen?" I said looking sideways to Ranka. The look of outrage on Stateira's face made me smile and I felt Ranka's hand hold me back as she must have been worried I was about to do something stupid. Well there were no worries about that unless she…oops, it looked like I was about to talk too soon because here she came, storming over to mark her territory. I had to wonder if she was also going to cock her leg up and piss over the little posse that followed her.

"What did you say to me!?" she demanded coming to stand before me like some over feathered peacock. I mean really, I thought some of the girls could overdo the makeup in my time but this woman looked as though she had used pig's blood to dye her lips red!

"I think you heard me the first time, precious."

"Are you mocking me?!" she snapped, actually stamping her foot like a toddler would. In fact, I had seen Ella behave better than this spoiled brat.

"If the shoes fits," I said causing her and her friends to look down at her sequined slippers.

"Of course my shoes fit! Are you simple?" I rolled my eyes and muttered,

"Jeez what is it with these people... Yes, I am mocking you!" I shouted this last part at her face, this time making it perfectly clear what I was doing.

"How dare you! Do you know who I am?!" I couldn't help it and blurted the first words that came to mind.

"A whore in sparkly pants?" I said looking down at her blue glittering pants that reminded me of something out of an Aladdin Christmas pantomime. It was at this point that her face turned crimson and she stepped forward obviously about to lash out at me. Ranka decided that enough was enough and stepped in between us making her now think twice about her actions.

"You have no authority here, now get out of my way!" she snapped at Ranka.

"No, but the King does and I am the King's right hand. So I suggest that you back away before I inform his Lordship that you just attacked his next chosen concubine, one I will add *he chose personally.*" Hearing this from Ranka obviously had its desired affect because she sucked in a sharp breath of disbelief. I gathered it was an unusual custom for the King himself to pick who became his next concubine, as he probably only went as far as picking one from the end of the beauty assembly line for his bed! The thought had me seething once more.

"The King wouldn't replace me!" she shouted, but that high pitch in her voice didn't sound as if even she truly believed in what she was saying.

"No? Then I suggest you don't force his hand and displease him with any unsavoury acts against a fellow concubine whom he chose." At this she huffed once and before spinning on her heel, she gave me a predictable warning,

"This isn't over."

"No? Wow, I'm gutted I truly am because I really thought we would become best of friends." I said as she walked away.

"Okay so what crawled up her ass and made camp?" I asked Ranka and she choked on a breath at what I just said.

"That is Stateira."

"So?" I asked looking back at her over my shoulder and curling up my lip in disgust.

"You don't understand," she said shaking her head, making her plaited Mohawk shake from side to side.

"Then explain it to me."

"There is not just hierarchy in royalty or within the Gods of my world but there is also one set up down here." I frowned and then looked around to see if I could see it for myself. It quickly became apparent that the divide I had seen when I first walked in was now screamingly obvious as to the cause. The highest and most luxurious section was where bitch face sat and was currently being fanned by one of her adoring fans. And on the other side were those who weren't as expensively dressed, looking awkward, timid and most likely afraid of one of those bratty outbursts being directed at them. I had to wonder if these girls were just waiting on the side-lines like substitutes hoping to be picked for their chance to play in the game.

"And let me guess, she is the boss," I said in an unsurprised tone.

"After Parmida, yes she is the boss."

"And I know I am going to hate this answer but just to be clear, who exactly is the crazy fool that gave her that title?" I closed my eyes and braced myself,

"She is head concubine because she is a known favourite of the King's." Ranka said softly trying to minimise that particular blow for me. But I decided to torture myself with the truth once more and say the words I myself needed to hear being said aloud, even if it did come out as a whisper,

"So Draven picked her." I saw Ranka nod her head and then add the next bombshell, which was something she thankfully thought I needed to know,

"It is said that she will soon become..." she paused a second as if second guessing whether or not she should tell me this, but I gave her pleading eyes and pushed for it.

"Become what...? What Ranka, tell me?" So she took a deep breath and uttered my worst nightmare...

"Queen."

CHAPTER THREE

VIOLATED

"He's lost his mind." I muttered to no-one in particular, unable to comprehend how Draven could even stand to be around her, let alone consider making her his queen!

"She is also the only other girl who the King has picked personally to be his concubine." Ah, so Ranka could see why Stateira was so pissed as she obviously thought I was here to replace her. Well, news flash bitch, I was intending to do more than just replace her!

"So that explains the claws then," I said and when she gave me that look I was getting used to, I meowed and scratched at the air. As you can imagine this didn't help to remove that look of confusion from her face…quite the opposite actually.

"You have to be careful, that viper is likely to strike without you even knowing it," Ranka said watching Stateira like a hawk as she swaggered back to her corner.

"I am not worried about defending myself against petty spoilt brats," I told her but obviously I wasn't taking this seriously enough, for she gripped my forearm and spun me around to face her.

"I am not talking about her attacking you, I am talking about her stabbing you in the back, poisoning your food or slitting your throat whilst you sleep." My eyes widened in surprise.

"She wants to kill me?!" I hissed stepping closer to her.

"Of course she does. In her eyes you stand to take her place as favourite and potentially as queen, for she is not blind," Ranka said and I frowned, not understanding what she meant. I looked down at myself only to see someone who looked as though I had fought my way through a desert and the desert had mostly won.

"Open your eyes Chosen and tell me what you see," Ranka said tipping her chin back to the room. I turned around but still couldn't see what she spoke of.

"I don't under…"

"Look at the girls," she told me and I did as she suggested. They were all beautiful and most were exotic without even trying to be. With their long dark locks smoothed to a high shine or pinned red curls over flowing floaty veils or…wait, why was there no…

"Blondes…there are no blondes," I said frowning at the room before facing Ranka once more in complete shock.

"No, there are none and those girls know it too. You are the first golden haired girl to be chosen and by the King himself, when in the past he has strictly forbidden girls to be chosen with this hair colour by Parmida… now can you see why you hold such a threat?" Ranka said and I looked back seeing that all eyes were on me which only managed to strengthen Ranka's words of warning. I couldn't answer her but I didn't need to as my look said it all.

"Great, so I have been thrown to the wolves dressed in silk

veils...*perfect."* I think I could officially say my situation had just got worse. So just to recap, I was in a foreign country, over two thousand years in the past, without my friends, where Draven had no clue who I was and somehow I had to get him to break one of the biggest supernatural rules and sleep with a human in hopes that he will knock me up so that I could save the world back in my time.

Oh and let's not forget now trying to survive getting lynched by a room full of jealous beauties. Beauties who probably had vials of poison stashed away in their cleavages and knives sewn under their tasselled pillows! Great, well no pressure Keira, I thought mentally shaking my head.

It was at that point I would have liked to retire from the position of Electus, move to the Swiss Alps and become a goat herder...surely those guys had a peaceful life...right? Well it must be better than watching yourself being surrounded by a group of ancient beauticians who looked as though they could also beat up a rugby team because that was what was happening to me now.

"We have a lot of work to do but I want her stripped and bathed so I can see what damage I am working with!" Parmida said circling around me like a vulture that was interested in dressing my meat not eating it.

"I want her separated from the rest, Parmida," Ranka warned, only Parmida just waved a hand around and said,

"Yes, yes." But thankfully this wasn't good enough for Ranka so she took her by the arm and forced her to listen to her final warning.

"Heed my words odalik, for in the eyes of the King she cannot be replaced *but you can.* Do you understand me now?" Parmida paled slightly and then nodded, telling me that she finally understood.

"Good, then do as I ask and keep her guarded day and

night. I will be back every day to check on her progress as the King is anxious to see his prize, so I suggest not to keep him waiting too long before he can claim it," Ranka said and I knew she was only playing her part but I had to say that I was getting tired of being treated like a new toy that needed polishing.

"You think in pleasing the King I will be rewarded?" Parmida asked quietly and I couldn't help but snort, which only earned me a dirty look from my new headmistress.

"I do indeed," Ranka said grinning and I had to say it was an unnerving sight. Ranka was killer first and foremost, that was clear for all to see. It wasn't just the way she looked, like some warrior who could mount a horse in one swift movement or draw a bow quicker than taking a breath, but it was also in her eyes. It was that dangerous glint that told a person she didn't even need to think about her next move but could kill them quicker than thinking about it.

But then I had to wonder how many people had ever got to witness the softer side to her as I had. It may have been brief but for someone who obviously cared a great deal for my husband, then she had shown nothing but kindness to me. She'd tried to comfort me in her own way and even now she was doing everything to try and ensure my safety. I knew one thing for sure and that was I was definitely lucky to have her on my side in all of this.

"I want a word with the girl." Ranka ordered as one of the servants tried to drag me away by the arms.

"Very well but if urgency is as you say then do not take long for I have much to do and no time in which to do it," Parmida warned. I looked down at their hands as if silently telling them to let go of me but it was only when they received a nod from their mistress that they complied. I then walked back to my only friend in all this to no doubt hear her last few words of wisdom and if I was going to survive being in the harem, then I would need all the advice I could get.

"I must now leave you here and go and report to the King." Just at the mention of him my heart rate spiked.

"What will you say?"

"I will answer whatever he asks of me," she replied, giving nothing away.

"Yeah, but what is he likely to ask?"

"Knowing the King, he will want to question me further about when I found you. He will ask if I trust you and also most likely want to know my judgement on making you his next concubine."

"What will you tell him?" I asked excited and nervous at the same time at the thought of him asking about me. She raised an eyebrow as if to say, 'well what do you think'.

"I will be as honest as I can be but I will also explain my concerns about your safety down here and hope he will agree with my recommendation of moving you to safer quarters."

"Oh yes, that would be good, I like that idea." I told her, even more grateful to have her at my back.

"I thought you would. But until something can be done you need to be careful and consider all in here your enemy." I looked around seeing that all eyes were still on me and some looked on with outright hatred, but there were also those who looked on with pity, which had me wondering, could she be right, would everyone here be my enemy?

"The King waits for no man!" Parmida said clapping her hands to tell us that our time was up. Ranka frowned over my head and before the servants could drag me away again, she grabbed my arm and said,

"Remember, Chosen... *trust no one.*" I nodded and before I knew it I was being dragged away and the only reason I let this happen was because I knew all that Ranka had done to get me here. She truly believed this was the only way to get close to the King and whilst I wasn't exactly in the safest place, at least it gave Ranka the time to find my friends like she said she would.

She had also made some pretty dire threats to the one in charge so fingers crossed my chances at survival had just gone up significantly...or at least one could hope. And whilst I was hoping, I also included Draven taking Ranka's advice and moving me from this place sooner rather than later. I was in half a mind to ask if they didn't have a tower around here they could lock me in until Draven asked for me. Well he had always joked about locking me in a tower, so maybe this would be his only opportunity to do so. I smiled at the thought of fun times with Draven, whom I was missing as if someone had chopped off a limb.

They took me down some steps into a separate room and I looked back over my shoulder to Ranka until I was pulled out of sight. I would never forget the look on Ranka's face...she was obviously worried. Meanwhile my heart was beating wildly as I was quickly surrounded by so many slaves I couldn't count them all for all the movement that was going on around me. From what I could see of the room it appeared to be a tiled treatment room for it had a sunken bath to one side and a stone table at the other. It had a vaulted ceiling and as I looked up I started to feel dizzy as all the paintings seemed to be merging into one.

"Hey, easy there," I said as one of the brutish women tried to undress me, getting frustrated with the button on my jeans and bringing me back to my situation.

"Wait, just stop!" I shouted to another woman as she pulled at my T shirt as if she was trying to rip it from me.

"Get off me!"

"Now listen to me, girl!" Parmida suddenly came up in front

of my face and shouted down at me as she was taller by a good few inches.

"This body no longer belongs to you it belongs to the King! And as the King's property it has been entrusted to my care to see that it is fit for him to bed. Now I will do that anyway I can with or without your consent. But this will go a lot quicker and easier if you do not fight my slaves, for know this, we will do this by force if that is the way it is to be. Do you understand?" I took a deep breath and knew what she was saying was right. In their world I was no longer my own person but just another body to warm the King's bed and being in this world I now had to act the part. So as much as it pained me to do so, I nodded my acceptance and let my hands drop.

"Very good. With an attitude like that you will make it far in this harem and you never know, one day you may find yourself head concubine," Parmida said grinning, showing me a full set of yellowed teeth and when she took out a long wooden pipe to smoke I knew why.

"Okay but, but...*just let me do it.*" I told her pushing the slave's hands away from my private girl parts. I just knew this was going to feel like one violating moment after another and that I had no choice but to let it all happen. The slave looked towards Parmida and she only let go of me when her mistress nodded. So slowly I began to undress under too many watchful eyes to count. It was one of the most humiliating things I had ever done in my life and because of it I couldn't stop my hands from shaking.

I couldn't look at the others as I started to pull each item of clothing off my body and when I was just down to my underwear I heard Parmida cluck her tongue, telling me she wanted it all off. I reached around to my back and unclipped my bra letting it fall on the pile next to my feet. Then I slipped my briefs from my legs and added them to what was left of my time.

"Good. Very good, now into the bath with you!" she said clapping twice. I did as I was told and was at least thankful to find it warm as I slipped my leg under the water, followed by the rest of my reluctant body. I let my head fall back against the side as the flurry of hands started working around me.

"Add the salts and oils. You two work on the legs, you two on the arms and you and Mika on her hair, bring that bucket! And oils, where are my oils?" Parmida started barking her orders around me whilst I tried to drown it all out by looking up at the ceiling. Whereas the images had once merged into one when I was standing, now they were starting to tell a story.

I would wince and jump when my limbs were stretched out to be washed by hands I didn't know. The feeling made me feel sick to my stomach and the only way to get past it was to concentrate on those pictures above me. It took me a while to decipher exactly what I was looking at and as soon as I did I decided it was better to just close my eyes and start my mantra of 'there's no place like home'. It was that or look at the Persian version of porn painted on the ceiling.

"You must be wrong, get out of my way and let me see!" Hearing Parmida's agitated voice made me open my eyes to see everyone was suddenly backing away from me.

"Now show me!" she snapped at the servant next to her but looking down at me.

"There see, she has no hair on her legs or under her arms and she has hardly any hair between her legs." The servant said holding out one of my legs and I had to squash down the urge to kick out with my other one. Seriously, could this get any more embarrassing? I almost wished I hadn't shaved ready for my wedding now. Which made me wonder, if they didn't have razors then by the time I got back I could end up having legs and pits like Chewbacca! That wasn't a sexy thought at all.

"You have no hair, why?" Parmida asked obviously now convinced that she wasn't being lied to.

"I don't remember." I said deciding this was safer than saying a woman name Gillette shaved it all off. She raised a sceptical eyebrow at me but said nothing.

"The Gods have blessed you with the softest, palest skin I have ever seen and the King will be pleased. Now wash her hair and let us hope it too is in as good a condition as her skin." Parmida declared, then clicked her fingers to the two who had been brushing my hair for what felt like an hour now. I was just thankful that whatever oil they had put on it was making it easier to brush through the knots, as I hardly felt a thing.

In the end I don't know how long it was that I was manhandled for but it felt like a whole day by the time they were finished with me. I was exhausted and emotionally drained thanks to having nothing to do other than lose myself in my own mind. As it turned out my thoughts were more torturous than anything all those rough hands had done to my body because now all I felt was more alone than I ever had before. Even now, sat in a room full of people who all looked as though they belonged here, all I felt like was a sitting duck with a target on my back just waiting for that first knife to be thrown.

They had cleaned every inch of me over and over again until it felt as though I had lost layers of skin. Even my hair had been washed again and again until it felt stripped of any natural oils. After this and feeling more prune like than ever before I was allowed out of the bath and dried off. Then I was placed on the table and the beauty treatments began. Oils and salts were rubbed into my skin and then removed again, leaving softer skin underneath. My hair also received a citrus and olive smelling oil that tickled my nose.

The only time Parmida got involved and did anything herself was when she attended to my bruises. She plastered on a thick layer of pungent smelling paste, placed large green leaves on top and then wrapped my ribs in long sheets of hemp. She also rubbed a white sandy paste onto my bruised cheek and left it on for a few hours before the other servants were allowed to wipe it clean. I had no idea what was in any of this stuff but was surprised to find that it seemed to be working as it was taking a lot of the soreness away.

Which brought me to now and how I had been dressed in the finest red silks with a gold paisley pattern bordering the edges. I had on wide floaty trousers that were split up the sides but tight to my ankles and waist with bands of stiff gold that looked like shackles. Matching this was a little cropped top that was shaped like something you would wear to work out in and one so tight it acted like a push up bra, being very exposed with a deep V at the front. Thankfully though this wasn't the whole outfit as to cover up my wounds they had wrapped lengths of the same silk around one shoulder first and then tied it loosely at the waist, giving me back some of my modesty.

My hair was now dry and I was happy to report it looked like spun gold and was pinned to one side hanging down in perfect waves. I don't know what that hair oil was called but I could make a fortune back home if I got the ingredients before I left. All in all, I looked a lot better than I felt as I was now sat propped up against a mountain of pillows once the servants had come along and ushered everyone out of the space. Well if I wanted to alienate myself and add to my list of enemies then I was doing a bang up job without even trying.

"Can I sit here?" A small quiet voice spoke and in response

came the sound of clashing metal as two guards blocked her path with their spears crossing over.

"It's fine, she can sit with me," I said hoping they would let her through as I was slowly going crazy sat here on my own, wallowing away in my depressing thoughts.

"We have our orders," they snapped back and the young beauty shrugged her shoulders and gave me a sympathetic look before leaving. My own shoulders dropped and I let myself fall back against the cushions with a sigh. Lay like this I could see the top of the room and all around was a stone balcony with a carved trellis that carefully hid anyone behind it, which was precisely what it was doing now.

I could see a large shadow of a man stood there as if silently watching the room below. No, I had that wrong, because it wasn't just the room below he was watching but more specifically…*it was me.*

I braved looking straight back at him as if daring him to move to one of the open parts of the design in the wooden panels and show himself. I could tell the man was hooded and obviously taking steps to conceal himself, not just behind the beautiful trellis, but also probably in getting there as well. So this meant he was someone who wasn't allowed to be there or someone that was but didn't want anyone knowing.

I only broke away what I believed was eye contact when Parmida clapped her hands, making me jump.

"Time for rest, come with me King's Lamb," she said but my eyes quickly shot back to the balcony only to find the man was gone.

"Now!" she added when I obviously wasn't moving quickly enough. I pushed myself up from the cushions, wincing when the burn in my ribs came back and I was left hoping that I hadn't cracked one as I'd first suspected. Once up I followed Parmida through one of the arches that framed what I called the open communal room and soon found that each arch was a separate sleeping space. I couldn't help but notice that mine was further back from the rest and the guards that followed us situated themselves outside without any orders.

They didn't have doors but sheer blue curtains that cast a calming glow on the small room. They were only big enough to sleep in and not much else as they were about the size of a double bed. Large square cushions filled the space in the same calming blue and purple tones as the curtains that covered the walls and high domed ceiling. It reminded me of sleeping in a little one-man Arabian tent for the night and I quickly wished I wasn't alone, knowing there was only one man who I wanted to share this little space with.

"Now you will sleep for no less than twelve hours as your body needs to heal quickly."

"Yeah but twelve hours…!" I started to moan when she clapped her hands again, which seemed to be her favourite way of communicating.

"You will do as I say or I will drug you to make you sleep, it is your choice," she said folding her arms making her baggy shirt sleeves hang down past her big belly. I sighed and knew that her threats were as real as the threats on my life were back out there and I knew both could find me dead quicker than I would like, because being drugged was not an option for me.

"Fine, I will sleep." I conceded and she nodded once and grinned that yellow grin before walking out. Well at least I could see the silhouette of the guards still standing watch outside of the little bed space. But even knowing they were there it still took me forever to get to sleep and it was only when I could hear the others being herded off to their own rooms that I finally started to relax. It had been a long and traumatic day so in the end I wasn't surprised that when the communal room beyond mine lost most of its warm glow from lit torches, was when my eyes finally started to close.

But even through my exhaustion there must have been something in the back of my mind that told me to keep alert because my eyes opened the second I heard the sound of weapons being drawn from outside my door. I didn't move like I wanted to as I didn't want whoever was out there to know I was awake just yet. So I lay perfectly still holding my breath as I watched the two guards outside being approached by a large figure. Well, with someone of that size I could at least rule out it being one of the other girls.

I was expecting the guards to cross over their weapons like they did last time but I was shocked to see that this didn't happen. Actually it was the complete opposite, because the second the figure spoke they not only lowered their weapons but actually lowered their bodies to the ground. Suddenly my nerves shot through the roof and I had to grip onto the cushions with my fists just to steady my hands.

I wanted to sit up and face the man about to walk through that doorway, finally getting my chance to say what I wanted to say. But then my mind thought things through and I realised that I just couldn't do it. How could I tell him the things I had been dreaming of saying most of the day. It just wasn't possible.

So in the end I knew it was better not saying anything and let him believe I was asleep. Because as soon as I saw those two men bow to the hooded figure that's when I knew who it was that had come to see me…

The King.

CHAPTER FOUR

DREAMS OF THE PAST

As I waited for the faint whoosh of the curtains to be pulled back I held myself perfectly still whilst trying to appear asleep. I had to remind myself to breathe as I felt his presence enter the small space and for a moment I wondered what he would do first. Would he wake me? Would he touch me? Or would he simply look at me to see if I was worth all this fuss after all? I had no answers because like any other smart person I had my eyes closed as I feigned sleep.

It felt like an eternity before he actually moved and I was almost tempted to look as the suspense grew too much for me to bear. Thankfully though I felt his knee dip into the pillows next to me, so I knew he was getting closer. I took this as a good sign for if he hadn't liked what he saw then surely he would have left by now.

I braced myself for his touch so that when I felt it I wouldn't jump and react to it. But that didn't mean when I felt his fingertips push my hair back on my forehead that my heart wasn't beating wildly in my chest. It felt like when we first met and Draven used to come to my bedroom when I was asleep. Of course back then he used to make me believe it was all a dream, but now I knew better. Although I had to wonder what would happen if I opened my eyes right now, would he do the same?

His fingertips felt so gentle against my cheek, as if he was scared of not only waking me but also breaking me. I don't know why but every small breath felt like my chest was heaving up, straining against the tight top I wore underneath the layers of silk. I was certainly on the bustier side of most the woman here as I guessed a lot of them came from backgrounds where food wasn't as easy to come by, as it was usually in abundance for the rich and wealthy. In fact, that was another way you could tell who had been here longer, as on one side their bellies were rounder and hips wider and on the other side they were obviously much skinnier not yet having the time to fatten up.

Draven seemed to be working his way down my body because next he seemed fixated on my hair. I could feel him gathering it up in his hand and stroking it as if he couldn't believe how soft it was.

"My golden fleece." I heard him whisper into my hair as he raised it to his lips. Trying not to react was getting more and more difficult, especially with him calling my hair 'His Golden Fleece', something he had also said to me back in my time. It felt like such a profound moment that if I'd have opened my eyes tears would have been seen shimmering on the surface.

He released my hair, letting it fall to the side and I felt him lean down towards my face. I wanted so badly to suck in my bottom lip, not only from habit but also to stop it quivering. Was he going to kiss me?

"I know you are awake Little Lamb, for I can hear your heart beating wildly in your chest," he said above me and my breath caught in surprise. Of course he knew, he wasn't the human in this scenario, I was!

"Now open your eyes and look at your King," he ordered gently and I had no other choice than to obey. So I did as I was told and opened my eyes to find him now sat back looking down at me curiously. Once again seeing him with a full beard, darker tanned skin and a scar on his face was a surprise that took me a second to recover from. It was almost like seeing the man you loved for the first time after years of being apart. However, it was his eyes that were my anchor in this emotional storm as they hadn't changed. Dark and soul consuming, they still had the same affect over me and I swallowed hard before being able to speak. He watched the motion, not missing a thing, which only made it harder to know what to do next.

"You have no words for me I see," he said raising an eyebrow in question and I couldn't help but blush for reasons unknown.

"I…uh…what are you…" I started to say and you could see he was starting to wonder where this question was going and for someone of the supernatural I gathered he didn't get many question of who or what he was, so I quickly hurried on.

"…doing here? I meant to say what are you doing here?" I asked in a flurry of words that didn't seem natural at all. He didn't yet answer me but with his eyebrow still raised I knew now what I had missed in that sentence.

"I mean My Lord, I meant to say My Lord I promise." I told him and that expectant look quickly turned to one of great amusement. And wow, if I thought Draven smiling was sexy back in my time, then now with his rough exterior and barbaric look, it was simply off the charts sexy!

"I must agree with Ranka, you are certainly different and I confess that intrigues me greatly," he told me honestly and I was left hoping that I intrigued him in a good way, one that would keep him interested for as long as possible.

"Is that why you're here…um, My Lord?" I asked

remembering at the last second to add on 'My Lord'. This made him smirk at me before saying,

"Good girl, you learn quickly." This of course made me blush and bite my bottom lip which drew his eyes down to the action.

"Why do you bite your lip like that?" I quickly let it go hoping he would do the same with his question but when he nodded I knew he was still waiting for his answer.

"You make me nervous," I told him truthfully and he seemed surprised by my response.

"Because I am your King?" he asked obviously curious to know. I shook my head and once more told him the truth, which reminded me that the reasons I was about to give him were the same as when we first met.

"No, because you are a man who could hurt me." He seemed truly affronted by the idea and sat back putting a small amount of distance between us.

"You think I want to hurt you?" he asked in a harsher tone that held a hint of anger. I decided to sit up so that I could be on an equal level to him because I couldn't stand him looking down at me and how overpowered it made me feel. So I pushed myself up with my feet and tried not to wince as it hurt my ribs. He frowned watching me struggling but thankfully remained quiet on what was obviously his displeasure. Once I was sat up and had also put a little more distance between us I replied to his question.

"Not physically, even given your size against my own. No, there are other ways to hurt a woman and they can sometimes be more painful than being struck…trust me, for I have felt both before this day," I told him looking down at my lap, not trusting myself to look into the eyes of the man who in my past had both broken my heart and made it whole all over again.

"Of that I have no doubt," he said reaching out to lift my face up to look at him so he could caress my sore cheek.

"Having the face of a Goddess comes with a price as much as being King does. But trust me Little Lamb when I say that I have no cause to hurt you. You will be safe here in the palace as no one would dare touch what is mine." I wanted to tell him so many things at that point but knew I couldn't as I hadn't been here long enough to prove what I feared would come true by being here in his harem. But there was one thing that I couldn't help but ask,

"Am I?"

"Are you what, Little Lamb?" he asked me as his hand moved further into my hairline and his thumb stroked the apple of my cheek.

"Yours?" I uttered on a whisper looking deep into his eyes and quickly getting lost in them as I'd always done. This was the first time I got the smallest hint of purple that heated his eyes for a second before he answered me with an intensity that couldn't be mistaken.

"Yes, *you are now mine.*" His eyes and his words both held me captive for what seemed like the longest time and we shared a silent moment together that I was too scared to break for what may happen if I did. In the end it was neither of us that broke it but the outside world had other ideas.

"I demand to see who is there! There were strict instructions. Now let me in there!" We both heard Parmida's voice ordering the guards outside and I winced knowing this wasn't good. I looked to the doorway and then back to Draven to see his eyes had grown hard and it was a chilling sight.

"Let her enter," he ordered sternly and I jumped at the new tone in his voice.

"I told you Little Lamb that you were forbidden to…Oh My King!" She stopped her scolding as soon as she saw the

King turn his head to her, realising her mistake. She quickly dropped to her knees in the doorway and lay her forehead to the pillows.

"Forgive me My King, for I had no idea to expect you or I would have prepared her for you, I beg your forgiveness for she is not ready to..." She started rambling her apologies and the King quickly put a stop to it with a curt,

"Enough!" This made Parmida jerk in fear and seeing Draven this way was enough to make me want to shake in fear right alongside her.

"I am not here to take her to my bed odalik, for I am aware that she is injured." On hearing this I knew I was slightly insane for feeling disappointed that he didn't want me that way yet and how crazy was that considering that he was also currently scaring the shit out of me!

"Yes my King of Kings, of course you did, forgive me," she said getting up when he motioned for her to raise the top half of her body, so that he was no longer talking to the back of her head.

"Tell me of her injuries," he demanded in that harsh tone but then when he looked back at me he did so with softer eyes.

"It looks as if she has been kicked hard by a mule in her stomach and ribs but the bruising should heal quite quickly, My King." Draven's eyes hardened when he heard this and he motioned with his two fingers for me to come closer. I wanted to as much as I didn't but in the end knew I had no choice but to do as he ordered. I scooted forward a little, shifting my bum down the bed.

"Lie back," he ordered and again I swallowed hard at what that commanding voice did to me.

"Do as your told, girl!" Parmida shouted behind him and Draven turned his head to the side in a threatening way to glare at her over his shoulder.

"You do not speak to her in my presence again, am I understood odalik?"

"Oh yes My King, please forgive…" Draven ignored her grovelling apology and turned back to me to cut her off.

"Don't fear me, my Lamb," he said nodding for me to do as I was told and this time I quickly lay back. He seemed pleased and I could tell that he wanted to say something more but thought better of it whilst we had company. However, what he didn't think better of doing was reaching down to my waist and pulling free the loose knot of silk at my side. He slowly pulled up the material through his strong hands and my heart stopped beating for a moment. Then once it was free he started to pull it back, about to reveal my body to him. I don't know what came over me but in that second I forgot which Draven I was looking at and my hand shot out to grab onto his hand that still gripped a fistful of silk.

Parmida sucked in a horrified breath that I had just restrained the King from doing as he pleased, but right then that sound was lost to the both of us. Because this was the first time I was touching him of my own free will and there was something so profound in that single moment in time that it's strength affected us both. A first and simple touch for lovers destined to be together for the rest of all eternity was a powerful thing indeed, even if only one of us knew the real strength behind it. Looking into Draven's eyes in that moment and I knew there was an unmistakable connection that was unfortunately something he didn't understand.

And that's when it hit me. This was just like history repeating itself only now the roles were reversed. When we had first met back in my time he knew what I was to him and he knew the importance of that first meeting. But to me, I was left in the dark and feeling confused at the intensity of it all. Well looking at Draven now he was experiencing that first touch as I had done. And when he looked down at my hand over his it was as though he was trying to figure out what it was he was feeling.

"I know you won't hurt me." I told him softly, hoping that only he could hear my words as they were just meant for him. He looked back up at me and for the first time it was as if he was seeing me as the girl who was always meant to be his.

He nodded as if he didn't trust his voice and I removed my hand from his, breaking the connection for a short time. But when he pulled back the silk and revealed my body underneath then the connection was back in the way of invisible sparks that seemed to crackle between us like little electric forks that licked out at our skin.

His eyes scanned up over my body as if he was trying to burn the sight to memory and I blushed at how lustful his gaze became. Then after spending enough time looking at my breasts with heated eyes, his look hardened once more when his gaze returned to my wrapped torso. He ran his hand along my side and I squirmed making him stop.

"Did that hurt?" he asked me with a rough edge to his voice.

"No, sorry My Lord, it just tickled." I said giving him a little smile which was nowhere near as powerful as the grin I received in return.

"I will have to remember that," he said smirking at me and once more proving that sometimes two thousand years didn't change a man from being who he was. I blushed again and when I went to bite my lip he placed his thumb on it and shook his head.

"I don't think my restraint will last, Little Lamb," he confessed and I felt my cheeks get even hotter.

"How long before she is well?" Draven asked Parmida after turning his attention back to my wrapped stomach.

"A month," she stated and I almost choked when

swallowing. A month! I couldn't wait around here for a bloody month, I would turn into a raving lunatic!

"You do not agree, my beauty?" Draven asked me and I must admit, I preferred it to Little Lamb.

"It is not my place," I said because I knew it was the right answer to give in this time but he raised an eyebrow again and this time it was joined with a playful smirk.

"I am making it your place," he told me and at that moment I wished we were alone again so we could continue the playful banter.

"Then in that case I don't agree."

"Good because I cannot wait that long. Make sure to have her ready for selection in three days' time," he demanded and Parmida looked as if she was choking on a bug.

"But my King, it cannot be done, there is still so much work to be done and she is…"

"Perfect as she is." Draven finished off her sentence for her whilst looking back to me and once he saw me go for my lip again he shook his head silently telling me of the risks in doing so. I was almost tempted to push and see where it got me…*underneath him I hoped.*

"Then you are pleased, My King?" Parmida asked in a hopeful voice.

"Indeed," he answered, making Parmida relax her tense shoulders.

"Now leave us for a moment but wait for me outside for I wish to speak further on a matter that concerns me." Parmida nodded and said,

"Of course, My King." Then she rose up and quickly left the room, leaving us alone once more. Draven looked back down at me scanning my body once more and when his eyes reached mine he surprised me with his honest question.

"What are you?" In that moment I wanted nothing more

than to tell him who I was, or more importantly what I was to him. His Electus. His Chosen One. But even greater, that I was his wife from another time. I wanted him to know everything, but I knew that I would also be risking everything if I told him any of these things.

"Your servant, My Lord," I told him trying to keep as much pain from my voice as I could. He gave me a look that told me he very much doubted my words and panic almost set in...did he know something?

"You are something to me it is true, but I am not sure if it is as my servant yet...but we shall soon see," he said as if talking to himself and trying to understand our connection, which again begged the question...why hadn't he figured it out?

"My Lord?" I said playing the part as a naive little slave girl, one I could tell he was quickly trying to unravel to find the real girl underneath.

"I will take my leave of you now," he told me and my face dropped. I didn't want him to go...*I never wanted him to go.*

"Now what is that face for?" he asked obviously liking the idea that I was disappointed that he was leaving me.

"Do you have to leave?" I braved asking him and his grin told me I hadn't made a mistake.

"No, I am King and can do as I wish but as a man looking down at a broken body I want to take to my bed, I know that in order to heal such wounds then what my Little Lamb needs is rest and plenty of it...and as your King it is my command, understood?" he added sternly and I knew I couldn't argue as I would have done in my time. But this was his time and he was my King, one I had to obey if I knew what was good for me.

"Yes, my Lord." I told him in a quiet voice and it was obvious to him that even though I said the words he wanted to hear, I still didn't like it. He grinned enjoying my neediness.

Then he leaned down getting closer to my face and I could only hope that the night would at least end in a kiss.

"I can see that your hidden defiance will amuse me greatly and your reluctance to see me go is even more pleasing, but be warned my little beauty..." he paused, this time getting closer to my ear so that he could whisper his threat,

"...once I have you in my bed, I may not want to let you out of it again." I sucked in a breath showing him without words how much his own had affected me.

"Goodnight...*My Golden Fleece,*" he whispered over my lips without touching them and I was tempted as never before to reach up and kiss him, knowing that once I did, I would capture him as he often did to me. But I couldn't risk it, not yet, so instead of acting on my impulse I let him lift himself up off the cushions and watched as he left my room. I didn't want him to go and after seeing this softer side of him that I knew before, my mind was at least put more at ease from when he had been holding a knife to my throat. Yes, I would definitely say this was a big step up from our first encounter.

I listened for a moment and scooted closer to the entrance so that I could hear what was being said.

"Ranka has concerns for her safety and believes I should have her moved out of the Harem." I heard Draven say back in that stern voice he obviously used when speaking with his servants. I heard Parmida cluck her tongue against the roof of her mouth before saying,

"What does a warrior know of such things? Your Harem is a peaceful place, my King." I would have liked to have seen Draven's face if I'd have acted on my impulse and stuck my head out through the curtain to say... 'Uh, I beg to differ with that one'.

"That is quite a different account from the one Ranka expressed to me a short while ago. I believe Stateira was involved?" 'Yeah I'll say' I thought frowning at the way that bitch acted. I could tell by the way Draven asked this that he had his arms folded and no doubt was trying to catch Parmida out to see if she was lying or not.

"Nothing but a bit of healthy competition for your affections, My King and after all, Stateira needs to state her position as head concubine. She is known as your favourite and has been for some time, so I believe this was all she was doing." I held my breath and waited for Draven's response, hoping that he would deny this claim and at least give me a small shred of hope that her position wouldn't be what it was for much longer. I was almost cocky with it, grinning behind the fist that I held at my lips. Surely any minute now he would tell her his obvious feelings for me.

"Whatever her reasons for this hostility are not my concern but her actions are. I want her kept away from my new concubine, is that understood?" I smiled hearing this, but it turned out to be too soon.

"My King forgive me but Stateira is still your favourite, is she not?" Parmida braved to ask and I unfortunately braved to listen to his crushing truth…

"She is and will be for the foreseeable future."

CHAPTER FIVE

BACK STABBING HEARTACHE

Once I'd heard this brutal statement from Draven I no longer wanted to listen. I threw myself down on the pillows, wrapped myself back up and revelled in the pain these actions caused my body, needing some physical agony to mask the emotional one. This way I could pretend the tears I cried that night weren't down to the heartache I felt piercing my chest.

I woke the next morning only to find myself disappointed that this wasn't all a horrible dream as I'd hoped. I was still trapped in this nightmare and the person who seemed to be pulling all the strings was someone I couldn't yet reach. I just wanted to go home and feel safe in the knowledge that Draven still loved me the way he always had done. Because even back in the days when we were separated I still knew deep down how much

Draven cared for me but this...well this was a different type of torture!

But I knew I couldn't just sit like a plump chicken in my gilded cage waiting for my golden egg to hatch. I needed to act and I couldn't do that here. No, I needed to formulate a plan now and as much as it pained me to say, that plan no longer included Draven.

Sure he may have given me some attention and shown me that at least he cared about his new prize getting hurt before he could sample the goods. And in whatever way that was for a supernatural King to do I didn't yet know and didn't want to for that matter. Because for someone forbidden to bed humans where exactly did that leave me?

Again I had no answers but one thing was certain and that was I definitely wasn't going to stick around to wait and find out. Not now I knew there was no hope for me to be the Chosen One to him like I was back in my time. For I knew that falling in love with me was the only way to get him to break his own rules and the reality of that happening now after last night looked impossible. Not when he already had someone he cared for in his life. No, it was time to jump ship and swim as if a shit storm was coming...one that was named 'the prophecy'.

So now all I had to do was escape this underground fortress and find the rest of my time travelling party before making my way back to the ocean, or in my case whatever the Hell it was we had jumped into in the first place. It wasn't as if I could find some tourist office on a street corner and pick up a map to the nearest Janus gate. No, I needed to be clever about this and to do that when I had two guards watching my every move was going to be difficult.

However, the one thing on my side was that I definitely had enough time to think about it considering I was being treated like the leper of the group. If only I had someone on my side who could help me in all this and as grateful as I was for Ranka, right now who I really needed was Pip, Sophia or Ari.

"Where are you guys?" I whispered to myself.

"What did you say?" Parmida snapped from the corner of the treatment room I was currently in. It was another day at Hell's spa and once more I was laid out naked on the stone slab feeling like a bruised piece of meat. Some of the servants were washing the mushy gunk off my ribs, whilst two other girls worked on rubbing oils into my feet.

I didn't answer her but instead just turned my head the other way to stare at the wall. I heard her huff and I knew another lecture was on its way, as I had already heard quite a few today.

"You don't know how lucky you are to be singled out by the King like this." I rolled my eyes which one of the younger servant girls saw and smiled down at me. She must have been no older than sixteen and I had to wonder what unfortunate life choices had been made to bring her to this point. Had it been a case of wrong place at the wrong time or more likely had she been born into slavery?

"You had better heed my warning child for you could very easily be cast aside and resold to the highest bidder should the King choose to do. And understand me now when I say that not everyone with wealth is as easy on the eye as the King is or as gentle with his women." Of this I had no doubt but she didn't need to hear me say that. I knew that to have such a handsome King with the reputation of being good to his women was like winning the royal lottery for girls in a harem but for me it meant nothing. He was my husband first and foremost and no matter how much I tried to distance myself from that fact, I just couldn't.

"You should listen to her, for she speaks the truth." The young girl whispered to me once Parmida had given up trying to get through to me.

"Look, I know you mean well but I am not going to be happy until I get out of here." I told her for no other reason than to test her. Her big dark eyes widened in surprise.

"But why would you want to do that?" she asked freely when the others had finished wrapping my ribs up again in fresh bindings and had their backs turned, cleaning up their supplies.

"It's complicated," I told her, not trusting her with anything that could potentially turn around and bite me in the ass later on. She looked thoughtful for a moment before helping me up off the stone table. Then she leaned in to me and whispered,

"I might know a way." This surprised me enough to ask,

"But why would you help me?"

"Because I too was sold into this life," she said, confirming what I already suspected.

"And what of your family?" I asked softly but she just shook her head telling me all I needed to know...*she had none.*

"Alright, so you say there is a way out?"

"Yes, but not here," she hissed looking towards the others who she obviously feared would overhear us.

"Then where?" I asked looking around in the hope that the others would leave but then I saw the young girl's shoulders straighten up and I knew whose voice I would hear next.

"Take her back to her room. She needs to eat and then to rest before she bathes." Parmida ordered and I was at least thankful that unbeknown to her she was giving us the perfect chance to speak.

"Yes, my Mistress," the girl said bowing once before leading the way for me to follow. I couldn't help but notice the imposing presence of the two guards who quickly fell into step behind us. We walked back through the large space and I couldn't help but notice that the looks I received weren't all ones of bitter hatred as I expected. Some even looked full of pity and I had to wonder about that, but then one look at the bitch and her posse in the corner and I didn't have to wonder long. It was obvious they must have known the dangers that came with being chosen by the King for special treatment and the thought made me want to hiss.

Of course I decided against growling at her as I walked past and instead started laughing, knowing this would annoy her much more. The young servant looked at me as though I had lost my mind but I didn't care as one look at the head Bitch and I knew my work here was done. In fact, she looked close to choking on her own tongue she was so enraged. Obviously she had never come across someone who wasn't scared of her position in this place. Good, it was about time she met her match as bullies were something I loathed in life!

"Why do you choose to anger her so?" The young girl asked me in a hushed voice and once we had passed them I told her the truth.

"Because if you show a person like her fear they will only feed from it but if you deny them it, then they themselves soon become afraid." She looked thoughtful for a moment but didn't say anything and I only hoped that she took the advice I gave her, as I had no doubt that one day she would need it.

We waited until we made it back to my little room and the guards had situated themselves outside before she started speaking.

"The only ones who come and go as they please are the servants and guards." It didn't take long for me to know where she was going with this and I looked up and down at her grey tunic so that she knew we were quickly on the same page.

"But how do I get…?" She cut me off with a wave of her hand already knowing what I was going to ask.

"You will have to give me time to think of something but it may be possible for you to escape the palace dressed as one of us but it will have to be done at night so it is harder for anyone to see your face."

"Wow, you have really thought this through, haven't you?" I watched the young girl blush and look shameful for a moment which had me worried.

"Why have you?" I asked frowning, now doubting whether to trust her or not. For a moment she looked as though she wouldn't answer as she turned her back on me.

"There was another not long before you who also didn't want to be here." Okay, so this made more sense.

"What happened?" I asked knowing it wasn't good given the slight emotion in her voice.

"She was resold to another before we could carry out our plan." I could tell even without asking that this person had meant something to her but I asked anyway because I wanted to know who.

"And she was a friend?" The girl looked back to me and I could see the unshed tears in her eyes when she uttered one heart-breaking word,

"Sister."

She left quickly after saying this and I couldn't say that I blamed her. I couldn't imagine the pain of seeing your own sister not only sold into a harem but to witness the misery of it each day would be even worse. Not everyone got to taste the sweetness of freedom to choose in life, but this was even less so throughout history. It was a brutal awakening and realisation of truth that was hard to swallow, one made even harder knowing that the man I loved had played his part in this cruel world just like so many others. I didn't want to learn about this part of his life but I guess in the end it was just one more test I had to face in the eyes of the Fates.

I remembered Draven once telling me about how humans had to forge their own path through history and that included making their own choices. His kind couldn't change the nature of humans as much as we could change theirs. So when playing a part in man's history it had to be done just as they chose to live. After all, it took the will of man to stand and fight for what they believed in and more often than not, it was the fight between good and evil and between right and wrong. Whether you faced an army standing in your way or just one man. Because in the end the most powerful weapon of all was the belief that burned like an inferno in your heart. One that was so strong it could defeat the Gods or in turn give them the power needed to aid us as we passed into the Afterlife.

Yes, this certainly felt like a test and one that I knew was to be my *last*.

Thoughts like this stuck to me throughout the rest of the day like muggy air that just wouldn't clear without the storm, which in itself had me wondering when my own storm would come. I felt something was coming but without being prepared for it I felt more like I was fumbling around in the dark looking for a way out. Would I have enough time to escape before Draven called for me? And even if I managed to break free from this madness, what dangers lay outside of these walls for me? What of Ari, Pip and Sophia? So many questions and as usual, I had no bloody answers for any of them!

It was so frustrating, just sat here waiting and feeling utterly clueless. I also didn't like the idea of involving a girl I barely knew and knowing that there was the possibility of getting her in just as much trouble as I would be in if caught. It was at this point that I decided I couldn't go through with it if it caused any risk to her at all. If there was even the slightest possibility of her being implicated in my escape, then I would just have to think of something else.

What exactly I had no clue, but at the moment that was a moot point until night fell and I could find out what she had planned. Which was why I was more than thankful when I was finally told to go back to my room and sleep before eating for the last time today. Hell, living in this place I just felt like I was fattened up ready for an apple to be stuffed in my mouth before I got a good roasting...*no pun intended.* And with the amount of oil that had been rubbed into my skin in the last twenty-four hours, the idea wasn't that farfetched as I felt as if I had been marinating all day in a hot sweaty room.

If anything, by the time I made it back to my little tented room, I almost collapsed onto the pillows, feeling utterly exhausted from doing nothing all day. Thankfully before this I had been allowed to cool down in the main pool before returning as I felt like a sweaty mess after being in that heated plunge pool that they had forced me to spend most of the day in. I had protested countless times only to be ignored every time so in the end I'd just shut up and endured it like a good little slave girl.

It was no wonder then that when I was finally allowed out that I jumped in the cool pool so fast, I must have looked like a child on the first day of their summer holiday...well, not that any of the others knew what that looked like but it was at least how I felt. So much for playing the dainty flower like the rest who would simply dip their toes in first before slowly sinking the rest of their bodies in like graceful synchronised swimmers. No, not me, I was only a few steps away from dive bombing in there saying to hell with the others.

And it was whilst I was in there that I received my second warning from Draven's favourite after she slithered her way into the water like some anaconda lurking in the shallows. Well

I had seen the true horrors of what were hidden away in those shadows for most of my life and there were things that would scare the shit out of the bravest of people. I had also dealt with bigger bitches than this pampered princess wannabe and I knew from experience that they had bigger claws than this spoilt brat, so when she approached she obviously wondered why I didn't look worried.

"I don't know what you are smiling at but I warned you that it wouldn't last long," she snarled making my smile grow to what I imagined was an annoying level. I had my arms out casually along the sides of the pool as I let my legs float out in front of me. As usual she was accompanied by the two girls she had with her before and I tried to supress a chuckle at how old these school ground antics really were…*ancient obviously.*

"Oh I don't know, because it looks pretty damn funny from where I am." I told her adding a wink for good measure.

"And what is that supposed to mean!?" she demanded going red faced and puffing her naked chest out as though it would intimidate me. I guessed 'boob envy' was also another tactic used, one that was as old as time in the history of bitchism! Well unlucky for her I won in that department as well, I thought with a satisfied smirk.

"Just that worried look on your face at finally being replaced…tell me, what will you do with your early retirement? May I suggest getting some cats, they make great company." I told her and I don't know what was funnier, the face she pulled at the part she understood or the twisted confusion on her face at the parts she didn't. In the end she must have decided to focus on the only part she did understand.

"I am not worried!" she screeched angrily, sounding similar to an angry bird.

"No? Oh I must be mistaken then because I just assumed that by you coming over here threatening me that you yourself must be feeling the one threatened." It was at this point that the other two looked at each other behind her back and that knowing exchange spoke volumes, they were thinking the same thing.

"How dare you! Do you know what my name means?!" she snapped and I laughed once and said,

"Okay, not sure what that has to do with the price of dates around here but I will take a wild stab in the dark and say that it means a bulldog chewing wasps." From the look on her face she hadn't understood the insult, which was a shame as it was one of my best.

"It means 'creation of the stars' and do you know who gave me that name?!" She spat out her words and I held my entire body ridged so I didn't flinch at the hurt she inflicted. She had no idea what Draven meant to me as she was merely trying to prove a point but in reality the powerful blow she had inflicted cut me to the core.

However, my face must have given something away as she decided to go one step further and drive her point home with a razor's edge.

"And from what I hear he named you after a piece of meat!" she laughed once and added,

"And you think I am worried that he will replace me!" She leaned forward and spoke the words that no longer had me smiling but instead looking close to murdering her.

"I am merely worried for the spectacle my King makes in lowering his standards enough to take you to his bed!" Now she was the one smiling and I knew I had lost my edge with the anger I had shown on hearing this. She knew her words had got to me and that was one of the worst things you could do when dealing with a bully, but all the will in the world couldn't have had me reacting any other way.

After this heated exchange that was witnessed by everyone

surrounding the pool, we were ushered out of the water as soon as Parmida could see what was going on and the fact that she was obviously failing in her task of keeping Draven's bitch away from me. But the last thing heard out of Stateira's mouth to me was a very obvious threat, one even Parmida couldn't ignore.

"Watch your back for soon you might be able to see the reflection of your death from the blade sticking out of it." I wished at this point I had come back with something witty or at least equally as threatening but Parmida put a stop to it before it happened. Which brought me back to now and the conclusion of another full day down in this stink hole of poisonous beauty.

I was at least thankful that I didn't have to wait too long before the young servant girl came through my curtains with a tray of food, which as usual mainly consisted of fruit, nuts and something strange they called sweetmeats, which wasn't meat at all. In fact, it was the opposite of meat and more like their version of candy that tasted of dried fruit caramelised in honey or crystallized brown sugar.

"I have thought of a plan," she informed me as she put down the tray on one of the flatter pillows that looked to be there for this purpose. I scooted closer and whispered excitedly,

"You have?"

"Yes but first you must memorise the instructions I give you as getting out of here will be the easy part, but finding your way to the palace above will be the biggest challenge you face." At this point I wanted to say 'Yeah no shit' because even coming through that stone bridged maze was enough to make my head spin so I was more than thankful that she had thought ahead.

"You can't be found with this so memorise it and then burn it otherwise they will know you have been helped," she said pulling a small scroll from under her sleeve and slipping it into my hand. I unfolded it and frowned looking down at the ancient text I couldn't read.

"What's wrong?" she asked knowing by my frown that there was a problem.

"I can't read this." I told her looking up from the tiny piece of parchment in my hands.

"I don't understand, do you not read?"

"Not this, no." I said making her frown.

"But the King likes his Concubines to be educated." If it was any other time I would have been offended at the assumption that I was a dumb blonde but I didn't have time for this.

"I can read and write but not this language," I told her holding it open for her to see.

"But you speak our language flawlessly, so I just thought…" She let that sentence trail off and I felt like rolling my eyes knowing how strange this must have seemed. But what could I say, that Ranka had worked her magic Voodoo on me to make it so the English my brain told me I was speaking was obviously coming out as ancient Persian. In the end I just shrugged my shoulders and said,

"I don't know what to tell you." Thankfully she got the hint and after giving the curtains a quick look to check that the coast was still clear, she knelt down beside me.

"I will help you."

I received a quick lesson in what was left and right in something that looked like lots of little arrow symbols which they obviously used as an alphabet. She explained that the grouped arrows next to each left and right was the number of turns I was to make. It took me a while but I thought I'd got the hang of it. She told me that she would return once everyone was asleep as it was her job to collect the empty plates when the evening meal had been eaten. She would tell Parmida that I hadn't finished mine when she last checked, which she knew would mean her being ordered to collect it once I was asleep.

Then when she returned she would strip out of her tunic and into my clothes, lying on the bed covered pretending to be me. I agreed but only if she let me tie her up and make it look as though I had forced her into doing this. I wasn't surprised that she didn't argue with this part of the plan, not considering what the punishment might be for her if she was caught helping me.

After this I couldn't relax as I waited for the servant girl to return. At least I had something to keep my mind occupied, if only for a short while. I decided there was no way I would be able to memorise all the turns I was supposed to make in time and I knew I couldn't take the scroll with me as she had warned. So in the end I did the next best thing I could think of. I split open one of the pomegranates with the sharp knife provided and used the juices to draw marks on my arm. I decided to do this on my upper arm so that they would easily be hidden under the tunic if I was found. Hopefully, even if the worst should happen and I was caught, at least no one should know what they meant.

My code was simple. I would start near my elbow and draw a red line across to symbolise a turn. My left would indicate to take a left turn and a right line would indicate to take a right. So that it didn't get confusing I decided to leave a gap in the lines I made so that I would know it meant for me to look to the other arm for my next move. Then I would simply lick the lines clean at the end. In theory it seemed like an easy system to follow but I didn't really know how it would work until I was outside of those big double doors and free from the Harem.

"It is time," the girl said after creeping back through the curtains and once again checking that she hadn't been followed.

I had to wonder if this would have worked for her sister and couldn't help but feel a sadness for her.

But instead of showing these feelings I said the one thing I wasn't sure was entirely true…

"Alright, I am ready."

CHAPTER SIX

HIDDEN TRUTH

I wasn't sure if I was ready for this but what choice did I have? Not only did I have my friends counting on me but also what of the world I'd left behind? I had no clue what faced me when I finally made it back just like I had no clue what faced me once I made it through those doors…or should I say *if* I made it through those doors.

I noticed that this time my new friend was wearing a wrap over her head that kept her hair from view and it was the same style which some of the other servants often wore so this wouldn't look out of place. She nodded down at my body and I knew it meant it was time to get undressed and switch. I hurried knowing time wasn't on our side as we didn't want the guards to get suspicious. It was only when I had finished that I looked up to see the girl looking down at herself in what I can only describe as awe. I gathered that this was the first time she had ever worn anything as fine and expensive as the silk she was now wrapped in.

"It suits you," I told her and she jumped a little as I had

obviously jolted her from her secret moment of desire. She blushed and looked away as if feeling ashamed of something she didn't want me to know.

"I need to tie your hands and legs together," I told her, feeling guilty but knowing it was also for her own good. I picked up one of the fancy cushions and ripped off the gold trim from around its edges knowing it would do for a makeshift rope. Then I wrapped it around her wrists and ankles before asking her to try to get out of it. When she managed to slip one hand free I redid it, knowing this time the best way to tie it so she couldn't break free again. Then I helped her lie back against the cushioned bed and covered her up so at first glance you wouldn't be able to tell it wasn't me.

"What's your name?" I asked her not realising until now that I still didn't know. She gave me a sad look I couldn't read and then told me in a quiet voice,

"My name is Farrin." I nodded, then I tied a piece of silk over her mouth, leaned in close and whispered my farewell,

"Thank you Farrin, I wish you well my friend." Then I pushed myself up, secured the wrap around my head and grabbed the empty plate. I had to make sure none of my hair was on view seeing as the blonde would have been a dead giveaway in this place. Then after one last deep breath I placed the plate up on my open palm as I had seen the rest of the servants do and looked down at the floor as I ducked through the curtains.

I held my breath until I made it far enough away from the two guards who hadn't bat an eyelid at me leaving. In fact, it was almost laughable on how easy that had been. I then followed what the other servants did and walked towards the double doors with our empties in hand and waited for the guards to open them for us. Still keeping my head low, I walked through trying my best to copy exactly what the girls ahead of me did and it was only when I heard the doors close behind me that I let my shoulders relax.

I hung back for a moment as I watched the short line of servants ahead of me turn down the side, which I'd learned from Farrin was where the kitchens were. But I didn't need the kitchens, what I needed was the exit to this marble watery maze that looked as endless as it had the day I walked in here with Ranka. This had me wondering what Ranka would think of my disappearing act and I could only hope she thought the reasons behind it were ones of self-preservation. After all, that wasn't far from the truth all things considered seeing as I had been threatened with waking up to find a knife in my back more than once.

But the truth was, I wasn't running from Draven's bitch flavour of the decade but more from Draven himself. Which had me thinking…

Just how many times had I run from Draven in the past? And did that mean that this was simply history repeating itself? Well, considering technically it hadn't actually happened yet, I think asking myself that question was enough of a minefield to give me a year's worth of headaches.

So, shaking these impossible questions from my mind, I looked down at my arms and knew that at the first junction I was turning left. I rubbed my thumb through it telling myself that I had already made that turning and didn't want to get confused. I would then lick away the evidence when I knew I hadn't messed up somehow. The worst part about this was every noise seemed to echo throughout the huge space that was mainly stone pillar after stone pillar, no doubt holding up the foundations of the palace above. I could tell that this place was secret and had probably been built this way by supernatural means as just looking at the incredible structure compared to the one above and they looked years apart. Actually in truth it looked more like something I would have expected to find in Heaven than this time in Earth's history. Zeus automatically came to mind and no wonder considering the fallen temple I had witnessed for myself back when I was taking that not so delightful trip into Tartarus.

It also reminded me of Draven's temple back in Afterlife and how different that also looked compared to the rest of his home. I guess now looking at this place that it had been nothing new and I had to wonder just how many of these secret places Draven had built throughout his many years upon this Earth? Well I could only hope that, unlike the temple I knew intimately, it didn't have the same horrors hidden behind prison doors as Afterlife did. After all, Draven might have been playing at human King but he no doubt still had a job to do amongst his own kind and that usually meant having some supernatural prison of sorts.

I shivered just thinking about it and suddenly it felt as though I had a million eyes all watching me. I stepped quietly along the marble footpath seeing no one walking in the same footsteps but my own reflection in the surrounding water. It was an eerie place that was for sure and not one I fancied getting lost in anytime soon. I decided to quicken my pace and found myself once more pulling up my sleeve and looking down at my arms to figure out my next direction. Once I made my choice, I swiped a thumb through the line and carried on, only the second I moved I heard footsteps coming from in front of me. I panicked and hid behind one of the marble pillars, holding my back against it and trying not to breathe.

I waited for the echoing sound to trail away into the distance before chancing that it was all clear. I peeked my head around and half expected to see a face staring back at me. Thankfully though there was nothing but the still unnerving room that apart from myself was empty. I closed my eyes and gulped in the air I needed before turning back around only to open my eyes and scream at the hooded figure before me.

A man's hand shot out and covered my mouth, pushing me back against the pillar with the force of his action. I froze as the mystery man stared down at me with his face still hidden by the hood of his cloak. However, he was not happy that I was doing the same so with his other hand he snatched off my wrap and threw it away angrily where I watched as it floated down into the water.

For long moments neither of us said anything but just stared at each other, although he was the only one who could see my face and what it showed was obvious…

Fear.

"Please don't…" My plea was cut off when the sudden sound of guards echoing through the underground cavern came charging our way and I knew there was nothing to be done now. My escape had failed. The man in front of me startled me as he quickly grabbed me by the arm and dragged me out from behind the pillar and into the view of the guards. Then, as if furious with finding me hiding here, he yanked my arm and swung me at the closest guard. Thankfully he caught me before I slipped into the water, which is where my body had been heading.

The guard seemed as surprised as I was by the action but quickly resituated himself within his ranks and held me firm, not letting go of his prisoner. I soon found out that it didn't take half as long to get back to the harem as it had taken me getting away from it. I had no idea what faced me when I got there but from the looks of all the guards surrounding me, I didn't think it looked good. In fact, it looked as if I had been caught out a lot sooner than I first thought. Which had me worried for Farrin… had she been discovered sooner than we expected?

Well I was about to find out because the double doors were

right ahead of me and opening up like doomed fate spreading its arms wide ready to swallow me whole. I couldn't help but look back to see the hooded man still following and he must have seen the panic on my face as it wasn't something I was trying to hide.

Who was he anyway?

Well I was sure to find out as we walked through the doors and he followed us all back into the harem. This was the point that my mask of bravery slipped back into place as all the girls had come out of their rooms to see what all the commotion was about. It was humiliating but I knew it would be even worse if I showed my true feelings especially when included in that audience was none other than Queen bitch face herself. Hell, even that sadistic smile was enough to set my veins alight with rage. I ignored her sneers and raised my head up showing her no shred of fear and hopefully disappointing her sick and twisted mind.

The room was surrounded by not only the harem girls but also the servants and guards making this a real spectacle. And stood there at the centre of it all was Parmida looking close to spitting fire she was that mad. But right now I couldn't care less about receiving another lecture or a smacked wrist because I simply felt drained in every way possible. I just wanted to crawl into my little room and pretend that curtained door was a steel door barricading me off from this barbaric world. But what I didn't yet know was that it was about to get a whole lot worse and a whole bucket load more barbaric!

I was just wondering why the guard hadn't yet unhanded me even though I was now considered safely back within my marble cage when I noticed he looked to the hooded man. And it was when he nodded that my nightmare really began.

"But the healing..." Parmida protested, now looking extremely worried, but a silent hand shot up and abruptly put a stop to her concerns. Concerns which quickly became my own, especially when the one word I was now focused on was 'healing', which could only mean one thing...*punishment.*

This was when things started happening very quickly and before I could do anything to try and stop it, my hands were yanked forward roughly.

"NO! Get off me!" I shouted and pulled my weight backwards which only managed to cause me more pain from my earlier injuries. My hands were quickly tied in front of me which only left my legs to try and defend myself with as I kicked out at anyone near to me. I was actually surprised that I wasn't being hit back as I got a few in the shins hard enough to cause them to jump back or grunt in pain. Well I wasn't going to let this happen without a fight that was for sure!

At one point I broke free by stamping on a foot and then when his hold loosened I pushed all my weight into him sideways and knocked him out of the way. Unfortunately for me though this escape was short lived as there were just another four of them there ready to catch me. All the while the hooded figure just stood watching this whole scene play out with his arms folded.

In fact, when one grabbed me around the waist to pull me back, I cried out in pain from my injured ribs and he looked ready to intervene for a moment. He unfolded his arms and took a step forward but as soon as they had me back under control he went back to watching, telling me he was only going to aid them, not me. For some reason this got me so mad that I couldn't help but scream out at them all in anger as everyone in the room did nothing to help me,

"Enjoying the show everyone!?" I wasn't sure but I thought I saw some of them flinch or look away in obvious guilt. But it wasn't the rest of them that I was interested in...it was the hooded man. I didn't know what it was but something in my gut told me that he was someone I knew but not just that,

He was someone I trusted.

I don't know how I knew this or even if I was right but I couldn't help but feel it somewhere deep in my soul. But it didn't matter as whether I trusted him back in my time or not, I wasn't there now and that man obviously didn't yet know me. Which only meant one thing, he wasn't here to help me, he was simply here to watch as I was dragged back to the wall where one man was throwing chains and shackles over one of the torch hooks. This caused my panic to double as I knew once they got me into those things then they would be free to do anything they wished to me.

"Parmida stop this, tell them!" I shouted, pleading with her but she just looked away as if ashamed that this was being allowed to happen. Well great help she was! Fine, I would do it myself.

"The King would never allow this! He wouldn't hurt me!" I shouted trying everything to get them to stop and something in this worked because suddenly a voice boomed from behind us all.

"STOP!" I felt a huge sigh of relief as I would know that voice from anywhere.

"Draven." I uttered secretly, knowing I was saved. The guards took their hands off me as they had been about to raise my wrists to the bands of steel. I turned slowly and looked around expecting to see their King of Kings looking as furious as he sounded but he was nowhere to be seen. This was when the truth started to sink in and my heart right alongside of it.

The one who had caught me.

The hooded man...

He was Draven.

CHAPTER SEVEN

TESTED HEARTS

In that surreal moment of half disbelief and crazed reality the look I gave Draven was one that spoke volumes, even if he didn't know who I really was. It was as easy to read in my eyes as the whispered *'It can't be'* from my lips and that was my crushed heart and now battered soul.

It was done.

It was finished.

It was over.

And I had failed for good this time. Because how could I love a man who was about to give the order for my torture? How could I lie with this man and be expected to give him the piece of myself that I had only ever reserved for one man? Because having sex and making love were two entirely different things and with Draven, even at the hottest and wildest of times, it had always been done with the deepest of love between us. I could give a lot in my life but I couldn't ever taint the love I had for him, not even to save the world...*because I just didn't know how.*

It would be like sleeping with a different man just because the Fates told me that was what I needed to do. And right now, looking into those cold black eyes, I knew there wasn't one shred of the man I knew looking back at me. And then he spoke and sealed my fate, along with what could be the future of the world.

"It is time to show our newcomer what happens to those who disrespect their King and one who has shown them such generosity." I ripped my gaze from his and unfortunately it landed on his poisonous bitch. The evil grin rivalled any Demonic being I had encountered who had been intent on killing me and I had to wonder in that moment if this hadn't been her plan all along. Maybe if she thought she had scared me enough with her threats that she could get me to run from Draven? Because either outcome would have worked for her. If I had made it then I would simply be one less female to worry about stealing her King's affections. And if was caught, well I didn't really need to state the obvious as that was happening now. But from the sick look of glee on her face then this choice was definitely the more favourable one for her.

Well I wasn't about to give her the satisfaction she craved and I certainly wasn't going to let this darker version of Draven see my tears. No, I was stronger than that...*or at least I would try to be.*

But then Draven spoke and sparked a glimmer of hope,

"Unless the act was committed for reasons I do not yet know...a threat of life perhaps?" I looked up and in his eyes what I saw was clear, he was willing me to speak up, which made me wonder...did he know what had been said to me in the pool? Was this a test? I looked towards the guard who was standing at the ready and had his hand on the whip coiled against his thigh. So that would be my punishment if I didn't speak up? If I didn't lie and blame his chosen favourite for her actions, actions that in my heart I knew wasn't the reason for me trying to flee.

I couldn't lie and say that the thought didn't appeal to me...*greatly.* She was a bully and quite possibly a murderer but did that give me the right to condemn her to the same punishment I was about to receive? Draven always spoke about my kind clean soul and up until this point I never really thought much about the true meaning behind those words. Yes, I had sought revenge against those who had hurt me and those I cared for but that was from direct actions taken by another. But now I had the choice to hurt someone and draw that first line in the sand before stepping over it and becoming someone I knew I wasn't. Could I really make the man I loved a liar by my actions? Could I darken my soul to save myself some pain?

It felt like another test and this one I *wouldn't* fail, because...

I wouldn't lie.

I don't know who was more shocked when I shook my head, Draven or Stateira, who up until now had looked almost ready to bolt for the door. I watched as Draven took a deep breath in defeat and said,

"Very well." Then he nodded to the guard and this time I didn't fight. I just let myself be pulled over to the wall like last time and when my hands were raised, I didn't resist. Because I knew that this wasn't just my test but it was Draven's as well because if he let this happen, then I knew within my heart of hearts that he would have failed, just as I would have done if I had lied. After all, he had picked this clean soul of mine to love and now he could choose whether to darken his own or not. And as the shackles were firmly shut around my wrists I knew the soul I had chosen to love was growing darker by the second.

My front was pushed against the stone and I couldn't help but yelp out in surprise when I suddenly felt my tunic being ripped open from behind, baring my naked back for maximum punishment. I took a deep breath trying not to think about the burning slash of pain that I knew was coming and instead raised my head up in a forced bravery, gripping onto the chains to hide my hands from trembling. I tried to block out the sounds of the guard behind as he obviously uncurled his whip from his belt. I heard it snap against the floor as if he first needed to test his swing. I tried not to flinch but couldn't help it.

Then I heard it. That mighty swing overhead cutting through the air at speed and I tensed waiting for the lashing pain to hit me…

But it never came.

Instead I heard the crack of the whip landing on skin but it wasn't mine that it hit…

It was Draven's.

"ENOUGH!" He shouted and I looked to the side and over my shoulder to see he had stood in front of me like a protective barricade, putting himself between me and the guard. He yanked the whip from the guard's hand and uncurled it from the arm he had used to take the blow. Then he threw it to the side angrily and I started breathing heavy, my chest heaving as my heart beat wildly at the knowledge that he had just saved me.

"My King?" The guard questioned, obviously confused.

"I think I made my point," he said in that authoritative tone that was not to be messed with…well, by smart people anyway.

"But my King, she needs punishment! Think of the disrespect she shows you! The disloyalty, the…"

"Like the disrespect you show me now as you question my judgement?" When he said this Stateira instantly started to back track and I couldn't say I blamed her, not with the barely restrained anger in his voice that was clearly directed her way.

"I…uh but no…I just worry for others who will see such

mercy as a weakness," she said sounding surer of herself as she continued.

"Is that so?" Draven asked her, crossing his arms over his chest and even I could tell by the sound of his voice that he was leading her into a false sense of security.

"I do my King, for my loyalty is always by your side." Hearing her kissing ass this way meant I had to force myself not to make a gagging noise.

"Then perhaps your devotion and loyalty are easily proven. Tell me, should I have you take her place and receive the same punishment for showing me an equal level of disrespect?" I wasn't the only one who seemed shocked by his threat as there were a few in the crowd who sucked in a surprised breath, but it was Stateira's reaction that held my attention. She looked as though he had slapped her as she took a step back as if recoiling from the mental wound he inflicted.

I couldn't see his face but the look he gave her must have been one that required an answer. Knowing Draven, if I had to make a guess, it would be an expectant raised eyebrow, one that prompted her to shake her head indicating a firm no.

"Clearly those feelings of devotion and loyalty don't run as deeply as you would have me and everyone else believe. I suggest in future you pay more attention to your own actions and be less willing to relish the punishment of those whose actions could well be by the force of others." Draven said cutting straight to the point and no doubt doing so in a way that made others believe what he himself obviously wanted to believe...that it was because of her threats that had got us all here in the first place. Of course, only I knew the truth and that it was actually through his own actions that had made me run from him, but I didn't think it wise to voice this now...or ever for that matter. Hell, my soul might be clean but I wasn't saying it was squeaky!

"Now get out of my sight before I change my mind!" he snapped turning his back to her and focusing his gaze on me. I met his dark eyes for only a few seconds before he looked down the length of my exposed back and when he fixated on my bound ribs that's when his expression turned hard once more.

I didn't know what to do or say, not that there were many options for me to do right at that moment. But what I tried *not* to do was flinch when he took those few strides needed in order to reach me. He didn't touch me, not right away and I wondered if it was because he was worried that he might frighten me. I don't suppose my reaction was going to help him dispel that thought as I purposely looked down, unable to meet his eyes with him standing so close.

He towered over me and his body became an imposing force behind me. I could feel the wall of solid muscle at my back and as much as I hated to admit it, I couldn't help but find a familiar comfort in knowing that such strength stood between me and this brutal world. Let's just say that the feeling was more than a little conflicting considering it had only been minutes ago that he was the man calling the shots in this brutal world against me.

"I hope you have learned your lesson, little Lamb of mine?" I still couldn't look at him when he asked me this but knew it was not the time to push the limits on his mercy, so I decided a nod would be the safest way to respond. But this wasn't enough for him as it was obvious he wanted to look into my eyes. His thumb and forefinger gripped my chin gently as he raised my head up so that I had no choice but to look back up at him.

"Then I suggest this time you tell me the truth," he warned and everything about his demeanour told me I was in big shit because he wasn't letting this go. I was just thankful that we were interrupted.

"Should we take her back to her room, my King?" A guard

asked approaching from behind. Draven's reaction was a protective one as a hand shot to my uninjured side so he could pull me closer to him, yanking me back hard against him as if feeling a threat. He no doubt didn't miss the sharp breath I took.

"No! She remains with me. Order your men back to their posts, Commander." And as much as his actions had been one of protection his voice was clearly one of a possessive nature.

"Yes, my Lord," the obedient Commander said before bowing in respect and doing as he was told.

"That's enough now, the King has spoken! Get yourselves back to bed all of you!" Parmida shouted clapping her hands and reading the signs that her King had obviously had enough of an audience.

"Ready to sing, little bird." His voice in my ear was like a warm caress against my skin and I could feel his smirk an inch from my neck as he felt me shiver at his touch. He knew how much he affected me even after witnessing this frightening side of him. But being only a second away from experiencing his wrath as a violent lashing against my flesh wasn't something I could easily forget or forgive.

I bit my lip to hold in my whispered plea and given his greater height he could easily see it.

"I warned you about that lip once before and also what it would do to my restraint," he told me and I instantly let it slip from my teeth, telling him without words that I didn't want him to lose control. Once again he must have found this amusing because I braved a look back at him and saw that smirk for myself this time.

"What is it, Parmida?" he asked not taking his eyes off me but obviously hearing her approach before I did.

"My King, if I may speak with you a moment?" Draven didn't reply to her but instead ran a single finger down my cheek and said,

"Don't go anywhere." And then with his other hand he rattled the chains I was still attached to. I wanted to growl back at him but didn't think it wise to show my sass, not in a place so open as this where I knew prying eyes still watched.

I looked to the side as Draven walked a short distance away to speak in private with Parmida and I couldn't help but wonder what was being said. Thankfully whatever it was it didn't take long before he was back as my arms were quickly starting to ache being held above my head for even a short time.

"Is the room ready?" I heard him ask as they both approached and suddenly my pulse rate doubled. What room was he talking about?

"It was prepared the moment you informed us of your late arrival, my King."

"Good. See that we are not disturbed," he told her curtly in reply.

"Yes My King of Kings," she said and was swiftly gone, no doubt to issue her own orders. Well whatever it was I didn't have long to think on it as Draven's presence was once again behind me, making himself known with a power that simply pulsated from within him.

He didn't say anything but when he ran his hands softly up my arms I knew he was finally releasing me. I didn't know what it was about the act that made it feel so sexual or whether that was just nature's way of saying that two souls meant for each other would find that sexual chemistry in anything they did. But being this close to him and having all choices taken from me whilst being completely in his control was doing strange things to my feminine core. Even the skin on my arms felt hypersensitive, leaving tiny bumps in a trail he left behind from his touch.

I expected to feel the weight removed from my wrists but this didn't happen. Instead he simply lifted me high enough so that the chain that connected the shackles was freed from the unlit torch it was hooked over. I winced from the ache I felt in my shoulders as my arms were slowly brought down.

"The ache will ease," he told me so softly it was hard to believe that it belonged to the same man who had been so harsh with me not so long ago. But that hard temper was long gone and had been replaced by gentle hands that were currently rubbing the ache from my shoulders making me want to moan in pleasure. In fact, I was getting so lost in the feeling that I had almost forgotten my current situation and the realisation that I was still chained up and half naked in preparation for my punishment. One that never came thanks to Draven passing his own test. But what now? Well that was what I was about to find out when Draven turned me around to face him.

The beauty in that raw masculinity was almost staggering. The Draven I knew had always been handsome in that dark and dangerous way but I was used to seeing him issuing his orders and commanding his people wearing a suit. That clean cut serious look that told you this was not a man to be messed with even though he was wearing Armani. But now? Well this was something else entirely.

If I was to look at him as just a man, then I would say he looked more born to fight than to rule. To look at him as I knew him I would say he was born to rule without the fight. But to look at him now I would say every part of him, Angel, Demon and man were born to fight for the right to forever rule and that fight wasn't just one that meant spilling blood. Because wasn't that what we were doing right now…forever fighting for the right to be together in our future? Looking at him now and I would say other than our timespans being millenniums apart, nothing had changed between us.

This had me wondering if the reasons for me running weren't just down to discovering my greatest fear and the second I had felt a hint of it I bolted. Fear can consume you enough to replace rational sense for insecure madness and the fear of not being meant for Draven in any time was one I wasn't willing to stick around and live through. Well, that was until he caught me and gave me no choice. Which brought me back to the man himself and me gulping down a lump named lust when he revealed his body by removing his cloak.

Even though his torso was mainly covered by a metal chest plate his arms bulged from his strong square shoulders and his large biceps looked to be created mainly from swinging a heavy sword around in battle for hours on end. Thick leather straps crisscrossed up one of them where a small dagger sat in its sheath against his forearm. On the other side he had a well-worn studded gauntlet fastened to his other forearm and he almost looked as though he had stepped straight off the battlefield. Did this man ever wear anything to relax in? But if I was being honest I didn't know what I found sexier, the way Draven could fill out a pair of jeans from behind or him looking like Conan the Barbarian.

Without a word Draven threw out the cloak and wrapped it around my shoulders in one swift motion. I was just thankful that the front of my tunic had survived the rough treatment and was hanging down in one piece staying there thanks to the sleeves which had remained intact.

Once he was satisfied what he did next was something even more unexpected. He gripped the chain that was dangling down in between my hands and pulled it up until my hands had no choice but to move up with it. Then he dipped his head enough to loop it over his neck meaning I had to take a step closer and rest my shackled hands against his chest as they had no other place to go.

The look he gave me was unmistakeable and it felt as if he was trying to brand the memory of this moment to his very soul. He leant his head down so he could tell me his own thoughts.

"There is little chance of you escaping me now, Little Lamb." Once more this left me swallowing hard and the slight spark in his eyes told me that he didn't miss it. After this he lifted me up into his arms being mindful of my injuries and not jarring my ribs too much. I had always been amazed with Draven at how such obvious strength displayed by just the look of him could be so gentle. But I think seeing him this way and that amazement doubled. Someone who looked so capable of causing so much destruction with his bare hands and here he was handling me like some delicate flower wilting in his arms.

He strode towards the back of the room giving no mind to those who saw us or the many servants we passed. They would scurry along with their heads lowered as if they feared bringing forth the beast they were obviously used to seeing in their master and the thought wasn't a happy one. I wanted to believe things were different now in my own time and even though the respect Draven was shown by his people, I still knew that many walked on eggshells around him.

Hell, his temper was something his own brother used to poke fun at and that was when I first knew him. Since then of course, I had seen it first-hand, many times in fact. However, the difference was that I was in the position to easily fight back against it knowing there wouldn't be any dire consequences to face other than adding fuel to his purple flame. None say, that could get me whipped and punished anyway. Which is why being here I had to tread carefully, which basically meant not acting like my usual hot-headed self and more like his submissive 'Little Lamb'.

Okay so it meant going against the grain doing so but until I knew more about the man I was dealing with I couldn't fight him. Which is why I let myself just be carried off still chained to him like some willing sex slave and if I was being honest, that thought wasn't one I hated…quite the opposite in fact. However, when I saw Farrin being escorted away by a couple of guards it was enough of a sobering sight to diminish these lascivious thoughts pretty quickly.

We looked at each other over Draven's shoulder as we passed and I wanted to call out for her. The remorse I felt was like a weight crushing me from above and I could only hope that she wasn't being implicated in my escape. At first I didn't realise that Draven was looking down watching me and I wondered if he was trying to gauge my reaction at seeing her or not. It was obvious she had been found long before I was discovered, which was why the guards were already half way to finding me back in the marble maze.

"What will happen to her?" I couldn't help but ask in a small quiet voice that spoke volumes of my guilt.

"That all depends on you," he replied unsympathetically as he looked ahead and while he wasn't looking down at me I freely bit my lip, only in worry this time. I remained silent as he walked to the back of the room where the wall was lined with small arched doors situated either side of a much larger, grander one. It was an elaborately carved door that was arched with beautifully painted pillars either side and above. Unlike the others it had a complicated locking system on it that looked to run the full height of the door, making me wonder if it was keeping people out or keeping something in.

At first I thought Draven was going to turn and when I saw Parmida standing there as if appearing out of nowhere holding one of the smaller doors open I thought this was where we were headed.

"All is ready for you, my King," she said bowing but for some reason Draven was hanging back as if he was changing his mind about taking me. Doubt clouded my heart for a moment and that shadow of insecurity came haunting back. He looked down at me as if trying to find something he was desperately looking for. I had no clue what he was thinking but when something obviously clicked within him he spoke,

"Not this time," he said to me and I felt strangely crushed that he had decided that he no longer wanted to be alone with me. At first I had been fighting with myself as to what would happen the second we were alone together and if it would mean what I guessed it would mean. I had worried the time wasn't yet right but that had been the self-doubt talking. Because I knew that the second I was back in his arms the truth would remain and that was that I wanted nothing more than what that door represented.

Draven and I alone.

"My King, have you changed your mind?" Parmida asked looking confused and surprisingly slightly disappointed for me.

"I have," he stated firmly and then turned back to the larger door once more. I didn't understand what was happening, was he returning me to my little bedroom or not?

"But my Lord, you have never..." Parmida seemed to know what was happening and the panic in her voice wasn't at all comforting.

"Leave!" he snapped abruptly, cutting her off and silencing her concerns. But I couldn't get her face from my mind. That last look of terror as if she was preparing herself for never seeing me again. I had no clue what was behind the door as I had never been in there before or heard any of the others talk about it, but for some reason it transported me back through my own history. A flash of images played out like an old movie reel taken straight from my memories.

It was when Layla had stabbed me that night in the VIP and Draven had picked me up to carry me through to his home for the first time. Back then I had been drawn to those doors like a moth to the flame but for unknown reasons. I had no clue back then what such an action represented just as I didn't now but for some reason my brain had brought that replayed time back to the forefront of my mind. And when he walked me through the door I finally knew why it felt so familiar.

It was Draven's first act of love towards a human girl by breaking his own rules as he did now by stepping us through to his own ancient version of his true home…

Afterlife.

CHAPTER EIGHT

FIRST TIME

I wasn't scared, just as I wasn't the first time I entered Draven's domain, but instead it felt more like a piece of the world I knew. I don't know exactly when it was that my own human world started to become the foreign one and the supernatural one felt more like home to me. But I just knew it had been a long enough time to take root and hold me there as if it never wanted to let me go.

So when Draven walked inside this hidden part of his home, I didn't want to do as I was told and close my eyes like he commanded.

"You are not to look Little Lamb, for this world is not meant for your tender eyes…*not yet,*" he told me when we approached a gold door after he had walked deeper underground, deeper than even the Harem was. I knew what he was doing and what scenes he no doubt wanted to shield me from. I knew why he was trying to protect me but there was no hiding what my other senses were telling me.

As soon as we walked through I could smell the burning

incense that acted as a drug to the mind and I could hear the beat of drums and jingling sound of gold coins as they tapped against the skin of erotic dancers. But most of all I could smell the sweat dripping from heated bodies and hear the moans of where that heat was being generated from. There were very little sordid acts of sexual content that I hadn't seen in the supernatural world and thanks to the likes of Lucius and Jared, well, let's just say I was far from being a prude.

But the King over it all who held me now knew nothing of this and must have thought me as innocent as I suppose I looked.

"My King, will you not play with us tonight?" A woman's voice purred, whilst another added,

"Yes, come play Arsaces, you're welcome to bring your new pet." And once more a different voice spoke up and agreed with the others,

"We promise not to bite...*hard.*" I shuddered against him, hating the green serpent of jealousy that coiled tighter in the pit of my stomach.

"Silence your tongues, all of you!" Draven roared at them as we passed and I found myself gripping onto his breastplate as his body tensed in anger. I heard the little moans of disappointment from behind us as they knew they weren't going to get what they wanted tonight. Which was when the dangerous cogs in my mind started turning. Suddenly the horrible truth hit me and no amount of being used to his world would prepare me for it. This right here, in this very room we walked through, this...

Was his real Harem.

It all made sense now but why then had he brought *me* here? He knew I was human and I was probably the only one he had carried through this room we were in. Why would he risk me seeing this hidden life of his? It made no sense, even if I had my eyes closed, I still had ears to hear but more importantly, I still had lips to *speak* with. He didn't know me enough to trust I wouldn't speak of this to others. That I wouldn't gossip about the King of Kings' hidden rooms, vast depths below his city and one that was closer to the demonic side of him that I shouldn't yet know about. Or did he believe he could simply wipe the experience from my mind? Which begged the next question... could he control my mind in this time?

This was a frightening thought as I had been forced to endure a taste of this when we first met and I hadn't cared much for it back then. I like to think that it wasn't a possibility after everything we had been through but of course I was forgetting the worst part about all this and that was our time together hadn't yet come to pass. And another fact that only seemed to back up my theory was that I had entered his world with no power of my own.

It was a scary thought and one it would seem I was left to worry about for some time to come because he didn't seem as concerned as I about any of this. Not considering he was carrying a human girl into the depths of his secret world as he continued through and there was no denying the screams of pleasure or the howls of the supernatural climax that was found by the males in the room.

I had to ask myself, was this another test? To see how I would react to hearing all this? Was it to feel every jump or flinch my body made so close to his or was it just to test my willingness to comply with his order to keep my eyes closed against such tempting circumstances? I didn't know it then or if I ever would but in the end it didn't matter because soon we were through the room and silence was all that greeted us... well, nearly all.

"Just what do you think you are doing, Brother?!" Sophia's voice turned out to be more of a temptation for me than anything else and before I could stop myself my eyes snapped open to find my dear friend looking back at me. However, it only took a second to realise that it wasn't the Sophia I knew and like her brother, I was faced with a very different version of her. The look she gave me was only to be described as one of pure loathing or in the very best case, one of disgust.

She even looked different and it wasn't just down to her ancient Middle Eastern attire. Her hair was pinned back in a harsh bun at the back of her head, one with gold rope coiled around it. Even the thick black makeup around her eyes gave her a cold, unfeeling appearance and it was more like looking at an evil twin than the lovable Sophia who I had come to know like a sister.

"Not now, Saphira." Draven said calling his sister by what must have been her name in this time.

"Not now? More like not ever! Brother you do realise what it is you have just brought into our…?"

"Enough! Now do not question me or my reasons again," he told her sternly, cutting her off from what she was about to say. Then he continued to walk and this time I could see where we were going. I was also left both dumbstruck and heartbroken at hearing my friend speak of me in such a way. I knew it wasn't the Sophia that I knew and loved like a sister but still it was a hard bitter pill to swallow, even if I had an ocean to drink it down with.

This reaction only ended up strengthening what I already knew and I couldn't then for the life of me understand why no-one knew who I was to Draven in this time yet they did when Draven and I first met back in the forest. It didn't seem to make any sense, for the only person to know of me was Ranka and I feared that without the Oracle I would never find out.

I was so lost in my own thoughts that I didn't even realise

which room I had been brought into until the sound of the door slamming shut behind us jarred me from my dark mind.

"Where are we?" I couldn't help asking, forgetting myself momentarily.

"I would have thought that obvious," he told me honestly and I guess looking around the room and seeing his bed, then yes, it was obvious. But he didn't know that I had been here before, just not in the physical sense. This was the room I had not only dreamed about the last time but also the same one I had dreamed about all that time ago after first meeting Lucius in my room. It had been when he had retaliated against me after his mind control hadn't worked and Draven had to heal me. Well I can certainly say that when dreaming of Draven back then I would never have thought I would ever be seeing it in real life, that was for sure.

The way he spoke to me rendered me unable to look at him. It sounded like a combination of restrained anger and breaking point lust. That thick rasp in his voice told me to watch myself carefully as I didn't know what he was liable to do next. It was a bit like approaching a wild animal for the first time and being unsure of what they would do, bite your hand off or nuzzle you affectionately.

"I take it that was your sister?" I asked thinking this a safer route to take the conversation. However, his reaction told me I was dead wrong. He suddenly dropped my legs, gripped my waist with one hand which was enough to turn me roughly to face him. My hands were still shackled behind his head so I instantly went up on tiptoes so I wasn't hanging with my feet off the floor.

"I didn't bring you here to talk about my sister," he growled taking a step towards me with every word until he backed me up against a sandstone pillar. I could barely move quickly enough to catch up and would have tripped up many times had it not been for his hands spanning my ribs and holding me up.

"Then why did you?" I braved asking, letting just the hint of annoyance spark in my voice. He raised an eyebrow down at me as if my bravery surprised him. I didn't suppose he was used to being spoken to this way or having who he would consider a slave question his motives. Like he said, I knew why I was here as it was blindingly obvious but at least now he knew that I wanted to hear him say it out loud. And I had to confess, I was intrigued as to what his answer would be.

His hand quickly snapped out and circled the column of my throat in a heartbeat.

"Why do you think?" he growled applying pressure. My eyes widened in surprise and I wondered if he would let me breathe before I passed out. However, I wasn't left wondering long because he must have been watching me for signs that I needed air. I felt his fingers loosen their grip just in time before I would have been coughing thanks to the burn in my lungs. Instead I simply sucked in little gulps of air which he quietly let me do whilst watching my every move. He seemed so angry that it had me questioning where the root of it lay?

"Time to confess, Little Lamb," he told me after I couldn't answer him and it wasn't the reason I had first thought as the obvious one. Looking at him now and getting lost in the same eyes I had all those years ago I wanted to confess, but much more than he knew. I wanted to confess it all like so many times before. All my sins against him starting with the very reason I was here.

He was so dangerous to be around and not just in the physical sense. I couldn't help but crave this man in a way that made me not want to think why. I didn't want to question the reasons because there were no words that would describe the type of power he held over me, even like this, in this brutal time. I just didn't care and I was fooling myself to believe otherwise. Oh yes, running from him had been just another form of running from myself.

"Why did you run from me?" he asked me and I knew it was now or never.

"I...I...I..." I stumbled out that one letter word and knew I had to tell him something because that one look alone told me my time for stalling was up.

"Tell me why!" he ground out between gritted teeth.

"Because being around you is dangerous." I blurted out, telling him the truth and that look of lost patience soon became one of surprise.

"You still believe I want to hurt you?!" he snapped. I pulled on my chained hands to make my point which in turn pulled against his neck.

"I keep you where I want you, but make no mistake girl, if I wanted you punished then I would have whipped you myself!" he shouted down at me and I winced looking away from his angry stare.

"Then why didn't you?" I threw back at him, no longer acting cautious. I didn't know why I was pushing him the way I was but I knew that the adrenaline I felt when doing so was almost addictive.

"By the Gods girl, I am questioning you as either having a simple mind or a bravery that can only be explained as welcoming death to act in such a manner," he told me and my mouth dropped open in shock.

"I am not simple!" I told him angrily, letting my temper get the better of me.

"No? Then tell me which is it to cause such stupidity in speaking to a King that has your life in the palm of his hand?" he asked squeezing his hand once more to emphasise his point.

"Only if you tell me why a King who has such a simple life

by the throat isn't yet taking its last breath for speaking to you this way?" I asked knowing he felt every word force its way passed his palm. The look he gave me was one of both respect and confusion. He obviously had never met his match in a woman before, or at least other than his own sister.

We seemed to remain in this silent stand off for I don't know how long but I knew it was finally over when his eyes softened and his hand relaxed. He released my neck only to move it slowly to my exposed side before caressing my bruised ribs.

"Because I think it is quite possible to endure enough pain by the hand of a man, even if that hand belongs to a King," he said looking down at my injury before finishing his sentence locking his intense gaze with mine. I took a shuddering breath before giving him my own answer.

"And I speak to you now not as my *King* but as a *man*, for where I am from, men and woman stand together as equals." Saying this certainly piqued his interest as he raised a questioning eyebrow at me.

"So you do remember?" he asked me and I quickly bit my lip forgetting myself. That flash of purple was unmistakable and so was that hungry look at my lips which spoke of only one thought…

Carnal lust.

I let my lip slip from my teeth and swallowed hard before quickly thinking my way out of this one.

"I haven't forgotten what morals were ingrained in my upbringing, no." At this he gave me a one sided smirk and I could tell he was finding the way I spoke amusing.

"And what did your father think of your mother's teachings on the subject?" he asked and I wanted to laugh myself at his question but more at the answer I was all ready to give him.

"Who said it was my mother's teachings and not my

father's?" His eyes grew wide for a moment before he threw his head back and burst out into laughter, one that unmistakably belonged to *my* Draven. I had to reach up and grip onto his shoulders to keep myself steady as his laughter was causing the shackles to pull at my wrists.

"But of course. It is only a father's teachings on such things that can spark such a brazen fire in a daughter's belly...I bet if someone put a dagger in your hand then you would rather fight to the death than see yourself beaten by a man...am I not correct?" he said with a spark in his eyes that told me he was both serious and pleased. I couldn't help but blush which he took as his answer.

"Ranka told me of your bravery in fighting back against the man who did this to you, with nothing but what the Gods gave you," he said raising his arms up to his neck so that he could cover my fisted hands with his own.

"But take heed little one, I may like seeing such a fire glow behind those beautiful eyes of yours. However, I will not accept that fire being hissed my way again when I am your King," he warned and my natural instinct was to argue back but in the end I decided against it, asking him a question instead.

"Then tell me... who are you to me when we are in this room?" I could tell my question had caught him off guard by the look he gave me. It seemed I was quickly making a habit out of surprising him.

"Who am I in this room?" he asked, repeating part of my question and stepping further into me so that he was pressed up against me. I looked up as far as I could, which forced the back of my head to brush up against the pillar. His lips came down to mine and I held my breath in hopes that they would meet my own.

"I am the man who owns you, Little Lamb," he informed me on a firm whisper and the effect was strong enough to render

me under his control if he but asked me to surrender. And this was all down to the feel of his lips that finally met my own in what was our first kiss in this time. The second we came into that delicious contact with each other it was as if all that time between us started to just crumble away into nothing but a cavernous black abyss.

I opened myself freely to him and in doing so he tasted me for the first time making him groan the way I loved. I had never fit this way to any other man before in my life and I didn't want to with anyone but Draven. But I wanted him to feel the same way and if his reactions were anything to go by, then I would say that it was mission accomplished. He held me locked to him with one arm banded around my torso and I didn't care about the pain I felt twinge in my ribcage as nothing else mattered but the feel of no barrier between our bodies.

His other hand gripped the back of my hair using it to keep my head back and my position as open to his erotic assault as I had first made it. It felt as though he was not only fanning the flames he spoke of in my belly but he was creating an inferno deeper down that not only touched my soul but also my sexual core. I wanted to give him everything right then and there and by the desperate way his hands held me, I would say that he was as close as it gets to taking it.

He let go of my body and ripped the cloak from my shoulders startling me before pulling me back to him. I let my mind wander for a second into wondering if he growled when undressing the others in his harem but then quickly let that thought fade away before the jealousy became a sticky residue that I couldn't get rid of.

He was devouring me in his kiss and if I didn't know better it seemed as though he had never felt this way before or maybe that was just my hope talking. His hands were everywhere and neither one felt like it wanted to stop discovering my body. I moaned in his mouth as his tongue battled with mine in what seemed like a fight for greater passion. The taste of him was sweeter than usual, as if he had not long ago been eating fruit dipped in honey and this, along with his masculine scent of leather and steel, was utterly intoxicating. In fact, I was getting so lost in his touch and the power he had over me that I didn't realise just how much of himself he too was getting lost in and the power I obviously held over him.

But there was one staggering difference between the way we lost control and only one of us had a Demon that wanted to break free. Of course I was used to Draven's demon side coming out to play but right now, he just wasn't used to me being there to play with.

I heard the first rip of material and saw that darkness in his eyes start to glow with purple fire and I knew he was close. I found myself with the unshakable need to push him further until he could no longer hide this side of him from me and I knew just how to do it...

So I pushed.

I moaned even louder and threw my head back, arching my neck and baring it to his Demon in the ultimate sign of submission. His hands pushed up my back either side of my spine so that I arched further against him, pressing myself into him. I wondered if he heard himself growl the way I did or if he just no longer cared. Did he want me to see this side of him?

Well I soon received my answer, even if it wasn't the one I wanted. I had just barely closed my eyes when I first saw the signs of him losing himself to his other side. He threw his own head back and looking up I saw his fangs emerge ready to plunge them into my offered neck. The primal rumble that then emerged told me he was mere seconds away from taking that last step needed but that's when something stopped him.

What happened next did so in seconds and in a wild, still

lustful heartbeat he gripped my wrists and yanked hard enough to snap the chain between the shackles. By the time I opened my eyes I found my arms had dropped to my sides like heavy weights and I was left panting... *alone.*

"No." I whispered to the now empty room. I let my legs slide out beneath me as I slowly slid to the cold hard floor. I pulled my knees up to my chest and lifted my sore chained wrists up so that I could hold myself in this protective ball. Then I let my head rest back against the pillar and let go of all the tears I had stored up.

I felt more lost now than I ever had before and it was all down to a love only one of us felt. Because no matter what we had endured over the years, we had done so knowing one simple truth...our love had carried us through it together. Sure there had been times we had fooled ourselves in thinking otherwise or times we had faced our battles alone but in the end it had been the love we had for each other that allowed us to conquer not only our fears but also our enemies.

Every action taken by both of us had been done out of love. Even now by taking this quest into an unknown past, one where I would never belong, I still held on to the shred of hope that Draven's everlasting love was strong enough to travel through space and time.

But I was wrong because at the moment of truth...

Draven had left me

CHAPTER NINE

JOURNEY'S END

I don't know how I did it but I must have passed out from emotional exhaustion. I didn't remember much after Draven left, not that there was much to remember other than my tears and looking out to the dark city wondering where it all went wrong. I had come so far only to fall at the first hurdle. I felt broken and worst of all, I'd finally allowed all my old fears to come flooding back. I felt like I did that day when seeing Draven on the balcony with Celina, when he pretended she was his fiancé. I knew now that it hadn't been real but the feelings I felt at the time certainly were and it was the same as I felt now…

I wasn't good enough.

At least not for the Draven of this time. And why should I be considering the pick of beauties he had lined up and waiting for just a look from their handsome king? I knew that somewhere in the back of my mind there was a part of me trying to break through with some shred of reasoning, but right now I wasn't letting it in enough to take shape. I didn't want to give him excuses, I just wanted to sit here and allow myself the time to wallow in self-pity like anyone else would. I was getting so tired of being strong and pushing through the hurt until it looked brighter on the other side. No, I just wanted to live out a few simple moments of my life thinking like most would. Sod being the Chosen One! I just wanted to play the heartbroken girl that felt crushed by rejection.

Was that really so much to ask?

Well I didn't think so as I spent the rest of the night sitting there crying myself to sleep. Or even when I allowed my dreams to mirror my feelings into the subconscious. Because instead of just allowing him to leave me behind in my dreams, I chased him. I reached out and tried to grab onto the figure of him running away from me. But as it was in life it was in my dreams and he was too fast for me to catch.

I would run until my legs were close to crumbling. Racing first down the corridors of this sandstone palace before it started to merge into a better world I knew. But even being back in Afterlife brought me little comfort as I still chased Draven down the corridors of a place I considered home.

Why was he still running from me?

I felt like I would never reach him and even when I lost sight of him I didn't give up. I spun around and around looking everywhere for just a glimpse of his shadow, casting shapes and pointing me in the right direction to go. I knew I was calling out for him as I could feel my lips moving but yet I heard no sound echoing along the walls. I even asked why he was running from me, hoping that the question would travel these old walls. But there was nothing but silence.

I asked myself what it was that I had done wrong or I would shout out what it was I could do to make it right but again the emptiness around me didn't answer. So I did the only thing that my heart told me to do and I let it lead me into the Temple.

I was shocked to see what faced me there and even being surrounded by the smoky images of my past was the last thing I expected to see. I watched on in amazement as they acted out as if they were stuck to live out the misery in some morbid play like ghosts that couldn't cross over. The mystical show started with scenes of my first steps into the sacred tomb. I couldn't help but feel sorry for the scared little girl who was so naive back then and who looked around in terrified wonder.

Then I watched Lucius battling the skeletons of Supernaturals once laid to rest and my former self building up the strength to help him. I shuddered at seeing Alex again even if it wasn't in the corporal sense. Just seeing that evil sneer through the floating vapour was enough to have me running away from the nightmares of my past. I didn't want to see Lucius die for a second time, the first time still haunted me to this day.

And even though I made it without witnessing it, I stepped through just as I heard my past screams of pain behind me. Of course, I didn't need to look to know what I would find. It made me wonder if ever given the opportunity to go back and warn those we love what would happen? Would it change the past enough to bring peace or would it backfire and only cause more pain? Well running into the next room had me thinking about what I would tell the foolish girl hiding from Draven's temple guards as she waited for a demon girl to be dragged from her cell.

I thought back to that night and realised now how much I still had to learn. How much pain and heartache I would endure over the coming years and not just by the mistakes I made but also by the mistakes of others. Was that what I was doing now? Was I dreaming of all this as a way for the Fates to try and tell me something. It did often feel like history was repeating itself and chasing Draven as I was now felt like life on replay. So much so I was almost too scared to find out what the Temple itself had in store for me. Thinking back on all that had happened within its elaborate walls was too much for anyone to deal with, let alone for a second time.

So I wasn't surprised when I walked through years of memories all bombarding me one after another. Life on fast forward and flashing through a smoke screen. A room full of hooded figures all fading into the next like dominos until reaching their master plunging a knife into a wasted vessel.

Lovers experiencing their first dance then replaced by the gruesome truth of Draven's responsibilities as a misty crowd looked on and cheered. Then happiness too quickly evaporated into a great battle between good and evil fought with equal amounts of love and hate and ending by a brother's blade forged from dangerous loathing and magic.

But last and most important to date was a wedding of the likes of no other, one consummated under a pair of wings belonging to the two sides of Heaven and Hell. A union of chosen hearts merging as one under Heaven itself to witness. It was painfully beautiful really and it made me grip my heart as if it was being pierced from behind. But as I watched that last image fade another pair of wings took its place, one belonging to the same man, only this time...

He was alone.

It was a haunting sight as the smoke cleared to reveal the broken shell of a man beneath. The figure of Draven on his knees and praying to the very Gods he was at the same time cursing to damnation. His wings outspread and shaking with both anger and utter anguish. I couldn't stop the silent tears as they fell with each step I took closer and I dug my nails into my palm if only to keep the sobs at bay. I wanted to comfort him. To run to him and tell him all would be okay now, I was here. But for some reason I didn't...

I couldn't.

That's when I finally realised why.

One by one the room started to fill with the last of my memories yet to come and each of them held the same shadowy grief on their faces. The room started to change too and looked just as broken as the people I loved who all looked on at the depressing and final scene that played out in front of them. However, I was the only one to brave stepping closer to see what it was that Draven now held in his arms.

I gasped into my hands as I took that last step as it all started to make sense now. The reasons Draven ran from me were not for the reasons I first thought. The life the Fates wanted to show me as I journeyed to where I knew I must go. For what was waiting for me when I got there was the cold slap of reality I never wanted to see. The horrific truth that faced my future no matter what paths I travelled down.

The destination was always to be the same place…

Dead in Draven's arms.

CHAPTER TEN

WE WILL BURN

Hearing Draven cursing my choice to leave him as I lay dead in his arms was by far the worst of my nightmares so far. In that moment I could almost feel my heart shatter within my chest as I tried to grip onto it with both hands. I looked down at myself and saw that it wasn't just my heart that was fading away into a million pieces but also the rest of my body. It was as though I was made from thousands of pure white skeleton leaves and someone had opened a window. I was slowly blowing away in this painted underground tomb with nothing to hold onto but my broken soul.

And as the last pieces of me floated away the memory of Draven throwing his head back and roaring his fury up at the Heavens would stay with me like a punishment for my unintentional sins. It was the way he held my bloody broken body in a crushing hold to his chest as black tears fell from the eyes of a Demon in utter agony.

"No…no…please…" I pleaded down at him, but it was no

use as it was drowned out by his demonic rage. I was floating so far now that it almost felt as though the pieces of me were being carried away by Angels.

"I didn't want to leave...I never wanted to leave you..." I whispered down at him because I was desperate for him to know this as my last goodbye.

"Neither did I, Nāzanin." I gasped when I suddenly heard his voice whispered back in my ear as it broke the spell. I tensed my body which was once again whole and when I opened my eyes I was no longer locked in my nightmare...

I was back to being locked in this reality.

"Ssshh now, don't be scared for I will not harm you," Draven said looking down at me with concern. Seeing him this way immediately after seeing him in my dreams was like swallowing a bitter pill and having no choice but to force it down just so that I wouldn't choke. I loved him but he wasn't the man I fell in love with.

"I...I am not afraid," I told him after clearing my croaky voice.

"Then why is it you shake like an arrow in the storm?" he asked as he lay me down on his bed made thick from the piles of furs. I looked down at my hands and frowned when seeing them not only still shackled but like he said, shaking like a leaf. I had obviously fallen asleep after he had left me and from how sore my eyes were, I gathered I had done so crying. I decided to answer him with the truth, no matter how childish it made me sound.

"I had a nightmare." His reaction wasn't what I expected it to be and when his eyes softened I could relish these few foolish moments to allow myself the time I needed believing I was looking at the Draven I knew...*the Draven from my time.* It was the same look I always woke up to when he knew I had suffered from what my dreams had put me through.

"Then I am even more sorry that I left you alone," he told me sweetly after he joined me on the bed and I blushed as he stretched out beside me.

"Why did you?" I braved asking, too curious to let it go. He had his head propped up on his hand and bent elbow and I was flat on my back so had no choice but to look up at him. At first I didn't think he would answer me as he seemed too lost in his thoughts to even hear me. He had started playing with strands of my hair and wrapping them around his thick fingers like he had so many times before back in a bed I called 'ours'.

"Because I know that I should stay away from you as being with me will only bring you a heartache I will never be free to soothe." The truth of his words surprised me as it sounded like a heartbroken confession. Therefore, I couldn't help asking,

"You are destined for another aren't you?" His eyes snapped up to mine with his own shock. He looked thoughtful for a moment as though he wanted to explain but then how would he? So in the end he settled for something else and unbeknown to him, it was equally as painful.

"The Gods have their plans for us all," he told me and I wanted to laugh out loud only it would have been without humour and more out of irony.

"Yes and I often wonder what they will throw my way next," I told him honestly before turning over and facing the other way, knowing that I couldn't look at him any longer. I knew I sounded bitter but really, how could it be helped? I wanted to scream out at the same time that I wanted to run away. I think he was also thankful that he no longer had to see the underlying pain in my eyes for he let me turn from him without protest. Instead he put his arm under me, pulled me close and moulded his front to my back, making me feel even smaller than usual.

Thinking about what he'd said and combining this with his

actions I knew there was no hope, even lying here in his arms the way I was. He was waiting for his Chosen One and even though he was obviously conflicted with how he felt about me, it made no difference and his statement about the Gods only confirmed this. Because if his reaction after just one kiss was to rip himself away from the moment, then I couldn't see how we were ever going to take it further?

I couldn't help but think about how much simpler all this would have been if he knew who I really was.

"I should leave," I told him as I looked out onto his balcony into the night, wondering how many more people out there felt as lost as I did right then. I felt his arms get tighter before he growled in my ear,

"No, I do not permit it." I released a sigh before saying,

"You may not permit it but that doesn't mean that it isn't the right thing to do," I told him softly, wishing the sound of my voice didn't break the way it did.

"Time is all some of us have in this life and right now, having you here in my arms is enough to consider as a gift and the right thing to do is not ignore such a blessing," he told me and I was just glad he couldn't see the tear that trickled down into my hairline. They were such beautiful words but I knew the time he spoke of was only mine to lose, as I was mortal…*he wasn't.*

"Then I will stay," I told him knowing this was what he wanted to hear, at least enough to make him relax his hold on me.

"Good. Now you can tell me why you were ready to take such a punishment in place of another?" he asked, stroking the hair off my neck and surprising me with the sudden switch in conversation. This time I was the one to tense in his hold and with it he could tell that it was a conversation I would rather not be having right now…*or ever.*

"Parmida told me of what happened earlier with Stateira and her threats," he added after I still wouldn't say anything. I had a feeling this is what she had needed to speak with him about as it wouldn't have looked good coming from anyone else, not when so many people had witnessed it. Again I didn't say anything which no doubt prompted him to roll me around to face him so I was once again on my back with him looming over me.

"Explain this to me," he demanded in a sterner voice. Right in that moment I so wanted to lie but once again I opened my mouth and the truth came out.

"I am not afraid of her." I told him and this time my voice didn't waver.

"Then why did you run from her?" he countered and this was where things got complicated. I knew I had to carry on what I had started to say and just hoped that he would keep his temper in check long enough for me to explain.

"I didn't run from her…*I ran from you.*" I whispered this last part not taking my eyes from his. I knew the exact moment he started fighting with his temper and therefore the other side of him which began to show when the tiniest specks of purple started sparking through the black.

"Why?" he asked through gritted teeth.

"Self-preservation," I told him making his eyebrow arch, so I continued.

"After all, it's like you said, you will only bring me a heartache that you're not free to soothe…I knew this before you said it, so therefore thought it best to run before I experienced a taste of it for myself, *although it's too late for that now.*" I muttered this last part even though I knew that he would hear it. Well it didn't matter if he did or not, he'd already witnessed it for himself when he walked back into the room and found me in the same position in which he left me, only the tracks of my tears were definitely hard to miss.

He obviously didn't know what to say as he silently stared down at me before shifting to allow me more space. He sat up and it was only now that I could see he was bare from the waist up, unlike before. I quickly realised it wasn't just the scar on his face that he had kept on his vessel, not allowing it to heal but also the ones on his body as well. I guess when you were injured in battle in front of an entire army, it was a little difficult to explain making it through those injuries without a mark to show for it.

I didn't care either way, as it wasn't like I was without my own scars, strangely ones he hadn't yet asked about. I knew he was frustrated when I saw him bend his head and push all his hair back with both hands. I couldn't help but smirk having seen this same action a hundred times before and usually because of something I had said.

I decided to move and when I started to pull myself up he shot me a look over his shoulder. As a human who had no knowledge of the supernatural, I would have naturally questioned how he moved his hand so fast when he suddenly grabbed me. It was obvious that with one look he thought I had been about to run, but after seeing that I wasn't going anywhere he relaxed enough to let me go, so that I could continue to sit up as was my first intention.

"You told me that you think I am dangerous to be around," he said out of the blue after long moments of silence and he did so without looking at me. I pulled my legs up to my chest and let my head fall back giving me that sense of déjà vu from only an hour ago. I looked up at the flames dancing in the oil lamps and knew it might have been safer putting my hand in one than the fire I was currently playing with by being here.

"You are," I eventually answered. He looked back over his shoulder once more and the undiluted lust I saw heating up his gaze caused me to gasp. He looked up and down my body as though eyeing up his next meal and once more had I been any normal girl I would have been running in fear from the purple flame I saw spark in his eyes. Did he not realise how much of himself he showed me? I didn't have long to question it further because he grabbed my ankle and yanked my body down quicker than human eyes could track. In the same swift movement, he was holding himself above me keeping me caged in by his large muscular frame.

"You're wrong," he told me in a tone that gave away far more than his words ever would. No doubt he was angry at his own lack of self-control although he probably wanted to blame me, but in the end he knew that he couldn't.

"You are the dangerous one, for the power you hold over me feels like a dagger in your hands held firmly over my chest and one simple push is all it will take to destroy…" he stopped himself before he said it but I couldn't let it go. *Not now, not ever…not with this man.*

"Destroy what?" I asked on a fearful whisper. He closed his eyes and finished his sentence over my lips before falling into his own trap once more and kissing me.

"Everything." I gasped in the agony of just that one word and he swept right in there to taste it for himself. I allowed myself to lose the hurt in his touch for just a few seconds before I could stand it no longer. This time I was the one to break the kiss as I turned my face from his lips and started to push at his shoulders to stop him. It didn't take him long to get a clue but the look of shock was almost laughable. It wasn't hard to guess that this must have been a first for him.

"Get off me!" I shouted when he only allowed a few inches between us. He frowned down at me before I lost my mind and gritted out my threat,

"Now." Something very serious must have shown in my eyes or heard in my voice because after this he lifted himself

off me very slowly. The second I saw the gap was big enough I, on the other hand, flew off the bed like Banshees were nipping at my heels. I could feel the night air cool my bare back but it did nothing to cool my temper. I wanted to hit something and could feel the familiar tingling in my fingertips which told me that I needed to calm myself down. And I needed to do this pretty quickly before I started to give him a show I couldn't explain. Well, there was my answer as to why I didn't have my powers, it was obvious now what my catalyst was…

Draven.

Why was it that heartache, pain and anger walked hand in hand and undoubtedly ended up with one fuelling the other?

"I have upset you?" he asked and I snapped, forgetting the part I had to play and this time being nothing but myself.

"You're Goddamn right you have upset me!" I shouted and the shock in my outburst was easy to see for someone who wasn't completely lost in their own anger yet.

"You dare damn the Gods because of me?" he asked of me in utter astonishment but I was too far gone to try and find the caution in all this.

"After all they have done to me in my life, you're damn right I will!"

"You are not in your right mind and know not of which you speak," he replied obviously trying to find a reason for what he must have considered irrational behaviour. Well this Draven didn't know me and if he did, he would be the one walking on caution right now.

"You're right, I must not be in my right mind now if I am still here talking to you!" I snapped and walked straight up to the door ready to walk through it and never look back…well at least until I had calmed down that was. This is when he finally started taking me seriously.

"Stop! I do not permit you to leave!" he demanded, getting up from the bed behind me.

"Like I give a shit!" I said and opened the door only to find it being slammed shut with his hand coming out from over my shoulder.

"Do not forget your place little lamb, for I am still your King," he warned in my ear and I shuddered before my anger shook off the affects he had over me.

"Then do your worst, because as far as I am concerned, you already have." I snarled back at him looking to the side he was on. I could feel his panting behind me as his own anger was building but this time I just didn't care.

"You think I won't punish you?" he asked me and I looked back to the wooden door before closing my eyes, taking a deep breath and speaking the truth,

"You already are by keeping me here."

"Then I intend to punish you a great deal longer for you are *not leaving,"* he told me, whipping me around to face him and pushing me back against the door. The face of Draven was quickly getting lost to his demon side and I had to wonder what his excuse was going to be when he lost his last shred of control completely.

"Fine, then I do so as your prisoner and as a slave... *not* with a free heart." I told him and after seeing his eyes narrow on mine for a second he pulled away.

"Then so be it."

"I don't understand." I told him shaking my head as he walked away from me.

"It is simple, I am your King, I give you an order and you obey," he answered arrogantly and I wanted to growl at him in response. However, I replied,

"What I mean is, I don't understand why you would want me to stay considering how you feel about me. If I am so dangerous, if I am such a threat to *everything*...then tell me this...why am I even here, *why chance it?"*

"Why do you question me like this?" he asked ignoring my question with an aggravated one of his own.

"Because I have a right to know." I told him but at this he scoffed and said,

"As a slave you have no rights to anything." I would have been hurt hearing this if I didn't know who I was to him.

"Maybe not, but as a woman about to give her heart to a man, then I have every right." I countered and I could tell by the look he gave me that he wanted to argue but hearing that kind of admission on my part, then what could he really say?

"One thing is for sure, your bravery is never to be questioned," he said shaking his head at himself as if still trying to fully comprehend my brazen behaviour.

"That's not an answer," I told him, folding my arms across my chest and he turned back to me, slashed a hand through the air and snapped,

"That's the only one you're going to get!" I decided this wasn't getting me anywhere so I made the decision to play this power exchange to my advantage.

"Fine!" I said before reaching up to my sleeves and pulling them down as they were the only part of the tunic that was keeping the shredded dress in place, keeping the front part of my body covered.

"What are you doing?" he quickly asked unable to keep the startled tone from his voice.

"You won't let me leave?" I asked pausing my actions and looking up at him across the room. He folded his arms and said,

"I will not permit it." To which I tilted my head in a way of saying, 'so be it' and then I pulled my dress off and threw it to the floor leaving myself standing naked opposite him.

"W...why...?" he started to stutter and I wanted to laugh at the sight of this mighty warrior king lost for words. Then I reached up and pulled the pins from my hair letting it rain down my back as I slowly walked towards him. The power I felt from such a bold action was like sucking down an aphrodisiac elixir that heated my belly before dipping down in between my thighs.

His hungry eyes drank in the sight just like I knew they would and I looked down slightly to hide my smirk just before coming to stop directly in front of him.

"Because I am not sleeping in that... just as I am not sleeping in these..." I said first looking back at the discarded dress before then holding up my shackled arms to him and giving them a little shake.

"You play with fire, Little Lamb." Draven warned looking down at my wrists as if now only just realising that I still had them on me. His eyes spoke volumes as to what he would prefer to do and for a moment I held my breath stuck in a luscious limbo. And it was lucky I did for it meant I was slightly more prepared for when he snapped...

And snap he did.

First his eyes widened at the sight of the chains dangling down that he had broken getting free of my kiss and this no doubt only managed to bring back how it felt to have me chained to him, which from the look of things, he very much wanted to experience again. Then he looked back to my eyes to see if I had heeded his warning but whatever he found there told him all he needed to know when he said,

"Then we will both burn together!" And with that he grabbed my wrists and spun me around to raise them to pin to the wall before he kissed me and this time he was right...

Our passion burned.

CHAPTER ELEVEN

IGNITE THE INTERRUPTED

Kissing Draven this time felt as though I could have opened my eyes and seen us standing in the middle of our room back in Afterlife. It felt like I was finally *home*. There was no resistance and no holding back this time because whether it was right in the wrong time for me or wrong in the right time for him, it didn't matter because it could no longer be denied by either of us…destiny just wouldn't allow it to be.

His hands still circled my wrists adding flesh to iron as he held the shackles pinned above my head. My head was thrown back enough to reach his lips and his muscular back was arched so that he could dip his head to reach mine, but it wasn't enough. He knew I needed more when my moaning could no longer be ignored.

"Impatient, little one?" he asked on a chuckle, pulling back enough to look down at my body trying in vain to mount his.

"More," I whispered as I strained against his hold to get closer to him. His eyes blazed for a millisecond enough to let

me know what that one word did to him and I looked down to see the other effect for myself. He watched my wandering eyes until they came back up to meet his and we spent those intense couple of seconds trying to read each other.

There were no words needed to explain what was about to happen as we knew if we crossed this line then it could change the world, for me the prophecy but for him...well, it was nothing short of an eternity of damnation for his sinful soul. Because if he did this, then in his mind he would be breaking the number one rule for all Supernaturals...

Sex with a mortal.

And I would be letting him because only I knew the truth. Could I really do this? Could I really let it get that far knowing what he thought of me or worse, what he *would* think of me when he found out who I really was? God I was so confused! It suddenly felt wrong no matter how much I wanted it...and by the Gods but that kiss...I felt like I was drowning in it and pretty soon I would be so far under that I would never see the surface again, let alone have any chance at reaching out for it.

I felt his fingers uncurl from my wrists before he ran them down the length of my arms. It felt so good that I closed my eyes and let my head fall back again on a moan. He must have liked this reaction because I heard his growl before he suddenly embedded his fists into my hair, roughly forcing my lips back to his. The warmth of his kiss as his tongue battled against mine was intoxicating. I felt drunk from it and knew I was losing the sense to tell him what I needed to. Of course, this didn't help when he ran two fingers down my bare spine making me arch my body further into him, which was his intention.

"Your body is so responsive to my touch, as though it was made for my hand to control," he told me and to emphasise his point he gripped my side causing me take an uncontrollable step into his frame, which had me pressing up against his very hard and obvious erection.

'Tell him Keira...tell him now...' A voice in my mind spoke to me and I almost jumped in surprise. *Was it her? Was she back?*

"Katie?" The question slipped out and Draven froze. My eyes snapped open to find his own narrowed my way and just as his mouth opened to ask the question there came a banging at the door. He closed his own eyes in what could only be described as frustration before he snapped out angrily,

"I warned you not to push me on this, Saphira!" That's when the door swung open to show Sophia standing there taking in the scene with nothing short of utter rage which she obviously tried to mask but I knew better.

"Well your new Pet will just have to wait for you, for there is news from Rome," she informed him calmly but like I said, I knew better. She was quietly seething inside, which quickly made me realise how lucky I was to have Sophia on my side from the very beginning. I couldn't, or more like *didn't want to* wonder what it would have been like any other way as seeing her like this, then I had to be honest, Sophia kind of scared the shit out of me.

"He is here?" Draven asked looking over his shoulder at her but thankfully still shielding my nakedness from view with his body.

"He is and as always he is as impatient as ever," Sophia said looking at one of her nails which looked as though they had been dipped in gold paint.

"Very well, go inform him that I will be there shortly," Draven ordered and for a moment I didn't think she would do it as she just looked at him as if to say, 'excuse me'.

"Now, Saphira!" Draven reiterated in one of those 'do as I say' tones. She rolled her eyes like a spoilt child before leaving

on a huff. Draven turned back to me once the door slammed shut and released a heavy sigh.

"I must leave you," he told me and I could tell not only by his voice but also the way he held on to me that he didn't want to follow through with his words.

"That's alright, I can just…"

"No!" he shouted, stopping me from slipping out from his hold. Then he closed his eyes for a moment as though he felt pain before he said,

"I want you to stay here."

"Why?" I asked causing him to look down at me once more.

"Because that way I know you will be safe and that I will also have you waiting for me in my bed for when I get back. That way my meeting will no doubt go much quicker." I couldn't help but smile at not just the compliment he gave me or even the obvious concern he showed but also the slightest hint of a sense of humour. I was so touched by the gesture that I braved raising my hand to his cheek and running my fingers down his bearded face before reassuring him.

"I will stay." He looked so touched by the gesture that it was easy to see his surprise. He took my hand in his before I let it fall away from his face and he raised it up to his lips to kiss. Then without warning he lifted me up in his arms and started to carry me back to his bed of furs. He lay me down gently as though I was easily damaged and ran his fingers across my bruised ribs proving that yes, to him I guess that was true.

"I wish I could have punished them myself," he told me in a thick voice that spoke volumes of his displeasure and the underlying anger that burned there. I covered his hand to draw his attention elsewhere and pulled it from my ribs up to my lips as he had done. I kissed him lightly on the palm and heard myself say,

"There is nothing to be done about the past." Straight after this I wanted to laugh aloud at my words as they didn't feel like my own. In fact, they felt like poison as I don't think being a person who has travelled back in time in order to change the future could be any more of a hypocrite.

"Maybe not, but there is much to be done about the future and with you laid upon my bed like the goddess you are, then there are many plans to be made in my mind about what I will soon do with this beautiful body of yours," he said softly, making me blush as he ran his fingers around my breasts and up to my sensitive nipples that quickly pebbled under his slight touch. I closed my eyes and moaned, once more so close to begging him to stay and show me these plans.

"I could easily become addicted to those little moans of yours but even more so to your taste." He said this at the same time he snaked a hand down my belly before dipping his fingers down in between my legs. I cried out and arched off the bed as I felt him swipe a finger through my wet opening and up against my sensitive clit.

"Mmm, not just the beauty of a Goddess but also one blessing me with nectar from the Gods," he said after putting his finger in his mouth and sucking my juices off it. I felt my cheeks burn and he smirked down at me knowing my embarrassment.

"I look forward to drinking from the source, my Nāzanin," he whispered down against my heated cheek and I wanted to ask what he meant by that name, one I had heard him call me once before but again I was too overwhelmed by his sexual words and what they obviously did to me.

"But what is this?" he said turning his head and focusing on the top of my arm. But before I had time to question what he was referring to I felt him lick across my arm expectantly. Then he looked to my other arm to find the same red markings I had made earlier to help me find my way out of the harem. He pulled back to look at me and what I found in his stare could only be described as...*admiration?*

"What a clever little Lamb you are, I had wondered how you found your way so far from the flock. And you call me dangerous." I frowned up at him and asked,

"What do you mean?"

"Like I said, you are the dangerous one, for with a body and mind like yours combined you would certainly make a king a formidable queen and no doubt be a force to be reckoned with...but by the Gods what fun that king would have." I couldn't help but bite my lip at his words and how playful he could be when teasing me. He growled when he saw what I was doing and said,

"I warned you." Then without another word he was quickly kissing me again but this time he started by sucking in my bottom lip and biting it for himself. Now this really did make me moan and soon without thinking about it my legs were wrapped around his waist and I was once again close to begging him to enter me.

"By the Gods woman!" he shouted suddenly, pulling himself back and panting like a wild animal after the kill.

"Did I do something wrong?" I asked timidly, wondering if this wasn't the way to behave for a woman of his time.

"Something wrong...what with your exquisite body all hot and slick ready to take my ready cock and clamp it tight like you never want to let go...answer me little one, does there sound anything wrong about the image I create?" I shook my head unable to speak after hearing his erotic and deliciously crude description.

"The only thing wrong with it is time and the length of which I will have to wait until I can bury myself in your wet sheath...and I warn you again my sweet one, once there I will be in no hurry to leave such a treasure unguarded." Okay so I had to say that I certainly liked the sound of that as just hearing his dirty words and I was close to exploding and he had barely touched me down there.

"I wish you didn't have to leave," I said honestly, glad that I did if the pleasure on his face from hearing it was anything to go by.

"No more than I, sweet girl," he replied running his hands down my sides, spanning most of my torso and grazing his thumbs along the sides of my breasts. The action was so dominating, as if proving what he could do to such a body with a pair of large hands and a commanding presence.

"But before I go, lets free you from your restraints, considering we won't be needing them any longer," he said smiling down at me. He lifted up the first one and pulled out the pin releasing the thick iron bracelet. Then before letting it go he examined the skin and frowned.

"I left these on too long, forgive me."

"It's okay, they don't hurt," I told him which was a bit of a lie considering they were most likely bruised. I don't think I was fooling him when he gave me a sceptical look.

"I will have to make sure to have some padded ones specially made for you for next time." I choked on a breath and questioned,

"Uh...next time?" He smirked up at me with playful eyes and said,

"Oh yes, I rather enjoyed having you chained to me and will certainly be reliving the moment, only for longer this time... *much longer.*" My eyes widened at the unexpected comment and I suddenly flashed back to Draven's cave where he had once done something similar. I was about to bite my lip once more simply out of habit when the pad of his thumb stopped me.

"That lip is no longer yours to bite," he told me with a stern and dominating look that I had no choice but to take seriously. I didn't know why but hearing him say I was *his* made me feel sad. I couldn't help but think of the man who truly owned my heart and was back home waiting for me to walk down the aisle and become his wife for the second time. And even though I was here in those same arms, I knew they weren't the arms I craved to hold me. I couldn't help but think about it as I missed him.

I missed my Draven.

"Come back to me, little one," Draven whispered down to me and I shook off my melancholy before I had to explain the tears I could feel coming.

"Sorry, I was just thinking about someone who used to tease me when biting my lip." I told him and he frowned.

"I hope this wasn't by another man?" he asked sharply. I smiled up at him and told him the truth,

"No, it wasn't by another man." Then in my mind said, 'It was by you.' Hearing this made him relax and I knew now to remember that jealousy was also a big issue with him in this time as it was in my own.

"Good. Hearing this pleases me for no other man is to touch you...*do you understand?"* The way he said this I could do little *but* understand as the hard edge to his jaw and purple tint in his eyes told me he was as serious as a heart attack, let alone the growl in his voice.

I don't know why but I couldn't help the vision of all the other men in my life popping into my head and I thought back to all my friends, wondering where they were in this time? I knew Jared hadn't been born, let alone been turned into Lord Cerberus yet and it was the same for Sigurd and Ragnar as they too hadn't yet been born as humans but what of Lucius? Where in the world was he? Because I knew that he had been changed after the crucifixion of Christ not long after being tortured as a traitor. This closely followed by being chosen by the Devil to serve as King of the Vampires.

So surely this must have happened by now? This is where it would have really helped knowing what year I had made it back to but even then...what would Lucius be like in this time? Was he working with Draven yet or was he out there on his own? But more importantly, why did that thought worry me as it did?

I tried to replay the history the two of them had together in my head but without knowing the dates it was hard to comprehend. I knew that they had been not only allies but also brothers at arms for the longest time, but when did they first make their alliance? Lucius had been Draven's right hand man for a small forever before they became enemies and, other than Vincent, had once been the only man that he had once called brother.

Which bombarded me with even more questions and this time they were about Vincent. I hadn't yet seen him but knew he must not have been far from his brother's side, so where was he? I was so curious that I almost asked him, but then how would I explain my reasons for doing so? No, it was better left for the likes of Ranka, who would know why I asked...of course now all I had to do was find her again to get the chance to actually ask her.

"What is that pretty little mind of yours thinking?" he asked me giving me a quizzical stare and it was only when he said this that I wondered how he must feel about not being able to read my thoughts the way he could with most humans...or had he simply not tried? I found that doubtful somehow.

My god there were just so many questions I felt like my head would soon explode!

"Just that the sooner you go the sooner you can return to me." I said instead and this worked, as what else could I tell him? Thankfully his eyes softened from their intense stare as he heard what he wanted to and I was saved from telling him the truth, which felt like madness since arriving here.

"And return for you I will," he said as a way of goodbye before placing a light kiss on my lips. Then he covered up my naked body to ward off the night's chill. After giving me one last look from the door, he left knowing no more words were needed for his eyes said it all…

He was falling in love with me.

CHAPTER TWELVE

LOATHE TO BE FRIENDS

I knew I was asleep when I felt a presence enter the room and it was one of those times when your dreams seem to merge into reality confusing your mind as to what was real and what was make believe. I stood upon a rooftop and looked out to a vast space of unsettled sand that had been transformed from desert to battlefield.

The sun was close to setting but before it could cast these horrors back into darkness it showed me the death and destruction that I knew my actions had caused. I didn't know what those actions were yet but I just knew from the tears that I shed upon looking down at the dagger I held, that there was an army's worth of blood on my hands.

"There was nothing you could have done, Keira." A familiar voice came from behind me as I wasn't alone on this rooftop. I looked down and to the side as way of acknowledging her without having to meet the same tears in her eyes.

"Maybe not, but what about you…could you have stopped this?" I asked the famous Oracle of Delphi.

"Some wars are destined to be fought, no matter the cause that fuels the hearts of men whose swords cast the first strike." I closed my eyes knowing whose heart she spoke of and whose hand was behind that sword.

"But am I always destined to die?" I asked feeling the tears fall for a very different reason.

"That I cannot answer for it is not my heart you fight for, Electus." I released a held breath knowing I would receive an answer like this as I always did. I knew what I had to do, I could feel it pulsing in my palm as though I held a live heart that still continued to beat in my hand. It was almost as though the dagger was speaking to me the way that Lucius' sword once had back in the Temple. Only this time instead of telling me his own story, it was trying to tell me mine. Now if only I could decipher what it wanted me to do.

I had heard its legend and how it came to be, but now gripped in my hand none of it mattered. It was now an extension of my soul and had fused itself to me in a way I couldn't describe. As though something I didn't yet understand held it with me and wouldn't let it go until our destiny had been lived through and we had battled together.

"And if he knew I lived, would that end the death?" I asked watching as hundreds fell with every second I stood here waiting, trying to figure out the right thing to do.

"I am afraid the sun has set not only on the day we faced but also on our King of Kings, for he has only darkness left in his soul to fight with." I knew she was right, he wouldn't stop until he had killed them all. For he was coming to claim his queen, whether she breathed or was bathed in blood, I was his and he would stop at nothing to reach me.

"Then I think it's time I go keep my promise." I said gripping my dagger tighter, knowing that it was what I would use to deliver that promise.

And a blood coloured blade was just the thing when cutting the head off a snake…

A snake that had betrayed a King.

I woke on a scream because when I opened my eyes I knew I was no longer dreaming and the horror I faced was real. Sophia was stood over the bed with her face close to mine. She had her head cocked to one side as if trying to make me out and if this in itself hadn't been enough to give me a fright then seeing her in her demonic form doing so certainly was.

"Why so frightened? You look as though you have seen a Demon," she said smiling and in her demon form it wasn't the usual endearing sight I was used to. Skin like sand cracked and peeled from her face like dead flesh that had turned to ash. The slashes either side of her lips gave her grin a sadistic craziness that told me not to make any sudden movements. I knew this was a test by the way she studied me and my reactions.

"I just…just didn't expect to see you." I said trying to keep my voice as even as I could at seeing her this way. She raised a flaky eyebrow and I knew she didn't believe me. But what could she say, 'I know you can see me human'… not likely, so in the end she rolled her demonic eyes before clicking her fingers and snapping back to the Sophia I was used to seeing.

"Come with me." She snapped out the order after she obviously didn't get the reaction she was hoping for, which was no doubt to scare me to death or make me run a mile.

"Why, where are we going?" I asked having a bad feeling about this.

"Do you know who I am?" she asked with such arrogance it made Draven look like a kitten compared to her.

"Yes." I said quickly, deciding it best not to piss her off any more than I obviously had done.

"Good, then stop asking questions and do as you are told, slave!" she shouted and then threw some clothes at me. I caught them and twisted them in my fists trying to dispel some of the anger I felt towards her. I wish she had at least warned me that she was an utter bitch in this time but then again, she obviously saw me as a threat of some kind. Which had me wondering what her attitude would be to me if she knew who I really was? Would she have welcomed me as she once did when we first met? Was I actually someone she considered a threat...*to myself?*

The thought was almost laughable, considering she was trying to eliminate any threat to her brother finding his Electus, when here I sat. I was almost tempted to tell her who I was but as I watched her storm out, slamming the door behind her I knew it was unlikely she would even believe me. After all, if her own brother didn't recognise his own Chosen One, then I doubt she would believe me telling her otherwise. Which meant I could only hope that her version of making me disappear didn't include Stateira's version of making me disappear, where I ended up dumped in the desert somewhere with a knife in my back.

I decided I had little choice than to do as I was told so I slipped from the safety of his bed and dressed myself in the long plain kaftan she had given me. There was also a long scarf which she obviously wanted me to put on to hide myself away. So I knotted my hair behind my head using the pins from the floor I had discarded earlier and wrapped the scarf around my head. Then after a deep breath I opened the door to the viper waiting on the other side. Well, if I was ever curious as to what it would feel like to piss Sophia off then I could consider that curiosity well and truly fulfilled.

There were four guards standing around her who I hoped were only there to escort me far from here and not to find use for their curved swords which hung in their leather sheaths. Sophia gave me a seething look that almost curled her lip and reminded me of an aggravated jungle cat.

"Let's go," she said throwing over one length of her silk scarf which hid half of her face from view. I didn't say a word as I followed her with guards either side of me and I couldn't help but feel that sickening chill creep up my body as though I was being led to my death and not to my freedom. Strange then how my mind wasn't panicking as though when the time presented itself I would know what to do or was it simply misplaced trust in a girl I still loved like a sister? Whatever it was I followed without emotion and without judgement for I knew this wasn't *my* Sophia doing this to me.

I don't know how far we walked but it was obvious how big this palace was when I didn't recognise any of it. We were walking down a long corridor of open arches on one side that showed the sun was rising in front of us. I must have slept longer than I thought if it was the start of a new day…and what a start this was, I thought bitterly. But then who was this now stepping out from the shadows…

"Ranka." Sophia hissed the name answering my silent question. With the sun to the back of her she looked quite formidable with the blades at her sides and the large bow at her back. Almost like some warrior elf ready to do battle in the most graceful of ways. She kept her stance at the ready and even with her arms folded you just knew that she could have had an arrow embedded in your skull in a heartbeat if she chose to do so.

"Going somewhere, Saphira?" she asked with deadly calm.

"And what is it to you? I have the right to go where I please in my own home!" Sophia replied in anger.

"But not with the King's new head concubine you don't," Ranka replied cool as a cucumber and I wanted to do a fist pump shouting 'Boo yeah!' but thankfully I refrained, thinking it would totally ruin Ranka's bad ass moment. Sophia looked back at me and snarled as if this was all my fault…which in her mind, then yes, I guess it was.

"This is no business of yours, so leave now before I make you answer for your insolence," Sophia threatened venomously.

"I answer only to the King of Kings," Ranka reminded her and this was when Sophia lost her temper.

"Fine! You want her, then take the little whore, for you will soon see what will happen to your King of Kings when he beds her!" The pain of her words was far worse than the pain of her nails digging into my arm as she grabbed me. Or even when she suddenly threw me across the room, causing me to slide sideways the rest of the way to where Ranka stood. I had to say I didn't really care for the way Ranka chose to prevent me from knocking her over like a pin at a bowling alley when she just calmly placed a foot on my back to stop me.

"Princess," Ranka said bowing in reply and with an aggravated huff Sophia stormed off having just stamped on my heart.

"I must ask but do you manage to get yourself in this much trouble in your own time?" Ranka questioned as she helped me stagger to my feet. I winced as I straightened up knowing that thanks to my old friend turning new enemy, it had set my healing time back by at least a week.

"You have no idea," I answered her truthfully as I walked past, knowing it was a good idea to get out of here.

"I thought as much," she said pushing both blades back in their sheaths at her thighs telling me that she had been expecting a fight…or at least ready for one.

I then held back letting her take the lead as she knew where we were going much better than I.

"So I am going to take a wild stab in the dark and say that the Princess isn't my biggest fan?" I said as we walked along even more arched sandstone corridors.

"I don't understand…why would you want to fight in the dark and what has a large fan owned by the Princess got to do with it?" I rolled my eyes before repeating to myself 'simple thoughts Keira, simple thoughts'.

"What I mean is, the Princess doesn't like me."

"I would think that was obvious considering she was just about to have you murdered," Ranka said bluntly causing me to miss a step.

"She was?" I asked surprised and I didn't know why. For starters I myself had suspected as much but I guess just hearing it being confirmed by someone else was enough to make it more real. I mean this was Sophia we were talking about here!

"What did you think would happen, that she would merely allow you to just leave the palace?"

"Well, yeah…kind of," I replied feeling like an idiot but even more so when she said,

"She knows as well as the rest of us do what would happen if you were to leave here a free woman." I stopped her from walking any further by grabbing her forearm and asked,

"And what is that exactly?"

"You would quickly be declared property of the King and hunted down until found." Christ, but that did make me sound like a damn pet!

"He would do that?!" I asked in astonishment. Ranka smirked at me as if she found my bewilderment at her King amusing.

"I think it is quickly becoming common knowledge of the obsession that infects the King and come tomorrow night it will be confirmed when he chooses you as his new head concubine in front of the entire kingdom."

"He is going to do what?!"

"I must say Electus, you do work fast," she said on a laugh and it was as unnatural to witness as it sounded.

"Well I didn't intend to, I tried to run remember." I reminded her of what she obviously already knew. This was when she no longer looked amused and gave me a stern glare.

"Oh save it, I thought it the best thing to do at the time, alright." I snapped at her and carried on walking.

"Lucky for you I forewarned the King of Stateira's intentions," she said not knowing what I had already confessed to Draven but she didn't need to know that, so instead I asked,

"And what of the Princess…will you tell him of her same intentions also?" She frowned and I knew why as this wasn't exactly something that could be considered a giddy prospect to look forward to. What would she say, 'oh yeah, I just caught your sister trying to kill your girlfriend, just thought you should know before that shit gets ugly but hey, good luck with that can of worms your Majesty.' …uh no, I didn't think so somehow.

"I am not sure that is wise," she answered and I had to cough to mask my laugh.

"No, I didn't think so," I muttered after she walked past me to lead me down a darker passageway.

"So you said the rest of you?" I asked referring to her earlier comment. She raised an eyebrow at me as we walked side by side and at first I didn't think she would answer me.

"My kind has been warned to stay away from you." Now hearing this did surprise me. It almost felt like history repeating itself, only in reverse. In fact, the similarities were mounting if not just working at a much faster rate. Which had me wondering how Draven would have reacted taking away the Western ways of the world I grew up in. Because Draven as the

King was only ever used to being obeyed by both his own kind and mine, so this very much included me and what he expected of me.

I remember him telling me about how he wanted to claim me without a second thought when we first met. I laughed saying how I wished he would have, but looking back how would that really have gone down? Meeting a stranger in the woods and then being taken by him back to his castle without any say. Well, in my heart I knew that no matter how handsome he was or how swept up I was by him, in the end it was all about free will. And even though now I wasn't afraid of Draven back in my own time, back when we first met I had been, if only for a short time, just as I was now because it was the unpredictability of it all. He was the same man as much as he wasn't, just as Sophia was the same loving girl as much as she was the utter bitch in this time. The difference was simple…I just didn't know them and they didn't yet know me.

And even though it wasn't just all about time, it certainly had its part to play. Even when I think back to how much I myself had changed in just a few years then what would a few thousand years have done to me?

"This doesn't surprise you?" Ranka asked when obviously trying to read what I was thinking and getting nowhere.

"No, he did something similar back in my time," I told her and she nodded looking thoughtful.

"So what now?" I asked when I still had no clue as to where she was taking me.

"I have arranged for some private quarters for you until the King decides for himself what he has in mind for you as he will agree that the harem is no longer safe for you." I frowned wondering what Draven would do when he went back to his room and found me gone.

"Okay, not that I am complaining about being let out of the

Spa from Hell but I am not sure the King is going to be too happy when he finds me gone." I told her, ignoring her confused look about the 'Spa from Hell' bit.

"After I have escorted you to your new room I will go in search of the King and tell him that your safety was compromised. He will decide what is to be done after the choosing." I wanted to roll my eyes at the barbaric event that would essentially be a King choosing his new girlfriend from a line of dressed up cattle...did I sound bitter much?

I decided not to look a gift horse in the mouth and just keep quiet and go with the flow. After all, I was going to get my own room and no longer be surrounded by an army of beauticians who wanted to scrub my skin off and call it therapy.

"I have picked out one servant for you and guards I trust who will stand outside your door at all times," she told me as we finally approached a door that I was happy to report wasn't too far from her own quarters.

"And I am only a few doors away, one scream and I will hear you." Well one look at this warrior woman who had thankfully appointed herself my personal bodyguard and I can honestly say I felt more at ease.

"Thank you, Ranka," I told her sincerely because I honestly knew that I wouldn't have made it this far without her.

"It is my honour to do so and the will of the Gods," she answered bowing and as much as I blushed I was just happy that she hadn't called me Electus. She was about to walk away when I shouted out after her, knowing this was one of my only chances to ask,

"Ranka wait, I have to ask...any news of my friends?" I knew how vulnerable I sounded when asking this but I didn't care. I was so worried about them that with everything going on in my own time here I could only hope that theirs was far less dangerous...in other words they didn't have half as many people trying to kill them!

She gave me a sad smile that unfortunately gave me my answer before she voiced it and not surprising it wasn't the one I had been hoping for.

"I am afraid not...but do not fear for I will not give up." I gave her a smile that I didn't feel and opened the door to my new room.

"Don't give up hope...*Electus.*" I nodded, closed the door and groaned at hearing that damned name again. I certainly didn't feel like any Chosen One, not here in this world that was for sure. Look what had happened so far, it just seemed as if I had needed saving at every turn, but what about my friends? Who was out there saving them? I couldn't bear to think about it, for if anything happened to them then I would never forgive myself. Speaking of which, I looked up to see another friend of mine who I had no doubt got into a whole world of trouble...

"Farrin?!"

An hour later and I was close to falling asleep I was that tired. After seeing Farrin waiting for me in my room she quickly explained that Ranka had intervened before any blame could be directed her way, which we were both thankful for. Ranka then thought it best to appoint Farrin as my servant considering she had gained both our trust with what she had done for me when trying to escape. She hadn't ratted me out but instead remained silent, even in the face of receiving punishment for doing so. Well I knew how that felt, so the respect I had for her definitely doubled.

"You didn't have to do that for me, you don't owe me anything." I said to her when she told me how she was about to be whipped herself if Ranka hadn't stopped it. She just looked away as if searching for reasons she couldn't explain in words.

"You did it for your sister didn't you?" I asked causing her to jolt as though I had electrocuted her with a live wire or something. Did the memory of it all still affect her so?

"What do you mean...I..."

"Farrin, it's okay, I understand. I have a sister too and there isn't much I wouldn't do for her. So I get why you are helping me...the way you couldn't help your sister." I added this last part in a quieter voice as I knew it must have been such a painful subject to speak of for her.

This was when her face changed and softened in understanding, no longer looking as though she was ready to bolt for the door. I was surprised that she would rather run from me than talk about this but then on the other hand it wasn't as if we knew each other very well yet.

"I'm sorry but it is still painful," she said looking away once more, as though she couldn't look at me because I reminded her too much of that horrible time. I reached for her hand and gave it a squeeze before saying,

"I understand and if you ever need to talk about it then I want you to know that I am here for you." Once again she looked at me in disbelief, as though she couldn't believe I was being this nice to her, which had me wondering how many harem bitches she had to deal with on a daily basis.

"You are too kind."

"Not at all, it's just us good girls have got to stick together that's all," I told her laughing and wondering what Pip would have said to that.

"You should get some rest, that's the third time you have yawned," she said nodding when my brain yet again needed the extra oxygen.

"I guess you're right, a nap wouldn't hurt but then again

neither would some food, I am starving." As soon as I said this I felt guilty as Farrin suddenly jumped up and said,

"But of course! I will get you some food, for I do not want to disappoint Ranka and fall short in my duties."

"No Farrin I didn't mean…" I started to say but she was out of the door before I could finish. I shrugged my shoulders knowing that there would be just another thing I would be apologising for when she got back but until then a nap didn't sound like a bad idea. I could barely keep my eyes open and no wonder for what a night I had been through.

"Good job, Keira," I said to myself as I pulled myself up to walk to the bed like a zombie saying to hell with brains, I need a nap!

I don't know how long it was before I heard the door opening but if felt as if I had only been passed out for a few minutes. Had Farrin come back that quickly with food? I smiled just about to label her an angel when I rolled over and that nickname died as quickly as I was about to. For I was right in one sense, Farrin had come back into the room but it wasn't with food to feed me but instead it was with a knife…

To kill me.

"But why?" I asked utterly stunned at the sight of her now stood over my bed holding the killer blade with both hands directly over my pounding heart.

To which she simply answered…

"As I said, you are too kind."

CHAPTER THIRTEEN

NOW THAT'S WHAT I CALL A FRIEND

I could barely believe my eyes, to the point where I thought I could still be dreaming. I blinked twice but no, the sight of Farrin holding a deadly looking blade over me was still there to be seen.

"I don't understand?" I said frowning, but when she started smiling I knew this went a lot deeper than just simply being ordered to kill someone she didn't want to.

"And you were never supposed to. Say hello to the others I sent there before you!" she said raising up her arms and I got ready to roll at just the right moment but in the end I didn't need to.

"Hey bitch, your date's here!" A familiar voice shouted making Farrin turn her head just in time for a gold bowl from the dried fruit to connect with her face. She screamed just as her nose exploded inwards before falling backwards away from the bed.

"Was it just me or did that sound exactly like hitting a dinner gong?"

"PIP!" I shouted launching myself off the bed and into her arms.

"Oh thank God!" I said holding onto her so tight I was most likely suffocating her.

"Well to be fair on all Imps, God didn't really have much to do with it, but I get what you're trying to say…how you doing my Tootiepop?"

"How am I doing…? How am I doing…? Pip, I don't think I have ever been happier since before I arrived in this Hellhole!" I said holding her back at arm's length to look at her. She gave me an awesome grin before moaning from the ground drew our attention away from our happy re-union.

"There are always those who just want to spoil the moment," Pip said to me before walking over first to pick up the fallen knife and then to the fallen servant girl. Pip looked down at the blade in her hand before getting down on one knee.

"Pip." I said her name in warning but she raised the back of her hand, gave me the peace sign and said,

"No worries Toots, I've got this." Then she grabbed Farrin's hair and lifted her head up so that she could deliver a hammering punch across her face. Just as she did this the door burst open and Ranka, quickly assessing the scene. completely got the wrong idea.

"Get away from her!" Ranka roared at Pip before launching herself at my friend, thinking that she was the one who had come here to kill me. And to give her some credit, it did in fact look that way, considering she had just seen my servant getting knocked out by a girl who was dressed as an Arabian ninja with a knife in her hand.

"Ranka, no!" I shouted but neither could hear me over the racket they both made as they instantly started fighting. Then when the guards who had been stationed outside my room appeared, I quickly decided it was best to put myself between them and the two girls having at it, before Pip was quickly outnumbered.

"No, don't! She wasn't the one trying to kill me, it was my servant!" I told them before they could simply push me out of the way as they were no doubt about to. Thankfully the one who looked in charge held up his hand telling the others to hold back as he took in the bloody scene.

Now that I had that under control I turned my attention back to the other two fighting it out and was at least happy to see neither looked too worse for wear yet, with all limbs still intact…but for how much longer was anyone's guess.

They both looked pretty evenly matched that was for sure but at any minute one of them could gain the upper hand and do some real damage. Ranka had already disarmed Pip of her borrowed knife and was just about to use her own, attacking Pip with her curved blades. She slashed out at her torso, but Pip skilfully jumped back in time and ducked as the second blade came at her from above. She twisted her body around on one foot so that she could kick out with the other, hitting Ranka's weapon straight from her hand and propelling it through the air. It whizzed passed me, missing me by inches and I turned my face in time to see it embed itself into a wooden carving of a naked man landing right between his legs. I heard the guards wincing behind me and as Ranka got Pip in a head lock, she still had time to look up at me and say,

"My bad." Then she shrugged her shoulders before dropping her body weight suddenly by doing the splits and quickly taking Ranka off guard. The move took her by surprise causing her to lose her grip of Pip. Pip didn't waste her advantage as she spun her legs around at the same time swiping Ranka's last blade from her thigh. Then in the same move she spun herself up with enough momentum to bring her to a standing position and held the blade at her neck.

"Poo, poo bitch, I win." Pip said cocking her head to the side but Ranka wasn't without her own victory and looked down at Pip's stomach. This caused Pip to do the same thing only to find an arrow in Ranka's hand held firmly to her gut at the ready to skew her like a shish kebab.

"You were saying?" Ranka said raising a cocky eyebrow and smirking down at Pip.

"Whoa there! Wait!" I shouted at both of them, running over ready to pry them apart.

"Stay back Electus, I will handle this." Ranka said scowling down at Pip and Pip snarled back and said,

"Yeah Toots, I have totally got this!"

"Pip! You know who this is so lower the damn blade!" I shouted at her but she just shook her head and said,

"No way Jose! I will drop it when lesbo here drops hers first!"

"PIP!" I scolded and was just thankful that Ranka didn't know what she meant.

"Ranka, this is my friend, you know, one of the ones I had you looking for. Please drop the arrow…she isn't here to kill me." I told her and I started to get worried when she didn't look convinced.

"I saw her attacking your servant," she stated and Pip groaned,

"Hello! I was saving her ass you Dingbat! Bloody Nora but where are Columbo and Jessica Fletcher when you need them!"

"She had just stopped her from killing me and the scream you heard was her hitting her with a…uh…"

"A bowl filled with dates." Pip filled in and I tried not to laugh thinking back to Pip's one liner when hitting Farrin in the face. Ranka didn't look impressed but it was at least enough to convince her that those were the facts, as strange as they might be.

"Very well." Ranka said retracting her arrow and sliding it back into its holder at her back. Pip removed the blade from her neck at the same time and mimicked what she said in a whiney voice,

"Verrryyy welll."

"Pip...not now," I grumbled at her and she threw up her hands and said,

"What? You want me to say sorry for the lesbo thing, because everyone knows how much I like lesbos really, especially the really butch ones like her," she said winking at Ranka and I couldn't tell whether she was joking or not, which was the norm around Pip. Ranka frowned and obviously didn't know what to make of her but thankfully at the same time having no clue as to what she was talking about. So instead of taking Pip's bait, she cleared her throat and held out her hand to her.

"Oh right, happy stabby woman wouldn't be much good without Mr pointy." Pip said handing her back her blade. Well if she didn't understand most things I said then she had no bloody hope being around Pip! Hell, half of the time even I didn't have a clue what the crazy Imp was talking about.

"You may leave." Ranka said dismissing the guards before walking over to Farrin who was still out cold on the floor. Once the door closed Ranka lifted up her head by her hair and asked,

"Did she say why she wanted you dead?"

"We didn't exactly get to that part but I did get the impression that I wasn't the first harem girl she's tried to get rid of." I told her also walking across the room to stare down at the murderous girl.

"Yes but why, it doesn't make much sense, for what would she gain? Someone must have put her up to this." Ranka said still down on one knee as if waiting for her to jump up at any moment and explain it all to us.

"Yeah like her nut job bat shit crazy sister, that's who," Pip said and we both turned our heads to look at her in utter astonishment as she was currently examining her handy work from where she had kicked the blade that had castrated the poor carved man.

"Guess there's no more getting wood for this guy," she said pointing a thumb over her shoulder at him giggling. Meanwhile I counted to three and said,

"Please explain, Pip."

"Well I hit him in the balls and see, he's made of wood and…"

"Not that Pip, the other thing, the part about her doing this for her sister." I said interrupting her quickly before Ranka lost it completely and tried to kill her again.

"Oh that, yeah didn't you know, her sister is in the harem and is as deranged, demented and as schizo as they come!" Ranka and I both looked back down at her no doubt wondering the same thing…how the hell had we missed this.

"So it's her sister that keeps putting her up to killing the others?" I asked and I didn't need to look sideways to know that Pip had already skipped her way over to us.

"She sure as shit is! Well…anyone who gets close to her lover boy that is…ooops, sorry Toots, my bad." I shot her a look and frowned feeling like I was missing something big here.

"Wait a minute, are you telling me…?" I started to say who I thought it was when Ranka had finally caught up and figured it out herself by spitting out her name,

"Stateira."

"Bingo! And our prize goes to…our gold medallist in sticking arrows in people! For our wicked killer, people is none other than the King's head concubine, Stateira, Aka Bitch face and her twisted minion, her sister dearest…I bet Christmas is a hoot in their house, all knives, pointy shit and deadly poisons before a game of fight to the death for the last turkey leg. Hey I wonder if they would have actual human feet in their stockings or if…"

"That's enough Pip, I think we get it." I said, only Ranka shot me a look to tell me otherwise. I doubt she got even a quarter of what Pip was trying to say.

"So what do we do with screw loose number one here?" Pip asked and this time I looked to Ranka for guidance as I had no clue.

"Leave her to me and I will soon get a confession out of her." I shuddered to think about how Ranka planned to do this even if the bitch had just tried to kill me, I was still very much on the anti-torture side of the fence.

"Ooo…can I watch?" Pip said clapping her hands and proving I was the only one in the room with this mentality. Ranka raised an eyebrow at her before shrugging her shoulders and saying,

"That would be acceptable."

"Fabuloso! I do like to think that I am quite cultured in all manner of things…*and I have never been to a Persian torture before.*" Pip said leaning into me and giving my arm a nudge. I shook my head and tried to rid myself of the image I had of Pip sat with a bowl of nuts and swinging her legs grinning as she watched something like this girl's skin being peeled off with a giant cheese grater.

Well at least the silver lining in all this was that Ranka and Pip were actually getting along with one another. I guess there was nothing quite like spilling a little blood and inflicting pain upon an enemy to bring a friendship closer together.

"So okay, this may sound like the obvious question but what are we going to tell Draven?" I asked trying to get past the torture point of the conversation and skip right to the part where we had a plan.

"She means the King." Pip said to Ranka and for once translating for me this time.

"He needs to be informed of their crimes and the attempt on your life," Ranka said firmly and I didn't exactly see this going down well at the moment.

"What, like his sister just did?" I said and I knew I'd made my point when Ranka looked as though she'd just discovered someone breaking wind which, given enough jalapeno peppers, gummi bears and strawberry mojito's, Pip often did.

"Wait a freaking nanosecond and back the juggler's balls up! Come again?" I winced at Pip and told her,

"Draven's sister tried to kill me."

"Oh okay then, so in this time Draven has a crazy ass sister too?"

"Pretty much." I nodded but no surprises Pip wasn't about to let it go so soon.

"Seriously Toots, is there anyone out there that's *not* trying to kill you?"

"I don't know. I am starting to think there is a club." She laughed once and said,

"Possibly," shrugging her shoulders.

"I know not of what you speak but we still have the …" Ranka never got to finish as I shouted in shock,

"AHHH Shit!" I don't know what happened but instinct took over and I kicked out when Farrin moved, which connected once more with her face, one that was already looking pretty battered from the amount of times she had been hit there.

"Okay I think that did…uh, Pip?" I was stopped short when Pip started hitting the unconscious girl over the head with a strange shaped bowl that she found next to the bed.

"Yeah?" she asked stopping with the thing held high above her head ready for the next blow.

"I think we are good." I told her making her lower her arm and look at what she held.

"What is that thing anyway?" I asked Ranka knowing from the confused look on Pip's face that she didn't know.

"It's what we pee in."

"Eww!" Pip said dropping the brass bowl causing it to once more land on the girl's head before landing with a thud on the floor next to her.

"Ooops."

"Well it looks like she will be out of it for a good while longer now." I said dryly in response to Pip's 'Ooops'.

"I will take her. Will you be alright left with just your little friend here?" Ranka said giving Pip a doubtful look making her growl.

"Look here Miss killer personality, I have saved this girl's life more times than you have pissed in the wind, so trust me when I say, I have totally got this!"

"We will be fine." I elaborated not really understanding the 'piss in the wind' bit but knowing what she meant all the same.

"Very well, I will take my leave of you now and send word when it is time for me to get my answers." In other words, she would let Pip know when the torture show started. We watched as she ducked down and flung the unconscious body over her shoulder before walking out the door like she was only carrying a handbag.

"I'm getting the feeling that she has done that way too many times." I said to Pip once the door closed.

"I hear ya! Maybe she's a shit driver and has problems with roadkill?" Pip's comment made me laugh and I turned to her and said,

"Don't think that's going to be an issue for quite some time yet, Pip."

"Oh right, so just an issue with dead bodies then," she added nodding.

"Looks like. God Pip, you don't know how happy I am to be having this conversation with you!" I blurted out as I grabbed her to me for another hug.

"Umpf! Wow Toots, if you're happy talking about dead people then you really must be bored, that or you really do need a check-up from the neck up." I laughed and gave her a sloppy kiss on her cheek before letting her go.

"Definitely not bored." I told her looking down at all the blood that could have quite easily have been mine.

"Are you ever? Besides, I already know what you have been up to, you naughty minx you!" she said making me frown.

"What do you mean?" I asked her and she giggled before running towards the bed and jumping onto it.

"Hell on a hot day, there is zero gravity to this bed, what's it made of, sandstone like the rest of this pale joint?"

"Pip, focus. How do you know what I have been doing?" I asked her again, only this time trying to be a little more forceful. She dropped to her knees and mouthed a small 'Oww' before sitting down quietly ready to tell me.

"I have been watching you."

"Uhh, come again?" I could barely believe my ears.

"Okay so I can see how this shit might make you angry but I had no choice." I slowly sat down to try and absorb what she was telling me thinking back to how worried I had been about her.

"Might? Slight understatement there Pip, I am close to furious so let's skip the dancing around the subject and just come out with telling me your version of events from the beginning."

"Alright, but you have to understand that I had my reasons," she said unwinding the scarf she had wrapped tightly around her head to no doubt hide the mass of green hair she'd just unleashed. I don't suppose it was easy to blend in covered in tattoos, body piercings and mad hair that looked like a beacon for all that was crazy. No wonder she was covered from head to toe in black.

"I am waiting, Pip." I told her on a sigh.

"When I arrived and the Janus Gate decided to dump my ass in the middle of the desert, I took some time to find my way to the city after searching for the others."

"Did you find them?" I asked quickly but seeing her face drop told me the answer to that one.

"I didn't but at least we know they made it through like we did and no doubt with panties full of bloody sand!" Well she was right about that but what of them now?

"So you made it to the city?"

"Yeah, I stole some clothes and sneaked into the palace thinking this is where I would find you first. So imagine my utter dumb struck luck when I heard you crashing into some random dude with a stick up his ass before the King found you." I couldn't help but think back to how that first meeting between Draven and I went and how quickly he held my life in his hands.

"You were there?"

"Yeah a bloody good job I was otherwise we would now be in mission fucked up street right about now!"

"What are you talking about?" I said shaking my head and once again trying to understand Pip speak. But this was when she decided to drop a bombshell on me.

"Why do you think he doesn't yet know who you really are?"

"Oh no…please don't tell me that has something to do with you Pip, please don't…" Pip gave me a sad smile and said,

"I had no choice Toots, it's why I am here."

"I don't understand." I said in a sad tired voice before

letting my head fall into my hands.

"He can't know that you're the Chosen One, it would be too dangerous."

"But why? Do you know how much easier it would be if he did? For starters we would have done the deed by now and be scot free to then find the others and leave this God awful place!" I snapped raising my head to look at her.

"That's not what would have happened. Think honey bunches, did you ever wonder why the Fates chose the three of us misfits to come with you on this quest in the first place?" she said softly, putting a hand on my shoulder. I angrily wiped away a frustrated tear and asked her to explain.

"Sophia is here for her knowledge of this time, something none of us have. I am here to mask the true side of ourselves as is one of my gifts, so the King doesn't find out you are the Electus."

"And Ari, what of my sister?" I asked still not seeing the picture she was trying to paint.

"Well without knowing who she really is, it's only a guess but I think that she needs to be around in order for you to get up the duff preggers." My eyes widened in astonishment before quickly narrowing again with my scepticism.

"But that would make her..."

"One of us." Pip finished off for me and I guess it made sense that she wasn't fully human, not considering she was obviously fated for Vincent.

"Alright, if what you are saying is true then tell me why Draven can't know who I am because I am struggling with that one, Pip."

"You're asking the wrong person," she answered cryptically making me groan as my stress levels rose to new heights.

"Look call me a pain in the ass or a freakin' tease but the truth is I don't know why. But one thing I do know is what the

Oracle told me and that was if he finds out who you are then its mission over and we blew it!"

"You're kidding me!" She raised an eyebrow at my stupid question and I rolled my eyes.

"Bloody marvellous! So she told you to keep who I am masked so he doesn't find out, making my job a hundred times harder because to him I am just a human girl that he has to break the number one rule of his kind to be with! Oh yeah this is going to be easy...*not!*" I ranted but once more Pip squeezed my shoulder and said,

"But you're *not* just any human Toots, you're *his* human and whether I am around to mask you being his Chosen One or not, he is still going to know who you are to him or he wouldn't have acted the way he has done already. You got this, honey." I gave her a small smile and nodded knowing that she was right. He had already acted out of character going to the lengths he had done for a human. And it was only hours ago that he had me in his arms telling me all the things he wanted to do to me, so it didn't look as dire as I was acting it was. I needed to do as Pip said and see the positive in this.

"You're right but I will tell you one thing, the Oracle is going to have a lot to bloody answer for when we get back."

"Damn straight!" Pip agreed.

"So what do we do now?" I asked thinking we needed a plan of action but what she said filled me with dread.

"Well you have that 'Chosen' thingy tomorrow night, right?" I nodded on a wince making her clap with glee anyway.

"Then we need to get started!"

"Started? What do you mean, what are we doing now?" I asked knowing that I needed to brace myself but even then, it would never be enough for what she said next...

"To teach you how to dance."

CHAPTER FOURTEEN

CONFESSIONS OF THE HEART

"This isn't looking good." Pip said with one hip cocked out and a hand to her lip looking at me like I was trying to master the funky chicken.

"No shit! I feel like an idiot!" I said letting my arms fall to my sides in defeat. It felt as though I had been trying to learn this stupid dance forever!

"I think it's the scarves that are confusing you." Pip said grabbing one and then flicking it out the way I just couldn't master.

"See, it's all in the wrist action, flick and snap, flick and snap…got it?" I rolled my eyes at her and said,

"No, I haven't got it and I don't think I ever will…it's hopeless." Then I deflated to the bed on a sigh.

"Oh I know, just think of it as a whip, so in the past when you and Draven have…" I quickly held up a hand to stop her and said,

"Don't even go there Pip, our kinky shit doesn't include weapons." This made her frown at me as if *I* was the crazy one.

"By the Gods why not!? You really don't know what you're missing."

"Well if it helps and eases your mind, the Draven from this time obviously has a thing for shackles." I replied sarcastically shrugging my shoulders.

"Ah that's beginners crappy snappy. Now good rough rope is where it's at." I raised an eyebrow and added,

"Maybe you should write a book when we get home, but in the meantime what are we going to do about my utter lack of co-ordination and inability to dance like some Bollywood dancer?" Pip gave me one sad look before also deflating next to me with a big sigh. Then she patted me on the knee and said bluntly,

"Sorry honey, but I think you're royally screwed and not in the way we all hoped."

"Yep, pretty much." I agreed thinking back to the conversation we had before the dance practice even began. I had asked her what the point of this whole charade was in the first place.

"Well, from my short career as a harem spy then it's simply to make a show of the King's next chosen favourite who will play Head Concubine until he requests for there to be another 'Chosen' to replace them."

"So like a cattle market?" I snapped hating the idea of it all. Pip burst out laughing and said,

"Well yes, if the cows danced to a ditty tune in front of the royal court wearing jingling bikinis." I had to admit that I couldn't help but laugh at the thought, well that was until she mentioned the bit about 'jingling bikinis'.

"Oh God, this just gets even worse." I groaned letting my head fall into my hands.

"Anyway, I don't know what you're worried about, not after the sassy performance you put on back in Wolfman's club." Okay so she had a point but I wasn't about to admit that.

"That was different." I argued making her jump off the bed and face me with her hands on her hips.

"How so?"

"Alcohol." I was quick to reply but she just rolled her eyes at me and said,

"You weren't drunk, so try again."

"Alright, how about the fact that I had three backing dancers and the dance we were doing didn't have bikinis and bloody scarves!" I said standing up myself and mimicking her stance.

"No it had fans and we were half naked in corsets and if I do recall, you did a solo act at the end singing Dolly Parton." Oh she would have to go and mention that, damn her!

"That's totally different!" I argued again getting louder this time.

"No it's not!" she said laughing.

"It is so!"

"How so?"

"Well for starters it's my favourite song and I have not only been singing it for years in the shower but it's also my drunken go to song if I find myself in a Karaoke crisis, so you see, it is totally different." I told her crossing my arms over my chest, as if this would somehow help my case.

"Oh yeah...*totally different,*" she said making fun of me.

"Look Toots, the fact remains that everyone does a dance for the King on the night of the 'Chosen' as it makes everyone feel as though they have a fair chance at getting his attention or some shit like that...so you're just going to have to suck it up and make Shakira's 'Hips don't lie' your new favourite. Now let me see you shake your ass!" I knew she was just trying to help but the thought of having to play performing monkey or more like *learning how to play one* was making me feel sick. What I had done back home the night of our stag and hen do might not have seemed any different but as far as I was concerned it felt a million miles from each other.

Back in my own time I had the advantage of so many things and even though I was no dancer or singer, I still knew the words and I could still shake it on the dance floor to the songs I knew. But here I was utterly clueless and trying to learn how to dance a certain way without the music…well it was like learning how to swim without water!

It was no wonder then that when Pip suggested we call it a night I nearly kissed her feet. I couldn't help but worry about tomorrow night but also wonder what Draven was doing now? How did he react to finding me gone or to the news that an attempt on my life had been made, which were the reasons for me not being there?

"I can almost hear your mind ticking over and it sounds like rice in a tin can being rolled down a hill." Pip said once we had called it a night as we were both obviously faking sleep.

"I can't sleep." I told her.

"Try flicking the bean, it always helps me when Adam is asleep and won't wake up." I spluttered out a cough at the thought.

"I am not doing that with you here!" I told her, mortified by the suggestion.

"What? It's not like I am going to help you out. Jeez…prude much. Look I will even turn the other way," she said getting snippy and rolling over to face the other side. I rolled my eyes before saying,

"I am not a prude, but there is still a line you don't cross with a friend."

"Line schmine. And anyway, how else are you going to get to sleep?" she asked me and this was when I chose my time to ask her what I really wanted to know.

"Well…"

"Oh here it comes." Pip sighed as though she knew what was coming.

"What! You don't even know what I am going to say." I complained thinking there was no way she could, but what she said next surprised me.

"Toots, you are my best friend, of course I know what you are going to ask me, it's like BFF code or some shit the cosmos can't even explain." I giggled and said,

"Alright, lets test your theory, what am I going to ask you?"

"You were going to ask me about what I did when we were in Germany and I sent you back to Draven without him knowing," she said after a big sigh and my mouth dropped open before I said,

"Holy shit."

"Yep, strong stuff that friendship mojo. So you want me to send you to Draven without him knowing about it, so you can see what he is doing right now because it is driving you crazy *not* knowing…right?"

"Seriously Pip, you have got skills…are you sure you're not an Oracle?" I said propping myself up and looking at her over her shoulder as she still had her back to me. She rolled over on a laugh and said,

"Oh Hell no, I'd freaking hate that job!" And I had to agree with her on that, as it certainly seemed to be a suck ass gift to have most of the time.

"So can you do it?" I asked and her cheeky smirk told me my answer before she did.

"Totally."

"So how did we do this last time?" I asked her and in that instant she launched herself at me, landing in my lap and because of it a memory came flooding back to me.

"You know you could warn me before just launching

yourself at me like that." I said, speaking the exact same words that I had done all that time ago. She looked down at me and winked before doing the exact same.

"Oh Tootie cake, you're no fun. Good luck, honey." Then she gave me the same gangster sign before slapping both hands to the side of my head and just before I was plunged into a world only half a palace away, I saw her eyes turn white before misty smoke filled them like bubbling storm clouds.

"Pip?" I whispered her name just to check but as I reached up to touch her face everything around me started to fade into nothing. My hand went straight through her and landed on the stone floor as I was now knelt by someone's throne. My world had flipped upside down and I looked up slowly to see an unfamiliar room. She had done it. She had sent me to Draven once more and I only hoped that this time it would be worth the journey, unlike the one in the past. For I knew that somethings were better left unseen. I had learnt that lesson the hard way but for some reason this felt different…it felt somehow,

Important.

"What do you mean there was an attack?!" Draven's angry voice cut through the silence and I looked up to see him facing off with Ranka. Like before it quickly became apparent that I couldn't be seen or my presence couldn't be detected. I looked around the huge open space and it didn't take a genius to guess that I was now inside Draven's throne room.

"There was an attempt on her life as I predicted, my Lord."

"Was she hurt? Where is she now, is she safe?" Draven snapped out these questions as if he was ready to explode if he didn't receive his answers just as quickly.

"She was unharmed my Lord and is currently situated in the quarters next to my own, under trusted guard." Ranka answered calmly at least giving Draven peace of mind enough to take a deep breath.

"Who was the traitor?" he asked next in an exasperated voice that spoke of his unease.

"That is where it gets complicated, my Lord."

"How so?" His head whipped up and I held my breath right along with Ranka. What was she going to say?

"I…" Ranka started to speak but just before she could say a second word the large double doors at the very end burst open and in strode Sophia in all her finery. The sound echoed through the painted walls and marble pillars as each step brought her closer to the three thrones at the end of the room. Her shimmering dress trailed along the floor like liquid gold pooling around her legs and following her motions like a living entity.

"Sister?" Draven sounded just as surprised to see her as I did. Ranka had no choice but to take a step back and bow as you would to any royalty entering the room.

"But what is this that I am hearing of talks of treachery around the palace?" Even I knew that the heavy sound of disbelief in her voice was put on for show. From the looks of Ranka I would have said if she could have gotten away with growling at that point, she would have.

"Saphira, it is none of your concern." Draven tried to say but Sophia just waved her hand around saying,

"Nonsense, what concerns you brother surely concerns us all." This time it was Draven who growled because *he* could always get away with it.

"Well no doubt it will not concern you once you know whose life was put in danger from such treachery," he commented dryly, knowing full well of his sister's instant dislike to me. Sophia hearing this feigned being hurt and placed a hand to her chest as though his words had wounded her.

"Brother, you insult me so. It is true I may not approve of your choice to ruin us all and all that the prophecy stands for, but I am not without some compassion, even if it is for humanity." This didn't exactly sit well with Draven and he let it be known when he hit out at a burning lamp sending what looked like hot coals scattering across the room. Neither Sophia or Ranka even flinched at their King's outrage, unlike me who jumped back and scrabbled up another step, placing a hand on the side of his throne to steady myself.

"So in return you insult me and dare speak to me of the prophecy, as though I am clueless on the matter?!" Draven roared in outrage.

"Ranka leave us." Sophia ordered looking sideways but she didn't move, instead looking to Draven for guidance. When he nodded she bowed again before leaving through the same doors Sophia had entered, once again filling the room with a deafening bang before plunging it back into deadly silence. Even I held my breath and as far as they were concerned, I wasn't even in the room.

"I swear brother, if I didn't know any better I would say you had been bewitched." I rolled my eyes the same time I saw Draven did as he turned away from her and walked back to his throne. I froze as he came closer but then relaxed once more when he sat down and released a heavy sigh.

"I must confess but the way I feel about her is too strong to ignore." I sucked in a sharp breath just hearing his confession as I felt my heart soar. The look on Sophia's face didn't look as bitter as I thought it would but instead it simply looked sad.

"But ignore it you must, for you know it is for the good of your people." Hearing Sophia say this in a sympathetic tone was more heart-breaking than I wanted to admit. But what was worse was how I could understand where she was coming from. After all, she was only looking out for her own brother and her people and as far as I was concerned, I was standing firmly in the way of that.

"But how can I?!" Draven asked like a desperate man half close to breaking into that famous temper of his.

"Send her away Brother, I implore you." Sophia said taking a step closer but Draven tore his gaze from hers as if the very idea repulsed him.

"Out of the question," he stated firmly.

"Then you will not only lose every chance of meeting your Chosen One, but you also condemn us all to damnation with you, for you know of what the prophecy speaks." This was when Draven hit his limit and let his fist slam down on his armrest cracking the carved black stone it was made from. I watched as the lightning bolts made in the throne snaked along until stopping just before touching my fingers that were still placed against it.

"Of course I know of the damned prophecy and this fated girl for whom I am expected to give my life up for," he thundered bitterly and I winced knowing I was both causes behind this curse.

"You know that it is not meant to be that way," she said softly, obviously feeling bad for her brother's given predicament.

"No…then tell me dear sister, for how is it meant to be?" he lashed out the question resentfully.

"You are fated to fall in love with this girl," she said lowering her voice to barely above a whisper.

"And what if I have already fallen in love with another!" he shouted confessing the way I could only hope he felt. Sophia and I gasped at the same time but only one was heard.

"You can't mean…" she started to say having taken a staged step back from shock.

"And why not, because she is mortal?" I looked from Draven asking the question to Sophia who was almost too dumbstruck to answer.

"But how could this have happened? It was never fated to be this way. The Oracle said…"

"I don't give a damn what the Oracle said, for she must have been wrong," he ground out, slicing a hand through the air.

"Wrong? But that is impossible! An Oracle as powerful as she is never just *wrong,* Brother, you know this!" This time it was Sophia's turn to snap.

"All I know Saphira, is how I feel and how there is nothing *wrong* about it. I cannot simply ignore it and trust me, I have tried for more than the sake of my own people but for hers as well," he told her reining in some of his anger and doing so with more reason in his voice. Sophia hung her head and shook it as though she couldn't believe in what she was hearing.

"But you don't even know this girl or anything about her!" she said trying to cast doubt in his mind and call it reason.

"I know what I feel and that is enough."

"And what if she was sent here…um, have you thought of that?" A rumble came from Draven's chest as the idea angered him, so Sophia jumped on it.

"For all you know she could be here as a spy for our Roman enemies, one to tempt you into bedding her to get close to you for information or worse, a temptation sent from the enemies of our own kind hoping to cast doubt upon your rule and make you a mockery for your past judgements sentenced down upon our people." Sophia said trying with one last attempt at planting enough seeds of doubt to cast at the very least a shred of suspicion or mistrust as to my intentions.

"I will not hear of this…" Draven started to say calmly and obviously trying to keep a lid on his rage but Sophia took this as an opportunity to push further.

"I mean, all you need to do is look at how she came to be here and the mysteries around it. By the Gods brother, think about it! She doesn't even know her own name or where she came from and for all we know that 'attack' on her was staged. Planned from the beginning so that Ranka just happened to come across her just in time, giving her instant access not only to the palace but more importantly to *you.*" Well I had to say that by time Sophia was done, even I was almost convinced as half of what she said wasn't exactly all that far from the truth. But one glance at Draven and it didn't take a genius to know she was fighting a lost cause.

His face had turned a deeper shade of tan giving his scars an even more startling contrast to the rest of his skin tone. Veins in his neck became more prominent as his muscles tensed and I could see him grinding his teeth from where I was hiding in plain sight.

"That all sounds a very likely cause…"

"Good, I am glad you are finally agreeing…" Draven's hand shot up to silence her, cutting off her premature victory.

"I am not finished. What you say could be true or at least have some grounds for mistrust…"

"That's what I…" Once more she was celebrating too soon and finally got the message when Draven shouted,

"BUT…there are obviously factors in which your own palace spies have failed to tell you about our mystery girl. For I find it highly unlikely that someone sent here with the sole purpose of getting close to me, would then attempt to escape her guard and leave the palace just after I make it apparent to her that she is my new favourite. Can you explain that to me?" I looked to Sophia after Draven's cutting statement and compelling evidence given in order to clear any doubt from my character and she just looked shocked.

"I…well, it seems to me that those actions might have also been taken to cast any doubt aside so that…"

"Enough! I am tired of hearing anymore of your attempts at

convincing me to think ill of her!" Draven exclaimed and by the looks of Sophia's slumped shoulders, it finally seemed that she was admitting defeat.

"Then that is it…for there is nothing to be done other than to let you ruin all that you have worked so hard to set into place. Are you really prepared to show your people that you aren't a King to be trusted but instead a tyrant like our father who broke all the rules?"

"Be careful of which you speak Saphira, for those broken rules are the very ones that lead us to be here today." Draven said in a tone that spoke only of warning and it was strange hearing him sticking up for his father, someone I knew he wasn't on the best of terms with.

"Yes and we too were also classed as an abomination at one time, is that something you are really so eager to go back to?" she lashed out at him in a nasty snarl.

"They would not dare!" Draven bellowed standing up from his throne in his outrage.

"I would not be so sure brother, for they are plenty and we are but three. It took us a long time to get here and you are ready to risk it all for the selfish reasons of your heart, a heart filled with feelings as our kind you cannot even be sure are real!" she shouted back getting just as angry as her brother.

"You couldn't possibly understand for it has not happened to you yet and your lack of compassion for others is testament of that. But be warned little sister, for one day you too will fall under its spell and when you do, then you can preach to me about the selfish ways in which such a stolen heart beats for one person. But until then, I would think twice about reproaching me on this matter again!" My mouth dropped open and not just from the furious way in which he spoke to his sister, but also from how in such a short time he felt for me. The love he spoke of was exactly the same way that Draven from my time would have spoken about it, which utterly shocked me after such a short time spent together.

Had the same thing happened to him when we first met back in the woods that day? Had it been as instant as he said it had been, but I just never let myself believe it until now? Well if I had ever been worried before about him feeling the way he did just because it was fated, then those fears were now firmly out the window as he was ready to renounce his own people for me!

But really thinking about it, was this not the same as he was doing back home, by denying the Fates of what they asked of him? He was willing to give up the entire prophecy, something he had believed in since first meeting the Oracle, just to keep me alive when our future together was most likely going to come to an end anyway due to that very same prophecy.

Sophia looked as though she had been slapped before being banished by her own blood. To the point that I couldn't help but feel sorry for her because, even though I knew that in this time she hated me, she was still only doing this for what she believed in, just as her brother was.

At least one thing was confirmed and that was the Sophia I saw now didn't yet know what it felt like to fall in love. Zagan hadn't yet been introduced in this time so Draven was right, she didn't yet know how it felt to give your heart to someone and the selfish levels you would reach to keep that love alive and ultimately with you.

I watched as Sophia gave her brother one last look of despondency before composing herself when she saw the proof that she obviously had no hope of getting through to him. She straightened her back, took a deep breath and after smoothing out the front of her dress she nodded in respect. I could easily tell it was done more to her King than to her brother, who she had no doubt lost some respect for.

"And Saphira..." Sophia stopped by the door and waited, refusing to look at her brother.

"You will leave the girl alone and not interfere again, am I understood?" Draven's command somehow felt as if it came at great cost but as I was the only one to look into his eyes, I was the only one who knew this. Sophia glared over her shoulder at the floor but only for the second it took to say,

"Oh I understand *all too well, brother.*" And then she left the massive room as though it was closing in on her. It was hard fighting my instincts against wanting to run after her to offer my friend comfort but I would only be fooling myself into believing it was the same Sophia I knew. It was as I said before, two thousand years could do a lot to a person as much as it could *for* a person. And without yet experiencing love for herself, then that certainly could change someone, which in her case, was obviously for the better.

I hung my shoulders in defeat as she had done, knowing I was stuck between sandstone time and a hard place, one that was safer to stay in between than get emotionally involved. I think even Pip would have agreed that the Sophia here wasn't the same girl we both called friend back home.

"You may come back in now." Draven said and I was surprised to see Ranka when she came in from behind a hidden door.

"I take it that it didn't go as you hoped, my Lord?" Draven released a heavy sigh and let his head rest on one hand so that he could rub the top of his nose between his thumb and forefinger, as he so often did when frustrated.

"I want you to keep an eye on her."

"My lord?" Ranka's tone mimicked the shock on her face.

"I don't trust her." At first I thought they were talking about me but when he nodded to the door and said,

"She will not let this go." I knew then that he was talking

about Sophia. Ranka looked torn and I knew why seeing as this would have been the perfect opportunity to tell Draven about Sophia's first attempt at getting rid of me. But then again, Draven now knew to be wary of his sister's intentions and how far she would go, so I guess Ranka didn't see the sense in adding fuel to a flame that already burned at a dangerous level.

"I will do what is needed, my Lord." Ranka said bowing her head but Draven wasn't finished and hearing his next question made my heart pound.

"I wanted to ask you about the day you found her."

"My King?"

"You were hunting at the time, were you not?" Draven asked rubbing his beard as he obviously thought back on some of Sophia's claims.

"I was."

"So it would not have been easy to foretell your whereabouts?" I knew where Draven was going with this and so did Ranka, for she relaxed slightly.

"Not unless they could foretell the whereabouts of the stag I was hunting, for as you know when I hunt I do so vast and wide until I reach my prey." Draven nodded seemingly happy with her answer.

"As I thought."

"If I may my Lord, what I saw that day was no act but only the actions of a desperate woman whose sole intention was to survive. I truly believe that had I not made the impromptu decision to go out hunting that day then she would not only have been raped many times over, but that she would have only had death to welcome her at the end of such an ordeal." Draven listened to Ranka's words as I myself winced at reliving them, realising now how true they were and how close I had come to death at their hands. Ranka had saved me in more ways than one and from Draven's expression, he knew it too.

"Then I thank you once more and this time on my behalf, for not only saving her life but also bringing her into mine." Ranka looked taken aback by this and I had to wonder how many times she had been thanked by her King before, because if I didn't know any better, I would say that this was the first time.

"It is my pleasure to serve you my Lord, as it is my own pleasure gained in saving the life of an innocent girl from meeting a violent end." I couldn't help but shed a tear in thanks to my saviour who had exceeded my every expectation since coming to this place. Her help in this quest had been monumental and no matter the outcome of it all by the time we made it home, I would forever be in her debt because of it.

I swiped away the single tear that rested on my cheek knowing now the importance of being a witness to all this as I rested my head on the side of the throne in which he still sat. I released a deep sigh knowing that I could go back to my own bed and finally find a peaceful end to this turbulent day. Of course this in theory sounded easier said than done when the next thing out of Draven's mouth was an unexpected order…

"I need to see her, take me to her…*now*"

CHAPTER FIFTEEN

THROWING CAUTION TO THE WIND

"*Hey Pip, time to get me out of here.*" I whispered still in the same throne room as before. After Draven demanded that Ranka take him to see me, I knew my time was limited. I watched as they both left before chancing calling for Pip but for some reason she wasn't responding.

"Pip?" I said looking up at the ceiling as if I was trying to radio God himself.

"Shit, shit, shit…what to do, what to do?" I said pacing back and forth, not knowing what to do next. Should I wait and continue to try and hail Pip or should I just leg it and try to get back before Ranka and Draven? I knew that if I didn't make that decision soon it would be too late as I needed to follow them to guide me back to the room.

"Come on Pip, last chance…BEAM ME BACK NOW!" I shouted making my voice echo but then wondering if it really echoed at all considering I wasn't really here.

"Oh sod it, I can't wait!" I said making my decision and

racing towards the door hoping that I hadn't left it too late and lost sight of them already. I yanked open the door and scanned the open hallways both left and right. I thought all was lost but then from the corner of my eye I spotted Draven striding through a doorway across the open courtyard. Watching all the people coming and going who seemed completely oblivious to me, I decided my best bet was to cut through the elaborate looking courtyard or I really did risk losing them.

I felt like shouting 'what are all you people still doing here at this time?' or was this everyone's version of date night and instead of going to the movies, it was a midnight stroll around the palace fountain!

I zigzagged and weaved in and out of people, knowing that no one could see me but I wasn't so sure if anyone could feel me or not, so knocking people down wasn't an option. I looked up to see there was only one way of making this any easier and that was to simply go through the fountain itself!

"I can't afford to lose them." I said to myself and so without giving it another thought I ran towards the small wall surrounding the water and leapt over it landing ungracefully on all fours thanks to my clumsiness. I spat out the water like I was also blowing raspberries and wiped the remainder from my face as I got back up. Then I ran in the only awkward way anyone could when running in water until reaching the other side, where I then legged it to reach the same doorway I had seen him pass through.

It wasn't easy running in a soaking wet tunic down to my ankles as I felt as though someone had dumped a wet sack over my head, but I could only imagine the trouble I would be in if I wasn't in that room by the time they got there. How on earth would I explain any of it. Hell, I didn't even understand it! And Pip, what had happened to Pip?

These were all the questions running through my mind as I

ran like my life depended on it. I skidded around the pillar and through the door only to be left panicking even more when I had no clue as to which way they went.

"Come on, Pip!" I shouted looking up one last time before making the rash decision to continue forward, instead of turning down either of the two directions they could have taken. At first the odds didn't seem to be in my favour until I rounded a corner and saw them just passing through a door at the end. My heart pounded and my lungs burned from all the physical exercise, which made me curse my stupid aversion to the gym. That was it, as soon as made it back I was signing myself up to one, because this was getting ridiculous! I couldn't help thinking how much easier it would be when getting myself in these crazy situations if I was as fit as say, Zena warrior princess!

I pushed myself even harder making it to the door before yanking it open thinking that I would be faced with another hallway I would have to race down. Of course assumption can be the downfall for a lot of people, just as it was for me in that very moment, because directly on the other side I found Draven and Ranka.

They had obviously been stopped by someone as Draven, with his back to me, was busy speaking to someone in fine robes and a jewel encrusted turban. My mouth dropped open in shock as everything else started to happen in slow motion.

Ranka was the first one to turn around to face me and from the look of astonishment she gave me, it didn't take a genius to know that Pip's voodoo was wearing off. I looked down at myself and frowned as my body started to fade in on itself, now making Ranka's look of astonishment turn into one utter bewilderment.

Draven was still speaking so hadn't yet noticed Ranka's strange behaviour but this was about to change as he gave her a quick glance, as though he could feel something was wrong.

She looked to him but it was too late, he had already seen her reaction to the doorway so was now turning around himself to see what it was she had been staring at. I closed my eyes hoping that I could prolong the time before having to explain myself and why I was stood opposite them both, now ringing wet. To be honest I couldn't understand how they could now see me, unless...something terrible had happened to Pip?

That thought nearly sent me into blind panic and my eyes snapped open expecting to see the same look on Draven's face as I had done on Ranka. Only that didn't happen. No, instead I opened my eyes only to find my friend staring back at me and still in the same position as I had last left her.

"Pip?" I said her name in question and she grinned down at me, shrugged her shoulders and said,

"Uhh...my bad?" This was the moment I let myself panic!

"Shit! Pip what happened?! Never mind, we have to hurry 'cause he is on his way up here!" Pip's eyes widened but seeing that she didn't move and was still sat on me, I had to buckaroo her off so that I could get up. She rolled to one side with an 'umpf' sound.

"I fell asleep. What do you mean he's coming up here?"

"What do you mean you fell asleep?!" I shrieked back taking in her guilty look which at that moment she decided to combine with a yawn.

"What, I was wiped. Sending you palace hopping isn't exactly something I can do with my pinky tied behind my back and with only three shakes of a lamb's tail...no pun intended." I frowned having no clue what any of that meant let alone what the pun could have been.

"Look it doesn't matter but what does matter is that I am here now and pretty soon so will Draven!" This was when Pip finally got what I was freaking out about.

"Oh...OH! Oh okay, so keep calm...wait, why are you

wet?" she asked, suddenly noticing first on herself from where she was sat on me and then on me, as I was still dripping on the floor.

"Because I ran through a fountain!"

"Rock on." Pip commented giving me the sign of the horns, one usually reserved for rock concerts.

"Pip!" I shouted her name as she was still just sat on the bed, now holding her legs to her chest and rocking like a child.

"Oh right, panic...sorry, so what are we gonna do?"

"I don't know, for starters how do I explain why I am all wet?"

"I know, say you were sweating and not used to the heat." I stopped in my tracks to give her a look.

"What?"

"Oh I don't know, because the whole aim of this trip was to sleep with the younger version of my husband in hopes of him getting me pregnant and him walking in here finding me dripping wet with what he thinks is sweat doesn't exactly scream sex appeal, Pip!" I told her and she looked as if she was going to say something but then stopped herself and said,

"Good point...sweaty sex...good, sweaty before...not so much."

"Exactly. Now what are we gonna do because he can't find you here and me looking like this." I said holding out my wet hair after nodding to my ninja friend.

"Right! First things first, take off your clothes...quick, quick!" Pip said taking charge and after giving her a curious look she clapped her hands and said,

"Mush, mush!" After this I didn't question it, I just did what she said and pulled my tunic over my head, trying to keep my modesty covered.

"Good, now stand there...over a bit...yep, just there. Now brace yourself, it's been a while since I did this." Pip said after directing me in front of the open arch that lead onto a balcony.

"How long exactly?" I asked with trepidation.

"Oh I don't know, the last time I did laundry, so a few years." I gave her a raised eyebrow.

"What? I usually just buy new clothes when I need them… now are you ready?"

"For what?" I asked still having no clue as to what she was planning to do.

"This," she said coming to stand in front of me, then after raising her hands up above her head she shouted a word I didn't understand,

"AURA!" I didn't have to wait long before something happened for it seemed like she was drawing in energy from somewhere. I watched as her small dainty hands started to shake and her eyes started to turn into black smoke. Then before I could ask if she was alright, she flicked her wrists and shot the energy my way.

I sucked in a quick breath as a mighty gust of wind hit me with enough force to send me back a step as I fought to stay upright. The air started to increase until it whipped around me like a small tornado, lifting my hair on end and spinning it around like rope.

It only lasted seconds but it was enough to have me bone dry in a heartbeat and as the air was suddenly sucked back out into the night, I was left panting for breath. I looked up to see I wasn't the only one trying to get over the storm that just entered the room as Pip was also trying to catch her breath.

"Pip that was…wow…it was…" I was still trying to find the right words when Pip's head snapped up from where she was bent over and she said,

"Out of time." I followed her intense gaze to the door to see she was right, we were out of time. We could hear not only the footsteps outside but also when Ranka dismissed the guards from their duty.

"Quick, on the bed, pretend to be asleep!" Pip whispered desperately and I didn't waste time. I could just see the door opening as Pip did a running leap over the balcony, dropping out of sight. I sucked in a gasp not knowing where my friend had landed but the second I did, I also heard her voice pop inside my head.

"Don't worry about me Sugar Toots, I am fine but remember, no nookie for you, not until Ari turns up or shit will hit this time warp and our cover will be blown. Now have fun...but not too much...nighty night." I tried not to smile at her mindful farewell, along with her 'no sex warning' and closed my eyes just as I could hear them both walk through the door.

"You see my Lord, she is safe and well." Ranka said in hushed tones obviously believing that I was fast asleep or at least playing along with it after what she had seen only minutes before back in the hallway. No wonder she also sounded slightly relieved and I was sure Pip and I would be explaining that one tomorrow.

"Very good, you may leave us now," Draven said sternly and I had to wonder what had been said between the throne room and here. Had Ranka told him of the attack and how Stateira's sister had been sent to kill me?

"My Lord?"

"I must know that she is safe and the only way for me to know for certain is if I remain with her." He informed her and my heart skipped a beat. He was spending the night? I don't know who was more shocked, me or Ranka.

"I...uh...do you think that wise my Lord, it is just that if people find..."

"Do you think me to be more concerned with palace gossip

over the life of the woman I love?" he asked seriously after first interrupting her and again my heart was going berserk.

"No my King, forgive me. The grounds for my concern is only making her more at risk from those who learn of her importance to you through such actions." After this I heard Draven sigh because he no doubt knew she was right. It had been the same reasons for his caution back in my time as he knew once his people got wind of me then it would also be like asking me to live with a big target on my back.

At first I remember thinking that he was simply being over protective but now looking back at all that had happened, I knew he had been right. For I hadn't spent many days since then when some plot against us wasn't being hatched by our enemies and I wasn't in danger of some sort. Hell, it was exhausting just thinking back over the years of what we had been forced to endure just so we could stay together.

"Her importance to me will soon be known at the choosing tonight and once the announcement is made, then there will be no more opportunities to be had, not when she will remain by my side and therefore have my constant protection." This was the point I wanted to stick my head up and say…uh, what now? Because this wasn't exactly the Draven I had planned for. Yes, an overbearing protective cave man act I was used to but never letting me out of his sight…I think that was a little much.

And besides, how was that going to work when he had not only an entire kingdom to run but also a hidden supernatural race to rule? And when he thought I was mortal just like the others who had no clue as to what was lurking in the shadows of this secret world of his. What was he planning to do about that…tell me and hope for the best? Well whatever he had planned, I doubted very much it was based on using a logical mind and more on acting with an irrational heart. Not that I was one to judge considering half of the crazy shit I had pulled in the name of love...*one called Draven.*

I guess it was nice for a change watching it from the other side and knowing that the Draven from this time was being less cautious with being blinded by his feelings for me. For in the past, or should I say the future, it had always felt as if I had been the one ready to just dive right in there, saying to hell with the bad that could happen. Whereas Draven had been the one trying to shield me from the dangers as long as he could. Well it was quite obvious that this was the effect that time had bestowed on Draven's personality and no wonder after living through how many lifetimes worth of enemies to deal with.

"Then I will double the guard until then," Ranka said obviously foreseeing even more trouble ahead of me.

"Do so in the morning, for they will not be needed tonight. That will be all," Draven said his voice remaining firm.

"Yes, my King," Ranka replied obediently and I heard her footsteps take her to the door.

"And Ranka..." Draven said just as I heard her opening the door before she left.

"Yes, my Lord?"

"You have done well." Draven's praise was no doubt a welcome thing to hear considering all the trouble she had gone through in just keeping me alive.

"As always my King, it is an honour," Ranka replied respectfully no doubt bowing before she walked from the room. I heard the door close and waited for the sound of Draven coming closer but it never came. What was he waiting for? In the end I couldn't help it so I opened one eye just a crack to see what he was doing. At first I couldn't understand it, why was he down on one knee where I had been stood when Pip had dried me?

"Tut, tut little Lamb of mine," he said to himself shaking his head. He still had his back to me so I couldn't see half of what he was doing but whatever it was, it seemed he had found something out. When he stood back up I sucked in a silent breath at what he now had grasped in his hand...*my wet tunic.*

'Oh shit.' I mentally scolded myself for not thinking of throwing it over the balcony along with my friend. I then watched as he lifted it to his face before taking a deep breath as though he was trying to draw my scent from it. I heard the quiet rumble rise from his chest as if this time it was his Demon responding for him. His head snapped back around to me with barely enough time for me to slam my eyes shut and go back to faking sleep. I heard my wet tunic slap back on the floor before I heard his footsteps bringing him closer to the bed.

I really wanted to open my eyes again but I knew then that I would have no choice but to answer why there would be my wet clothes on the floor.

"I know you are not asleep, little Lamb." I couldn't help but jump a little when I heard his voice whispering in my ear calling my bluff.

"No one's heart beats that erratically when resting as soundly as you pretend," he said running the back of one finger down my cheek.

"So come on now, open those pretty eyes for me." I couldn't help it but I bit my lip as I did as I was told knowing I wasn't getting away with it any longer. His finger still travelled down along my neck but now he could see what I was doing with my lip he decided to use it to stop me. His eyes blazed into mine and the intensity of it nearly unravelled me. Why was it that with only one look this man had me almost ready to confess everything?

"Good, now hold still," he ordered and I frowned, unsure about what he was about to do. It didn't take long before I started to panic slightly with Pip's warning dinging alarm bells in my mind as he put one knee at my thigh before lifting his other leg so he could straddle me. Then instead of lowering his body over mine like I thought he would, he sat back on his haunches looking down at me. It was as though he was searching for something and wasn't happy with the results. He frowned as though whatever I was doing was insulting him but before I could ask him what I had done, he moved suddenly.

"My...Lor...?"

"Sssh." I started to question what he was doing when he whispered his command down at me before snaking an arm underneath my body, starting at the base of my spine. The further he pushed his hand up the more pressure he applied, which slowly lifted me up to meet him. Then with his free hand he walked his fingers up over my breast, gathering the covers that hid my nakedness from him as he went. All that was left was a gentle tug and the material slipped away leaving the top half of my body bare for his pleasure.

He held me still as he lowered his head to my neck where he inhaled a deep breath and continued to do so all the way down my shoulder and at the side of one breast. I wondered what he was doing but then it quickly fit into place as it was no doubt doing for him.

He was just confirming that I was the one wearing the wet tunic as he could no doubt still smell it on my skin, just as he had scented my skin on the tunic. Sometimes I forgot all of his supernatural skills which included heightened sight and smell.

Which meant only one thing...

I was busted.

CHAPTER SIXTEEN

MOONLIGHT ASHES

"It seems that my Little Lamb has been out wandering again," Draven said in what I knew was a dangerously soft voice. I didn't know what to say but thought desperately of what excuse I could use that would be good enough for having a soaking wet tunic lying discarded on the floor. I hated to admit it, but unfortunately it was looking like the best one was Pip's excuse and that was me being sweaty.

"I…uh…I got hot," I stammered out and he raised an eyebrow at me.

"Is that right?" he asked pulling me closer and making it even hotter. I gave him a series of little head nods letting him know how nervous he made me.

"And now?" he asked before grazing his lips against my shoulder as if testing the temperature for himself.

"Still hot," I said on a breathy sigh.

"Mmm, so you are… And what about now?" he asked after pausing to blow cool air along my neck. The shiver he invoked tingled all the way down my spine which he could feel for himself, if that smirk was anything to go by.

"I uh…think…" Actually, that was a lie because I couldn't think, not with the way he was teasing me. Especially when he dipped his head lower and blew air across my nipple making it stand to attention silently begging for his hot mouth.

"You were saying?" he asked after I threw my head back and moaned without restraint.

"I was saying?" I repeated back at him because as far as I knew I had been speaking in tongues.

"Yes, you were just about to tell me where my pale beauty dangerously wandered to, but more importantly…" This was where the sweetness ended and his voice turned hard and serious as though a switch had been flipped.

"How she slipped passed my guards unseen?" The restrained anger in his tone was easy to detect but even if it hadn't been then the way he circled my throat with one hand certainly was. He didn't hurt me but he definitely applied enough pressure to warn me that he could if he wanted to. My eyes widened in my panic because truly, what was I going to say?

Think Keira, think! But no matter how I shouted at myself for the answers it would do no good, so as the very last resort I couldn't help but call out to my friend, hoping she could hear me in my mind.

'Pip, what do I do?' When I didn't receive any guidance back I knew it mustn't have worked and had no choice but to try and explain what I had been doing. It was that or simply refuse to say anything, which might endanger my new position in his world. It didn't exactly scream trust if I said nothing.

"I…can explain," I said making the split decision to try and give him something. The look he gave me was a sceptical one as if he doubted that I could.

"I'm happy to hear it and more than ready for it." he said, in other words telling me to get on with it. Although what I was going to get on with was still left to be seen, for what single reason could I have to have left this room? But not just that, he didn't just want reasons, he wanted the 'how's' and no wonder considering the guards were stationed outside my room.

"I must warn you, pretty girl, I am not accustomed to waiting," he warned and I knew I could stall no longer.

"I am sorry but I just couldn't…" I panicked and started to quickly blurt out the truth when suddenly the door burst open. Draven was off the bed and stood like a sentinel in front of me.

"Pip!?" I shouted when I saw her entering the room dressed from head to toe like a servant and carrying the biggest urn of water I had ever seen.

"I am sorry my Lady, but once again the coolest water to be found was in the fountain, so I …oh dear, my Lord!" Pip said pretending to play the part of only seeing the King after setting down her heavy load. Draven looked at me trying to gauge my reaction to all of this before addressing it for himself.

"Forgive me, my King, for if I'd have known you were with my Lady then I would have waited in bringing her the water she requested," Pip said bowing gracefully.

"It's alright Pipper, the King's arrival wasn't planned," I told her softly trying desperately to get my heart to calm its erratic pounding.

"This is your servant?" Draven asked me and I nodded. I could see him trying to piece the evidence of what she had said, together with what he had been accusing me of doing. I felt bad for deceiving him this way but couldn't help that I also wanted to kiss Pip's feet for saving my ass yet again.

"This water was for you to cool down?" Draven asked me and I could see in the way his eyes started to soften that his trust in me was seeping back in there. I ended up blushing with my guilt but thankfully this worked in my favour as it was one he took for embarrassment.

"Yes and I do hope you take my advice this time by undressing first before asking me to just throw the water over you. Won't you look at all that pale skin, it must have been a cold place you travelled from my Lady for you can see that she is not used to the heat…why just look at her red cheeks now…" Oh yeah, they were red alright and if Pip didn't put a lid on it soon they were likely to explode. But on the other hand, at least the King was now looking highly amused at not only me but Pip as well. And like most people, he also looked at a loss what to make of her.

"A cold bath is what she needs but alas we have nowhere to bathe her and when mentioning the communal bathhouse, then by the Gods no! She will kick up a fuss and say that her body is for the King's eyes only…" This was the point where I popped my head to one side behind Draven and started doing the universal signal for 'cut it' by slicing my hand across my neck. She caught my action and smirked before saying,

"…Oh, but would you listen to me rattle on…I will be leaving you young ones to your lustful ways." Hearing this I thought I was going to choke when swallowing.

'Lustful ways?!' I mouthed to her making her just shrug her shoulders at me after Draven looked back at me. I gave him a little smile that I could only hope translated to 'Don't ask me, she's crazy'. Draven turned back to Pip and I couldn't help but smack myself on the forehead out of habit, which just so happened to be one of the side effects of being around Pip.

"My Lady, will you be needing my services again this evening?" she asked and in my head I said *'Oh Christ, but I hope not!'*

'Charming. That's the thanks I get for saving your 'can't lie for shit ass'.' Pip answered in my mind and I wanted to laugh.

"No, that will be all." I said out loud this time.

"Then I will take my leave. My King, My lady," she said bowing and then huffing as she straightened up as though she was much older than she looked. Which had me wondering if I was the only one seeing her like I was used to and for everyone else she changed her appearance to a sweet unsuspecting older woman? Well, she had certainly played her part well because Draven most definitely looked convinced!

She was just about to walk out of the door when I stopped her as I couldn't let her go before saying how I really felt.

"And Pipper…"

"Yes, my Lady?"

"Thank you for bringing me the water," I said telling her much more.

"You're always welcome, My Lady. Good evening to you both," she said in a way that told me that she understand what I was really thanking her for before she left.

"Your servant…she is…*different,"* he said after pausing to try and find the right word.

"That's one way of putting it," I said sarcastically, momentarily forgetting myself. Draven burst out laughing, obviously finding my comment amusing and then seeming surprised by it. Did he not have any woman in his life who had made him laugh before? I had to admit, I liked the sound of that, just as I did when finding out from Draven back in my time that he found me funny.

Draven came to sit back down on the side of the bed and looked at the urn of water with a sigh. Then he pushed all his unruly hair back with one hand before looking back at me.

"I fear I owe you an apology." This was when my guilt doubled.

"It is not necessary my…" I stopped talking when he held his hand up.

"I think it is. You told me yourself that you were hot and I thought it nothing but a feeble excuse. But your servant is right, it is quite obvious from your pale skin that you are not yet accustomed to our Parthian sun." Well, I couldn't argue with him there as I wouldn't have been surprised if the chickens here laid omelettes instead of eggs it was that hot and this was coming from someone who had been to Hell...*twice!*

"I am sure I will adjust in time, my Lord." I told him not knowing what else to say.

"You must remember to cover up when outside, for it would not please me to see this beautiful skin of yours burnt and too sore for my touch," he said running the back of his hand up my arm. I nodded as thanks to plenty of summer holidays in Spain, I knew all too well what could happen to pale skin under a burning hot sun...thank you, Aloe Vera, that's all I could say.

"This new servant of yours, is she a trustworthy one?" he asked looking at the door, which made me wonder if Ranka finally had the chance to tell him about what had happened.

"I believe so," I said smiling a secret smile, one put there when thinking of all the things that crazy Imp had done for me over the years. She was truly one of the greatest beings who ever graced this Earth and as far as I was concerned it was an honour to know her, let alone be privileged enough to call her friend. And one of these days I would get the opportunity to tell her that.

"Then I am satisfied," he commented obviously worrying about who he was entrusting with my care.

"Now let's see if we can cool you down, shall we?" he said surprising me and making me squeal when he suddenly plucked me off the bed in one swift move.

"Wait, I...uh...what are you doing?" I asked as he yanked the sheet from my body, leaving it to float back onto the bed. He lifted me up to get a better grip and thought that giving me a cheeky grin was enough of an answer. I wanted to demand where he was taking me seeing as I was stark naked, but when he only went as far as the balcony I relaxed slightly.

He stepped outside and he was right, the night air did manage to cool my skin somewhat. But being naked in his arms I feared I would need an iceberg to cool me down fully, for the heat he gave off would more likely burn me long before the Persian sun would ever get a chance to.

He lowered me down, letting go of my legs first so that I could stand. I couldn't help but frown in confusion as I had no clue what he was up to. I don't know why but being naked both added to the excitement and to my nervousness, which I guess only ended up with one fueling the other.

"Wait here," he ordered and even though it came as a whisper it was still commanding enough to make me do as I was told. I didn't dare look round but instead closed my eyes and let my other senses take over. I could hear his footsteps behind me and the slight scraping sound of something on the floor before obviously being picked up. Then I felt his presence enter my personal space once more, making my skin hypersensitive ready for his touch. So much so that when he traced his fingertips up my spine I jumped before shuddering at the sensation.

"I thought the view of my city at night was one that I would treasure throughout my lifetime but by adding your beauty to the picture it will no doubt stay with me, not only in this life but also on to the next," he told me softly and on hearing such a compliment I couldn't help but close my eyes and bite my lip after swallowing hard. It was such a beautiful thing to say I could feel the emotions inside me rising beneath my eyes.

"You do me a great honour my Lord, for your city is the most beautiful city I have ever seen," I told him remembering how I felt when first seeing it in my dreams.

Scalloped stone peaks decorated the tops of palace walls where guards could be seen manning their stations. Hundreds of tiny lights were dotted inside the outline of sandstone buildings like flickering candles defying gravity. The distant mountains created a dark vista all around us, the tips touching the sky as if trying to reach the full moon. And speaking of the moon,

"I love how your pale skin looks under the moonlight, but more so how it contrasts underneath my own," he told me, coming up closer to my back and wrapping his arms around my torso. Then he entwined his fingers with mine and lifted our joined hands up so I could see the differences in our skin colour for myself.

"It is almost easy to believe you have been touched by the Goddess of Light and her power still lingers on your skin."

"I…I…no, I just, uh…I'm just pale, my Lord," I said not really knowing what to say or how to take such a compliment. He reached around and lifted my face up so that he could look down at me from behind. Of course, given our height difference it was easy for him to see whatever it was he was looking for.

"Tell me, how is it possible for such a beauty not yet to be accustomed to hearing such things?"

"You're the only one who tells me I'm beautiful," I said in a quiet voice wanting so much to add…'that matters' on to the end of that sentence. He gave me a disbelieving look and said,

"I doubt that."

"It's true. Plus I didn't always look like this," I told him thinking back to how I used to hide myself away under layers keeping my head down. How my life had changed since being taken by Morgan and then once again when meeting Draven. It was as if before I was a closed rose bud, unwilling to open itself up and making itself vulnerable to the elements. But then someone came along and took the time to gently coax it from its safe cocoon, giving it the strength to bloom and open itself up to whatever the world had to throw at it.

"Sweetest one, you are stood in front of my world naked, hidden by nothing and graced by the moon. You can hide yourself away under layers of silk but it is *you* that brings forth its beauty, not the other way around. *You can hide nothing from me.*" He whispered this last part making me shudder against him. It felt like the sweetest of threats but one I knew I could only push for so long. For the reality of my situation pierced my chest like a thunderbolt when I thought of all the parts of myself *I was hiding from him.*

"Now let's see how good a servant I make," he said teasing me and giving my chin a little shake before letting my face go. It was such a common Draven gesture to make, it was getting harder to distinguish between the two of them.

He started doing something behind me and I couldn't help but take a peek over my shoulder. I watched as he untied a deep crimson coloured sash from around his waist, one that had tarnished gold disks attached to it. They were fastened like belt buckles and as he pulled the material through, he discarded them one by one as they clattered to the ground. I looked to see each held a different symbol of some sort and I wondered what each of them meant.

I looked back once more to see him winding the length of his soft belt around his wrist and then his hand before gathering the end to hold in his palm. Then he dunked his arm inside the water filled urn he had obviously carried over earlier.

It quickly became clear what he had in mind but even so, I still sucked in a startled breath when he started to cool my body with the cold water.

"Better?" he asked with his lips against the top of my shoulder before kissing and sucking away the droplets he had left there.

"Mmm." I made a noise that sounded anything but ungrateful for what he was doing and he laughed once as he dipped down again to plunge his arm in the urn once more. This time when he pulled it out he brought it to the front of me by my neck so that when he squeezed his fist, the water ran down over my breasts and belly. The feel of the water trickling down my skin combined with the sensation of the night's air caressing it further was enough to have me moaning louder.

"Addicted." Draven muttered to himself behind me and I wondered briefly if he was talking about how he felt about me or how he thought I obviously felt about him. It was certainly clear by my actions as I couldn't help but squirm against him wanting…no, more like *needing*… to make more contact. For short insignificant seconds I thought about Pip's warning but when his hand came up again to drip even more water on me, this time dripping down in between my thighs, my thoughts quickly became lost in only the man at my back.

I didn't even realise what my body was doing as I arched my back and pushed my body forward whenever his hand would grace my skin with his touch. It was as though I had no control over myself and the next time he came close to my breasts I pushed them even further against his fist, wanting him to feel for himself how hard my nipples had turned.

"I adore how your body responds to my hand. Like a finely tuned instrument that only I can play." I should have blushed at the comment but he was right and I was too lost in the erotic feelings he created. This, of course, increased tenfold when his hand dipped even lower and rung out the water right over my feminine core.

"Uh ahh mmm." The noises I uttered made no sense but spoke volumes as to what he was making me feel.

"Is that what you want…?" he asked in that velvet voice of his humming at my ear. To make his point and to get me to respond quicker he gently caressed the folds of my labia before grazing his fingers along my clitoris, making me arch back even further against him.

"Please," I moaned knowing there was no going back now, I needed the touch only he could give me.

"Your skin is getting hot again," he said and pulled his hand away and I couldn't help but release a small cry in regret.

"Don't fret little one, I am coming back," he told me, his voice thick with lust but also obviously amused. I released a deep sigh when he kept his word and brought his dripping wet arm back around me. This time he put his hand back to my mound and tightened his fist so that the water all gushed at once through my folds and down my legs, joining the liquid his touch had already created.

I was so close it was maddening and he had barely even touched me. It was easy to see why though, given the romantic setting of his city lying at rest in the moon's shade. The warm glow of the flames dancing shadows along the walls from the lamps lit in the room behind us. The smell of incense burning somewhere below and the scent of cold water on hot skin combined with the sexual musk my own body emitted was enough to drive me wild. But added to all this the feel of his fingers touching my most intimate spot and a tight bundle of nerves that was just desperate to be played with, well then I had no chance at lasting long.

"I can't wait to see you unravel beneath me just as you do now, only instead of my fingers..." At the exact time, he inserted two up inside of me making me cry out.

"It shall be my cock fitting tightly in your sheath," he said in a harsher tone, telling me just how close to the edge he was. His fingers continued to pump inside of me, stroking all the delicate nerve endings in just the right way so that when I started screaming it was from coming this way instead of stimulation to my clit.

"Yes, yes, yes...YES!" I shouted reaching up behind me so that I could lock my hands around his neck just for something to hold onto as I felt as though I was falling. The feeling was so intense that he also had to hold up my body with his other arm banded around me so that I wouldn't crumple to the floor. My legs had turned to liquid and my knees no longer wanted to lock and support my weight.

He rocked his fingers inside me a few more times so that he could feel my passage clamping around his fingers, trying to keep him there for longer.

"Calm that little heart of yours sweetness and take breath," he said clearly worried about me and I did as I was told, inhaling deeply and feeling lightheaded in the process. As if sensing this for himself he removed his hand from the firm grip he had of me down there and before we moved from the balcony, he dipped his hand in the water once more so that he could clean the mess he made. I could feel my own juices dripping down my legs but at the feel of the cold water hitting my overheated core I couldn't help but scream out once more.

"Easy now," he said as he swept me up into his arms to carry me back inside the room. I felt exhausted, as if the last of my reserves had been quickly swallowed up and now all that was left was an empty shell zapped of all energy.

"I think I have pushed you quite enough for one night. Time for you to rest now," he said laying me back on the bed gently as though I would easily break. I couldn't even find the strength to argue, not that I would have, given that I was half asleep as soon as my head hit the pillow.

"Sleep easy Little Lamb, for I will stay with you and guard over what will soon be mine," Draven whispered in my ear after he tucked me closer to him, resting my head in what was

usually my little nook. He draped my arm over his chest and wrapped his own arm around my back, pulling me in as close as I could get. Once he was satisfied he released a contented sigh just before I fell into a deep sleep.

"Time to wake now, Keira." I heard his voice but sleep still lingered on and wasn't in any rush to give up power over my mind just yet.

"Just a few more minutes." I moaned trying to roll over but something wouldn't let me.

"But it is time," he told me and after having more time to focus, I knew now that it was Draven's voice.

"Time?" I questioned still unable to fully open my eyes. And then logic started to slowly seep its way into my consciousness. I had fallen asleep in the King's arms but the man who spoke to me now wasn't the Draven I had travelled back in time to find, it came from the Draven I had left behind.

"You said my name," I whispered as it slowly dawned on me and upon opening my eyes I found I was right. I was back.

"Draven!" I shouted his name and threw my arms around him.

"Hush now," he told me holding my head to his chest and it was only when he said this that I realised that I was sobbing. I just couldn't help it. The emotions were overwhelming and without giving it a second thought as to how I had made it back, all I cared for in that moment was that I had.

"Say… it… again," I told him in a broken sentence due to crying around my words.

"Keira." He said my name again knowing exactly what I needed in that moment and it felt like I was breathing fresh air for the first time since making it back from Hell all that time

ago. Why was it that I felt suddenly haunted as if none of this were real?

I lifted my head up and saw we were, as I suspected, in our bedroom, one that was more familiar to me than any other room I could call home…yet, it wasn't the same. Yes, the furniture was the same, the bed, the tapestries and even the smell of antiques that followed you wherever you went in Afterlife but the truth remained…

This wasn't Afterlife.

"What is this place?" I asked looking back at Draven to see him staring straight past me and out of the glass doors ahead.

"Much has changed since you left," he told me and I followed his steady gaze around to see what he saw.

"Persia." I could barely believe what I saw let alone what I spoke of. For there all ablaze was the city that not so long ago I had found such pleasure in beholding.

"But it can't be…I…I must be dreaming?" I said shifting off the bottom of the bed to get closer, needing to see what trickery the glass must be portraying. I stepped up to the glass and tentatively touched it needing only my fingertips to open it. The glass slid open and the smell of smoke and fire burned my nostrils along with my lungs as I breathed in not only the scent of destruction but also the scent of death.

"What happened…what is this?" I asked taking in all around me as far as the eye could see the city of Ctesiphon and all it's glory now lost to smoke and ruin. A battle in the distance raged on but within the city's walls, there was nothing left after the brutal siege had penetrated the city gates after being long battered open.

I felt Draven come up behind me and his hands gripped the tops of my arms.

"Why didn't you do something?" I implored knowing that he had the power to stop this.

"He doesn't have the power to choose but he doesn't have the will to lose...remember that Keira," he whispered behind me cryptically and I turned round to look at him only to find my greatest fears come true.

"DRAVEN!" I screamed his name just as his body was turning to ash right before my eyes. I had never seen Draven die because Draven could never die...he could never die!

"Draven...come back to me...please." Suddenly I was shaken awake as if someone out there was answering my prayers.

"Draven?" I spoke his name as I opened my eyes only it wasn't the face of a man who loved me staring back at me like I expected. No, instead it was the face of a man who looked close to losing himself to a fury buried deep within him, one usually conquered by his demon.

Then the reality of the situation came back to me as I remembered where I had been when falling asleep. It wasn't in the arms of my Draven, it was in the arms of a Persian King. I knew this when the first words spoken through gritted teeth were ones that filled me with dread, for this time, I didn't know how I was going to get myself out of this one...

"Who is this Draven?"

CHAPTER SEVENTEEN

MASTER AT PISSING OFF A KING

Dreams can be a funny thing when the life you are living is the dream and the nightmare part is being ripped away from the life you want to be living. Take now for example. I was currently staring into the eyes of the King of Persia thousands of years into the past and he was furious with me at the very mention of another man's name…

His future name.

I had once had this very dream before, only then I was waking up to my own time and the Draven I fell in love with had been there to comfort me. But now the dream had been the Draven I had left behind and this angry King I woke up with was my reality. It seemed like a cruel twist of fate or was it just the only way the Fates could prepare me for what was to come? Was that what all my dreams were, in one way or another? Well, seeing Draven turning to ashes as his past world burned to the ground all around him was a nightmare I knew I would do everything in my power to prevent.

Or was it simply a painful way of telling me that I was running out of time…in both worlds?

"I asked you a question, girl." He snapped out the reminder as to why my brain was suddenly plagued with this new heartache and I jolted at the harsh sound of his voice.

"I don't remember," I muttered softly as tears slowly clouded my vision. Draven grabbed my arm making me moan at his rough treatment and forced me to look back at him.

"You don't remember yet you shed tears for such a man!" His disbelief was easy to hear and my heartbreak was easy to see, for I couldn't hide it any longer.

"You may not like the answers you hear but that won't change the answers I give you." I told him keeping my voice steady and trying not to break down in the face of the man I loved.

"You love this man?" he asked me and I couldn't help it, my hands flew to cover my mouth as a silent sob escaped me. My reaction to his question was obviously answer enough for him as he recoiled back from me as though I had stabbed him in the heart.

"This…I…" I don't know what was harder, seeing Draven's rage or witnessing him painfully trying to find the right words to speak of it. It seemed so wrong that I couldn't just explain to him that my heartbreak was over him. That this man I loved, this Draven, was the same man I was looking at now. That they were one and the same. But I knew if I did all would be lost and the reasons for me coming here would then be pointless. I hated myself for doing this to him, in this time and my own, but what choices did I have?

"I'm sorry." I told him for so much more than he would ever know. As soon as I said this I knew it was a mistake for his features grew hard and his eyes flashed purple.

"Only the guilty speak in such a way," he told me in a

cold unfeeling voice that spoke volumes to the amount of hurt I had inflicted. I reached out to him, needing to comfort him but it was once again a mistake. He snarled down at my hand the second it landed on his arm and I watched in slow motion as my fingers lost their hold on him as he moved away from me and off the bed. It then landed on the cold covers and as the first tear fell, I fisted the material as my own pain doubled.

"It's not what you think," I told him looking up and finding only pain, one that mirrored my own but for different reasons. He thought I loved another and the reality was that *I loved him* too much. I loved him enough to lie and the weight of those lies were crushing my soul.

"No?! Then tell me, who cries out for a man they don't remember?!" Well he had me with that one because he was right, who would shed tears for a memory they couldn't find?

"You don't understand," I told him because it was the truth.

"Oh I think I understand all too well! Now it's time for you to understand. You are never to see this man again. You are never to speak his name or even think of him, for if you do, then I vow to you that I will find him. I will hunt him down to the ends of the earth and make sure there is nothing left for you to love...now do you understand?!" he thundered at me and I knew that most of it was said out of anger and jealousy. I knew that no matter how brutal his threats sounded I couldn't judge him too harshly as how did I feel when I found out about his Head Concubine? Well for starters I had tried to run away because it was eating me up inside, so yes, who was I to judge? And besides, it was an empty threat considering who Draven was as he wouldn't exactly have to go far to find him now would he.

"Yes, my King," I said looking down at the bed in defeat for there was no argument there for me to fight.

"Guards!" Draven shouted as he wrenched open the door, nearly pulling it from its hinges.

"See to it that no one but her servant is to enter this room, nor is she to leave it without my say so. Am I understood?" he ordered once four guards had appeared and I winced at how humiliating it sounded. As though he was dealing with some naughty child, or worse, some prisoner who no longer needed protecting but now needed a warden to keep me in my place.

"Yes, my King." The one in charge spoke for the rest as they all bowed at the same time.

"You will remain here until Ranka comes to escort you to tonight's Choosing. So if I were you, I would use this time wisely and figure out a way to have my favour in you restored, for after this, I now remain *undecided.*" These became his parting words as after this cruel statement he slammed the door behind him and left me to my misery. I jumped as the door rattled in its frame and then finally let myself give in to despair.

All because of my dreams, I had gone from being the King's favourite and had him declaring his love for me, to one frayed thread away from casting me aside and having done with me. I had come so far in the short time I had been here and now with one whispered name my goal was crumbling around me. And ironically, the worse part about all this was that it was his name that I had been calling out for.

"It's alright, ssshh, I am here now." Pip's voice started to filter through the sounds of me sobbing as she took me in her arms to comfort me. I hadn't even heard her come in, that's how lost in my agony I had been. Because it wasn't just his harsh treatment of me that was causing this now but it was a combination of everything.

It was being in this strange place where I didn't belong. It was missing my life and not knowing for sure how much of that life I even had left to live when I made it back. It was feeling as though I was betraying not only this Draven but the one back in my time. But worst yet, it was doing all of this and facing it knowing that at some point I would have to say goodbye.

Because no one but me knew that there was only one destiny waiting for me. Only one outcome to it all, whether I succeeded or not. The only difference was choosing to do so where my life had meaning and that was always going to be enough to carry on. No matter the tears. No matter the pain. No matter the heartache. In the end I was simply a vessel as well, only I was the one who had the power to change the outcome of the future of not only humanity but also the Gods themselves and all they ruled over.

I got it now. I was starting to understand what it meant to be an Electus. I was the Chosen One not because the Gods and Fates deemed it so, but because I was choosing to save them all.

Just as they knew I always would.

After my emotional outburst to Pip I decided no more tears. I had finally accepted my fate and would now concentrate all my time in making it happen rather than crying over the things I couldn't control. It was time to take a stand and show the world, this one and theirs, what I was made of but more than that, what I was capable of.

I thought more on what I had done over the years and found it incredible to realise that it had all come from a mortal girl who was once broken before she stepped into Draven's world. I had fought Demons, Angels and all of those in between who called themselves my enemies. And up until now I had won, for I was still alive and what would that have all been for, if not this final mission? If not something as important as changing the course of history and making it better. Healing the wrongs that threatened to crack its foundations. I needed not only to be strong, but stronger than ever before.

Now if all that wasn't riding on me having to know this bloody dance!

"I think you're getting better," Pip said and I sighed out the opposite,

"I think I am getting worse."

"It's just such a shame we can't hit him over the head and tie him up…what? Adam always liked it," she said with a hand on her hip like everyone should have a bed with a cage around it!

"Yes and you're also married to the most dangerous Demon ever known who could destroy a city as though it was made of playdough." Pip smiled one of those loved up smiles before her eyes turned sad. She plopped herself on the bed next to me and sighed,

"I miss my boo pants." Then she looked down sadly at his name she had tattooed over her knuckles as she started tracing the letters surrounded by hearts and flowers. I hadn't taken one second to think about how hard this must also be on her as I wasn't the only one missing a husband.

"I'm sorry, Pip." I told her taking her hand and giving it a squeeze.

"For what?"

"For getting you into all this," I said letting my head hang with the added guilt.

"Hey, you didn't get me into all this…I chose to get myself into all this and you know what?"

"What?" I asked looking at her and frowning in confusion when I saw her smirking.

"I might be missing Adam but right now, honestly…well there is nowhere I would rather be. Plus, I would have shit bricks and smashed in your windows with them if I had found out you had gone without me!" I looked at her a minute and then couldn't help but burst out laughing at her comment.

"I love you, Pip." I told her grabbing her to me and she chuckled a girly giggle before she said,

"I love you too sugar Toots, but you're kinda squashing our boobies together...hey it's not a problem, just thought you should know is all." I laughed again before letting her go and said,

"Well we are the Boobeteers after all." She gave me a wink and replied,

"And I wouldn't want it any other way, Tittanian!" We were still laughing when the door opened to see a panicked looking Ranka on the other side of it.

"And watch out, here comes the Cardinal now," Pip commented dryly referring back to the Musketeers once again.

"Behave," I warned as Ranka closed the door.

"What has happened?" she asked once she was a safe distance from the door and any would be eavesdroppers we had close by.

"What do you mean?" I asked, first wanting to be sure we were on the same page before I admitted to pissing off her King.

"I, of course, speak of the King who is out there now laying waste to my warriors' efforts in fighting him." she told me and I gasped.

"What she means to say is he is training with her men and beating the crap out of them but not killing them." Pip said putting a hand on my shoulder, knowing I would have taken this bit of news the wrong way.

"Oh, well that's alright then," I muttered sarcastically.

"I have not seen him in this foul a mood since the Romans killed that Carpenter in the City of Jerusalem but that was nearly 200 years ago," Ranka said making my mouth drop open.

"Uh...I wouldn't go there," Pip said shaking her head to me as I doubted Ranka would understand the importance of that single event until many years to come.

"So what did you do?" she asked and Pip and I gave each other a look as if to say 'Where do we start?'.

"I had a dream and called out the King's name."

"Well that doesn't sound too..."

"Or should I say, my husband's name." I interrupted before she got confused. I watched as she slowly realised what I was getting at but just to be sure I added,

"His name in my time is Draven... Dominic Draven."

"But this can't be true," she argued looking at me in utter disbelief.

"Why not, because I assure you, that's his name." I told her.

"I do not know what this 'Draven' means but I do know that Dominic or Dominicus as it is more formally known, is Latin and my King would never choose a name from his enemies." I laughed thinking a lot can happen in two thousand years.

"He may feel that way now, but time can do a lot to a person and to a country at war." Ranka didn't look convinced until it became obvious something started to fit into place for her, to the point where I couldn't help but ask,

"What is it?"

"Well if what you say is true, then I wondered at its meaning and..." she paused which drove me nuts.

"What...what does it mean?"

"It means 'Of our Lord, he is our Master and belonging to God.'"

"Yep, that fits!" Pip said clapping her hands.

"So what am I going to do now because it isn't exactly as if I can say 'Ooops, sorry but you're the spitting image of my husband back home' won't you forgive me?" I said and Ranka's response made Pip smack her forehead after giving us both a look of confusion,

"Why would you ever spit on the image of your husband?"

"It's an expression Ranka, we don't actually do that."

"Not unless it's an ex-husband and that dude is a Grade A asshole!" Pip added trying no doubt to be helpful. Ranka just ended up looking even more confused and I waved a hand at her and said,

"Don't worry about it, let's just concentrate on what we all understand here and think of a way to get me…"

"Unfucked to get fucked?" Pip said jumping in there and coming right out with it in the only way Pip knew how…blunt and blunt.

"Pretty much," I agreed.

"The only chance you have left is at tonight's Choosing… how is the dance coming along?" I heard Pip clear her throat and I turned around to see her pretending to shoot herself in the head.

"Well that's a confidence booster right there," I remarked with a groan.

"What does this mean?" Ranka asked mimicking Pip's action.

"Oh right, guns haven't been invented yet. Okay how about this…" Pip said now pretending to pull an arrow from behind her back to then fire it with an imaginary bow under her chin.

"Ah, I believe I understand your little friend now," Ranka said to me and I rolled my eyes thinking this was getting us nowhere.

"Great, glad one of us does."

"Oi! I heard that!" Pip complained which I ignored out of frustration.

"Can we get back to the plan now?"

"What plan?" Pip asked and I groaned again.

"Exactly! There is no bloody plan, which is why we need one!" I snapped losing my patience and angry at myself that I couldn't just master this stupid dance.

"Alright, but let's leave the blood out of it should we…right Warrior woman…?"

"Don't call me that," Ranka answered wryly.

"Whatever you want Miss Stabby Pants, the point is we need to know exactly what happens at these shindigs," Pip snapped back and this time I translated for her,

"The Choosing." Ranka quickly understood and continued to tell us what we needed to know.

"First the women are presented to the King for him to eliminate any he sees fit. And then the ones remaining are all to dance for him one by one, then he chooses which one is to be named his next Head Concubine in front of the court. After this there is a great feast before he then takes his new Chosen to the royal bedchamber."

"I'm so screwed."

"You're screwed." Both Pip and I said at the same time once Ranka had finished her thorough walkthrough of tonight's events.

"You cannot dance?"

"That depends what you mean by dance because if we are talking cheesy disco music after a few tequilas and a bottle of beer, then sure, I can shake it. But if we are talking crazy shit with scarves that are pointless and keep getting tangled between my legs, then no, I can't dance," I told her, wishing I had a few of those tequilas right now as I could have done with some liquid courage. Ranka looked to Pip who simply shook her head and said,

"That's a no, Mohawk." Ranka didn't understand the reference to her hair but at least she got how hopeless our situation looked.

"What about an instrument? We once had a girl who played a Kamancheh and I believed the King enjoyed that greatly."

"Think of a little round guitar with three strings that you play with a bow," Pip informed me when I looked confused and I had to say, I was impressed.

"I asked for a book once on the history of sexual instruments but Adam missed out the 'sexual' bit as it was written on a used napkin that had guacamole over the word 'sexual'," she told me obviously reading my surprise.

"Turned out it made a good toilet book," she added and all I could do in response was give her a fake nod when really what I wanted to do was weirdly ask what other books she had in her 'Toilet Book" collection.

"Sorry, I never learned and I don't do tapestries or sing either, so both are a no, no."

"No, but you do paint!" Pip jumped up and shouted with one arm up in the air.

"You are a Master of Arts?" Ranka asked me in surprise, making me blush.

"I can draw and paint, but I wouldn't call myself a master at it." Pip came to stand next to me and bumped my hip with hers before putting her arm around my back and pulling me closer by the shoulder.

"Oh, would you listen to her, but she's just being modest! Of course she is a Master of the Arts …so do you think that will impress him?" she asked leaning forward and waggling her eyebrows.

"Well it would certainly be different," Ranka said and you could almost see the cogs turning around trying to picture it for herself.

"Leave it with me and I will see what I can do," she said

before walking towards the door, but there was one last question I wanted to ask her before she left.

"Ranka wait."

"Yes, Electus?"

"I wanted to know, when you said that he takes them to his bedchamber and…" I didn't have to finish my question.

"Ah, I thought you would wonder upon that. The bedchamber he takes them to is not his own but one staged as such. His real quarters are among his own people and to my knowledge, you are the first female he has ever taken to his bed there," she told me with a grin and thankfully through time, it was one that was getting less unnerving to look at.

"Oooh, that's promising," Pip said elbowing me.

"But when they are there…I don't…I mean I just don't see how…" Okay so my question wasn't coming out the right way but again thankfully she knew what I was trying to say, if her smirk was anything to go by.

"The King is forbidden to bed any humans apart from one… His true Chosen One. His Electus named by the Gods and sent to him…"

"Yes, yes she knows this…now get to the good part," Pip said urging her on. Ranka first gave Pip a raised eyebrow but then chose to ignore the interruption.

"But he is still King and like all Kings before him, there is a certain reputation to uphold. It would do no good if he were to have a harem of beauties without ever touching any of them." I nodded biting my bottom lip waiting to hear the rest and finally have my jealous fears confirmed.

"I wouldn't worry yourself over such matters Electus, for the King has dealt with…"

"Oh, just put her out of her misery woman, before she bites her lip off!" Pip snapped, making Ranka frown.

"They are human so he simply makes them believe they

have spent a night with their King," she said quickly and getting to the point.

"Oh I just bet he does, Mr Lover, Lover," Pip said, like that crap Shaggy song back in early 2000's.

"Not now Pip," I snapped.

"So there is no…uh…" I was trying to word the question when Pip jumped in and stuck two fingers in her fist making me roll my eyes once again.

"No! That would be forbidden," Ranka said affronted and looking disgusted. Well at least that was one bit of good news for today's crapathon.

"Now, I must be getting back to the King… and see what is left of my warriors," she added not looking too pleased by the idea.

"Oh, but I nearly forgot," she said opening the door and gesturing for some servants to bring something in.

"The King wanted you to have something."

"Ooh, goodie a gift, I love gifts, I bet it sparkles!" Pip said clapping and jumping up and down next to me.

"Think again," I told her as two servants carried in a large copper bath, followed by ten more servants carrying in urns of water, presumably enough to fill it. The last of the servants then carried in a wooden chest and layers and layers of folded silk, which was what I gathered was my outfit for tonight.

"The chest was sent from Parmida, seeing as although even she wasn't trusted with your care for tonight, she still wanted to ensure you were perfect for the King." This reminded me of something even more important that I wanted to ask her.

"Ranka, about what happened yesterday…" She quickly held up a hand to stop me and said,

"Now is not the time but we shall speak of these things later. Now you'd better start preparing yourself, for I will be sent back to get you once the sun has set." And with that she was gone and with it my answers for what had happened with Farrin.

Pip had never been called for the 'Persian culture experience' which was code for 'torture time' and she had complained about it one way or another for most of the day. But I had to wonder, had Draven been informed yet but more importantly, after this morning... *would he still care?*

Well we would soon find out as the day was quickly coming to an end and my night, well my night was only just about to begin.

Now all I had to do was...

Survive it.

CHAPTER EIGHTEEN

CHOSEN PICTURE

"I don't think I can do this!" I said in a panic grabbing hold of Pip and pulling her closer. She looked around, no doubt looking for Ranka to come back and save the day before murmuring down at me,

"It will be fine." This was when I knew to really panic because I had come to live by one fundamental rule when around Pip…if she ever looked concerned, then you should *really* panic!

Ranka had come to fetch us as she said she would when the sun had only just set. I had been bathed until my skin felt new and now smelled like a beautician's wet dream. We had used oils I didn't even know the name of but if they smelled nice then they went in. Thankfully the only thing we did recognise was soap, so at least I could wash my hair without it looking like it had simply been dipped in chip fat!

Once I was out and dried, I let Pip take over brushing my hair until it fell into the long waves it usually bounced back up into. Then she pinned it up to one side letting a long golden plait hang down over my shoulder. Once my hair was done she then added a long length of material to match my dress, securing it into my hair so that it trailed down my back and onto the floor like a cape.

The rest of the dress, I was surprised to say, was quite reserved and not as revealing as I would have thought. Not considering the whole point of this 'event' was to show as much skin as possible in order to entice the King into choosing them but maybe I was wrong.

The top was a long sleeved tunic style jacket that was tight across the breasts, so tight in fact I didn't think it would close up at first. At one point I thought Pip was going to punch my breasts in it but thankfully with some tugging here and there we finally got it fastened.

The material was a beautiful peacock blue colour adorned with large golden leaves throughout and framed around the edges. The design was a thick border of smaller gold leaves tightly entwined in lines. This border was used to edge wide cuffs on the sleeves, the bottom part of the top and also the collar running down either side of where the top fastened in the middle. The trousers I wore, which Pip told me were called Shalvars, were in the same shade of blue as the top but were plain without the gold design.

These had a high waist, held by a thick gold belt that could be seen thanks to the high split in the front of the jacket, as it only fastened just under my breasts so that it could show off my belly.

"Shame this outfit didn't come with any bling," Pip commented after standing back and taking a look at her handy work, which on her part was mainly man handling my breasts.

"I doubt anyone else will have any and will all be dressed like this," I said which soon became famous last words as the second we walked into the main hall, Pip turned to me and said,

"You were saying?" This was because not only was I the only person not wearing any jewels but also because all the other 'contestants' were all wearing red. As soon as I walked in the whole room fell quiet as though everyone already knew who I was.

"I guess gossip spreads quick in this town," Pip whispered to me before I was ushered up through the centre and to the front.

When Ranka had come to get us the first thing I noticed was the lack of art supplies she had in her hand and when I asked her about it she just gave me a look I couldn't decipher and shook her head. I didn't know what this was supposed to mean and with the guards there I didn't get the chance to ask.

This was pretty much when my panic started to kick in. And then this panic started to double when I first entered the room and saw that I was the only one out of the other girls who stood out like a sore thumb! Of course this was nothing compared to the triple, near passing out panic I had when being led down the centre of the massive hall, only to see a stern looking Draven sat on his throne waiting for me. I had to wonder if it hadn't been planned having me coming in last just to double my humiliation.

I tried to hold my head up and not give in to temptation to lower my head in shame but one glance at the front and that was easier said than done. Draven sat looking disinterested and important on his golden throne, which was different from the one I had seen him sat in last night.

This one had a high pillared back with thick red material curtained down from the top two peaks and cascading on either side. Draven was currently drumming his fingers on top of one of the snarling lion heads that decorated the armrests, looking just as mean as the lions themselves. Well I guess that answered my unasked question as to whether, given the day to calm down, he would be in a better mood than how he left this morning. That was certainly a big fat 'no' then.

I had to wonder if that scowl had only just appeared once I entered the room or had it been there all day? I also had to wonder what the other girls thought about their King's obvious displeasure at tonight's Choosing?

The whispering seemed to get louder the closer I got to the front and I had to walk around the large round shaped pool in the middle of the room that was covered in brightly coloured glazed tiles. Flower petals floated in the water and bowls of fruit framed both it and the walkway that had been kept clear for our arrival.

Men and woman either stood or sat amongst piled cushions on both sides as they were ready for the show that would soon begin. Scantily dressed servants weaved in and out of the guests holding jugs of wine, bowls of nuts and large golden discs filled with what they called 'sweetmeats' for the guests to enjoy.

I couldn't help but look at the wine being poured into goblets wishing I could steal the jug and drink the lot! I looked off to the other side to see Pip was walking parallel to me all the while keeping me in sight and nodding as if to give me encouragement. Ranka seemed to have quickly vanished after we first arrived, which didn't give me much hope at all.

Finally this first round of torture was over as I made it to the front and looking left and right saw that there was only one space left empty for me, which just so happened to be directly opposite the King.

I was just about to sit down in my desperation to get out of view when I noticed Pip from the side waving at me. I glanced her way to see her bowing like a mad woman, reminding me of royal etiquette. I then quickly bowed before the King but noticed that he too had just seen Pip reminding me of my actions…and once more, he didn't look impressed.

"Sit," he barked at me, making a few more people other than myself jump at the sound of his harsh tone. As I lowered myself to my assigned cushion the gossip doubled because of it and it was only when he stood that the room silenced. He was dressed in what I gathered was suitable attire for the occasion as was his sister who also sat in a smaller throne next to his. The one on his other side however, still remained empty which had me wondering where Vincent was.

Sophia wore a stunning purple dress that was made up of layer upon layer of the most delicate looking fabric. It was so fine that had she been only wearing one layer it would have been see-through. Draven wore the same striking purple colour but as a sash around his waist which was combined with leather straps that held an elaborate looking dagger to one side. This same colour continued in the open robe he wore that went down to his knees and the muscles on his bare torso looked hard enough to scrub clothes on…or better still, to lick and kiss all over.

"I invite you all here tonight, for the time has come for there to be another Choosing of my new Head Concubine. As is tradition the current chosen one, Stateira, can still hold claim to the title if she can still impress me as she once did in the past and yet again I choose her above any other." Draven said this to the whole room but when he looked down at me I knew who he was really saying it all for.

I wanted to get up, stamp my feet and shout, 'fine pick the murderous bitch, you're welcome to her!' but I knew that would have only been my anger talking. Besides I don't think I would have got away with it quite so much as I would have done with the Draven in my time. So thankfully, I kept my mouth shut!

At least that had answered one of my questions for Ranka, as it was clear she hadn't yet had chance to tell him of his precious Concubine's crimes or I doubt very much she would be sat among us as she was now. All I could hope for tonight's events was that at some point the evil poisonous smirk would be wiped off her face, preferably in the form of a slap from someone...please Lord let it be me, I thought to myself.

"Let us begin!" he shouted clapping his hands and all the other girls stood up at the same time...all except me, as I had no clue this was what we were supposed to do. I scrambled up as quickly as I could and frowned when I heard the few sniggers directed my way. Draven gave me an amused look and I suddenly knew what this was...

This was his version of payback.

He walked down the line starting at the first girl furthest away from me. She was beautiful just like the others and like the rest was scantily clad in red. So not only did I stand out for being the only one in a different colour and mostly covered up but I was also the only blonde in the room. Brilliant, just brilliant I thought sarcastically!

Draven smiled down at her making me want to growl with jealousy and this was only the first girl. I could only hope that by the time he got to me I wasn't so outraged that I just slapped him and stormed off! Now I knew how anyone felt knowing their husband was at a strip club for a night with their pick of beauties all lined up waiting to be chosen.

It was awful and I hated every damn minute of it, but wasn't that the point he was trying to make? Because I had certainly seen for myself his own reaction to jealousy and this was obviously the perfect way of teaching me that lesson, one that I remember he had cruelly taught me once before back in Sophia's playroom.

Draven reached one girl who looked too young and barely legal to be out at night, let alone be someone's Concubine. Draven gave the girl's cheek an affectionate stroke and whispered something in her ear. After that the girl looked as though she wanted to burst into tears as she left the line, obviously being told to sit back with the crowd.

His first elimination.

Draven continued down the line of half-naked girls having dismissed another two, which now left only seven of us to try and seduce the King with our skills at enticement. But first he had to cast his judgment over me, as I was the last one he faced. I didn't want to look at him. I was so emotionally drained from the whole experience and it was only the beginning. He must have seen something in my face that told him this because the next words out of his mouth weren't as harsh sounding as they had been or as I had been expecting.

"Look at me, Little Lamb." I did as I was told and slowly looked up at him, knowing I wouldn't have been able to handle his disapproving eyes like I was dreading.

"Breathe, Pet," he told me and I finally let out a held breath as his eyes softened as though he was finally taking pity on my fragile nerves.

"I have never done anything like this before," I whispered up at him, deciding to be honest. He gave me a small grin back, bent forward a little and whispered,

"I am happy to hear it." Then he put a thumb to my lip to pull it from my teeth and said,

"Now behave yourself." After he let me go he clapped his hands obviously for the music to start. He walked up the few steps back to his throne and after flicking aside his robe he sat down, waiting for the first dance to begin, which unfortunately seemed to be me. Once again he looked amused at the clear terror on my face as he beckoned me to stand before him to begin.

The panic really started to take hold and it was becoming clear as the sniggering and whispers started back up at my expense. Draven's stare was just as intimidating as the room full of people at my back. It was almost as though I was frozen to the spot. Even when he motioned me forward with his hand I didn't want to move. Why did it feel like I was being asked to walk the plank?

He knew I didn't want to do this, I could see it in his eyes and the way he gripped the lion's head as though he was fighting with himself to come down and rescue me from myself.

"Don't keep him waiting." Even the girl next to me whispered a warning and I knew my choices were down to none. So with a pounding heart I stepped forward as though I was facing a firing squad. I looked to Pip to see her looking just as panicked but then she spotted someone coming through the crowd and I could only hope it was…it was…

"Ranka, oh thank God." I muttered when I saw her, hopefully coming to my rescue.

"If I may my Lord, I believe she wishes to do something different for your entertainment." Ranka said coming to stand by my side. Draven looked intrigued and rubbed his beard with one hand as though he was taking his time thinking about it.

"This entertainment you speak of, explain it to me," he demanded but just as Ranka was about to speak he held up a hand silencing her.

"Not from you, Ranka." Then he nodded past her directly to me. Ranka looked back at me and motioned with her head for me to come forward and to go ahead and explain. I looked back at the room nervously and the second I saw bitch face laughing I knew this was where I was going to find my backbone. I straightened myself up and looked directly to the King, ready to seize the moment. For Pip had been right, I had something here that no one else was going to do and that in itself should be enough to find courage in and be proud of.

So I couldn't dance. So I wasn't looking as sexy as the others. But I was the one who'd had the King in my bed last night and I was the only one who could actually claim to be his real 'Chosen One'. Even if he didn't know it yet, I knew this gave me a power that the others didn't have. So let them dance! Let them flaunt themselves in vain! Because a dance lasted all of a few minutes but what I was going to do would immortalise his image forever by my hand. Not many could claim to have the same skill. I could do this!

"You can do this." I whispered my mantra to myself, forgetting myself and that Draven could also hear this. His eyes widened a moment but he didn't say anything.

"My King…" I said raising my head up and meeting his intense gaze with one of my own.

"Tonight I wish to bestow on you a great gift, one that I hope will last throughout the ages."

"And this gift you speak of…?" Draven worded it as a questioning sentence he wanted me to finish.

"A drawing of your image, my Lord, one done here in front of everyone whilst you sit and enjoy the others dancing," I said trying to make my voice steady enough to sound confident. He tilted his head to the side and ran a hand down his beard again as he thought about this.

"So you don't wish to dance for me?" he asked as though being clear on that and I couldn't help but blush.

"What good is a harem girl if she can't dance, My King!?" Someone heckled from the crowd and the others started laughing. Draven looked momentarily outraged and was about to stand when I decided to intervene by coming back with a witty reply.

"Oh I didn't say that! For the dance I have in mind is for the King's eyes only and not one I wish to share with the room… that is, if I am blessed enough to be the one Chosen." Once I finished the room's ruckus was now sounded out for very different reasons and mainly by the men who shouted encouragements, like, 'I would pick her!' or 'The King is in for a treat with that one!'

"Silence!" Draven roared obviously not liking the idea of other men lusting over me or thinking about my sassy reply. The room hushed in an instant and Draven sat back down from his outburst. It was a real confidence booster to know that I now had the approval of the room and some were on my side. Draven raised an eyebrow at me and asked,

"So you wish to dance for me privately?" I swallowed hard and he watched the motion like a hawk knowing what such a question would do to me.

"If My King wishes it," I told him bravely making his eyes widen in surprise before growing intense with the idea of it.

"Very well. I will accept both but for now, you may grace me with your artistic talents," he said motioning for Ranka to proceed. Ranka bowed and clicked her fingers once to tell the servants to come forward and place their items down that they carried. They set down a small table in front of my cushion and with it a number of supplies which Ranka had obviously been trying to find in time.

"Your station awaits you, my little Artist," Draven said nodding back to my cushion with a smirk he wasn't trying to hide. I bowed this time remembering my place and gave him a smirk of my own, looking up and saying,

"I thank you, My Lord." Then I finished this off with a quick bite of my lip just to tease him. He gave me a look and mouthed the word, 'behave' at me before I sat back down. I did so now unable to wipe the smile from my face, which didn't go unnoticed by the two females in the room who equally wanted to see my head on a spike. Sophia looked disgusted by my behaviour and Bitch face looked ready to rip my head off. Well she was welcome to try herself this time, for she would find a very different type of fight on her hands, as it was her own King himself that taught me how to punch.

I sat back down as the music started again and looked at what I had to work with. Bless Ranka but she had tried to give me a bit of everything in hopes that I could work with some of it. I unrolled one of the sheets of thick parchment paper that was a cross between ancient papyrus and dried bamboo, knowing this would have to do. I had no idea when paper was invented but looking at this and I would have said they were a long way off yet. I also looked at what I had been given to draw with and was happy to see that it looked like thin sticks of charcoal, which had me wondering if Pip had said something to Ranka as they looked freshly made.

I decided to use one of the pieces of paper to test the charcoal on and quickly found that I couldn't use the ends the way I wanted. They just weren't fine enough as they had all been squared off at the ends making them blunt. I looked around trying to find something to use to sharpen the edges and after finding nothing, decided I would have to try and rub them into a point using the paper.

I bit my lip as I worked, trying to shape the end but it was no good. I looked up seeing if I could get Pip's attention only to see that the first dance was underway. But what I wasn't counting on was that Draven wasn't watching the beauty dancing in front of him, *he was watching me.*

Suddenly he was up and out of his seat, shocking everyone as he walked directly over to me and got down on one knee. I had to stop my mouth from dropping open in surprise, which wouldn't have been a sexy look at all. Meanwhile the poor girl dancing just stopped not knowing whether to carry on or just return deflated and rejected back to her place.

I kind of felt sorry for her but Draven didn't look concerned for her at all, however for me was a different matter as he had obviously been watching me struggle. Therefore, he knew exactly what I needed and there was a collective gasp from the crowd as he pulled his dagger from its sheath before he handed it to me and said,

"Try this." I looked dumbstruck at the blade for a few seconds more before taking it from him like it was the greatest gift.

"Thank you," I whispered to him and made sure that my hand touched his fingers gently as I took it. He nodded once and then stood up to resume his place on his throne. Then he nodded at the musicians to continue and also for to the girl to do so as she had paused her dancing.

Well if I thought there was gossip before then now the whole room seemed to be talking about the King's mighty gesture as it seemed for a warrior to give his blade to someone was of great significance indeed. I could feel the heat rising to my cheeks as I tried to concentrate on my task and used the heavy blade to chip away at the end until I had it as I needed it. Then I tested it with a few lines to find that now it would work nicely. I placed the blade down next to me, took a deep breath before looking up at my subject.

As usual when drawing someone I started at the eyes and looking deep into his now was no easy task given the intensity in which they looked back at me. There were so many emotions hidden there that until you started really looking at him like an artist, they just belonged to a handsome man high up in power.

However, once you started breaking each feature down and putting it to paper, then his face almost started to tell a story. There was a respect for his people only seen in the quick glances around the room. There was the soft close of his eyes as he nodded his thanks when being handed a drink by a passing servant. But my favourite was the slight tilt of a smile when glancing my way watching me work and this combined with the small creases next to his eyes had me quickly smiling back at him.

I rapidly became lost working on his face and it was as if the whole room had suddenly evaporated around us. The music became a soft hum in the background, that could have easily become the trees swaying in a gentle breeze or water cascading over the rocks down a stream. There was nothing else in the world but those eyes and the gift I was given in trying to duplicate them. The intimacy found in these passing minutes was unlike anything I had ever known because I finally got the chance to study the man I loved in a way I never thought possible.

I didn't know how he felt as he was being studied this way but I can tell you that if his eyes ever left me then it wasn't but for a moment longer than it had to be. And one by one the beautiful girls all got up and had their chance to dance for his enjoyment but I was happy to say that none of them received half as much attention as I did just by sitting here drawing him.

I was just holding out my stick of charcoal, using it to measure the distances and thus gauging the size of his mouth, jawline etc, when the last of the dancers stepped up. I wanted to hiss at her as she walked past me and her grunt of disapproval of my work only fuelled my hatred more. It had been easy up until now ignoring all that had gone on around me and not getting swept up in the jealousy that would have happened had I not been concentrating on drawing Draven. But now that it was Stateira's turn to dance it was hard to concentrate on anything else. Thankfully, most of my portrait of Draven was finished but either way I decided not to give her the satisfaction of looking her way. Instead I just continued to tweak the picture here and there.

I was just rubbing his jawline with my thumb, creating some

more shadowing when I heard the room gasp after Draven thundered,

"ENOUGH!" I looked up to see that Draven was now stood and pointing down the steps back to where Stateira should have been dancing. She had obviously taken her entertainment too far as it was clear she had been brazen enough to start nearly lap dancing on him. This was obviously an attempt to hide Draven from my view and also me from his as it must have been clear where his attention was focused throughout her dancing.

She was utterly outraged to say the least. She looked back at me, snarled and then back at Draven with fury in her eyes.

"She sits there and insults me!" she shouted and Draven's eyes became disinterested as he sat back down and said,

"Your own actions insult yourself! Now sit down, for I grow tired of watching you." On hearing this I couldn't help but cough back a stunned laugh. She looked back at me again and it became very clear what she was planning. She was angry enough that if she had a blade in her hand she would have killed me right then, in front of all these people.

"And your actions insult me!" she roared back at him and it was then that I saw something no one else seemed to see. She *did* have a blade, only this time she wasn't going to use it on me...

She was going to use it on the King.

CHAPTER NINETEEN

A CRACKING END

The second I saw Stateira start to pull that small blade from behind her back, my instincts took over. I grabbed Draven's dagger at my side and ran towards her just as she raised the weapon high into the air. She was just about to throw herself at Draven when I suddenly yanked back her hair and held the deadly blade to her throat.

"I wouldn't do that if I were you." I told her in a surprisingly calm voice. The whole room gasped in horror at what was unfolding before their eyes and what had been an attempt made on their King's life. Well, if they liked my sass before then now they all looked ready to bow down to me and name me their next queen!

"Drop it," I ordered as she still held on to her weapon.

"Now!" I warned further, pressing the edge of my dagger harder into her skin making her hiss with pain before she did as I demanded. I looked to Draven who wasn't looking at all concerned with the mad woman who had just tried to kill him

but instead was looking at the 'crazy in love' woman who just saved him.

The whole room seemed to be at a standstill, almost as though everyone was too afraid to move.

"You saved me." Draven uttered these words in wonder as if having to speak them just to make sense of them. I knew they weren't exactly true as Draven wouldn't have been injured by this insane mortal's hand but still, I guess he knew what the gesture meant all the same.

"Of course. And if it is ever in my power, I would do so again," I told him honestly. At that moment something very intense I couldn't read passed in his eyes before they hardened on the traitor.

"Guards! I want this woman in chains!" Draven shouted and within seconds we were surrounded by Draven's men. I looked around slowly wondering what they were all waiting for when it was Draven who took that step closer to me and said,

"You can let her go now." I gave him a wide-eyed look before realising he was right, the guards couldn't get her as I hadn't yet released my brutal and punishing hold on her head.

"Oh…right," I said letting go of her hair and pulling the dagger from her neck, letting it drop to the floor with a clatter. She suddenly fell to the ground, clutching her neck as though I had slit it open and I wanted to call her a pussy and tell her to man up, when all of a sudden she reached for her own dropped blade and swung it at me. She wouldn't have killed me but she certainly would have sliced me good, that was if it hadn't been for Draven's supernatural fast reflexes. He had her arm in a lock before my eyes could fully register the move. It was held twisted out in front of him and she was crying out in pain as he applied enough pressure to get her to drop her knife once more.

"You're dead, Bitch!" She snarled the threat up at me but this was when Draven's patience had run dry, for with one swift move, he brought up his knee and broke her arm at the elbow. Now she was really screaming and the sickening crunch of bone combined with the gross way her arm looked as if it had been put on backwards, was enough to turn me green. Draven dropped her to the floor, knowing this time she was not getting back up to attack anyone. Then he took my hand and pulled me closer to him, first walking me around her broken body.

"Get her out of my sight!" Draven snarled down at her, commanding his guards of their new task. Her screams of agony could still be heard long after she had been dragged out of the hall and the doors closed behind them.

"Are you alright?" Draven asked, hooking me under the chin and raising my face up to look at him. He seemed to be studying me to check for any signs of stress and I blushed under such a penetrating look of concern.

"All is fine, my Lord." I said shyly looking down at his chest.

"Not yet it is not, but it soon will be," he replied cryptically. Then he spun me around to face the room and placed his hands on my shoulders. Seeing as I was the shortest girl in his Harem and he was a very tall man, he could easily still address the room by looking over my head.

"Tonight we feast to honour not only my new Chosen One but also the guardian the Gods have bestowed upon me, gifting me with both her beauty and loyal courage! I give you my new Head Concubine!" he shouted before spinning me back around to face him and bending me back slightly to kiss me in front of everyone. The whole court roared with their cheers and clapping, loving their King's open display of affection towards me.

I didn't know if this was a common thing for him or not but at that moment I didn't care. I simply let myself get lost in his kiss and the happy knowledge that I had gained his favour once more…now all I had to do was keep it.

Draven finished his kiss and set me back to standing straight but when I turned to step down, ready to retake my seat he wouldn't let me go.

"Oh no, you're not going anywhere Little Lamb, for your place is now here by my side," he said pulling me backwards to his chest before putting an arm across my torso from behind.

"Where you will remain," he added, whispering the promise in my ear and making me shudder against him. Then he decided to reinforce this decision by picking me up and walking back up the steps to his throne. Once more the room looked utterly shocked to see such behaviour from their King but it was obvious he didn't care, just as he never did in Afterlife.

He turned around with me in his arms and faced the room as if daring anyone to reproach him on his actions but not only did no one say a word, they actually all got to their knees and bowed down to us both. This was obviously what Draven had been waiting for because it was only after this that he sat us down himself, readjusting me so that I was comfortably on his lap.

Therefore, I couldn't help but wonder about our fate and ask myself the question, was it rooted in our destiny to always be this way, no matter which time in history we were to meet? Would Draven always find himself acting this way towards me whether he knew who or what I was?

I didn't have the answers from his viewpoint as I only had my own feelings to go on, but using that logic then I would have to say yes. Because no matter which Draven I faced, my heart had no will of its own but to give itself over to the man without question. It was as if I was hardwired to fall in love with him over and over again, no matter how many lifetimes we lived through.

And for Draven, well one look around the room and you could tell he was acting out of his normal character. And looking up at him now, it was blindingly clear that he didn't give a damn about the world or what they thought. He was willing to deny his own people their Prophecy's Chosen One so he could have his own Chosen One. The fact that they were one and the same in this case, just didn't matter because he didn't know. To him I was just a human girl he was falling in love with and it was a strong enough force to get him to give up everything he had ever known…it was enough to get him to forgo his own people and even his own morals. His own rules. His own judgement. Everything but his own heart.

So my conclusion,

Love was without a doubt a powerful force, no matter which time we lived in.

"You look deep in thought, Little Lamb." Draven said bringing me back to the room.

"I don't think your sister approves." I said nodding to her empty seat. Sophia must have crept away at some point and whether this was before Stateira's attack or after, I couldn't say. All I knew was that her seat now remained empty and she was nowhere in sight. Draven sighed and looked to his side where his sister should have been.

"It is complicated," he told me and I wanted to laugh and say, 'yeah no shit,' but thankfully refrained.

"I understand," I told him and he shot me a surprised look.

"You do?" He probably wondered how on earth I could understand such a thing, considering as far as he knew *I* knew nothing of their world.

"Can I ask you a question, my Lord?"

"But of course," he said looking intrigued.

"Now I am not fishing for a compliment when I ask this but…"

"Fishing for a compliment, upon my word little sweetheart of mine, I have never heard of such a thing!" he said clearly very amused by my comment.

"It's just a saying I use sometimes and means…"

"I can comprehend what it means sweetness, but you are the very last person I would say fishes for anything, let alone for compliments," he told me before I could finish. I blushed making him laugh,

"To begin with, an easy blush like yours doesn't appear through modesty but more through lack of confidence." I frowned at him causing him to laugh at me again before explaining,

"Don't misunderstand me, you hold a courage to rival my generals as you must be the only female I know who would run towards the blade, not away from it." Well he had me there.

"Yes, but I had your blade," I told him but he just smiled back at me and tapped my chin twice saying,

"You did but are you trying to tell me that if you hadn't then you would have run away or would you have attacked her anyway and taken the chance?" I didn't need any time to think because I knew he was right, and he knew it too.

"Exactly. You are a fighter. It is rooted in both your heart and in your soul…*I can see it,*" he told me, whispering this last part to me as if it was a secret and I guess it was. Because he *could* see it in my soul. It was something all supernaturals could see. They could read your soul as easily as though they were reading it from a manuscript.

"You may blush all you want, as the colour undoubtedly suits you, as it did last night when you *came all over my hand."* Hearing this teasing I completely forgot myself and where I was. So just being myself and being around my Draven I turned around and smacked his arm playfully and hissed,

"You can't say that!" I didn't realise that I was actually

hitting a King in front of his court. My eyes widened for a second as realisation seeped in and I waited for his reaction. He looked shocked for a moment as did everyone else in the room who had witnessed it, but I think his next reaction they were most surprised at, as it beat mine.

Draven suddenly threw his head back and burst into uncontrollable laughter. His reaction forced me to grip onto him tighter as I was being bounced up and down on his knee but thankfully before I could fall off, he pulled me closer to him.

The room soon followed suit and even though they may not have understood the reasons for him laughing, they were simply responding to their King's happiness…that was, *all but one.*

I was scanning the crowd when I saw him. One person who was watching us both with no expression on his face whatsoever. I had never seen his face before but I knew I would never forget it. Those cold dead eyes seemed to pierce straight through the crowd and I frowned back at him, telling him silently that he was caught. I had seen him and the second he realised this he backed away and slipped back into the crowd before disappearing altogether. I didn't know who he was but I knew enough to know that he was sent here with one purpose…

He was a spy.

"Oh you will pay for that one later, little warrior of mine," Draven told me, his voice still thick with humour from his outburst. I was in two minds whether to tell him about the man I'd seen in the crowd but decided it would sound more paranoid than anything else and besides, the man was long gone now. So not wanting to kill his good mood I smiled back up at him.

"I wouldn't underestimate me if I were you." I teased back.

"Oh I wouldn't dare. The lack of confidence I speak of was referring to the shy girl I saw standing opposite me, terrified she would have to dance for me."

"Ah well, yes." I had to agree with him there.

"And any girl who knows her own beauty as you should, knows the worth of the power she holds. So when given the opportunity to show off such beauty in the form of a dance, she will take it. This isn't rare to see…" He paused and placed a hand to my cheek and continued,

"But what is rare to see is a beautiful girl who uses the strengths of her mind and of her heart to reach her goals…" He let his hand run down my neck and tapped on my heart when he said this before then letting his hand run gently over my breast when getting to his next point,

"…She doesn't use them to manipulate, as Stateira does using her beauty." This he was referring to the way she was dressed with most of her body on show.

"Men can be easily fooled by such a woman but a real King doesn't want to be led around on a leash whilst letting himself believe he is free. For a King may pick such beauty to look upon but only a foolish King picks such beauty to sit upon his throne with him…do I look like a foolish King to you?" He finished by asking me this question and I finally understood what he was saying.

"No, you don't, my Lord," I told him making him grin back at me. This was his way of explaining to me why in the past he had someone like Stateira as his Concubine. Which made me question, had tonight's 'Chosen' been merely a test of character?

"But I do believe you had a question for me," he said reminding me that he was right, I did have a question for him, one that tied in with our current conversation.

"Out of all your other Concubines, have you ever had them sit upon your throne with you like this?" Draven looked taken aback by the question and raised an eyebrow at me.

"No…Why do you ask?"

"Well I told you that I understand the reasons your sister

doesn't approve and you seemed surprised by this, but it's obvious."

"How so?" he asked clearly intrigued, which is why he shifted me around so that he could see my face more clearly.

"Because if I am the first as you say, then she must see me as a threat." I knew I was really pushing it here but I couldn't help it, I wanted to test the waters on this one.

"A threat you say...A threat who saves my life?... Explain this to me," he asked trying to make a point but no doubt doing so to try and throw me off where I was going with this.

"I am not a queen and I am not a princess. I have no royal blood to offer the likes of a king. She is no doubt worried for your reputation and if what you say is true, that there is power in my heart and mind, along with unknown beauty, then sat up here upon your throne, in her eyes...My Lord, would that not be reason enough to see it as a threat?" I asked straightening my back and showing him the mind he spoke of with such respect. Well let's see if after all that he still thought of it that way.

"And you, do you consider yourself a threat to my throne and royal bloodline?" he asked me seriously after taking the time to think about the point I made. I couldn't help it but I laughed and blurted out,

"Oh, Hell no!" Then I covered my mouth realising what I had said and his eyes grew wide before they crinkled with humour.

"And pray tell me, for what do you know of Hell to speak of it as such?" he asked in jest.

"You would be surprised," I told him dryly unable to say anything else, for I doubted he would believe me if I told him that I had been there twice, each time done so to save his ass!

"I certainly would be, for if you were to tell me otherwise, a face such as yours only ever came from the beauty found in Heaven." I gave him a small smile, knowing of the same beauty that could also be found in Demons. For the downfall of having a good heart wasn't always from looking to find an Angel in a Demon, but sometimes it was from trusting that Angels all had good hearts.

But Draven thought he was only speaking to a girl who knew what she was told and not of the hidden world he lived in, that was one I discovered long ago. And more importantly, one that was discovered long before Draven ever entered my world. I wondered what he would have said if I had confessed to him of seeing Demons most of my life?

"So let us return to why you don't consider *yourself* a threat," he said going back to what prompted my 'hellish' reply.

"It's simple. I have no ambitions of becoming queen or any other royalty for that matter." Now this did surprise him. He jolted back a little as if doing a double take and looked at me as if he was trying to detect a lie.

"You wouldn't wish to become queen?" he asked as if needing to hear me say it again just to be sure.

"No, not at all. Not unless it was something that was expected of me so that I could be with the person I loved. I respect anyone who chooses to take on the responsibility of an entire nation upon their shoulders but only when they do so for the right reasons."

"I must confess this is surprising but what you say also intrigues me. I have never met someone with this view when asked such a question." Well one look at Stateira back in the harem that day and I wasn't surprised, as right there was my first example of someone wanting that power for the wrong reasons.

"Do you want to hear my honest opinion?" I asked making him smirk back at me.

"Oh very much so. In fact, I am very much looking forward

to hearing your views on such a subject." I gave him a little grin and asked,

"Are you teasing me?" At this he laughed once, lifted up his hands and said,

"I wouldn't dare, for I fear what your mind would make your lips say." This time I laughed and teased back,

"Or what you may learn from it." At this his eyes grew soft and he ran the back of his hand down my cheek before saying,

"I have a feeling that would be a great deal from you. Please continue and let us see what I can learn this time." Then he nodded for me to continue. I took a deep breath and decided to give it to him, as he couldn't then say he didn't ask for it.

"Power isn't found in simply being in a position that allows you to tell people what to do, but is more powerful when found in the freedom of *asking* people what to do and having them choosing to do so through respect, not fear…that's where real strength lies. Like having your men join you in battle because they believe in their cause for fighting. Those are the men you want at your back, not because they have been ordered to die for another man's cause…Because in the end it is belief that holds the power and the strong union in that belief that is more powerful than any royal command." Once I had finished he looked stunned. All the time while listening to me prattle on and preaching my views he had an elbow to his armrest, supporting his hand that covered his jaw as he stroked his beard out of habit.

"What?" I asked after I could no longer stand it. He was just staring at me as though he was waiting for me to disappear in a puff of smoke.

"I am just trying to figure out if you're real or not," he told me gesturing with his hand as though he couldn't believe it. I laughed and said,

"Yes, trust me, I am annoyingly real." He frowned and said,

"Annoying, No. Real, well I am still not sure of that yet."

"Why not?" I asked unable to help myself.

"You may not understand what I am I about to tell you but I fear I have no other way to explain." I nodded for him to continue.

"My idea of promised perfection is not everyone else's idea of it. I never knew when it would happen or how long I would have to wait but I feel as though with you sat here on my lap, telling me how the ways of the world should be, that the wait is over. So yes, in sight of such perfection, I am indeed finding myself questioning it, for it is not every day the Gods gift you with such a promise and grant it so quickly."

"I…I…I don't know what to say." I told him too overwhelmed to speak. Tears filled my eyes and threatened to cascade over with the sheer amount of emotions his words had created. He believed I was his Chosen One, even when others did not. This was what he was trying to tell me and only someone who knew what he stood to lose could really appreciate what this meant.

He didn't care that I was human. He didn't care that I wasn't who everyone else thought was the 'Electus'. All he cared about was that he had found me and that he believed I was his Chosen One. That's all that mattered to him.

"You don't have to say anything, Sweetest one, for it is how I feel when I have you here in my arms," he said smiling at me as he swiped away a few stray tears that had slipped down my cheek. It was a beautiful moment and not one I would ever forget, as it was like having Draven tell me that he loved me for the first time all over again.

"And besides, whether you are of royal blood or not, from the sound of such worldly wisdom you hold, I will indeed be seeking your council on certain matters." I grinned and nudged his arm, saying,

"What, like matters of war? Because I'd better warn you now, I am more of a 'let's all get along' kind of girl" At this he burst out laughing once more, again showing everyone in the room that their King obviously did have a sense of humour and also, someone else for that matter...

"By the Gods! Why, in all my years I didn't know you could even make that sound!" A voice suddenly shouted from across the room as the doors were opened to grant him entrance. I looked up trying to make out the man but he had a helmet on that covered half of his face.

But Draven on the other hand didn't need to see him to know who it was and after first grinning at me, he set me down off his lap before standing up to greet his…

"Brother!"

CHAPTER TWENTY

WHAT TO DO ABOUT FAMILY

"Brother come, there is someone I wish for you to meet!" Draven shouted, beckoning his brother from across the room. I don't know why but my heart started beating wildly in my chest as if something very bad was about to happen. I didn't really have a reason for this as it wasn't as though his brother could recognise me in any way and with Pip around, I was safe from having my real side discovered.

Then what exactly was I afraid of?

I couldn't say and had no more time to think about it as Vincent was currently making his way through the crowd to us. I didn't really know what to expect when seeing him but the last thing was who faced me now.

"Arsaces, you old goat! Was that really you I heard making that awful noise, for no wonder you never did it before!" Vincent said taking off his golden helmet and showing me the same handsome face I was used to but with a very different personality to go with it.

He seemed so young at heart and so full of life. But where

was the reserved Vincent I was so used to? The Vincent who was the very epitome of cool, calm and collected to the point that if he was threatening you, you probably wouldn't even know it until his blade was protruding out of your body.

Even his hair seemed unruly, as wild curls bounced around his head barely being contained by the tie he had used to try and tame them. His eyes were the same crystal blue but now with an added mischief to them, they almost glowed with excitement. He was stunning and still looked all Angel, but one who was now out to find trouble and certainly not one for helping maintain order.

"Vardanis, I wish to introduce you to my new Head Concubine." Draven said informing me of his brother's name in this time. He stepped to one side as he was mostly blocking me from view and Vincent's eyes widened when he saw me.

"Why brother, you surprise me," he said pushing Draven further to one side before circling around me like a predator.

"How so?" Draven asked sternly, crossing his arms over his chest.

"Because this one is not only beautiful but she also looks intelligent, which is something new for you!" Vincent joked, nudging his brother's arm as he openly teased him. He also grinned at me and said,

"A damn sight better than that Harpie you had as your last Concubine, that is for damn sure!" I couldn't help but laugh considering I had met a few Harpies in my time and he didn't know how right he was about that statement.

"Ah well, about that..." Draven started to say but Vincent held up his hand and said,

"No need Brother, for I have heard of her murderous actions already."

"How? You have only just arrived," Draven asked incredulously. Vincent tapped the side of his head and teased,

"Ah yes, but you should know by now Arsaces, that gossip travels faster than a sandstorm in this city."

"And you have spies," Draven added dryly.

"And I have spies." Vincent confirmed light-heartedly.

"But come now, someone has to keep an eye on you," he said slapping his brother's back and I couldn't help but giggle at his playful behaviour.

"Oh, she is adorable but wherever did you find her?" he asked as though I was some lost kitten found wandering on the streets.

"That is not something I wish to discuss right now. I take it your hunt was successful?" Draven asked, quickly changing the subject, thank God. Vincent shot Draven a look in disbelief.

"And this is something you *do* wish to discuss?"

"There is nothing that can't be said in front of her," Draven replied coming to stand next to me, obviously not liking the way Vincent stood so close. He raised a cheeky eyebrow at him and tested that theory,

"Nothing?" When Draven merely glared at him Vincent burst out laughing and said,

"Good! Glad to hear the rumours are finally true for once." Of course, I knew the hidden meaning behind all of this, which had me wondering if Draven ever did plan on telling me what or who he really was?

"So this beauty saved your life I hear?" he asked looking down at Draven's dagger, before kicking it up with his foot and catching the forgotten blade in his hand. Then he looked back at me with something that looked an awful lot like respect.

"She was very brave," Draven said resting a hand on my shoulder as though I was his star pupil, which meant this was yet another occasion where the real Keira came out, as I let my mouth run away with me.

"I don't think so, if I am honest I have been itching for an excuse to slap that evil smile from her face since I first saw her, but it's not like you can just go around hitting people for being a massive cow bag, bitch face…uh…I mean…" *Shut up, shut up!* I scolded myself as I turned to face Draven who must now be thinking very differently of me.

"Cow bag? Bitch face? I do not believe I know these terms," he said smirking at me and Vincent laughed.

"No, but I for one will certainly be using them! Oh I like her! I declare you must keep her brother, for if you do not, then I certainly will, for she is most amusing," Vincent said joyfully only this was the wrong thing to say in front of Draven. He growled at him and came to stand in front of me protectively.

"I assure you that I intend to keep her…for a very, very long time, *if you get my meaning, brother.*" Draven gritted out these words like he was also carving the declaration in stone. It was a warning and nothing else, one that from the looks of it, he was starting to take very seriously.

"So it is true what they say?" Vincent asked with wide eyes.

"Enough! We will discuss this another time, but in the meantime let us sit for I wish to hear of your success," Draven commanded looking back to his throne.

"You might be needing this again sometime, or should I give it to your lovely Concubine here, whose name you still haven't told me." Vincent joked as he was about to pass me Draven's dagger. Draven took it off him before I could take it and gave his brother another glare, one Vincent didn't take seriously.

Then without answering him straight away, Draven simply wrapped an arm around my waist, picking me up with one hand as he sheathed his blade with the other. Then he casually walked up the steps to his throne as though he wasn't carrying a small person with one arm.

"Uh…I can walk, my Lord," I commented on a laugh.

"Yes, but I find pleasure in carrying you. *This way I can keep you close,"* he told me softly before he turned to sit us down at the same time using his other arm to swing up my legs to position me on his lap. I couldn't help but notice the way Vincent watched us with an openly displayed smirk, as he too made his way to his own throne.

"I have named her Nāzanin," Draven told his brother and I couldn't help but wonder what it meant, seeing as I'd heard him call me this a few times before. Thankfully I didn't have long to wait thanks to Vincent.

"Ah but of course, 'Sweetest one'. Well, no one would doubt it after one look at that face." I blushed at both Vincent's compliment and what Draven had named me. Vincent burst out laughing the second he noticed my red cheeks.

"And she even blushes! Why brother, I would say I am surprised at seeing you with such an innocent beauty but after hearing for myself of her fiercely protective side, I dare say she would make you a fine wife!" This time I couldn't tell whether Vincent was joking or not but from the looks of Draven I would say he at least was taking what his brother said seriously.

"Ah but just wait until you hear her political views on war…then you will be declaring her my queen before long," Draven teased back, squeezing my sides and seeing if I had a ticklish spot, which of course I did. I grabbed his hands and tried to stop him from being so mean, which he simply found even more amusing.

"So tell me of your hunt, did you catch the Roman spies?" Draven asked after finally giving up on torturing me. Vincent didn't answer at first as he seemed captivated by watching the way his brother was with me, as though he had never seen anything like it.

This took me back to Afterlife when Draven and I had first got together. I couldn't help but notice the surprise on everyone's faces as they watched their King and the way he was with me. I never really understood it at the time but after travelling back through all these years, then it quickly became plain to see. For when you wait for something for decade after decade, living through the years that eventually merged into one millennium after another, then what would you do when that wait was finally over?

"Vardanis?"

"My apologies, Arsaces, your little Nāzanin is somewhat distracting," Vincent said making his brother laugh.

"I often have the same problem," Draven replied before continuing with his questioning.

"I trust Avis was of some use to you?" I couldn't help but smile when hearing of my old feathered friend that was no doubt causing all sorts of mischief in this time.

"Do not speak to me of that pet of yours! You know she terrorised my soldiers…Oh and you owe my Captain a new helmet!" Vincent said shaking his head at her antics.

"Oh come now, surely she wasn't that bad?" Draven asked trying to hide his smirk behind his hand.

"Oh no, you don't think so! I was just glad his head wasn't still inside the thing when she flew off with it!" At this Draven laughed and said,

"I will make it up to him."

"Yes you must, or I will no doubt have his wife yapping at my heels for I believe it was a gift. In fact, I believe he was more afraid of returning home to face her, than he had been facing that damn bird of yours!" Vincent said making Draven roar with laughter once more.

"You have a pet bird, my Lord?" I asked knowing that it would seem odd if I didn't.

"I do. A gift from our father." I smiled a secret smile, when thinking about Draven's horny Father.

"Yes and a cruel one at that!" Vincent commented wryly.

"I would like to meet her sometime," I told him making Vincent laugh once without humour this time.

"Oh no you wouldn't! Take heed Brother, if you wish to keep her pretty then keep her far from that menace of the skies."

"Avis doesn't like many people," Draven told me after his brother's warning but I couldn't help but grin at him.

"Try only one person she likes and that is her Master," Vincent told me and I had to wonder what they would think if she reacted to me the same as she did the day I first met her. Would it be giving too much away when it didn't end in my blood being shed?

"But I trust she found her targets with little trouble," Draven said defending her and Vincent huffed before agreeing,

"Oh she found them alright and had my horse not felt up to the task, then by the time I got there, there would have been nothing left for me to question." Okay so…Eww! I didn't really want this image forever imprinted on my brain as it was bad enough seeing her tearing apart Gorgon Leeches!

"Did you find all three?" Draven asked getting back to business.

"Sadly no. One took the mountain road and disappeared, but we believe this is where he had planned to rendezvous with his own people, for we found many tracks."

"And the prisoners?"

"We have yet to question them further, for shortly after their discovery, we made another," Vincent said and this time his bad boy grin reminded me of Draven back in my own time.

"Ah yes, so I heard. Then let us feast, for we have much to celebrate," Draven said obviously drawing a close on such matters.

"Ah but indeed we do, for I have not shown you my own prize found in the desert." I frowned wondering if their version of hunting was finding people. I would like to say no and think better but considering Draven just had us all lined up like cattle not long ago, well to be honest it looked like I couldn't put anything past them!

Vincent looked up and gestured with his hand for something to be brought to him. Shortly after this the doors at the end opened and a girl was brought in. I gasped and Draven held me tighter to him as if expecting me to move. I couldn't see her clearly from this distance but one thing was for sure…whoever she was, she didn't look happy.

"She needs to be bound?" Draven asked his brother who was looking at the girl as though she was his next Messiah!

"Unfortunately she is somewhat confused and believes I have kidnapped her," he said shrugging his shoulders and smiling as if this was all very amusing.

"I take it this is not the case, for I would not have said you of all people needed to force a woman into your bed," Draven commented ironically telling me that Vincent was obviously a womaniser in this time. Vincent shot him a look to the side and said,

"No but this one is slightly unstable…" He paused for a moment as if remembering something and the woman must have kicked him in the balls considering the way he placed a hand on his package momentarily.

"But I am putting this is down to the sun's heat for I found her wandering in the desert, heading away from the city."

"Oh my God." I muttered before I could help it as the girl they spoke of started to come into view. Thankfully neither of them took notice of me and Vincent continued to tell his brother how he came to find the girl lost and wandering.

I could barely believe my eyes!

"Ari?" I couldn't help it when her name slipped from my lips and this time the brothers both heard it. The next few

moments started to play out in slow motion as I tried to take in the sight of both her and Pip in the background shaking her head at me like a mad woman, telling me no. But it was too late for that, not now, not when Ari saw me.

"Keira...is that really you?" I bit my lip to hold back the sob at seeing her this way. She looked as though she had been through Hell and back. Her body was bruised and covered in dirt and sand. She looked utterly exhausted and the second I saw the rope around her hands I couldn't think of anything else.

"ARI!" I shouted and suddenly found myself struggling to get to her. Draven held onto me and shouted,

"What is the meaning of this?!"

"Let me go!" I shouted back, twisting my body in hopes of breaking free of his hold.

"You know this girl?" Vincent asked but it was Ari who shouted,

"Let go of her! She is my sister, asshole!" This was when I saw Pip smacking her forehead as if this was the very thing she didn't want to happen.

"Is this true?" Draven asked me and finally I stopped struggling enough to look back at him.

"Please...let me go to her," I begged him and his eyes grew hard before he asked again,

"Answer me, is what she says true?!" I briefly saw Pip in the background shaking her head but it was too late, the tears in my eyes gave him my answer. I lowered my head and said,

"Yes, it is true." He watched for a second longer as the tears fell before letting me go. I scrambled off his lap and raced to Ari, taking her in my arms as she collapsed to the floor. She sobbed into my shoulder and I held her head there, letting my own tears land on top of her head as I tried to comfort her.

"It's alright now...Ssshh, it will be alright." I told her,

lifting her face to mine and wiping away the dirty tear tracks down her cheeks.

"I was so scared, Keira, I woke up alone and couldn't find you! I couldn't find anyone and then these men came, and he doesn't know who he is or who I am...why doesn't he know...?"

"Hush now, we will talk about this later." I looked back at the thrones and tried to ignore the stern glare Draven gave me and instead looked to Vincent.

"Has she eaten or drank anything?"

"She drank some water but did so too fast and brought it all back up, despite my warnings of such." I heard Ari growl next to me and I gave her a little shake of my head, telling her,

"Please, you have to trust me here. Count to a hundred and pretend to pass out." She gave me a small nod to tell me she understood. I then stood up and faced Vincent before seeing just how far I could push having the pretty face he claimed I had.

"I ask that you entrust her care to me, for she is clearly scared and confused about all that has happened." Vincent was about to speak when Draven beat him to it.

"So are you telling me that you remember now?" Draven asked clearly irritated by the thought.

"Some of it, my Lord." I answered softly but from the hard lines of his jaw, I knew that it would take more than a few softly spoken words. I couldn't understand why he was so angry.

"You sensed it too, brother?" Vincent muttered, leaning to his brother's side so they could speak more privately.

"Yes, when she first walked in, but now it has strangely disappeared, as though something is trying to mask that side of her," Draven replied furiously and I didn't understand what they were talking about.

"Well I can assure you, it has only just happened, for it may account for why the girl has no knowledge of what I speak." At

Vincent's odd reply Draven rubbed his beard and looked first to Ari and then to me. This was when Ari reach a hundred. I heard the gasp of onlookers who had gathered around the guards and knew this was my cue. I raced to her and looked up at Draven to try my luck once again,

"Please, My Lord…let me help her." At first Draven looked as though he was going to deny me but after receiving a small nod from his brother, he gave me a nod in return with the added gesture to continue with his hand.

I was just leaning down so that I could put her arm behind my head when Draven suddenly roared out.

"STOP! Guards, take this girl to my Concubine's quarters!" I let go of her arm and stood back as one stepped forward to take my place in carrying her. Vincent suddenly had a face like thunder as she was being carried from the room and I half expected him to go racing after her. However, one look from his brother and he remained seated…for the meantime anyway.

"I thank you. I will just go and…" I was about to finish when Draven obviously had other plans for me.

"You will go nowhere!" He thundered the order at me making me wince. I looked back at him like a wounded puppy but in that moment his anger was overtaking any chance of patience or reasoning.

"Ranka!"

"Yes, my King?" Ranka said, quickly coming to his side.

"See to it the girl is looked after by the same servant who cares for Nāzanin." Okay, so at least it wasn't so bad seeing as he was entrusting Pip with her care.

"It will be done, My Lord," she said bowing and giving me a small troubled look before disappearing off into the crowd.

"Come here!" Draven barked an order at me and even Vincent looked sorry for me, giving me a small encouraging smile in the place of his brother's angry glare. I reluctantly did as I was told and walked back over to his throne.

"I think it is about time you answered some of my questions." The way he said this filled me with dread, as until I had seen Pip and Ari, I had no clue what to tell him.

"Yes my…"

"My Lord!" I quickly found my sentence was being finished off by another, as a servant came running through the doors and down the hall as fast as he could.

"What is it?!" Draven roared back, obviously not appreciating the interruption.

"Riders my Lord! At the gates."

"And what of it?" Vincent asked frowning down at the man.

"They say they have seen an army heading this way, coming from the west, my Prince. They believe they recognised the Roman banners." Hearing this Draven released a low growl that made the poor man scurry back a bit, fearing his King's wrath.

"Very well, let me see for myself what these riders have to say. I will meet them at the gates… Go!"

"Yes, my Lord." The man couldn't seem to get away quick enough.

"I will accompany you…"

"No, stay with her. I will send for you when I know more." Draven said, in a way that broke no argument for Vincent didn't even try to insist. Draven walked down the few steps to me and came an inch away from my face when he caressed my cheek before issuing me with a promise,

"Soon we will be alone and then I will get my answers. Even if I have to chain you to my bed and make you beg for mercy to come again by my hand or tongue. For one way or another, you will tell me all I want to know." Then he sealed this erotic threat by yanking me hard to his chest and finishing it with a kiss that was almost bruising before letting me go.

"Well I think it's obvious he likes you," Vincent said on a chuckle as he came to stand next to me as we both watched him leave.

"How can you tell?" I asked sarcastically making him laugh again.

"Well, this is the most passionate I have seen him around a woman, and trust me when I say, it is not from lack of trying from the woman." This time it was my turn to laugh.

"I bet."

"Go easy on him, for this is all new to him," Vincent said nudging my shoulder and I looked at him with surprise.

"What is?" I couldn't help but ask.

"Falling in love," he whispered down at me and just before I could say anything else, his name was being called.

"Vardanis!"

"Saphira?" Vincent turned in time to see Sophia running over to him just before she threw herself in his arms. So there was at least one person she loved then. She quickly took note of me and scowled over his shoulder before he placed her back on her feet.

"Why little sister, is it me or are you getting shorter?" At this she playfully punched him on the arm.

"But even prettier…*and stronger so it seems,*" he added rubbing the top of his arm.

"That's better. So I see you have met our King's new favourite," she said curling her lip up at me. Vincent didn't see what most would have been able to see, which was pure loathing but instead he pulled me closer and said,

"I have indeed and isn't she utterly charming?"

"Um, charmed I'm sure," she responded mockingly but again Vincent seemed to miss it.

"I heard brother has gone to the gates, but I am surprised

you're not with him," Vincent looked longingly at the door and said,

"He wanted me to..."

"Babysit?"

"Saphira, now be nice," Vincent said finally getting a hint of her hostility. Unfortunately, this didn't last long as Sophia plastered on a sweet smile and said,

"Why don't you go and let me get acquainted with our brother's new Chosen One. I promise to take care of her." Vincent's eyes widened with glee and said,

"That sounds like a good idea and one no doubt our brother would approve of, for he would want you two to form a good friendship."

"Indeed," she said looking to me with her fake smile. I, on the other hand, swallowed hard and said,

"Oh that's okay, I should be getting back to my sister..."

"Nonsense! And besides, you wouldn't want to upset your lover's sister now would you?" Sophia hissed, taking me by the arm, digging her nails in and pulling me towards one of the open archways.

"Don't worry brother, I will take excellent care of her," Sophia said over her shoulder to Vincent who had no choice but to watch us leave.

I gave her one look and said,

"You're going to kill me aren't you?" I don't know what was more chilling, her smile or the answer she gave me...

"Let's have a chat first, shall we?"

CHAPTER TWENTY-ONE

A POISONOUS REUNION

I have to say that those unfortunate times when I thought about death I think the very last thought on my mind was seeing it coming by the hand that had hold of me now. Sophia continued to drag me from sight and I dare say she had been waiting for a moment just like this before making her move.

The second she had pulled me from the great hall, she spun me round to face her and with the hatred I saw in her eyes, I half expected her to just strangle the life out of me right there and then. But instead of snapping my neck like she wanted, she grabbed hold of the long piece of material down my back and used it to wrap around my head and across my neck to conceal my face.

I wished in that moment that I had the strength to do something but my mind was numb. It was stupidly too busy fooling myself into believing that when we reached our destination that she could be reasoned with. And if not, what then I thought, playing devil's advocate with myself. My only option left would be the truth. I would have no other choice but to tell her who I really was and hope on all that is holy that she believed me, because if she didn't then more would be lost than just my life.

So I let her drag me to where she had murder in her mind, all the while hoping that there was a shred of the Sophia in there that I knew. Something inside her that I could appeal to and I feared that the only part of that would be her supernatural side, for I think it was clear that her humanity had yet to develop.

"Inside," she ordered me, once we finally reached an elaborately carved door that looked too feminine to belong to anyone else but Sophia. She pushed me inside after checking that we weren't followed and I fell forward, only just righting myself in time before I landed on my knees.

I looked up and under different circumstances I would have smiled when seeing Sophia's room for the first time. It was like a movie set as if any minute now an Arabian princess would walk in the room and start singing about her love for Sinbad. Of course an Arabian princess did walk in the room but I think singing was the last thing on her mind at the moment, that was unless it was a song about happy stabbing.

The room was covered floor to ceiling in expensive fabrics of every colour that hung down in swags. These were then held to the wall with a golden border that had fan shaped shells in the moulding and golden pillars with the same design to match in every corner. Beautiful exotic art work from around the world decorated most of the walls and these were all framed with the same expensive luxury.

Furniture, both carved and handcrafted, was dotted around the place amongst other worldly treasures. Such as a stuffed peacock standing on a plinth and a tiger's head which hung over a Japanese screen. These I couldn't help but scrunch my nose at as I didn't believe in using animals as trophies. To feed a starving family, then yes or to clothe them so they didn't freeze to death, sure thing. But just for sport... then I say take up a hobby that doesn't include killing a living creature and let's make the world a better place...but hey, that was just my opinion.

Other items included scatter pillows in every colour, shape and size all positioned around a low hexagonal table that only stood a foot high. All of its feet were carved in the shape an elephant's head and this was where she wanted me to sit. I did as I was told as I didn't think it wise at this juncture to piss her off even more, not if I was going to try and convince her not to kill me.

I sat down amongst the pillows and anyone walking in now would be fooled into believing we were just about to have a friendly chat over some freshly brewed tea and cake...or at least that's what that plate of soft looking sugary bread looked like because for all I knew it could have had razor blades hidden inside it!

"You know I envy you in a way." Sophia surprised me when this was the first thing out of her mouth and I couldn't help but reply with,

"I highly doubt that." Deciding to cut the 'time warp' bullshit here and just be myself.

"You don't believe me?" she asked almost acting insulted.

"No, why, do you like having everyone trying to kill you?" I responded sarcastically.

"Ah, well that is a misfortune indeed. But alas no, I was referring more to your freedom to love, something my brother unfortunately does not have the privilege of," she said lifting up her long skirt and gracefully folding her legs, coming to sit down opposite me.

"And you think being sold into a King's harem as a slave is freedom to choose?" I asked her, trying no doubt in vain to get her to see life through the eyes of a mortal living in the real world.

"Correct me if I am wrong but I believe that didn't happen to you, that you were in fact rescued from getting raped to death," she snapped but my come back was even better.

"Yes and imagine my luck when finding myself no better off being sat opposite my death now, because either way, there are people determined to kill me because of that freedom to love you speak of." Sophia didn't have much to come back at with this but simply growled at me.

"So I ask you…do you still think I am free?" Sophia tore her gaze from me and looked down at the floor deep in thought.

"I think you are free enough to make the right choice," she said and after giving it sometime she finally looked back up at me.

"And that choice you speak of is walking out of here and leaving your brother." At this she laughed once and it wasn't exactly what I would call a joyful sound.

"By the Gods no. I am afraid the time for that has long passed. No, no, my brother is so besotted with you that it would be no use if you ran," she said waving her hand around as though we were merely discussing the weather.

"You think he would find me?" I asked raising an eyebrow at her.

"Oh, undoubtedly," she agreed but this was when her demeanour started to change. Sophia was always so regal looking in this time, holding herself up tall and straight, even given how small she was around her brothers. If anything, seeing the way she had run at Vincent had been a shock but now, with the way her shoulders seemed to slump in defeat, I knew she was at least finding this hard. Or so I liked to think when she released a big sigh.

"It is true that I have never seen him like this or looking so happy. And if circumstances were different then I may have even thanked you for it at one time. But we do not live in a different time…" I had to hold back from muttering 'no shit' at this point but thankfully she carried on before I had the chance.

"We live in this one and in this one I find myself the unfortunate task to act on what is best for my people and you my dear, are not what is best for my people." Wow, way to suck it to me right in the gut, Sophia.

"You don't hold back do you?" I commented making her laugh, for real this time.

"Not usually, no. I am afraid I don't have that luxury in my position."

"Can I ask you a question?" I boldly asked my soon to be murderer.

"I guess I don't see the harm in it, as we have a few minutes yet," she said shrugging her shoulders after giving my death a time frame.

"Have you ever been in love?" Now this question certainly threw her off as she seemed to do a double take.

"It would not matter if I had been or not."

"Oh I beg to differ with you there, for I think it would matter a great deal. If you had ever experienced love, like I doubt you have, then what you are about to do would not come so easy to you." I said calling her out and by doing so, it obviously made her angry. She banged her fist on the table making the little golden cups shake and the tall silver teapot rattle.

"You think this comes easy to me!?"

"You said it yourself that you have never seen him this way or looking so happy, yet you are still prepared to take that all away from him, just because of what you *think* you know of the future." I told her, trying to get through to her before I was forced to tell her the truth in order to save my life.

"I may not know much about love but I know that nothing is without its sacrifice!"

"And you, what would you be willing to sacrifice to achieve the same goal? Would you give up that kind of happiness so easily?" I asked pushing her for an answer.

"I would give up everything for my people!" she snapped, standing up in her outrage.

"Then are you saying that your brother is unworthy to rule his people because of the choices he makes?"

"I did not say that!" she shouted and I knew I had her caught in her own net.

"No, but you will be by killing me and taking away his choice!" I snapped back getting angry myself.

"He is blinded by you! He cannot see the truth of his actions with you standing in his way!" At this I laughed and said,

"And now you are saying your brother is weak in the shadow of a woman!"

"ARGH!" Sophia had no come back other than to let her rage build and get the better of her.

"You are merely trying to prolong your life and trick me into letting you go."

"I am not trying to trick you into anything, I am just trying to get you to see sense and to realise that you too have a choice. You can kill me and devastate your brother or you could have faith and see what the future holds, as you may find it not to be as dire as you think."

"You want to be queen, is that it?!" she said quickly turning my argument back on me and using some deluded quest for power. I jolted back in my own outrage and said,

"I couldn't care less about becoming queen and sitting on a throne!"

"You lie! Why else would you try and convince me to let you live out your days by my brother's side. If it was merely to spare your life, you would be trying to convince me to let you go and get as far away from the palace as you could. For that would be the smarter choice, for if all I wanted to do was be rid of you, it would make sense to convince me of such." This made me furious as she still hadn't got it!

"What and you think he is the only one who can fall in love!" I shouted back banging my own hand on my side of the table. Now this bit of news did take her back and for a moment she was silent. Had she not thought my love for him would be even the slightest possibility?

I wondered in that moment whether I had finally got through to her but when she shook her head at the floor and said softly,

"Then you will die a tormented martyr."

"Better to die a martyr than to live a thousand lifetimes knowing the one I loved was cruelly taken from me by my own flesh and blood!" I shouted back placing both my hands on the little table and leaning forward. Sophia looked back at me utterly enraged and was panting because of it as we continued our showdown. Looking at her now was like looking at Sophia's evil twin and it was hard to put them together, let alone go as far as saying they were the same damn person!

"By the Gods I should first rip out your tongue for daring to speak to me that way!" I laughed again and said,

"And what, you think someone intended on murdering me in cold blood deserves my respect!? Get a clue! You're angry because you know what I say is true!" At this she snarled at me and turned away, knowing she had no come back once again. Was I really wearing her down?

"Tell me, for I am curious. How do you think your brother is going to react to the news that you killed me?"

"Ha! You're a fool if you think I would ever let him find out." Oh so her plan was finally coming out.

"Oh and you don't think he will simply put two and two together when he knows you pretty much forced your brother's hand in letting you bring me here." At this she huffed and just waved her hand around the air, as she paced the room.

"All he will know was that I was trying to get to know you in an effort to please him."

"What, even after Ranka tells him that you attempted to have me killed once before, is he really going to believe that you had so much of a change of heart in only one day?!"

"My brother will trust in whatever I tell him to believe."

"Oh please! You are deluding yourself if you think that is true. He told you himself to stay away from me, and now here we are drinking tea at a knife's edge!" She snapped her head back to glare at me and said,

"And how do you know that?!" I had to think for a second as I couldn't exactly tell her the truth.

"He told me himself."

"You lie!"

"Then how would I know, if it was not he who told me?" I waited a minute for this to sink in before carrying on,

"He even expressed to me how he didn't trust you and told me to stay clear of you." Okay so this was all a bare faced lie but right now, fighting this battle of wills and doing so where the prize for winning was my life, then hell yeah, I was fighting with my own claws!

"I don't care what the consequences are, for I will not be swayed any longer!" Okay, so this sounded like it was backfiring pretty quickly! I knew now for certain that I wasn't going to get through to her, that much was obvious. So it was time to play my last and only trump card...*the truth.*

"Alright Saphira, have it your way. Time to..."

"NO! I will hear no more of what you have to say!" Sophia shouted and then snapped her fingers. I rolled my eyes to express my frustration but this quickly turned into panic as the long piece of fabric around my neck started to tighten. I instantly made a grab for it and managed to get a few fingers in there before it could strangle me completely.

"Li...st...en...to...me," I said trying in vain to get her to just let me say a few words but she simply tightened it further, making it almost impossible to speak again. I pulled down as hard as I could, trying to give myself even an inch in which to draw breath but the most I could manage was a centimetre at best.

"Stubborn girl! Even to the last few breaths you wish to fight with me and your will to survive. Um...maybe you do love my brother after all, as you say you do. At least it has to be said, I do admire your courage and bravery," she said leaning forward and letting her other side come forth.

"I want you to die knowing what we truly are, my brothers and I. I want you to see what it is you give your life for in the name of love!" She snarled cruelly as she tightened the scarf to the point it was cutting into my neck.

Seeing her this way didn't shock me as I had seen it many times before, which meant her sadistic slitted grin didn't last long. My eyes may have looked panicked but that wasn't at the sight of Sophia's demon, it was merely in the face of death and something deep inside of me wanted her to know the real me she was killing. So drawing in all of my strength I pulled even harder, straining my neck muscles and those in my arms, trying to get just the tiniest bit free.

"It's a shame really, I had really wanted you to just drink some tea and die painlessly from poison but like you and my brother, I guess it was never meant to be," she said picking up her cup and drinking back her own tea after tilting it my way to toast me,

"Here's to immortality." This was when I finally managed to pull it back enough to utter three tiny words...

"I...am...E...lec...tus." The second the words escaped me the scarf dropped from my neck and Sophia launched over the table grabbing my hand,

"What did you say?!" she shouted shaking me and trying to get me to say it again but I couldn't say a word for coughing. I was desperately trying to drag air back into my burning lungs, barely keeping myself from passing out as it was, let alone speaking.

"WHAT DID YOU SAY?!" she screamed and then suddenly her eyes widened in panic and her hand flew to her neck.

"Wh...what...have...you done?" she stammered out as she continued to clutch her neck as though she no longer knew how to breathe. Then before I could do anything her head hit the table, knocking over the cups and spilling tea over each side of the hexagon. She looked dead! My hands flew to my mouth as I couldn't believe what I was seeing...

Was Sophia really dead!?

I sucked in a deep ragged breath, having no clue what to do or how I would explain any of this when Draven found out. But worst of all, fearing for my friend, the Sophia of the future, who was still out there somewhere and I was just praying that having her other self die in this time didn't affect her now? What if she just disappeared!

"Oh shit, oh shit...she must have drunk from the wrong cup!" I said on a gasp thinking she had drank from the one intended for me. However, I wasn't given long to think on this as a familiar voice spoke up from behind me...

"No, she drank the right one."

CHAPTER TWENTY-TWO

DOPPELGÄNGER AMBUSH

I could barely believe my ears as I must have been dreaming, for it couldn't be...could it? The figure slowly walked up to stand next to me and looked down at the body of a princess sprawled out over the table like one of her stuffed decorations. I looked up at her and gasped, needing to see for myself. The woman suddenly whipped off her head piece and said,

"Man, I was such a bitch!" I think other than passing out from shock, my mouth dropping open was the right first response and then the second was to shout her name...

"Sophia!" Then I threw myself in her arms and hugged her close. I had been so worried about her!

"Thank God you're safe!" I told her making her laugh as she hugged me back.

"I think I should be saying the same about you," she said nodding down at herself. I followed her gaze and this was when panic set back in.

"Oh my God, oh my God, oh my God." I couldn't help but repeat this over and over knowing what had just happened.

"Calm down, it isn't that bad."

"Isn't that bad, Sophia, you just poisoned yourself!" I said looking back at her in astonishment.

"Well yeah I did, but she deserved it." Sophia responded as though we were talking about someone else that was currently sprawled out on the table.

"She deserved it? Jesus Sophia, you killed yourself!"

"Now let's not go that far." she said holding her hands up in her defence.

"Well, is she dead or not?" I asked edging closer to see if I could see signs of life.

"Uh…I'm not really sure," she said squatting down next to herself.

"You're not sure!" I shouted close to losing it.

"Calm down, let's just think about this sensibly and…" Sophia was saying just as two people burst in the room.

"Don't you lay a hand on her you bitchnugget!" Pip shouted stumbling into the room as her and Ranka looked to have been fighting to see who could get in the room first. They both righted themselves, scowling at each other before taking in the crazy scene in front of them.

"Nice of you to join us," Sophia commented with a smirk and hand cocked on her hip. Pip did a comical double take which turned into a triple take.

"I uh…okay this is so not the party I was expecting to crash." Pip said, whereas Ranka took a more logical approach.

"There are two of you?" Okay so when I said it was more logical, what I really meant to say was blindingly obvious!

"And the prize for the 'No shit Sherlock' award goes to…oh and wouldn't you know, Captain Obvious here!" Pip said sarcastically dragging out her words. Ranka turned to her and said,

"I don't know of this Sherlock."

"No but give it a millennia or two, Mohawk." Pip said patting her on the back.

"Okay, so if you two are finished bonding over there, can we move on please?" Sophia said nodding to her other self. Pip then shook herself and said,

"Pluck a turkey! It is good to see you home, girl!" And then Pip came over to Sophia and gave her a big hug, then she turned to me for a fist bump and said,

"Glad you're not dead again."

"Me too," I said and then laughed when she said,

"But buck me off your back and shit on a stick, you have more lives than a damn cat!"

"She's right you know," Sophia said agreeing.

"…Any later and you would have been one dead Keira." I hugged Sophia again and said,

"Thank you for saving me…well, from yourself."

"Speaking of dead and bitches, did you really kill yourself?" Pip asked and Ranka stayed in the background looking as though she was still trying to figure out what the Hell was going on, which kind of made four of us.

"I don't think so."

"Let's check," Pip said lifting Saphira's head back by her hair and when her wet open mouth twitched she dropped her head, making it smack back on the table with a deafening thump. Our own Sophia groaned, folding her arms and Pip just shrugged her shoulders and before she could say it, we both said it for her,

"Yeah, we know, 'You're bad."

"Well, at least we know she isn't dead now and plus more

importantly…what the hell was you thinking! Have you never seen Back to the Future 2! Do you know nothing about the space time continuum!?" Pip shouted after smacking Sophia's arm, getting irate.

"Oww and no, unfortunately my science fiction is a little rusty!" Sophia said sarcastically, rubbing the place she had hit.

"Why don't you explain it to us, Pip." I suggested calmly.

"I knew I should have forced the issue before we left," she commented to herself shaking her head and I couldn't help think we didn't really have the time for movie night before our grand and stupid idea about travelling back in time.

"Right…how does it go again…Oh right. 'Great Scot, Jennifer could conceivably encounter her future self. The consequences of that could be disastrous. I foresee two possibilities; one…Coming face to face with herself 30 years older would put her into shock and she would simply pass out or two… The encounter could create a time paradox, the results of which could cause a chain reaction that would unravel the very fabric of the space time continuum and destroy the entire universe… Granted that's the worst case scenario."

"How the hell does she remember shit like this?" I asked Sophia who shot me a look as if to say, 'It's Pip we are talking about here'. But instead of saying that she decided a more important question to ask was,

"Who's Jennifer?"

"Marty McFly's girlfriend." Pip answered with a grin.

"Who's Marty McFly?" she then asked and this time Pip lost her grin and snapped,

"Really?!"

"I think I understand this," Ranka said shocking everyone from where she still stood near the door.

"Oh great, the only one in the room who didn't get on the time travelling express understands the space time continuum!"

"Your little friend here is clearly lost in her own mind and needs to be put to rest," Ranka said to us both, making Pip lose it.

"Hey! Yo Bitchmuncher, I am not a damn dog!" I placed a hand on her shoulder and said,

"I think she just meant you might need to sleep Pip, not get put down."

"Oh, well that's alright then. Peace Out," she said giving Ranka the Peace sign that wouldn't have mattered if she had given her a Nazi salute, because she had no clue what it meant. I decided not to explain this but found myself asking something that was equally as unimportant as most of this conversation was going,

"Bitchmuncher? Bitchnugget?"

"I dunno, it was the first thing that came to mind, plus I think I am going through a 'bitch phase'. I was half tempted to go with Knob jockey or Ass clown. Man I wish I was more like Bond, he has all the best one liners." And I was half tempted to say that I couldn't really see Bond saying words like 'Bitchnugget' and Ass Clown' but I decided to leave it be, considering we had more important issues at the moment, like the dead doppelganger currently lying in a pool of tea.

"Sorry to interrupt this pointless crap we keep chatting about but can we at least address the fact that my other self is lying unconscious in a puddle of tea," Sophia said nodding at herself yet again.

"Hey sure sister, it isn't like you're the one who poisoned her or anything," Pip replied rolling her eyes.

"Yes well, next time I will just jump out of my hiding place and shout 'surprise, surprise' hoping that the whole space continuum thingy doesn't happen and she simply passes out like Jennifer, Marty McFly's girlfriend!" Sophia shouted and Pip broke out into a massive grin before she bumped hips with Sophia, saying,

"Aww shucks, you *were* paying attention in time paradox class." I gave Sophia a sideways glance and she shrugged her shoulders at me and whispered,

"What, it was quite an interesting theory."

"Yeah, one we thankfully proved wrong, unless the Universe is crumbling as we speak," I commented cheerfully just being thankful we hadn't yet got to Pip's/ Doc Brown's worst case scenario.

"No, but it just might do if we don't hurry up!" Sophia said in a sudden panic.

"Why, what's up?" I asked when she started grabbing her unconscious self from the table and trying to tear her clothes off.

"My brother is on his way! And man, he sure is pissed!" she hissed.

"Bollocks!" Pip said jumping in and helping her.

"Ranka, can you stall him?" I asked looking up at her to see her version of looking panicked was very different from our own. I could only hope that inside she was screaming 'Shit!' like the rest of us and not just standing there with one raised eyebrow.

"I'm sorry, let me rephrase that, STALL HIM NOW!" I shouted when she didn't move. She groaned at me and unfolded her arms.

"I will see what I can do," she replied sedately before leaving.

"Is it just me or is that woman hard work?" Pip said as we all tried to lift a very wet Sophia off the table.

"Ooops." This time it was my turn to say 'my bad' as she slipped from my fingers and her cheek slapped back on the table once again.

"Look, I know she was a bitch but can we at least try not to break her further," Sophia asked shooting me a look.

"Yeah and now you mention it, why were you such a raving bitch head, in this time?" Pip asked grabbing her under one arm as I did the same on the other side. Sophia then stopped what she was doing and put her hand on her hip and said,

"Really, you're asking me that now?"

"She has a point," I told Pip looking up over Sophia's floppy head.

"Fine. Just saying the heads up would have been nice." Pip grumbled before hoisting our burden up further so we didn't drop her again.

"So where are we putting Miss Arabian Bitchy Nights here?" Pip asked changing the subject.

"Stuff her in that trunk over there," Sophia said trying to tear her own clothes off.

"We can't do that...! Uh…can we?" I asked thinking this was wrong on so many levels.

"Look, I get overall say on what happens to her," Sophia said and Pip made a whiny noise.

"Aww no fair."

"I will make you a deal, if we ever have to go back in time to save the world again and we encounter your younger self, then you get a say but right now, stuff her ass in that trunk!" Sophia said calling the shots and I was just glad someone other than me was doing it.

"Oh and pull her dress off," she added, just to make the day even stranger.

"Holy shitballs, but this mission just went from weird to screwball in a heartbeat," Pip said meaning we were totally in agreement here. We then did as Sophia asked and started to undress the soggy girl. I had to say undressing an unconscious wet woman had officially made it to my top ten 'most difficult shit' list and with the likes of 'dealing with Harpies' and 'getting into Hell', let's just say it was a hard list to get onto!

"Jesus, it's like undressing a fish!" Pip commented obviously finding it as difficult as me.

"Give it to me," Sophia said, holding out her hand when we finally got it free from her body. Pip then threw it at her and it ended up slapping her in the face. I couldn't help my reaction because I burst out laughing.

"Don't say it!" Sophia warned holding up a finger at her, just before Pip said her famous 'my bad' line. Meanwhile I still couldn't stop laughing.

"I think deliria has set in," Pip said shaking a thumb over her shoulder at me and she was probably right. Of course, watching Sophia struggling to get this wet dress on and the way she had to wiggle around just to get it down her was in itself enough to set me off into wild hysteria once again, not even taking into account how crazy the whole situation was. Added to this was also the next task of trying to swing Sophia's body in the large chest and then fold her limbs in a way that we could get the bloody thing closed!

"I give up! She can stay looking like a hoopla game for all I care!" Pip said slapping her hands together like she was getting the dust off.

"Seriously, I am starting to question how we get ourselves into this crazy shit." Sophia agreed after taking one look at her other self with her legs and arms sticking up once she had the dress finally on.

"You and me both," I said after I had wiped away the tears of laughter.

"So what now?"

"Pip you have to hide, you sit there and let's have some tea." Sophia said answering my question.

"Tell me you're joking!" I screeched in what was no doubt an annoying voice.

"Look, he will be here any second and if we don't sit down right now, then how else will this look?" she said holding out both her arms to the mess on the table.

"Like there has been a struggle," I agreed.

"Exactly! At least this way we can just pretend you had an accident," Sophia said folding herself down as gracefully as her former self did and doing so in a sopping wet gown no less.

"Me?! Why me?" At this she just raised an eyebrow at me and replied dryly,

"Let's see, out of the two of us who is more like to have a clumsy moment and do something stupid like say, fall backwards off some cabin steps and hit her head on a rock… umm?"

"Hey, now that was one time and that was freakin' years ago!" I argued.

"Yeah but there was that one time you also fell into an icy lake and almost drowned," Pip said adding to the unfortunate list.

"Oh come on, I was pushed in by that bitch Layla!" I said defending myself.

"Oh yeah, man but you really do have a problem with people trying to kill you, don't you?" Pip said looking up at the ceiling as if trying to remember them all.

"You think!?" I replied sarcastically.

"Yes, well at least you have an equal number of people trying to save your ass, which I have to say, is what I am trying to achieve now, so sit your sweet ass down and drink some damn tea!" Sophia said almost panting when she was finished.

"Okay, okay, jeez, no need to get snippy," I said sitting down and doing as I was told. She smiled at me before blowing a kiss my way and Pip had all her fingers bent out like she was still counting.

"Wow, I think I lost count! Holy Harem girls but you have more enemies than Batman!" Pip said making me giggle and also feel a little paranoid. As if reading my face Pip said,

"I wouldn't worry...I'm sure if they just got to know you better then it wouldn't be half as many." Sophia smacked herself on the forehead and said,

"Oh brother."

"Speaking of which, Pip get outta here!" I said hearing them behind the door. She was just about to run into the next room when I noticed the biggest flaw in our plan.

"Pip the trunk, you forgot to close the trunk!" Sophia looked up just as the door was opening and we both knew she wouldn't make it. I held my breath and could feel every muscle in my face tense as I couldn't bear to watch the next few seconds play out. However, with all the will in the world I also couldn't close my eyes.

The door swung open and two things happened all at once. Sophia righted the cups on the table just as Pip threw herself down on the trunk lid, slamming it shut and effectively stuffing the rest of the Princess' body down so it was out of sight... limbs and all.

All three of us simultaneously looked to the door to see a red faced Draven stood there looking both worried and furious. His eyes first went to me and after giving me the once over to check I wasn't stabbed, maimed or that blood wasn't pouring out of me, he then looked around the room, focusing first on Pip and then on the mess on the table.

Sophia looked back at me and after I didn't get her wide eyes as enough of hint, she then cleared her throat and stared at the spilt tea.

"Oh my I am so, so sorry Princess, how clumsy of me. It

was the door, it startled me," I improvised, thinking was this really the worst sounding acting I had ever heard or was it just me? My silent question was answered when I saw Sophia roll her eyes before looking back to her brother.

"Arsaces, I am afraid you startled my guest. Come join us, we were just having some tea as I was getting to know a little more about your new concubine here…I must say, Vardanis was right, she is most charming." I had no clue how she knew that was what Vincent had said but I knew one thing and that was her acting was Oscar worthy! Unlike mine, whose only award would have been a rotten tomato.

"See brother, I told you no harm had come to her." Vincent said coming up behind him to look inside the room for himself. It was obvious he had joined his brother at the gates and had to explain where I was or more like who I was with. And from the looks of Draven's frayed nerves, he had been more than a little worried. Well I can't say that he didn't exactly have cause to be, considering we had a little Imp sat on a trunk stuffed with his murderous sister inside.

"Are you alright?" he asked me, ignoring Sophia.

"But of course she is…"

"I was asking her!" he snapped, obviously not forgetting their last conversation about me. I gave him a kind expression, being thankful that he cared enough to worry about me and said,

"I am fine my Lord, your sister has been most kind." Hearing this was supposed to ease his mind but instead he frowned and gave her a look that said only one thing…'What are you up to?'

After this he quickly spotted the tea and his eyes grew wide. He stormed over to me and picked me up as though I was a doll. Then he placed me next to him as though at any minute one of his sister's stuffed animals was going to come alive and take a chunk out of me.

Then before any of us could say a word he picked up the tea and sniffed it before taking a sip. Thankfully the tea that had been poisoned was currently still dripping onto the floor off the table, so unless he was going to get down and start licking it, I think we were all good.

"Oh really brother, do you think so little of me?" Sophia complained, obviously still having a part to play.

"Why is she here?" Draven asked nodding to Pip and ignoring his sister's complaints.

"She came to tell me of my sister's recovery and how after drinking a little more, she is now sleeping peacefully." I jumped in to say before Pip could stick her foot in it. Draven looked at me as if trying to spot the lie but other than what I had told him, what other reason could there be? Because let's face it, the truth was pretty unbelievable, even for me and I was currently caught up in the middle of it all…Hell, I was the bloody cause of it all!

"Ranka!" This was Draven's only response to what I had said as you could see he was determined to find out the real truth of what had gone on.

"Take Nāzanin back to my quarters, I wish to speak with my sister," he ordered when she walked through the door and this didn't sound good. I gave Sophia a look of pity, one she just shook her head at as though trying to tell me not to worry. I suppose if anyone knew how to handle her brother, then it was her, because in this time period it certainly wasn't me!

"Very well, my Lord," Ranka answered and nodded for me to follow. I then looked to Pip who was currently watching the show like all she needed now was a bowl of popcorn and her world of entertainment would be complete.

"Pip." I hissed her name trying to get her attention and for a minute I thought she was going to just wave me off. Thankfully

though the look I gave her made its way through her funfair brain and she got the message...probably in big neon flashing lights knowing her.

"Oh, right...yep, that would be me then." she said throwing her legs off the trunk and not really acting the part of the old ailing woman. Thankfully though, Draven and Sophia were too busy to notice as they were having some kind of silent showdown.

We then quickly left the room after Vincent was also commanded to join them. It was obvious Draven had a few things to say and he wanted his brother to hear them also. The three of us walked down the hallway and I turned to Pip and asked,

"Do you think she will be alright." Pip gave me a nudge and said,

"Sure, why not, our Sophia can handle herself, just as long as..." Then she paused as if not wanting to say it to worry me further.

"What, just as what?"

"He doesn't open that trunk," she said making me frown at her.

"Why would he?" I asked on a laugh, one that died quickly when I saw her face.

"Pip...what did you do?" I asked as my dread caused me to drag out her name.

"Oh nothing...really, well it wasn't really my fault as I didn't have time and..."

"Pip." I said her name in warning, coming to a stop in the hallway, refusing to go any further without her answer.

"Well, see, I kinda...might of...possibly..."

"PIP!" I shouted and she then confessed,

"Got some hair and maybe a few fingers caught in the lid,

but only like one or two…three at the very most!" she confessed making my face drop in horror.

"Oh my God! Pip, what if he sees it? What if he opens that damn trunk!?" I screeched throwing my hands up in the air. And I had to say, Pip's answer didn't fill me with very much confidence, in fact, none at all…

"Space time continuum's worst case scenario."

CHAPTER TWENTY-THREE

PERTINAX

I paced around the room, one that was now Draven's private domain. Ranka brought us here a different way and after going through hidden entrances, we walked along a series of secret passageways that seemed to have been carved into the stone foundations centuries ago.

I think this was so that I didn't have to walk through any other 'supernatural' rooms like the last time he had brought me here, where he made me close my eyes first. I was actually surprised that he was even chancing it and didn't just treat me like every other 'Chosen Concubine'. I knew that he had a room set up for such occasions and it was obvious that they only saw this room when Draven requested their presence for the evening. Take Stateira for example, the first time I ever had the unfortunate task of meeting her was back in Draven's harem, where she was having a hissy fit because her presence hadn't been requested for the night.

When I first walked in I saw things that I didn't even notice last time, although that wasn't surprising seeing that Draven had also been in the room. He had a way of absorbing every ounce of attention from me, so that when he was around all I saw was him.

His quarters were divided off into different sections and each area branched off from a large circular room that was surrounded by spiral marble arches. I didn't feel comfortable enough to go snooping around, besides I knew what one of the rooms held and that was a big bed covered in furs.

The main room looked to be a sort of living space/study as there were tall tables with layers upon layers of what looked like ancient maps all laid out. There was also strange ladder style shelving that lent up against the walls and each level held different sized scrolls rolled up, which were piled high.

There was a small seating area off to one side that was sunk into the floor and covered in cushions of all the colours you would find in a desert sunset. What I first thought was a tall vase in the centre of a small table turned out to be some sort of smoking device, like some earlier version of a hookah pipe. I had to wonder who he shared this social setting with and hoped it was his brother, not some of the girls I had heard inviting him to their bed the night he brought me here.

The walls were mainly bare, unlike Sophia's room, with only a shield or weapon dotted around the place. I had to inwardly giggle as it looked like some ancient version of a bachelor's pad minus the bar in the corner, beer labels, sports memorabilia and car plaques on the walls…oh and not forgetting the classic pool table. Instead it was all about weapons and battle strategies in this room. There was even a corner dedicated to spears, all tipped with different lethal spikes, ready to do all sorts of bodily damage. It was the one that was shaped like a giant scorpion at the end that had me shuddering the most as it looked all kinds of deadly.

"So what now?" I asked Ranka and Pip who had been

silently watching me trying to wear a footpath in the stone floor for the last ten minutes.

"Chill out in the Royal pad?" Pip said as she was currently sat sideways in a chair and swinging what looked like a golden curtain tie around her wrist and back again.

"Chill out! How am I supposed to do that after we just stuffed his sister into a damn trunk?" I screeched.

"Pretend we didn't?" she suggested, shrugging her shoulders and making me groan.

"Seriously Toots, you just need to relax a little and try taking a load off," she said nodding to one of the empty chairs and I sighed before taking her advice. I deflated down into the seat wondering how on earth I was going to make it through the rest of this 'Mission'. What if Draven opened that trunk? What if he made Sophia confess? What if he was on his way here right now to make me confess?

"Oh dear, she's gonna blow," Pip said shaking her head.

"I don't understand," Ranka replied looking confused.

"Big shocker there. Look Toots, what's done is done. But look on the bright side…"

"The bright side?" I said eyes wide as I interrupted her.

"Well yeah. One of your biggest fears when you first got here was that you couldn't find anyone and was worried something bad had happened. Well at least we are all together now and everyone made it through okay."

"Alright, so you have a point there," I admitted.

"Yeah and try this one out. Even if Draven boy somehow finds out the truth, what then? Do you really think that finding out the woman he has already fallen in love with is in fact his Chosen One and that he's gonna be pissed that he now gets the green light from the Gods? Uh NO! I don't think so somehow," Pip said making sense yet again.

"See, so it's all good in the hood. Oh, but of course if none of that happens then you still can't do the mighty mambo with him yet." Pip added, causing me to freak again.

"Why not?!"

"Because Ari is still passed out from exhaustion and we have no clue how her shit works, so until we do know, then I am afraidamundo it's a no, no on the stuffin' in your cushion." I closed my eyes and shook my head a little as if this would somehow help matters…needless to say, it didn't work.

"Slight problem with this plan of yours Pip, as I don't think he is gonna want to come back here and play checkers or a friendly game of Kerplunk!" I said rubbing my forehead in the hope of easing some of the tension.

"I love Kerplunk!" Pip said missing the point completely and totally getting sidetracked as usual.

"Of course you do," I muttered just before she carried on.

"Only that game is so much better when you replace the marbles for bubble gum balls and then you have to chew the ones that fall and if you lose them all, then you have to stuff them all in your mouth and sing the national anthem of whichever country you're in…and trust me, that shit gets real hard if you're ever in Russia like I was!" The mental image she painted was certainly one I wouldn't be forgetting any time soon.

"So what do I say then?" I asked throwing my hands up.

"I dunno to be honest, I don't think I've ever said no when it came to sex." I can't say this surprised me.

"Don't mortal woman usually go with the whole 'I have a headache' deal?" she asked and to be honest, I can't say that I'd ever said no to Draven either, so I had no clue.

"I will just have to think of something," I told her, knowing this was easier said than done.

"But you think Sophia will be alright?" I asked just to be sure.

"He isn't going to hurt his own sister. Don't sweat it Tootie bird, she can hold her own, as we know." I rubbed my neck that was still sore from being almost strangled to death and said,

"Yeah, tell me about it."

"So tell me, what is the deal with these Romans that have turned up?" I asked deciding to change the subject, turning to face Ranka who would know better than anyone. She was currently sharpening one of her blades on some kind of stone which caused little sparks as she ran it off the end.

"The King has many enemies, but none like Pertinax."

"Pertinax?" I repeated his name making Pip swing her legs back around and slap her hands to her knees as she stomped her feet back on the ground at the same time.

"Wait…back up a sec…*The Pertinax*?" Pip asked in a serious voice that sent shivers down my spine. Pip was never serious, so when she was…well let's just say, you had cause to panic.

"Who is this guy?" I asked again looking to Pip and back to Ranka who nodded her head.

"He's a legend that's what he is and a fucking scary one at that!" Pip said and I looked to Ranka, surprised to see her nod her head in agreement, which again only added to the seriousness of the shit storm with this guy obviously was.

"But how is he a legend?"

"Do you wanna tell her or should I?" Pip asked Ranka making my frown deepen.

"Tell me what?" I asked getting inpatient now. Again I looked from one to the other and it was when Ranka nodded for Pip to speak that I knew this was even worse than I thought.

"Legend goes that he was once the most powerful Demon to walk the Earth and even though it wasn't officially recognised, he actually ruled the supernatural world and he did so with an iron fist." Pip said looking down at her hands that she held together almost in prayer. She tapped her middle fingers together a few times before looking up at me.

"That was until the most powerful unity was born. Now this story you know and know well. Three siblings, an Angel, a Demon and one more powerful as two powers combined for the first and only time in History…"

"Draven." I whispered his name and Pip continued,

"He was the most powerful being ever to be granted a soul and vessel and therefore became the most logical and recognisable King of all Supernaturals on Earth."

"And that pissed off Pertinax," I said finishing off the obvious.

"Oh, you bet it did. He believed it was his throne to fight for but it was never granted to him in the first place. See in the eyes of the Gods, both those from above and below, you don't just rule because you say you do…Gods are a bit picky about that type of shit. So when Draven was born into this life and was chosen by them, then naturally not to piss off the Gods, the Supernatural world fell into line and followed Draven's rule… So bam! Suddenly overnight Pertinax had lost his entire empire."

"And now he wants it back," I said finishing off for her again.

"Oh no doubt, he has been fighting to get it back for a long time but he was never successful as he knew he needed an army."

"Which he now has," Ranka informed us before replacing her weapon and then walking over to the window. Pip and I got up together and walked over to stand next to Ranka to see for ourselves what she had nodded towards. It was hard to see how big the army was in the dark but the one thing that wasn't hard to miss was the number of glowing torches that stood along the dark horizon, making it look as though it was on fire.

"Oh God," I whispered now looking at what Draven faced.

"Have no fear Electus, for no one conquers the Parthian army," Ranka told me with a proud little grin curling up one side of her mouth.

"It's true. The Romans tried for years to conquer all of Persia but never really got there…not until…"

"Until?" I prompted when Pip stopped.

"Well now, that's a story for Sophia to tell as she knows it best." I frowned trying to understand Pip's strange expression and when I was about to ask her about it, Ranka and Pip both looked to the door.

"Heads up, here comes Loverboy…ETA two minutes tops," Pip said looking at me sideways and even though she told me not to worry, I knew that from the way she too held her breath, that I hadn't been the only one feeling anxious for our friend.

"Oh and by the way, just to give you the heads up for when Kingy man wants to know why you now have a sister, you know after not even knowing your own name…I would go with the seeing her brought it all back, chestnut."

"Uh okay, but slight problem with that."

"Like?"

"Well for starters, I have no bloody idea what year I am in and not even sure if England was called England, let alone explain how I got here!" I said in frustration as I knew my acting skills were definitely not up to this one!

"My guess is that England is still currently controlled by the Romans and if that's right then is unsurprisingly named Britannia which is Latin for 'The Britain'," Pip said, weirdly sounding more like a historian than her usual quirky self.

"This is correct…my King has heard many things of this Britannia." Oh goodie, he will be able to tell me all about it then, I thought sarcastically at Ranka's confirmation of information.

"Look don't sweat it, just say you were a merchant's daughter or some shit like that."

"Uh, ya gonna have to be more specific here, Pip."

"Fine, how about this...Your mother died when you were young and your father brought you up...sad, sad story. Then you and your sister both worked in the market selling your father's fabrics, after all it makes sense that you would go into the family business," she said behind her hand for some unknown reason other than dramatic affect.

"But on your way back from selling your goods you all got ambushed. Oh no! Terrible, terrible. But you and your sister, because you were pretty and worth a high value, then got sold into slavery...Boom, also very sad...You are unsure of what became of your father and this makes you sad yet again, for these are sad times which we live in, yada, yada, yada... then after being bought by a Persian man, you were both put on a boat and brought to this far away land...ooh, all very scary and exciting. Then the man who bought you got ambushed...as a lot of people tend to get ambushed here these days, and wham bam thank you ma'am, you ended up here."

"Wow, that was specific," I said nodding my head and agreeing that it was actually pretty good.

"Not just a pretty face you know," Pip informed me pulling out her invisible lapels and just as the door opened she whispered,

"Now it's showtime...but remember, no boats down your fun canal," which made me groan as he entered the room. I sucked in a deep breath at the sight of him. He looked so masterful I was almost scared. I scanned down the length of him, taking it as a good sign when I didn't see any blood on his hands.

"Leave us!" he ordered and Pip turned to me and bowed her head, giving me a cheeky wink before she left after doing the same with Draven...all except the wink. Ranka was just about to leave when he looked as if he remembered something, so he stopped her as she walked past him.

He had hold of her arm but from the way that Ranka was looking down at his touch, it meant a great deal more to her than it did to him. This was all the reminder I needed to remember that her feelings for Draven ran far deeper than just the loyalty usually found between a subject and his King.

It hurt to look at and I had to turn away before my face gave any hints to what I was feeling. I owed a lot to Ranka. With all her help in this mission and for having my back when no one else could be there for me. And the added bonus in all this was that she must have been the only person in this time who loved Draven yet wasn't trying to kill me. Surely I had to find comfort in that somewhere.

I must have been too busy lost in my own thoughts because I couldn't help but jump when I felt Draven's hands on my shoulders from behind.

"Easy now, calm yourself little Lamb," he said sweetly as he leaned down so that he could kiss my neck softly.

"I guess I am a little jumpy, what with an army outside," I said looking towards the arched stone window. Draven looked briefly and then laughed.

"I am afraid having an enemy at my gates is something you will have to get used to, as it is a common sight to see when you are King." Oh he was certainly right about that, in fact, I was already used to it as I would often find them at my gates also.

"You're not worried, my Lord?" I asked knowing anyone else would.

"No, and nor should you be, for you will be safe along with my people behind these walls," he said sounding confident and I had to wonder if this also included the obvious threats that had been made to my life in that promise.

"I was worried about you," he surprised me by saying and swiftly changing the subject.

"You were?"

"Yes. I love my sister dearly but her intentions are not always as I would hope they would be. She has much to learn about the ways of the people," he told me and I wanted to laugh considering the Sophia I now knew used to tell me things like that about him when we first met back in my own time. It was funny the way falling in love could make you view the world differently and even if it didn't actually make it go around, it certainly had enough of an impact to make a difference...*even on the supernatural.*

"And now?" I asked trying not to sound like the weight of his answer could easily crush me considering it was now about my friend and not his 'In this time, crazy bitch sister'.

"Well, that is the surprising thing for your powers of persuasion must be great indeed, for she seems to have had a complete change of heart." My reaction to this wasn't as cool as I had hoped as I gave him a short nervous laugh, one that I could only hope he took for modesty.

"I don't know about any powers of persuasion my Lord, for I only spoke the truth," I said and he quickly turned me around to face him.

"And what was that I wonder?" Draven asked raising an eyebrow down at me as if trying to judge me for himself.

"You don't trust me?" I decided to come right out and ask him, pulling myself free of his hold and putting some much needed space between us.

"Trust and lack of knowledge are two very different things, yet combined they can give power to both those who ask and those who tell." I knew what he was saying as it was true, power was knowledge and knowledge was power.

"And you don't know very much about me," I finished off for him.

"I wish to know more about the woman I have chosen to share my bed with, yes, very much so." Hearing this I couldn't help but tease him slightly as I was too curious not to.

"And tell me, does my King usually want to know about each of the Concubines he sleeps with?" I dared to ask, raising an eyebrow at him this time. I wanted to laugh when he at least looked taken aback by my question.

"I think we both know you are much more to me than that," he said being serious and making me blush.

"But I confess you are right, until this point I never asked, nor did I find myself intrigued enough to know." I couldn't help but grin at how special his words made me feel. I should have felt bad for the others but being in love with the man enough to drive me wild with jealousy, then I just couldn't find it in me. I loved that I was different to him, as when you meet your soul mate that is exactly how it should be.

Because let's face it, every woman when meeting the one they love wants to be the spark that ignites that eternal flame. The very one that until now, no one had the power to achieve and deep in their hearts, they would never feel guilty about it.

They had nothing to apologise for or need to make any excuses for their success where others had failed. It was just the natural way of things and I firmly believed that with the right person you could achieve anything. The type of happiness that years of doubt of it ever existing could demolish in an instant. And Draven, no matter which time in history he graced by living in, well...*he was my happiness.*

"Then you compliment me greatly," I told him blushing and giving him a cheeky little bow before giggling about it. The look he gave me was the same one I would find often on him and it was as though he was seeing me for the first time and I guess in a way he was. It was that beautiful moment you experience when you were first learning of each other's quirks.

All those little mannerisms and tiny seconds that painted the unique picture of someone's soul. Whether it be a certain laugh, the way they played with their hands when upset or even the way they nodded when agreeing with something on the TV when they thought no one was looking.

The little sighs of pleasure when eating something they liked or wrinkling up their nose when eating something they didn't. What could be the most annoying noise to one, could just as easily be the most endearing to another. That was the crucial part of finding your soul mate and what it was all about. It was finding the puzzle pieces that fit and connected together unlike any other. And most of all it was about the picture you became when you were finally put together and for the first time in your life, you felt whole.

Which was why I was still grinning like a crazy woman even when Draven walked to the door and opened it even before Ranka had chance to knock.

"My Lord, the items you requested," she said first handing him an elaborately carved box and something rolled up in cloth. Then she asked if that would be all and left when Draven told her it was. He closed the door and walked over to one of the small tables to place the box down and I couldn't help but wonder what he was up to and was about to ask him what was in the box when he nodded to the sunken seating area and asked me to sit. I did as I was told and didn't have to wait long before he joined me. He sat opposite me as though purposely trying to put some distance between us, which had me worried for a minute. That was until he relaxed back onto the high cushions and said,

"Now, tell me about you." I couldn't help but take in a deep breath but it was in relief not because I was feeling relaxed like he was. In fact, I was surprised that he was feeling this relaxed considering there was an army awaiting him.

"Can I first ask why you're not worried about them?" I asked nodding to the window.

"Because it is not a battle they can win, if there is even a battle at all."

"You seem so sure, has this happened before?" His mouth quirked up at my question before he responded as to why he looked so amused.

"I must say that talking about war was not something I thought to be doing with you tonight but given your views on politics, then I am intrigued to see where this will go." I didn't know what to say to that so said nothing at all.

"In answer to your question, then yes, I have seen many an army at my gates and none more than the Romans, as like the Parthian people, they are ambitious, that much can be said. But they are arrogant and it is usually their belief in their own superiority in battle that tends to be their downfall."

"Ah, I see." I said smiling and forcing Draven to ask,

"Explain that look to me," as he leaned forward towards me.

"Someone once said to me that assumption is the mother from where most mistakes are born." I told him remembering the day he said this to me. Draven grinned at me and rubbed his beard as he leaned back once more.

"Those are wise words indeed. It is true the Romans assume victory too easily but as they travelled a long distance to get here, their soldiers are often worn out before even stepping foot in battle." I looked towards the flickering lights in the distance and had to ask,

"Then why do you let them rest, why is it you do not strike whilst they are weak?" At this question Draven burst out laughing and hit his hands on his knees in his amusement.

"Upon my word, for someone so against the acts of war, you

are surprisingly cut throat!" he said through his laughter. I couldn't help but blush knowing he was right, it had sounded bad and a complete contradiction to what I had said about war earlier.

"You're right, that did sound bad." I agreed.

"It sounded like the act of a desperate ruler and one I am fortunate enough to say I am not. My men are always ready to fight as they train daily and are the best at what they do which, first and foremost, is to defend their city. It was what they were born to do and it is what they choose to live for." I understood now why it must have meant something to him to hear me talking about my views of war. When I said about the man who fights by your side because he chooses to is the one you also want fighting at your back…well no wonder he had looked at me the way he did.

"To have that kind of faith in your army is answer to your earlier question and the reason I do not worry about such things. It is also the reason I allow the enemy this time to meet us in battle at their best, because I believe we can beat their best and I will have none of my men believing otherwise." I couldn't help but smile at him and then did something that was out of character for this time but not for me in mine. I got up, walked across to him and placed both hands on his cheeks before kissing him quickly then saying,

"And that is what makes you a great King." Then I sat back down. He looked utterly stunned by my actions and the look he gave me was one that could only be described as confused. It was as though he was trying to figure out who I really was without asking me but by asking the Gods. But this was the point where he decided to ask something completely different and it felt as though if he didn't ask it now then he would go mad without the knowledge.

"Whereas all the other girls cowered away, you ran to her

blade...why?" I was taken aback by his question, making me repeat it,

"Why?"

"Yes, why did you save me?" I looked away for a second, but this wasn't to look for the answer as it wasn't one I would ever need to search for. It was because I *knew* the answer.

And I knew the point had come to tell him the truth of it...

"Because I love you."

CHAPTER TWENTY-FOUR

BEAUTY IN A BOX

"Because I love you."

My answer obviously had hit its mark as he looked as though I had injected the very words of love straight into his heart. I'm sure that I hadn't been the first person to speak of my love for him but from the look of things, I had been the only one to do so that mattered.

"You love me, yet you were prepared to run from me... why?" he asked after we spent long silent moments looking at each other.

"Wouldn't you if you believed my heart belonged to another?" I asked and I could see his fist clench at the thought, no doubt thinking back to how he felt when I had foolishly said Draven's name.

"No. I would kill the other so there would be nothing standing in my way," he answered harshly and I had to hold back the urge to roll my eyes.

"Are you so sure about that?"

"I threatened the life of this *'Draven'* didn't I?" he snapped, obviously still feeling raw about it and proving my point.

"So if I'd have murdered your Stateira, your 'creation of the stars', then this would have been acceptable to you?" I asked making my own point and doing so by letting him know I knew what he had named her. He narrowed his eyes on me for a second but his smirk was easy to spot…he liked that I was jealous.

"A woman like her is motivated first and foremost by her own vanity and therefore expected a name like this to be bestowed on her." I gave him a quizzical look back and said,

"Just because a screaming child wants to eat nothing but sweetmeats you don't let it happen just because they want it." I told him making him laugh and remembering that their version of gummy bears and fizzy cola bottles were usually fruits covered in sugar.

"You say I was wrong to feed her vanity?" he asked looking amused.

"Yes. A person like that needs to learn humility and know that the world doesn't owe them a certain way of life just because they want it…or worse, expect it." I told him and this time he tried to hide his grin behind his hand but I could see his smile easily enough in his eyes.

"I am curious then, how do you believe it is that people achieve their goals?" I shrugged my shoulders and said,

"Simple, I believe people can achieve anything when they put their hearts and minds to it and when they apply enough hard work to get there, I think it makes their personal victory even more sweet."

"And that is why I named you the way I did," he told me looking proud and it made me blush.

"You think I am sweet?" I asked biting my lip.

"Oh I know you are, for I have tasted you for myself." Now at this I really blushed and he laughed, obviously watching my cheeks deepen in their colour.

"In truth you are unlike any other woman I have ever met. In fact, I believe I could listen to your intelligent views of the world for days on end and I would still be asking you for more."

"Now you're teasing me," I said smirking myself, making him laugh again.

"I wouldn't dare, for your lips are far too dangerous to battle against." This time I was the one to laugh and add my own brand of teasing when I said,

"Says the King who has won every battle when kissing them." Now this comment made him really grin and it was a breath-taking sight, enough to make me sigh.

"Explain that sound to me," he asked when he caught it for himself, so I told him.

"You are very handsome but when you smile it often takes my breath away." I loved the way his lips twitched hearing this as though trying not to give me another reason to sigh but loving the idea that this was what he did to me.

"You compliment me greatly," he told me, mimicking my own words back, making me bow to him in an exaggerated manner.

"Tell me about your life before you came here." This was when my faced changed and my good humour fled me.

"Ah, I see I am not in for a happy story," he commented and I remembered all that Pip had told me, which included words like 'ambushed' and 'very sad'.

"No, not really." I told him frowning but not for the reasons he thought. I hated that I was about to lie to him as I would have loved nothing more than to continue our flirty banter and make him laugh. I would also have loved to be able to be truthful, telling him about my family and the true home I came from. But I knew that would have been impossible as in this case the truth would have meant so much more.

That had been the beauty of 'I have no memory' for it was a lie yes, but one that was the lesser of two evils. I wasn't a good liar at the best of times and when I actually ever managed it without being caught out I often did so more shocked than most. But Pip was right, with the added appearance of 'my sister' Ari, then to not say anything would have been more condemning than the lie I was about to tell.

So I did as Pip had suggested and pretty much repeated it back to him, trying to do so as if I wasn't just reading it off a script Pip had handed to my brain.

"I must say I am surprised to hear so much intelligence coming from a simple merchant's daughter," he said and if I had been one, I would have been insulted.

"Well someone had to keep an eye on his accounts and besides, my father was an intelligent man and always encouraged his daughters to read from a young age," I said, hoping this reason would suffice.

"I don't doubt this but that is not the type of intelligence I speak of," he said rubbing his beard as he looked at me as though once again trying to read my mind.

"I don't understand?"

"It is the worldly knowledge that you hold that intrigues me and one not often found in a simple merchant's daughter but one normally found in that of an Emperor's," he said pushing his point. I frowned thinking how I would answer that if referring to my own father and I decided to say what I would if it were true.

"Make no mistake in believing my father could ever be

classed as a simple man," I said getting to my feet in the face of what could be taken as an insulting comment.

"Oh trust me little lamb, I am starting to understand where that passionate nature stems from and believe me when I say I am more than thankful for it," he told me then held his hand back out and said,

"Please Nāzanin, sit back down, for I meant no offense." I gave him a little smile and sat back down.

"I may have over reacted," I told him sheepishly making him smile back at me.

"On the contrary, I find you fascinating."

"Why?" I asked dumbfounded, as fascinating wasn't a word I would ever have used to describe myself or was it just down to the blinding differences between me and the other women from this time.

"Because you have not allowed your misfortunes to ground such a passionate soul into submission. You have not let your struggles in life taint strong views and good morals which makes you unique. Your faith in the good of others has been tested time and time again yet you still believe it is there to find, where others would not." He took a moment to look out of one of the windows before he continued,

"To not let the cruelty this world has forced upon you to take a hold and break your spirit is a rarity indeed, but to wake and see its beauty with every sunrise is astonishing. That is why I find you so fascinating." He finished and I was nearly in tears hearing how he viewed me. But I doubted he would think that way once he knew the truth. When he found out who I was and how I had lied about everything...what then?

It didn't bear thinking about.

"You do not trust in my words?" he asked after obviously being able to read the doubt on my face.

"I think you might be biased," I told him making him laugh in one short surprised burst.

"And I think that you are too modest, whether you think my feelings for you are classed as biased or not. Speaking of which, I think it is time for my prize," he said and I watched him get up to fetch the two items off the table. He then placed the box down on the small table between us before sitting down with the long item that had been rolled into a cloth.

"I haven't looked at this yet but as I am curious to know how it is you see me, I can wait no longer." After he said this I knew what was wrapped inside before he started to unroll it from its fabric. I bit my lip knowing it wasn't my best as I hadn't been used to the materials I had been given to use. In fact, I suddenly had the urge to run over to him and snatch it from his hand, which was exactly what my impulses made me do. He looked so shocked from my actions that he seemed too stunned to react, making grabbing it an easy feat.

"Uh...sorry but I just...well I think I need to explain and ... um, well I..." I started babbling and it didn't help that he was still looking at me as though it was the first time anyone had stolen anything out of his hand, which it probably was.

"Did you just take that from me?" he asked tilting his head at me and I couldn't tell if he wanted to laugh or bend me over his knee and teach me a lesson. Well at least only one of those options would most likely lead to sex... ironically something I was currently forbidden to have.

I gulped and then shook my head.

"Nope, more like borrowed...yeah, I borrowed it," I said, this time definitely making him grin, only it was all bad boy and mischief.

"It seems I will be needing what is in that box sooner than I thought," he teased cryptically then he leaned forward quickly to grab me but I was quicker. I jumped out of his way and from the looks of things he didn't expect that either. He raised an eyebrow at me as though trying to make sense of my actions but then he saw my playful grin and knew what to do. He shook his head to himself like he had never dealt with someone like me before and was still trying to twist his mind around it.

"You like playing with fire, little one?" he asked leaning forward like a predator about to spring for its prey. I licked my lips then held the bottom one in my teeth for a few seconds before bravely answering him.

"Only when I feel cold," I replied with a cheeky grin I couldn't wipe off my face. I watched as his lips twitched with amusement, which ended up being my only warning before he pounced. I shrieked as I turned around and ran from him but unsurprisingly I didn't get far. He grabbed me around the waist and hoisted me up over his shoulder as I giggled and snorted. Then he jumped back down into the sunken cushions with me like a sack over his shoulder, proving his immense strength as he made it seem as though I weighed nothing at all to him.

Then just as he was about to sit he brought me down from his shoulder and swung me around before placing me in between his legs. I tried to tease him further by lurching forward but he was much quicker than me as I knew he would be. And to be honest I just wanted to feel his arms wrapped securely around me, which was precisely what he did.

He first placed his left one across me so that he could trap one arm and reach the other to hold it down. This then left his right one free and I shivered against him when he used it to start touching my body.

"Still cold?" he hummed in my ear and I could only manage to respond with a little shake of my head.

"Mmm, I am addicted to your scent." When he said this I

didn't know whether he was informing me of this fact or just speaking to himself. It was the way he ran the tip of his nose up the length of my neck and inhaled deeply as though getting lost there.

"It makes me want to bite you," he confessed before taking my flesh in his mouth and holding me there by his teeth something, unknown to him, he had done many times before to me. I could feel the length of his fangs growing and I moaned back against him further letting him know without confessing too much how I loved this natural side of him. In fact, I arched my neck further in the ultimate act of submission making his chest rumble.

"Careful what you offer little lamb, for I may take it and never let it go," he warned after holding me immobile for a second longer then retracting his fangs before they had chance to pierce my skin.

"I am not afraid of you," I told him trying to keep my voice as steady as I could when he made me feel this way.

"Not yet you're not but I would rather not take any chances so soon," he said, not knowing that I already knew what he was referring to.

"Are you afraid I will run from you?" I asked, smiling a little when my words made him react by strengthening his hold on me.

"No…" He paused and then whispered the rest in my ear,

"…not when I am faster than you." I couldn't help but shudder again against him making him chuckle.

"Do I affect you as you affect me, sweet girl?" I blushed at his question and found that I could only nod in agreement.

"Let's see should we," he said and before I could ask he gave me a very stern command.

"Place your arms by your sides and *do not* move them…am I understood?" I obviously took too long to answer him as the next thing I knew he had a hand around the column of my throat and a hand moving my head back so that I was looking at him.

"I am not your King in this room but when you walk in here you choose to obey me...now, *am I understood?"* he asked again and after swallowing heavy against his palm, I nodded as much as he would allow, letting my eyes do my talking for me.

"Good girl, now do as I asked of you." He let go of my neck and this time I quickly did as he ordered and without hesitation. My heart was pounding but my sexual desire was through the elaborate arched roof! I loved it when he got off by dominating me and I could feel the evidence of it pooling in between my thighs.

"You looked beautiful tonight with just the hint of skin teasing me but there is a reason I wanted you more covered than the others," he said running his fingers softly down my cleavage making me moan again and bite my lip to stop me from begging for more.

"I have never felt the venomous bite of jealousy before but the thought of your body being seen by any other lustful gaze but mine had me intervening in your outfit choice."

"Is that why I wore a different colour from the rest?" I couldn't help myself but I had to ask.

"I am not interested in the others but you, well I wanted to make a statement that you had already been chosen the second you stepped foot into the room. And besides, the colour suits your milky skin and brings out the blue in your eyes." I couldn't help but smile to myself when hearing this. But if that was the case and I had already been chosen as he stated then why would he make me dance?

"I know what you are thinking as your eyes give you away. I wanted to see if you would dance for me..." He paused for a moment as he unhooked my jacket at my breasts, letting them burst free into his hands. I leaned back against him, happily pressing them further into his palms.

"But when you brazenly declared to the whole room that your dancing was for my eyes only, well then, how could I refuse such an offer." This was when I froze under his touch making him laugh behind me.

"Not feeling so brave now, little one?" he said and all I could do was shake my head a little, silently begging him not to ask it of me.

"Lucky for you then that I am quite content having you here against me so that I can freely explore what is mine to play with." Hearing this I finally took a deep breath after holding one in for so long, which again made him chuckle behind me. I wanted to come back with something sassy and was about to speak when he pinched my nipples hard, shocking me into silence.

"You were saying?" he asked, toying with me. I tested the theory and opened my mouth to respond only to have him do it again and harder this time. A little cry was all I managed to get out and he followed with,

"Good, you are understanding our little game now, for every time you speak without being asked, you will feel the sweet bite of pain, one I know you like for I can smell your sweet musk from here." I blushed feeling embarrassed by this but soon his hands quickly took away all other feelings other than lust.

He played with my breasts, working them to the point that was maddening and had me begging for more. But the second that word slipped out, he pinched me harder again, and I swear I almost came from it.

"Oh you like that, don't you?" he asked and when I didn't reply he did it again, making me cry out.

"I asked you a question, little lamb." I nodded in response only this wasn't good enough for him so he squeezed them harder still, this time adding the bite of his thumb nail to press against the sensitive tips. I cried out even louder and arched myself back, shouting,

"Yes! Yes, yes I like it!" This obviously amused him as I felt his laughter once again rumbling against my back.

"I think it's time to see for myself," he said letting go of my breasts and putting a stop to his sweet torturing of them. I have to say I was sad that it ended but also intrigued as to what he would do next.

"Lean forward and hand me the box," he ordered and I automatically pulled my jacket closed.

"Did I say you could hide your body from me?" he asked sternly, giving me a 'tutting' sound before grabbing me back roughly to his chest, spinning me around to face him and leaning down so this time his torture could continue with his mouth. He lifted my breast up to his lips before he sucked a hard nipple inside and then had me crying out when he used his teeth against it.

"Oh please, please!" I begged for something I didn't know or maybe I did know and was too ashamed to ask for. But despite this his biting continued as he worked me up into a frenzy. He would scrape his fang across before using his tongue to sooth the hurt and then lure me into a false sense of security before biting down hard enough to have me calling out again. I don't know how long it lasted for, but only when he knew I was close to coming did he cruelly stop.

"No, please don't." The moan slipped out with no way of stopping it and I could almost feel him smiling.

"Soon my sweet one, for I promise to let you come shortly but first, let me show you my gift…now do as you were told and this time, without trying to hide yourself from me." I nodded my compliance, turned and leaned forward feeling slightly embarrassed as the weight of my breasts fell forward into the hands he had waiting there.

"I love the feel of them filling my hands," he told me making the heat rise to my cheeks even more.

"Don't stop…continue," he ordered as I had paused as soon as he started to touch me again. I grabbed the box trying to stop from shaking, unable to prevent the effect he had on me.

"Now open it," he instructed once I had placed it down on my knees. I did as I was told and gasped at the beautifully erotic and scary sight that lay inside.

"I told you I would get you in chains again," he whispered seductively to me. I gulped down the hard lump as I let my fingers circle the stunning gold craftsmanship. In fact, if it hadn't been for the thick chain connecting them together I would have thought it looked more like two heavy pieces of jewellery than a pair of shackles. My mouth dropped slightly as I took in the sight of the most beautiful pair of thick gold bands sat nestled amongst the blood red silk.

Draven lifted them up for me to see better and I soon realised that the same red silk was used on the insides of them, to act as cushioning.

"I didn't want to see these delicate wrists bruised again from any rough treatment I had in mind for you." Hearing this made me swallow hard. I didn't respond, not knowing what to say but instead couldn't help but notice the striking contrast between the two vivid colours of gold and red. It gave them a royal sensuality that soon had me excited to see what they would look like clamped tight against my skin.

I let my finger tip trace the foreign writing across the band that was bordered by twisted vines and small intricate flowers that were also richly encrusted with small sparkling diamonds and larger purple jewels at their centres.

"What does it mean?" I asked, unable to help the way my voice sounded all breathy.

"It means you belong to me and that now…" he paused for a moment so that he could bite down on my ear before whispering the next part of his promise…

"…It's time to really play."

CHAPTER TWENTY-FIVE

CHAINED TO MY KING

Soon after this Draven took me by the hand and walked me into one of the rooms that branched off from the one we had been sat in. I wasn't surprised to see it was the one with the bed in but I was surprised by how little of the room I'd taken in last time. In fact, it soon started to dawn on me that this wasn't the same room at all.

I didn't say anything as it wasn't the time to ask, that much was obvious with the way Draven led me inside with one hand and held onto the shackles with the other. I only had a brief time to scan the room before he spun me around to face him, momentarily shocking me enough that my mouth slipped open.

"I like that look on you," he told me as he slipped his thumb inside for me to suck. Then he started walking me backwards until I was up against the wall.

"From the first moment I saw you chained up I knew that I had to see you that way again. I must confess that I have thought of little else than the sight of your body stretched out, naked and helpless in chains, ready to receive the pleasure I will soon force upon you." I couldn't help but close my eyes at the thought of the delicious image he conjured up in my mind.

"So let's see what we can do about making that happen now, shall we?" he said before pulling the jacket the rest of the way from my body and down my arms before discarding it on the floor.

"That's much better, now hold out your arms." I did as I was told without hesitation this time and I couldn't help but watch him in utter fascination as he ran his finger over the inscription making it unlock.

"Magic," I uttered smiling and receiving a mischievous grin back as he raised his eyes to mine. Then he placed the first band of gold around one wrist before clamping it shut and then doing the same to the other, pulling on the thick chain slightly to check they were secure. Once he was satisfied his grip on the links tightened as he started to raise up my arms until I had no choice but to lift them to where he wanted them to go.

"Trust me Sweetest one, for I promise to take care of you." he told me softly as my face must have given away some of my trepidation. I gave him a small nod, giving him the go ahead to carry on. With one arm he banded my waist lifting me up slightly and at the same time he hooked the chain around something I couldn't see above me. Then he let me down slowly making sure the length was just right so as not to cause me too much discomfort.

Once finished he took a few steps back to admire his handy work, doing so with a hand on his beard, causing my anxiety to hitch up a notch along with my libido.

"Perfection is but one step away," he said to himself and without any more warning he reached out, grabbing the waist of my trousers and yanking it hard, then he stepped into my body as it swung towards him to take a demanding kiss. The second his lips touched mine I opened my mouth with a feverish desperation to taste him. I couldn't help but moan against him, pulling at my shackles simply because I wanted more. He heard the noise and pulled back a little to lift a questioning eyebrow at me.

"You want more, little lamb?" he asked in a husky voice, thick with his own lust.

"Yes, with you I always want more." I told him truthfully causing his eyes to flash purple before he could contain it. Then he crushed his lips back to mine, this time taking our kiss to the next level. His hands entwined in my hair pulling my head back, opening myself up further to him and a small whispered 'yes' escaped inside his mouth.

I soon heard the sound of material ripping and when I felt the air hit my naked legs I knew my trousers had been snatched off. I kicked off my little slippers that no longer matched my naked outfit and soon my legs were wrapping around him in an attempt to get him closer. I briefly heard Pip's warning ringing in my head but my addiction for this man wouldn't let it sink in far enough to stop this.

"No, come back to me." I demanded as he tore his lips from mine. But it was only when I saw his eyes glowing purple that I knew why he'd stopped...*I was provoking his Demon to come out and play.*

"No, but you will come for me," he told me as he suddenly dropped to his knees before me. At first my naive mind asked itself what he was doing but then he started to lift up my legs, hooking them over his shoulders making it clear. I think my whole body started to blush as he spread me out for his view. My natural instinct was to close my legs but this was impossible with the way he had firmly situated himself in between my thighs.

"Oh Gods!" I shouted on a cry at the first swipe of his tongue against my clit making him chuckle against my mound.

Then he ran a finger along the insides of my folds and passed my opening, dragging the juices to his waiting lips.

"So fucking sweet!" he said on a growl before diving in and making a meal out of me. Suddenly he gripped both my cheeks with his hands and pulled me tight against his mouth as I fought against him, trying to pull away from the intensity of it all. But he wouldn't let me and instead drove me to screaming as he sucked my clitoris into his mouth and rolled it around with his teeth. I came like a firecracker, bucking against him and filling the room with the sounds of sweet cries of torture and the sound of my chains rattling above me.

"Please, oh God please stop." I begged as my body started to betray me as the rise of another orgasm started to build.

"One more I think," he told me looking up and seeing me almost in tears from it all.

"Oh no…no, no, no…yes, yes, YEEESSS!" I screamed changing my tune very quickly as I came again causing my legs to shake and my muscles to twitch against him. It was as if someone was injecting me with a drug and I could feel it seeping into my system causing a beautiful sweet euphoria.

I dragged the air into my lungs trying in vain to get my breath but this was made harder when he started lapping me up and growling because of it. When he finished he pulled back and rested his forehead on my stomach, looking down as he panted. He must have been trying to control himself before he dared looking back up at me, which sent a twinge of regret in my heart. I just wished for nothing more in that moment than for us to be able to be honest with each other and both reveal our secrets.

But I knew that we had come to a standstill because either way, once we both crossed that line and had sex, we would both discover the truth. Which was why I wasn't surprised when he stood up, and without a word lifted me up off the hook. Then he placed the chain behind his head so that I had to hold onto his shoulders as he walked us both to the bed.

"Are you alright, my King?" I asked him softly placing a hand on his cheek to get him to look at me.

"You were perfect," he told me sweetly, but this hadn't been what I had asked him, so I reminded him of the fact,

"That's not what I asked." He didn't answer me at first and I didn't think he was going to until he lay us both upon his bed, one this time that was more fitting for a King and not a barbarian ruler. Silks instead of furs and carved wood that raised up until it touched the ceiling and twisted into four sides of an arch.

"I do not want to push you too far." Or himself I thought silently, knowing in his mind this was what it was.

"I would never be afraid of you," I told him gently after he positioned us on our sides facing each other, my chains still firmly in place behind his neck as he obviously still wanted to keep me close.

He looked taken aback by my confession and for a moment incredibly touched by it but then the reality of what he would have to tell me must have set in. He frowned, obviously already convincing himself that I would run from him. Of course, when we had first met he knew that I had been seeing Demons since the age of seven, so he never had these fears until now.

"You don't know of what you speak," he told me, convincing himself of this.

"I know my own heart, even if others choose not to trust in it." I told him angrily, letting him know of the insult he caused.

"I trust in what you believe you feel little one, but I also know how possible it is for feelings to change," he told me running a thumb along my cheek.

"Then the feelings must have been false to begin with for

real true love only ever changes when it gets stronger, not weaker," I told him making him smile.

"Another lesson for me to learn?" he asked, quickly back to teasing me. I laughed and said,

"Only if it sinks in and stays there," I teased back only half joking. He looked me up and down smiling to himself this time and then as he found my eyes once more said something that was truer than he would ever know…

"Many things can be proven in time, so we shall see."

CHAPTER TWENTY-SIX

THE TROUBLE WITH BAD GUYS

The next morning, I awoke in a strange position and at first, because I faced an empty side of the bed, I thought I was alone. I wondered where Draven was for all of ten seconds until realising that having my hands both raised above me was an unusual way for me to fall asleep. I looked up to find both hands still wearing their shackles and a firm hand fisted around the chain in between. It had been as though holding it all through the night had brought him comfort and although I hoped he didn't make this a habit and insist on it every night, I had to be honest, it got me as hot as Hell.

It was just so barbaric being chained to him all night that I couldn't help but feel owned. That feeling should have felt strange, especially for an independent woman of my own day and age, but there was nothing demeaning about it. Quite the opposite actually. It felt more powerful than anything else and even though I liked the idea of belonging to Draven, I liked it even more that he wanted to own me. It was the silent flip of the power exchange that had me smiling and feeling happy with myself. And more than ever I could understand the strange but alluring ways in which a Dominant and submissive relationship worked.

Having two alphas just meant butting heads and having two submissives just meant that one would have to take the lead and then resent it. But giving your trust to someone enough to let them make important decisions felt a bit like freeing your soul, especially when it came to sex. It took overthinking and analysing everything out of the equation and just allowed you to feel exactly what the other person wanted you to feel. They themselves then got pleasure in knowing that only they could do that to you and to control something so powerful was considered a gift to them.

But would I have considered myself a submissive in everyday life? No, not at all or would I have even considered it with anyone else but Draven...? Probably not. Which is why I think it is that certain people must just bring it out in you, like a dark secret poking its head out of the shadows for the first time, while timidly entering the room. Then once it's out and freed, it is like a beast that never wants to be put back into its cage. And the truth of it is that any real love of yours should never want it to either, for it is part of who you are.

I truly believe that although you will have many regrets in your life, your sexuality is one that you should never feel embarrassed about or ashamed of, for it is like asking a flower not to bloom because the people around don't approve of its colour. I felt nothing but grateful for this side of me that Draven had awakened, so when I looked up at my chained hands now, I felt proud not ashamed.

"That's an active mind I hear for so early in the morning," Draven said in a throaty voice, wrapping an arm around me and pulling me back closer to the length of him.

"And is that part of your other magic my Lord, reading

minds?" I teased for more reasons than one. I smiled to myself when I felt his muscles tense around me before they relaxed after I spoke again,

"I do hope not for I would be forever blushing around you."

"Is that right? Maybe it is your lip biting that gives away your lustful mind." I laughed once and gave him a cryptic,

"Maybe," back.

"I wish I had the luxury of enjoying your naked presence for the rest of the day…"

"But you have an army to battle?" I asked making him turn me over so that he was above me.

"You worry about me?" he asked avoiding answering my question.

"Of course, just as you worry for me." My answer prompted first a smile that then led into a good morning kiss, one that unfortunately ended far too soon.

"That was goodbye wasn't it?" I said unable to keep the sullenness out of my voice making him chuckle.

"Not for long, I promise you. Ranka will take you back to your quarters to gather some things."

"Why? Where am I going?" I asked frowning and not liking the sound of this new plan.

"Just somewhere where I know you will be safe." He obviously felt uneasy about the look I gave him so decided to make it a command.

"This is an order from your King, do you understand?" he said in a sterner tone and instead of rolling my eyes like I wanted, I knew at this point that would have done nothing but got me a slapped ass or a pissed off Draven.

"Yes, my Lord."

"Now don't look at me like that, this is for my own peace of mind whilst fighting the enemy, for a worried mind can easily result in a lost head," he told me and even though I knew that

Draven could survive most things, I also knew not to underestimate this Pertinax guy.

Shortly after this and a few more stolen moments alone we both got dressed…and of course after he freed me from his personal choice of restraints. I was surprised I even had any clothes to wear after he had been his usual brutal self with my choice of outfit. They definitely had that in common, so it only confirmed my theory that there were certain aspects of your personality that you never grew out of.

Ranka soon appeared ready to escort me back to my room and, like the loyal subject she was, received her new orders to protect me with a bow and a confident,

"I will do so with my life, my Lord," making me want to slap her on the back and say, 'relax, how bad can it be making sure I don't die?' but I knew this would have been a joke lost on her and neither the present or future Draven would have appreciated it, considering the amount of trouble I somehow managed to get myself into.

I said my last goodbyes to Draven, which of course included issuing my own orders,

"Stay safe and come back to me." I will never forget the way he looked down at me in that moment, but it was his words that really rooted themselves to my soul. He leaned down to place his forehead to mine and whispered,

"I will always come back to you, my Queen." I sucked in a quick breath at his declaration, knowing what this meant, but instead of telling him how I felt, I placed a hand to his cheek and closed my eyes basking in our silent moment, telling him without words of my love.

So now here I was, walking back with Ranka and wondering why I felt as if there was something so very wrong. I looked sideways at her walking like she always did and acting no different to how I was now used to. So what was it? Was it because I knew what she had witnessed and how hard that must have been for her?

To see the King she loved falling in love with another and be willing to give up everything for them, after asking you to protect her with your own life…well let's just say how she hadn't been the first one in line to try and kill me yet was astounding to me. In fact, I think if I woke up to find her dagger at my throat my first reaction would have been to shrug my shoulders and say 'Um, it figures.'

Okay, so maybe after crapping myself first.

"You alright?" I asked once we neared my quarters as I couldn't bear it any longer.

"Yes, why wouldn't I be?" she asked me back.

"No reason, just that you look different." At this she seemed affronted and shook her head in an uncomfortable way that was a strange reaction to see from her.

"I am used to battling by his side, that is all," she finally admitted and it started to make sense…she too was worried about him.

"Ah, I see."

"You do?" she asked seemingly surprised.

"You want to be out there with him fighting and instead you're stuck babysitting me."

"Babysitting?"

"Looking after me or should I say protecting, as that's a better word for it." She nodded in agreement and I had to say, I felt better knowing this was the reason for her subdued mood.

We didn't say another word and after she opened my door for me she told me that she would soon return ready to take me to Draven's chosen 'safe house'.

"Sophia!" I shouted, surprised to see her there, but glad that she was and I showed her this when I ran over to her and hugged her to me.

"Whoa, miss me?" she said laughing and then I saw Ari sitting up in the bed and let go of Sophia to run to her and hug her also. I laughed when I heard Pip walk up to Sophia and say,

"Obviously a love ya and leave ya type of girl."

"Obviously," Sophia agreed folding her arms, making me roll my eyes at their little act.

"Well at least you got a hug, jeez, I didn't even get a head bob, finger click or a Yo Bitch."

"They have been like this all morning," Ari told me smiling and I had to say, it was a relief to see.

"How are you feeling?"

"A lot better mainly thanks to those two who have spent most of last night and this morning getting me up to speed. Jesus Kazzy, but is there anyone else out there trying to kill you, only no offense but you're a liability to be around," she joked and I smacked her on the arm lightly.

"Oi! Says desert girl here," I said looking back at the other two who were sniggering.

"Who are you calling desert girl, because from the sounds of it we all ended up in that stupid desert but on different sides of the city." Well this was something I didn't know. And speaking of things I didn't know…

"Wait what happened with Draven and the other you we stuffed in the trunk? I guess Pip told you about…" I stopped when I saw Pip slicing a finger across her throat to try and get me to shut up.

"Tell me what?"

"Oh nothing." I added but the second she turned around to look at Pip I knew her gig was up.

"Spill it, Imp!" Sophia demanded and Pip looked to me cocking her hip.

"Jeez, so glad you came back just now, what did it take you, all of two minutes to put a Tootsie roll in it?"

"Hey don't look at me, I wasn't the one who sat on the trunk and broke three of her fingers and caught her hair in the damn lid!" I said realising I had just given it away to Sophia, making me bite my lip and scrunch up my face before facing her.

"Uh…her bad." I said wincing and making her roll her eyes at me. Then she turned to Pip and said,

"You and me are gonna talk about this but right now, try not to break me anymore!" Pip gave her a salute and said,

"Sir, yes sir!"

"In answer to your question, it went fine. He believed that I'd had a change of heart and we are back on track with mission baby maker."

"And what about our little side mission named doppelganger?" I asked raising my eyebrows.

"She is fine, or at least will be in like a week or so, anyway we should be long gone by then so why should I care?" Sophia said obviously having a massive issue with her other self, which needed a bottle of Vodka to understand without getting a headache, saving it just for the morning after.

"Wow, you're so sexy when you're angry like that." Pip said sideways to her.

"I know," she replied, giving her a wink, making me laugh. But then I looked at her again doing a double take before asking,

"Why are you both dressed like that?" I looked them both up and down noticing that Pip had on her ancient ninja look, complete with long black hood she currently wore down and straps of leather across her chest and off to one side where an array of weapons hung.

Sophia, on the other hand, looked more ready for battle in an obvious way, dressed with a shapely bronze coloured breast plate that was made to fit her female curves. This, combined with the metal shoulder plates that fanned out in three different sizes and the silver gauntlets strapped to her arms, and she looked ready for anything. She also wore a long leather skirt that managed to add some class and Sophia style to the warrior woman outfit. Even her hair had been pinned back tight for the occasion.

"Well, I am protecting you," Pip said patting her weapons before she turned to Sophia so she could say,

"And I am protecting Dom."

"Okay, I think you need to explain," I said shaking my head wondering why Sophia would be going into battle if there was nothing to worry about.

"And it's your turn to take the stage," Pip said gesturing to Sophia dramatically.

"Okay, so you had better sit down as we are about to get into a shit storm here, for up until I saw that army, I had no idea what year we had travelled back to," Sophia told me and I whispered the name I kept hearing,

"Let me guess… *Pertinax?*"

"Yes and let it be known that had I been aware I would have suggested coming back to a time after he was long dead instead of only a few days before," she said as I did as I was told and sat down ready to hear this.

"So Draven did defeat him then?" I asked feeling much better if this were the case.

"No, he didn't." Hearing these simple words managed to have enough power to sink my heart in a sea of dread.

"What do you mean?" I looked first to Sophia and then to

Pip, knowing this was the part of the story she hadn't wanted to tell me herself and yep, there was that sheepish look of hers.

"Pertinax is what his vessel is named and who he is known as in the human world but in our world, he is known as much more."

"And much worse." Pip added grimly.

"Why, who is he?"

"He has many names, Angra Mainyu in Zoroastrianism but right now, in this time's history, he is better known as Ahriman...*the Persian Devil,*" she added delicately, knowing this was the part I would understand the most.

"The Devil! Draven is going to fight a Devil, as in a Satan, and Master of Hell!?" I shouted getting worked up.

"Easy there. Yes, he is fighting one of the former presidents of Hell but he was banished to Earth for even Hell didn't want him. And Satan and Lucifer are not the same being."

"They're not?" I asked feeling strangely betrayed by the mythology. Pip shook her head and I looked to Ari who shrugged her shoulders and said,

"Don't look to me, you know more about this shit than I do...I'm the supernatural novice in the room, remember." Pip looked about to say something but I quickly noticed the way Sophia shook her head at her telling her not to go there.

"Ahriman was like a brother to Lucifer and when Lucifer fell from the Heavens in disgrace he followed him there. But pretty soon he slowly became more bitter and enraged that *he* wasn't ruler of Hell. In the end Lucifer had no choice but to cast him out to Earth, just as his God had done to him."

"Hence one uber pissed off Demon Under Lord," Pip added being helpful and saying it in plain English.

"So he ruled Earth?" I asked hearing as much from Pip last night.

"Yes, but only because he had no domain anywhere else. I

think the Gods were simply expecting him to just go away quietly and fade into exile."

"Man, but they were so wrong!" Pip said shaking her head and continuing to add commentary to Sophia's story.

"For a long time the world just seemed to be at chaos with itself and with no balance of power, the Gods knew something needed to be done."

"Enter you three." I said this time jumping in before Pip could.

"Yes, we seemed to be just the answer they were looking for and even though placing us down there was a risk in itself, it was one they were willing to chance."

"Why was it a risk?" I looked back, surprised to hear this coming from Ari.

"Because they didn't know if by adding even more power to the situation it would cause more damage than good. They didn't know our temperaments or know of our loyalty to the cause in which we first had to battle it out in order to win control." Hearing this kind of made sense because the second they were reborn into their vessels then there were no assurances that they would be better off than having this Ahriman.

"So what happened?"

"The supernatural world didn't revolt against our rule like the Gods first thought they would. But instead they seemed to be drawn to us, my brother especially because to them being connected to that type of power was to gain power themselves."

"But this Ahriman was the most powerful…" I was about to ask when Sophia interrupted me knowing where I was going with it.

"Ah yes, but even he didn't have what my brother had and that was the power of both Heaven and Hell running through his veins." I suppose this made sense but then if Draven was so powerful then why couldn't he fight him alone?

"You must remember that Ahriman was still a God walking on Earth and my brother is not. But with our birth it was also prophesied that the power of three combined could defeat him in battle and that day…"

This is where I finished off for her…

"Is today."

CHAPTER TWENTY-SEVEN

SNAKES AND STONE

After this Sophia went on to tell me the story of how they defeated him the first time. Pertinax had gained his new army after taking his position as emperor only three months before and this was by suspicious means.

The previous emperor Commodus was a great fighter and proved this everyday as he fought as a gladiator, winning all rounds but on the 31st December year 192 AD there was a conspiracy to murder him. First one of the conspirators named Marcia poisoned his food but Commodus vomited up the poison, so the conspirators sent his wrestling partner Narcissus to strangle him in his bath.

After this Pertinax was declared the new emperor and that was only three months ago. This was when he decided to take his army and march them straight to the King of Kings who sat upon his throne in the Parthian capital, Ctesiphon. But really he was taking this fight to the King of the Supernatural world using a seven hundred year feud to mask his real intentions.

And the time of that final battle was today as the sun

caressed the mountains before setting on the day's bloodshed. With carnage lay wasted all around them all but three had fallen. The three heroes had fought against an evil King and finally brought him to his knees in the last hour. I, of course, asked how they did this and it was time for Pip to take over as it must have been her favourite part of the story.

Just as Pertinax was about to plunge his spear into Sophia, Draven took the hit, sacrificing himself. It pierced his flesh and in his rage Draven snapped off the end of his enemy's weapon that he still grasped in his hand. Then he ripped it from his shoulder just as Vincent came up behind him to hold Pertinax down, before launching himself up into the air and slamming back down, driving the bloody blade into his cold dead heart.

I had to admit it was dramatic stuff and I could only hope that it happened the same way as it did that day. Well one thing was for sure and that was that Sophia certainly looked ready to do it all over again.

Ranka, true to her word, came to get us and we all walked down the corridor together, Ari included as she too was being kept in the safe place, which had been Vincent's command.

Ari hadn't said much about him, which wasn't a big surprise considering she never did. But all she did say was that he visited with her last night wanting to check she was alright and being well cared for. I said this was sweet of him which was obviously the wrong thing to say and her reaction to it just made Sophia frown but not surprisingly, she kept quiet on the subject.

So here we all were, five women all making our way to someplace only Ranka knew where and three of us looked like warrior women. I didn't know about Ari but I for one was kind of jealous I wasn't dressed the same, as they all looked kick ass!

"So what will happen now?" I asked Sophia, still keeping an eye on Ranka in front leading the way.

"After I have escorted you guys to…" Sophia started to say but stopped abruptly when Pip placed a hand on her shoulder. Pip had come to a standstill and the look on her face was almost frightening but not as frightening as what she said next,

"You didn't do this last time." It wasn't a question but more of a statement. Sophia looked confused and quickly said,

"Well, no I was with my brothers when…" Sophia's face suddenly dropped as what Pip was saying must have suddenly dawned on her. I looked around just as she did trying to piece together what they were obviously so worried about.

"What? What is it?" I asked as Sophia looked to Pip and Pip looked to me.

"None of this is right," Sophia said.

"Agreed," Pip added and when she put a hand to her blade I knew to really worry.

"Will someone please tell me what the hell is going on?" I snapped getting panicky.

"Be on your guard, for it was about this time," Sophia said cryptically to Pip and ignoring me.

"Ari, come back to stand with us," Pip muttered quietly after she too had stopped up ahead.

"Sophia?" I whispered looking at her, finding a serious face that brought me no comfort.

"The last time I lived through all of this they tried to split us up but were unsuccessful as I was with my brothers. I had completely forgotten until Pip…"

"What do you mean? Sophia I don't understand," I asked interrupting her.

"Pertinax. He tried to separate us. But I wasn't here back then, I was…"

"What…you were what?!" I hissed out the question grabbing her shoulders to get her to tell me and stop pausing before finishing her answer.

"She wasn't with you," Pip answered for her and my heart dropped. *I* was what was different in this time and that meant everything had changed. History was rewriting itself and right now, with Pertinax as the biggest threat the three of them had ever known until nearly two thousand years later, then this had just become a lot more complicated than I first thought.

"Oh God," I whispered before covering my mouth with both hands. I looked back to Ranka down the long hallway who had only just now stopped up ahead. She cocked her head to the side as if trying to understand what we were all waiting for. Then she flung aside her long black jacket and released her blades, spinning them up in her hands before running at us.

I looked behind just in time to see armed guards running for us and knew these must have been the men sent by Pertinax to capture us. Sophia pushed me back and Pip did the same to Ari on the other side as Ranka charged through and killed four men in seconds. She spun with such speed and grace it was more like watching a dance than a fight as the guards didn't stand a chance.

I took a deep breath when I saw them all sprawled out on the floor, knowing the threat was over so we could get Sophia to Draven as quickly as possible. That was the most important thing right now. To hell with safety for what might happen, it was more about what *could* happen if we didn't follow history to the letter. Me being here had already changed things enough but we couldn't risk it getting too far. Sophia needed to be with her brothers charging into battle at all cost, for the costs were far too great to chance.

"Weren't they the King's guard?" Pip questioned, frowning down at the bodies on the ground and then before I knew it she'd pulled a dagger from her side and a curved blade from her back, pointing it now at Ranka.

"Fuck, I knew not to trust you!" she snarled and I shook my head before shouting,

"Pip what are you doing?!"

"We have been betrayed by Mohawk here." Pip answered and I looked to Sophia to find she was looking down at the guards trying to work it all out for herself. Then she pushed me back against the wall again and pulled her own long blade from her back before pointing it at Ranka's other side.

"You're right. Why would you kill the guards who were on their way here to…"

"To protect us." Ari spoke up and finished off her sentence finally getting it as well.

"Because the Bitch is working for Pertinax that's why!" Pip growled out through gritted teeth.

"That's why you wouldn't tell me where you were taking us." Sophia added looking down at the floor for a second and then bringing her blade back up to Ranka's throat.

"Why?! Why would you betray my brother this way?!" Sophia shouted, losing her cool. I watched as Ranka merely smirked back at her refusing to answer but in the end she didn't need to because I answered for her.

"Because he is in love with me that's why. She witnessed it earlier, when he called me his Queen. I saw her face and the hurt it inflicted." Ranka's eyes grew wide when I said this and I knew I had hit my mark with her.

"You are working for him, aren't you!? Answer me!" Sophia shouted backhanding her across the face so hard that her head snapped to one side. However, the last sound I expected to hear coming out of her mouth was that creepy laugh of hers, one that quickly started to warp into something much deeper… *and deadlier.*

"I am not working for him." Ranka snarled in a strange

voice that didn't seem to belong to her but instead someone else…someone…

"Oh God, she's right." I said figuring it out now and the others looked to me just as the rumbling on the ground started.

"SHE IS HIM!" I screamed just before I stumbled back. He threw his head back and started laughing up at the ceiling and just as Pip and Sophia both moved in to attack him, he raised up his hands. I screamed along with Ari as the walls all around started to explode in great pockets, throwing debris and large chunks of stone at us. I felt one piece slice across my forehead and another hit the top of one arm as I tried to lift it to protect my face better.

"Ari get down!" I shouted doing the same but that's when I noticed the movement coming out of the holes in the walls. They looked like stone snakes slithering their way towards us and suddenly Pip and Sophia found themselves surrounded as they slashed out over and over at the floor to stop themselves from being overrun.

"KEIRA GO, FIND DOM!" Sophia screamed at me and I didn't need telling twice. I scrambled through the broken stone to get to my feet just before the snakes could reach me and make a run for it. I saw the untouched hallway in front of me and knew I had to get there!

"LOOK OUT!" I heard Ari's warning but it was too late as I felt something tighten on my ankle. It started pulling and I looked down to see the stone snake had coiled itself around me and was moving up my leg, anchoring me to the ground. The bottom part of the snake merged into the floor so it acted like chains locking me in place. I looked up to see the same had been done to Pip and Sophia only they had so many snakes covering their bodies, that you could only see their heads from their shoulders upwards.

"Stay away from her!" Sophia shouted as Ranka slowly

walked towards me, but with every step she took she started to change. She would shake her head at a blurring speed that looked as though she was morphing into something else. It was as though she was fighting some invisible force. She threw her head back and screamed out, her jaw opening up like it was being dislocated and pulling away from the rest of her skull. It was a sickening sight and one that made me want to gag.

Thankfully it didn't last long and when she looked back at me it was no longer a she, but now a he...*it was Pertinax.*

"So you are what all the fuss is about," he said looking at me and tilting his head to the side. I was surprised to see a man who looked to be in his sixties wearing what was obviously a Roman military uniform, dressed like a general. His hair was cut short in a certain style that you would have expected to see and added to this was a dark thick beard that lengthened into a V shape by his chin.

I had to admit that he didn't look particularly terrifying but his eyes certainly gave you reason to be wary. They were piercing through me as though reading my soul before deciding how to pull it apart. They were so light in shade I couldn't actually tell you what colour they were but the dark ring that circled them was what set them apart from others. This gave them an eerie chill, matching the pin points he had as pupils. In fact, just having him look at you made you want to wince back and hide.

"I am a nobody, just his Concubine," I told him making him raise an eyebrow at me.

"And I would have believed this if it had not been for the new information you had just given me." I swallowed hard, silently cursing myself for being so stupid and basically telling him how much I meant to Draven.

"I think we have more than enough to use against him," he said and at first I thought he was speaking to himself. However, soon the rumbling grew back up again and I watched in fascination as all the snakes started to slither into one big pile.

In total six mounds grew in size as it looked as though all the snakes were fighting each other to get to the top. I looked to Sophia, Pip and Ari who all were still held in place within their stone prisons and I wondered why none of these had joined the piles.

Pertinax started laughing and I looked back to him just as he clicked his fingers. This was when the giant mounds all started to merge together as one before forming what started to look like winged rock demons, made up with thick stone skeletons. Their faces were twisted features, with wide thin mouths, stone fangs and slitted eyes attached to elongated noses. Now these things were truly terrifying as they looked like demon drones which had once been gargoyles on top of buildings and had just flown down to fight because they had no choice.

Pertinax nodded towards the other prisoners and just as the snakes released them one by one, a stone demon each stepped forward ready to grab them. Sophia and Pip started to fight which was when I was quickly yanked forward and I cried out when Pertinax grabbed hold of my neck.

"One snap is all it takes. Now lower your weapons," he ordered using me as bait.

"NO! Let her go!" Ari screamed and Sophia and Pip both stopped dead, turning around to see for themselves that unless they lowered their weapons, I was one dead and broken Keira. I closed my eyes in defeat once I heard the clatter of their blades, knowing now we had failed.

"Take them," he ordered his minions who each grabbed hold of my friends and started marching them down the hall.

"Now what to do with you? Let me see, I could just kill you now and leave you as a gift for Arsaces..." he said, suddenly spinning me back to face him and encircling my throat once more with his hand, using it to push me up against the wall as he started strangling me.

I desperately started to claw at his hand, trying in vain to tear it away from me, as my air supply started to run out quicker in my panic.

"But as tempting as that is, I think using you as leverage will be a far greater advantage to me at this present time." He looked back to see Sophia and Pip being dragged away and allowing this to happen because of what Pertinax currently held in his hand...*my life.* Then he pulled me closer until I could feel his breath hitting my skin, my own air quickly running out.

"It will at least keep his sister in check until the time comes to kill her but until then..." he paused so he could squeeze harder making my vision start to blur and I knew this was it, this was the end.

The last thing I heard was his sickening promise...

"Let's have some fun."

CHAPTER TWENTY-EIGHT

OPERATION DOMINIC

"Well that's another fine mess you've got us into, Stanley." Pip said laughing at her own joke.

"Hey, don't look at me, it was Sophia he wanted this time, so technically this doesn't count as a kidnapping." I told her as I slumped down in my own stone cell that looked as though it had been cut right out of a mountain.

"Yes and may I add that the first attempt had been unsuccessful." Sophia said adding her money's worth.

"Fifty/fifty odds then, not bad, much better than Keira's ninety/ten." Ari added, giggling when I shouted,

"Oi! What is this, pick on Keira day?!"

"No, just your usual snatch and grab day, with a little extra threaten Keira's life thrown in there for good measure," Pip answered on a chuckle making everyone laugh.

"Ha, ha! I am so reminding all you bitches about this when I am the one coming to rescue your asses next time!" I said, glad for the banter and keeping it going as long as it kept up our spirits.

"Yeah right."

"Like that's gonna happen any time soon."

"I won't hold my breath." They all said collectively but it was Ari's response that had me biting.

"Oi you! You can't say anything as I have already saved your ass once before, so you don't count! Oh and Electus here, so technically I save all your asses when the crappy prophecy ever happens."

"Yeah, she has a point."

"Totally got us all there."

"I guess that's true, she did save my life on that altar thingy when our uncle and mother tried to kill me, who weren't really related, thank God, just crazy cult people who wanted to take over the world…man, does anyone else think I might need therapy?" Ari asked making me smile.

"Oh that's nothing, try getting punished in Hell for accidently bringing a teeny tiny plague to Europe." Pip said as if this was nothing and Ari made a choking sound before saying,

"Tell me she is joking."

"Nope."

"Afraid not."

"It wasn't my fault!" The last one to speak was obviously Pip and she went on to tell Ari of how it wasn't too bad as this was how she met her husband, which must have stunned Ari to silence as there was no way anyone would have fallen asleep during this story.

Meanwhile I was still wondering where we were and if it was Ranka who had been the one to deceive us all along. Nobody else was sure on either question, so we quickly moved on to joking about our situation rather than freaking out about it.

The cells we were in were all bunched together but were

only big enough for one person to sit down in. They seemed to have been cut from the rock and each had crude bars made from stalagmites rising from the floor and stalactites that hung down from the ceiling, all interlocking as if the mountain had teeth.

I knew that these wouldn't have been enough to lock in the likes of Sophia and Pip and my first question would have been, 'can you not get out of them?' That was until I saw all the strange demonic symbols that had been etched all the way along the length of them.

I remembered seeing something like this before and it had been back in Draven's garage surrounding the large glass box that housed the strange silver Porsche. It didn't take a wild stab in the dark cave to know that these were some form of demonic spell to keep Sophia and Pip from escaping. Which then begged the question, how the hell were we gonna get out of this one?

"Anyway, it's been years since the last time I was kidnapped," Pip said as the conversation continued.

"Oh yeah, I remember that. It was the Cubans right, just after the Bay of Pigs invasion?" Sophia asked and I frowned knowing that I had definitely not heard this story.

"Yeah, the bastards heard about a weapon that was the most dangerous ever made!" Pip said, muttering *'Idiots'* to herself.

"What happened?" I asked.

"They were led by this dipshit Demon that used to be a somebody back when the Dead Sea Scrolls were a best seller." I laughed loving her reference to the ancient texts.

"I can't even remember the dude's name now but anyway he convinced these bloody Cubans that they could win the cold war by abducting me and letting who they thought was a weapons analyst know where they were keeping his wife and if he ever wanted to see me alive again…yada, yada, yada."

"Oh shit." I said and Sophia laughed,

"Oh shit indeed."

"Yeah they thought that he would be able to tell them where all the US hidden Nukes were kept or some shit like that. They had no clue that *he was the weapon,*" she said chuckling.

"I'm confused." Ari said and it was only now that I realised she had never seen the terrifying sight of Pip's husband in his Demon form.

"Adam is the most powerful Demon in history," I told her and no doubt Pip was currently beaming with pride hearing me say this.

"What, even more than Lucifer?" she asked and Pip made a 'Pah' noise before saying,

"That guy has nothing on my man."

"Then forgive me if I am being dim here but if this is the case then why isn't he ruling Hell or better yet, why didn't we bring him with us?" Ari asked making me laugh at the idea.

"Ever heard of the Hulk?" I asked making the others laugh.

"The comic book green guy?"

"Yeah, him."

"Yeah why?" she asked.

"Well think bigger, badder and more out of control…oh and did I say bigger because what I actually meant to say was think Godzilla bigger."

"Ah."

"Yep, that's my hubby," Pip said proudly.

"So what happened?" I asked getting back to the story.

"Well they nabbed me and stuck me on some deserted island in the Pacific Ocean and waited with their bait thinking it was gonna be an easy 'torture the prisoner until he talks' type of gig."

"And I gather it wasn't?" Ari asked.

"Not even close. But they got the torture part, just not the type they were hoping for," Pip said giggling.

"What she is trying to say was that the second Adam found

out she had been taken he went against every order to stop him and allow Lucius to handle it. It was the first time he knocked Lucius out cold...right?"

"Oh yeah, I'd forgotten about that bit, didn't he also do the same to Dom when he then had to intervene?" Pip asked Sophia.

"Oh yeah, I remember that. We tried to stop him at the airfield from getting on that private jet. He laid Dom out cold the second he told him that as his King he forbade his actions. I remember Vincent and I just holding up our hands in defeat after seeing Dom hit the floor and letting him go, before he could do the same to us." I could barely believe what I was hearing and was stunned just trying to picture it.

"Aww he's such a sweetheart... I miss him," Pip added in a forlorn voice.

"So what happened then?" This time it was Ari that was hooked.

"He took the plane, flying it himself after knocking out the pilot first of course."

"Of course," I said thinking this story included a lot of people getting hit by Adam, which I had to say surprised me as much as it didn't. Pip was without doubt his Achilles heel as were most women to the men who loved them.

"Then he crashed the plane after having nowhere to land it before jumping out of it mid Demon change. I remember those assholes' faces when they first heard his battle cry...*priceless,*" Pip said chuckling away to herself.

"Anyway, he not only killed every human waiting for him on the island, which thankfully didn't include any innocents, but he also destroyed the actual island itself," Sophia told us, helping Pip out with the story.

"Well you say destroyed but he did leave us a nice bit of

beach to have sex on until you guys turned up," Pip said in her husband's defence.

"Holy shit." I heard Ari mutter in astonishment before adding,

"Jeez, you weren't kidding."

"I will never forget Dom's face when Adam walked on the boat carrying Pip straight past him stating calmly 'I will never apologise for hitting you, for no one stops me from rescuing my wife, but I will thank you for bringing the boat'. Oh Gods it was priceless!" Sophia said laughing as my mouth dropped open.

"What did Draven say to that?" I asked flabbergasted.

"He took a step back and said, 'Understood.' Then I raised an eyebrow at him when he walked past me. I will never forget the way he just rubbed his sore jaw and said, 'What? Would you take him, 'cause I fucking wouldn't!' I think I saw Vincent near wet himself he was laughing that hard." Sophia told us making us all laugh as this time I could just picture it for myself.

"Trust us all to be locked up in a hopeless situation with a demonic banished megalomaniac, with an army of Romans waiting to destroy a city before taking over the world, and we are laughing about Pip's husband hitting my husband because he tried to stop his mass carnage and destroying an entire island!" I said near to tears with what I suspected was closer to hysteria than anything else.

"Forget about me, I think you lot need therapy!" Ari said before joining in.

"So I am curious, how did the world react to finding a King Kong attack on a Pacific island?" I asked after the laughter had calmed down.

"Oh now that's the genius part. See lucky for us the King knows high powered people in high powered places and considering things were still a bit testy with the US and Soviet Union in the early sixties, good old President John F. Kennedy was only too happy to help Dom out and drop a few 'test bombs' in the area. Am I right in saying he even named it 'Operation Dominic'?" she asked Sophia and I briefly heard her agree, however, I was still stuck on Draven asking the US President for a favour. And something as major as dropping a nuclear weapon on an island to cover up Adam's raging murder shit storm no less.

"You guys tell the best stories," Ari said and I had to agree with her there.

"Now if we could just figure out a way of making this a great escape story then we would have a real doozy to tell our grandkids one day," I replied and Pip sounded like she was choking,

"Seriously, did she just say the word doozy?!"

"What?" I asked.

"I am nearly nine hundred years old and even I don't say doozy!" Pip said laughing at me and I was surprised because I didn't know how old Pip was. Wow, nearly nine hundred years of causing trouble! I was surprised the world had survived her this long, I thought on a grin.

"Oh yeah, and I am getting stick from the girl who has called me every form of Toots since she met me!" I said making Ari giggle.

"Yeah but they're almost always sweet versions of it," she argued making me shrug my shoulders... mind you not that anyone could see me. Each of the cells were all on different levels with a slim cut staircase that interweaved in between each one and with us all being on the same side there was no way of seeing the one next to you.

"Good point. So any ideas about how to bust out of this joint?" I asked and after there was nothing but silence I couldn't help but say,

"Wow, that many."

"Well these symbols mean we can't touch them, so woman kick ass brute strength won't cut it this time," Pip answered and Sophia agreed,

"She's right, we would kind of just melt to the bone."

"And that's never pretty to watch," Pip added.

"Ssshh, someone's coming!" Ari hissed and she was right, from the sound of the footsteps above someone was coming, who though was yet to be seen.

"Which one did Master want?" I heard one of the voices snarl, which quickly told us all we were dealing with more than one.

"He wanted to play with the human bitch before she dies, the rest he wanted their heads mounting on pikes ready for the battle."

"Well I have to admit, that doesn't sound like much fun," Pip commented dryly and I couldn't tell if she just wasn't taking this new threat seriously or whether she just knew that she wouldn't be going down without a fight.

"Well, it's been nice knowing you ladies," Ari said in a wavering voice that told me how terrified she was but also how brave she was being by standing up to that fear.

"Always," I agreed.

"It's not over yet, just be ready to run," Sophia told us seriously and we heard the demonic laughter of whoever was coming. A sound that grated along my skin like a fork scraping on a china plate.

"Delusions of escape won't make it so, little girls." One said in a high pitched sneer.

"Yeah and we will just see how little I am when I am crushing your skull between my thighs!" Pip growled back. I think at that point I would have high fived her if I could, as if I was going to die right now then I couldn't imagine doing it any other way than standing tall with the girls I loved. I got to my feet, ready to take on the unknown enemy, as I refused to go down without a fight or still sit on my ass for that matter.

"I love you girls." I told them just before the first of the horrors stepped in front of my cell.

"Just keep that love alive, honey," Sophia said and I had to say that was going to be much harder said than done looking now at what we faced.

It looked as though burnt red skin had been stretched across the typical face of a Devil. He even had a chin that curled upwards mimicking the shape of his horns, that grew straight up from his forehead. These were also covered in the same skin and it was pulled so taut across the nose and high cheek bones that it created lines and ripples, flattening the nose bone underneath.

Its lips were none existent along his long slitted mouth, with only its teeth to be seen poking through the same reddish skin. Dotted glowing eyes grew brighter as they took in the sight of my fear.

His body was also covered in the same skin that had been stretched across a bony frame and each part seemed to be pierced with metal rings that all pulled painfully in the direction of the weight from the weapons they carried hooked onto them.

"This one has pretty flesh," said the one looking at me, raising a skinless finger that reminded me of sharpened bone in the shape of a spider's legs. The deadly long talon that had been carved at the end scraped along the length of the rock formation that was locking each of us in. The symbols all lit up one by one as he touched them.

I thought back to what Sophia had said about melting to the bone and wondered if maybe they were the only ones that could open the cells as they had no flesh on their hands?

Either way I knew we were all screwed if we didn't think of something and fast. I tried not to see them as they looked but view them as something else of this world that could be killed. I just needed to find a weakness and home into it. Focus on drawing up my energy and blasting it their way the second he opened the door.

Okay, so this was easier said than done as realistically when was the last time I could do anything helpful with these so called powers I had. Since I had been here that side of me had all gone to shit. No, I needed to think this through or at least hope that the others had a plan to win this fight.

My biggest worry had to be Ari who, along with the rest of us, still had no idea who she was. So as far as she was concerned, she was human and in this game that was not always a good thing. Power was the name in this game and without it, survival was the next on the list. I was surprised she had lasted as long as she had without falling to pieces. I sometimes forgot how hard this must have all been for her. After all I had been somewhat eased into this crazy life but for Ari, well she had been thrown in head first and then just expected to know how to swim upside down.

But her bravery at every turn had astounded me and for someone who was still on her own mission to figure out who she really was, then this just managed to make my respect for her double in size. Now all I could wish for was to see her happy and settled into this world I felt responsible enough for dragging her into and if that was with Vincent then all the better. Of course, these thoughts kind of went out the window considering my first wish was to see us all survive these ugly bastards and get the hell out of here and back to our men, speaking of which,

As I looked to the side to try and see how many Demons there were, that was when I first saw it...

A hooded shadow.

CHAPTER TWENTY-NINE

FLAMES THAT FALL

I blinked a few times just to check that my eyes weren't deceiving me. It had moved so swiftly I barely caught sight of it. But what I did see was one of the same demons fall silently to the floor behind the one that stood opposite me now. I only just managed to catch a glimpse of the blade sticking from its neck, glinting silver from the flaming torches as it went down.

My eyes widened in surprise when the hooded figure suddenly appeared directly behind the demon near me and his laughter quickly faded as he must have felt his presence standing there too. He turned quickly trying to catch him off guard but the hooded shadow was quicker. He simply sidestepped just as the demon tried to spear him in the gut with his dirty knife and instead, he grabbed his arm as it stretched out mid thrust, and snapped it down against the joint.

The demon howled in pain and held his dangling arm to his chest like a wounded dog tucking in his damaged limb.

"You will pay for that!" he promised but it quickly became an empty threat as the hooded figure spun around, kicking him to the bars, where his back instantly started to sizzle at the contact. The smell of cooking meat started to make me feel sick and I heard Pip briefly ask,

"Is someone cooking steak up there?"

The hooded figure ignored her and grabbed the demon's head towards him as he kicked out one of his legs so he fell to his knees. I heard the sickening snap of bone but had little chance to recover from it before another disgusting thing happened. He twisted the demon around and pressed his face against the stone bars making all the skin quickly melt off the bone and stick to the stalagmites. If I thought I was going to be sick before, then now I was actually having to turn around to *be sick*.

Just as I continued to heave up an empty stomach I briefly looked back just in time to see the hooded man grab the demon by the horns, positioning his hands ready for something. Then with one quick twist, he snapped his neck, killing him instantly and from the looks of things putting him out of his torturous misery.

The demon slumped forward still burning against the symbols, his flesh sliding away in great big chunks leaving nothing but bloody bone beneath. Then I watched as he placed a foot to the back of the demon's neck, grab the horns again and this time when he jerked his body sideways, he did so with enough force that he ripped the demon's head clean away from the rest of its body.

Unsurprisingly this had me heaving again but nothing would come up.

"Stand back!" The man growled an order and I did as I was told, placing my back flat against the far wall of my cell and wiping the spit away from my lips with my sleeve. The man stepped over the body and kicked back so that the headless demon rolled over the side of the steps and down to somewhere I couldn't see. Then with the head still held by one horn in his hand, he swung it up, gripped it a certain way so that he could place the horns through the rock formations sideways.

I had no clue what he was doing but noticed that the horns didn't burn against the symbols the way the flesh had done. Which suddenly dawned on me, was he using the demon's skull as some sort of key?

My question was quickly answered when, in one quick motion, he twisted his body downwards and the action caused the horns to break apart the stalagmites and stalactites, making them crack all the way to the top until they all started to crumble to the floor. My natural instincts took over as I covered my head with both hands.

"Get out!" he ordered in a stern voice before moving along with the skull still held firmly in his grasp. As soon as I heard the cracking sound of rock next to me, I knew that he was using this to open the rest and free us all.

"Cool!" I heard Pip shout after her cell was next.

"Hurry, this way," he said once we were all free. I looked back to see the guy had taken out the four demons that were sent to get us, five including the headless body that looked to be at the bottom of some ravine.

"Not exactly a man of many words," Ari said to me after I gave her the once over checking she wasn't hurt.

"No, but of many deadly actions, which right now is better than being able to talk them to death."

"Good point," she said agreeing with me, for it was true, I couldn't have cared if he didn't know more than the seven words he had spoken already. As long as he was good with the sword that hung from his waist, I was more than happy with that.

"Let's move," he snapped back and Ari leaned into me and said,

"Well, there's two more," before winking at me and walking on ahead. We followed the hooded man whose every step seemed to be with well thought out reason and purpose. His hood hid his face well enough for none of us to know who he was, but considering it was obvious that he could have killed us all before we blinked, then it wasn't farfetched to assume he was here to help us.

He was mainly wearing all black, with a long cloak that strapped across his chest. He also wore some sort of long tunic style jacket with thick metal clasps holding it shut. Leather straps crisscrossed around his chest and waist, each holding an array of different blades and weapons in place for easy reach. Black leather trousers were strapped tight around his legs with cord and he reminded me of some ancient looking highwayman, ready for a night's ambush.

We continued along a series of makeshift steps that had been chipped away in the stone to get us from one walkway to another. It was obvious we were inside a mountain or underground in some secret network of caves, because the only thing that lit our way were the burning torches that were anchored to the bare stone walls.

"Not the best place for someone scared of heights," I muttered as we got to a narrow part and had to hug the wall to fit along the jagged rock path that had a sheer drop on one side.

"How much further?" Sophia asked looking around and sounding all businesslike.

"Not...wait!" We never found out what he would have said as he raised a quick hand to stop us all from moving.

"They know, hurry!" he said and just after this we heard a

horn being blown that echoed through the honeycomb of tunnels using the walls to travel along. This was when we started to pick up pace and after turning a corner a space suddenly opened up in front of us. It brought us out into a gigantic opening that looked as though it had once been two mountains next to each other that had then fallen together from an earthquake and this was what space was left in between. Well, if I thought the drop before looked bad then this one was something else, for you couldn't even see the bottom.

There were natural bridges dotted along the cavernous space that joined the two sides but I think if asked to cross one I might have found myself the one at the back quickly wussing out. Some areas across them looked narrow enough that even a wheelbarrow would struggle getting across.

"Brace yourselves for here they come!" Sophia said looking back and pointing at what looked like a demon army heading our way. Another horn blew and this time it was followed by an echoing dong sound.

"A weapon! We need weapons!" Sophia cried as the first wave hit the stranger head on. He quickly made short work of them as he had done back in the cells. In three swift moves all three of them were down and falling off the side into the endless canyon. It seemed every move he made was a killing blow and it looked utterly flawless.

Then came the clash of weapons as he slashed out sideways at the next set but this time as each of them fell he would catch their weapon and hand it back until we all had one. He was just kicking a body off the side to make room for us to run through, when he looked back over our heads.

"Pip, you get at the back and I will get in between the girls!" Sophia shouted after following his line of vision, letting me pass her so that I was right behind our mystery saviour.

"Get ready, for here they come again!" Pip shouted back

before turning to face the demons. We continued to move but this way it was slower with us continually getting surrounded with each new wave. I looked back to see Pip was swinging her battle axe smiling the whole time. Forget clowns and strippers at her next birthday party, just give her a war to fight and she would have been as happy as a dog in a muddy puddle.

"COME ON, YOU FUGGLIES!" she screamed, laughing as she mowed them down, flinging them off the side like they were nothing but cardboard cut outs. I looked down at my own short blade that was slightly curved and shaped like a Gurkha knife. I tried to ignore the fact that the handle looked as if it had been made out of part of a femur bone and fused together with some thick black tar-like substance that had hardened solid.

Another horn sounded and this time it was for longer, which was quickly followed by a collective howling sound, like a horde of beasts had just been released. It turned out that I wasn't that far off as Sophia suddenly shouted,

"Gorgon leeches!" after she had effectively beheaded one of the demons.

"Oh no," I muttered and Ari gave me a panicked look.

"I take it we are not dealing with cute little demon puppies?"

"No, try the things that would most likely eat them," I told her and then Pip looked over shoulder at us and added,

"And then puke them back up only to eat them again." Then she swung her axe up, getting one demon in the man parts without even looking.

"Up ahead, we cross over there," the man said taking no notice of us as he sliced into the chest of one demon, causing him to fall into another, taking him over the side with him. Thankfully, there seemed to be a break in the demons ahead of us so we picked up the pace and ran faster to where we could see men battling it out on the other side.

"Friends of yours?" Sophia asked but unsurprisingly the man ignored her and continued on.

"Look out! Above us!" Ari shouted raising up her weapon just as the first wave of Gorgons hit us. I slashed out and ducked out of the way as the dead body of a gorgon leech fell from above me. These looked slightly different to the ones I remembered back on the cliff face where I first saw them.

Instead of cracked skin over twisted mangled bodies, they had slightly thicker limbs that split at the joints. Their skin looked to be dusted in ground stone and wet cement but their bleeding eyes were covered in dirty bandages, whereas their snapping teeth were entwined with spiked metal wire, making them even deadlier than usual. Some even looked to have their entire bodies covered with the stuff and these were the ones you had to watch dropping from above as both Ari and I got snagged by a few.

"Go past!" the man told us, ready to take them on alone. We did as we were told with Pip and Sophia now taking the lead and trying to get to where he told us to cross. I looked behind me just in time to see him unhook a wired glass vial from one of the many leather straps around his waist and throw it up as high as he could so that it smashed above the Gorgons, raining liquid down above them.

This didn't look as if it had done much damage until he hammered his heavy sword down on one of the torches, freeing it so that he could catch it. Then he swung it up like he had done with the vial and boom! The second the fire touched the first leech, the rest of them caught fire one after the other like a wave of flames was rolling over the lot of them.

"GO!" he shouted to me as I watched him following behind us running with the sight of flaming leeches falling from above and into the gorge below. They looked like blazing lanterns from a distance lighting the dark chasm below as they fell.

I did as I was told but found myself coming to a dead stop as the path in front of me started to crumble away. Thankfully the others made it ahead of me and just as I was turning around to tell our hooded saviour about our new problem, I felt myself being picked up by the waist and anchored under his arm.

"What are you...AHHH!?" My question was cut short as I screamed as I found myself suddenly flying over the deadly drop as he jumped us both over it. I thought I would fall forward and put my hands out to catch myself but never got there. He righted me before pushing me on the back to me keep running to join up with the others.

The rest were just getting to the other side of the bridge to join the armed men that were fighting the same demon foes as we had been. We were about to run over when I was suddenly yanked back and held against the wall by a strong arm across my chest. I was about to ask why when I followed his gaze up to see a huge jagged boulder come crashing down with ropes snapping all around it. I looked then to the other side to see where those ropes led to and it became obvious the demons had destroyed the bridge in order to trap us on this side by cutting the net that held it in place. The boulder smashed its way through the narrow stone arch from above, shattering it as though it had been made of glass.

"Is there another way across?" I asked.

"Come with me." He grabbed my hand and pulled me behind him, swinging me to his back and then to his front, whenever an enemy got near so he could fight them head on and I was out of danger.

"There, up ahead." He nodded to a single rope bridge that looked to have half broken slats across, obviously the one they used before the stone bridge was made. I did as he said knowing I had a better chance of surviving the bridge than I did the demon horde still headed our way. Although the second I stepped on it and it started to sway I couldn't help but take a step back.

"Go!" the man ordered but I started shaking my head, telling Mr Indiana Jones at my back,

"I don't think I can do this."

"Fucking Humans!" he snapped suddenly, placing a hooded shoulder to my waist and lifting me up and over into a fireman's lift.

"Oh my God, don't drop me! Shit, shit, shit! Don't die, please don't die," I repeated as I had no choice but look down directly into the terrifying drop below. We got to the centre of the bridge when he let me slide down the front of him. I looked up at him, noticing for the first time how tall he was and from this angle I could just see his sandy coloured stubble covering his chin. He looked one way and then the other and I followed his motions, quickly realising why he had stopped in the middle of the bridge. His men had moved down to meet us as they still fought against wave after wave of Pertinax's supernatural army.

I could see they were getting closer to the cave's opening and knew that if they just made it out then they had a chance. I would have liked to have said the same for us but the second the demons spotted us on the bridge I knew we were done for. I watched in horror as each of them started to grab the torches off the wall and run towards us.

"Occidere eos!" The man at my back shouted, ordering his men and pointing to the danger ahead. (means 'Kill them' In Latin) They saw the demons running for us and quickly started firing arrows at them. They all took shot after shot but kept running until all but one were dead. He fell forward just at the end of the bridge, setting it alight like he had sacrificed his life to do just this.

"We need to get back!" I shouted but just as we looked the other way, we saw some of the gorgon leeches he had set alight had managed to crawl their way back up the sides of the gorge.

"The bridge! We need to get off the bridge!" I shouted just as three of them reached over the ropes of the bridge, setting it alight as well. The blaze was travelling towards us at too fast a rate and I knew that we would either be burned alive or the bridge would soon give out and we would plummet to our deaths anyway.

I looked to Sophia, Pip and Ari on the other side, seeing them through the flames crying out to me. Ari was on her knees screaming, reaching out her arms to me. Sophia was shouting orders for the men to try and reach us in time and Pip was holding the top of her head in her hands, as though she couldn't bear to watch. I swallowed hard knowing that this was it. There was nothing more to be done. All I could hope for was that they made it back to our time and Sophia would have the chance to tell Draven all I had done to try and save his world and mine. This in the hopes that one day, in the Heavens maybe, we could be together once again.

It was only a dream but when you faced death as much as I seemed to do, then all we had left was our dreams to give us comfort. Our hopes that when facing impossible odds there was a place for us at the end of it all, one that would be a welcomed reprieve from the chaos and destruction that put us there in the first place. This was something I had to believe in.

I felt the bridge start to go, tipping to one side as the first of the ropes burned away. The flames were getting closer towards us and just before they could touch us, I felt the man grab me close and suddenly there was a darkness as I felt the floor beneath us start to fall as we plunged to our deaths. The rest of the bridge fell into the abyss and as the man tightened his grip around me he told me to,

"Hold on!" There was only one name that escaped my lips and for the first time in the face of death it wasn't Draven's, it was the man whose voice I'd just heard.

Our shadowed saviour…

"Lucius."

CHAPTER THIRTY

KILLER PERSONALITY

The last thing I heard was my name being screamed from above as we fell down with the middle section of the bridge. However, the only thing I could think about right now was dying in Lucius' arms, of all people. He had wrapped his cloak around me to protect me from the growing flames so all I could do was feel my death, not actually be able to see it when it came. I suppose I was glad of this for instead of being petrified of the fear, I was getting ready to say goodbye to my life and accept my fate.

I didn't know how long I had left to do this but in those short moments I saw a glimpse of Draven stood waiting for me at the altar. It was our wedding day and just as I imagined it would be, him standing there in a tux, looking as handsome as the day I met him and smiling at seeing his bride for the first time. The grin he gave me lit up his eyes and spoke volumes of the pure happiness he felt in that single moment.

Then it all disappeared.

The feeling of falling suddenly jerked to a halt and as it did the cloak that covered me fell away letting me see for myself what had happened. I cried out in fear as the deadly drop below was far from over. Now it simply loomed there below me as Lucius had one arm banded around my waist and was currently hanging off the rocks with his other hand gripped to a ledge.

He swung us both a bit before quickly flipping my body up with enough strength that it flung me up and over onto the ledge above. I landed with an 'umpf' jarring my not completely healed rib cage as I rolled a few times. Then I looked up to see not one hand but two grip the edge before Lucius hoisted himself up the rest of the way to join me on the ledge.

I stood up, wincing slightly but glad to feel the pain because that way I knew I was still alive. I walked over to Lucius and said,

"So what now?" In fact, what I would have preferred to say was, thank God it's you and thank you for saving my life yet again, but I had to remember that he had no clue as to who I was. He looked down at me as if only now remembering that I was still there and he took so long before speaking that I didn't think that he would answer me at all.

"Do you hear the water?" he asked and I took a moment to listen but it was obvious his hearing was far more acute than mine was. I gave him a look and shrugged my shoulders telling him no, which had me wondering if I could see his face would I have seen him rolling his eyes at me?

I looked down to see if I could see anything but it was too dark and I knew that if I couldn't hear the water, then it was still a long way down.

"Do you swim?" I frowned up at him and said,

"Yeah, why?" This time he didn't answer me but instead he just picked me up and tossed me over the edge without so much as a warning. I screamed as I fell down but at least had the good sense to hold my nose as I crashed into the freezing water below. The force of my landing meant my head went under the water but thankfully holding my nose meant that when I resurfaced I wasn't coughing and spluttering for air as I had held my breath.

I couldn't see anything but I heard something crashing into the water behind me. The current of the water was dragging me along but the second I felt something grab me I screamed. I started flinging my arms around in the dark as all I could think about was the gorgons that had fallen down here, wondering if one of them had survived.

"Be still, woman!" Lucius snapped, calming me enough with the sound of his voice, letting me know that it wasn't something demonic that wanted to take a chunk out of me in the dark! He didn't say anything else once I had stopped trying to drown us both and he had fitted himself securely against my back. Then he started manoeuvring us both through the underground river, moving us from side to side and obviously avoiding any obstacles he could see in the dark.

We both bobbed along silently with me shivering in his arms and breathing heavily as I kicked my feet underneath the water trying to stay afloat in the current. I had to admit I doubted I would have achieved this as gracefully as I looked, without Lucius at my back helping me stay steady.

Thankfully up ahead I could finally see a small speck of light that the further we travelled the bigger it got.

"Turn around and hold on to me."

"Uh…why?" I asked not liking the sound of that but doing as I was told anyway because in the face of all the things I didn't like, I still didn't want to be stupid enough not to listen and die from them. He didn't answer me as I faced him but just nodded up ahead. I turned my head to look over my shoulder knowing what I would see because I could hear it before I could see it.

"Oh shit." This was all I had chance to say before we both went crashing over the waterfall and I was sure my grip was so tight on his neck that I wouldn't have been surprised if I ended up strangling him before we hit the bottom.

"You asshole! You could have killed me!" I screamed at him after coughing up a reservoir of water and smacking him on the arm. I would have remained angry if it weren't for the fact that I was getting momentarily side tracked by the sight of him undressing. He had his back to me so I hadn't yet seen his face fully but the sight of his muscular tanned back was making me shake my head to try and get some sense back to my brain.

"Uh…what are you doing?" He looked back over his shoulder at me briefly and said,

"I thought that would have been obvious to a Concubine."

I was utterly outraged!

"I am not going to have sex with you! What did you think, that I would just drop my harem pants as a way of saying thanks for saving my life! Oh my God, somethings never change! Seriously will there ever be a point in history when you're not trying to get into my…"

"Undress."

"Excuse me?" I snapped putting a hand on my hip.

"To see a man undress is something you would be used to," he clarified making me go beetroot in colour with shame as it finally dawned on me what he had meant.

"Oh, I thought you…" I tried to back track and explain but he cut in and said,

"I know what you thought, woman." I mouth the word *'woman'* behind his back wondering if he always made it sound like a bad thing or was he always this much of an ass around the opposite sex?

"Well you still could have warned me before just throwing

me over the bloody ledge!" I grumbled turning my back on him just in case he decided to start taking off his pants.

"So what now?" I asked looking around at the endless barren land that stretched out for miles around us. When he didn't answer me I glimpsed back over my shoulder at him to see he was bent down on one knee doing something with his weapons. Well at least he still had his pants on I thought wryly. I decided this was getting me nowhere so I stormed over to face him and put my hands on my hips.

"I know you don't have any problems using words so I would appreciate an answer," I snapped, which after even more silence I realised it still had no effect on him. He continued to take stock of his vast weapon collection as he lay them all out in front of him. His cloak, tunic and under shirt had all been wrung out and were laid upon a rock so that the sun could do its work.

"Answer me!" I demanded getting pissed off with this pointless silent treatment. He simply raised his head up a bit and looked at me as if he had honestly just realised I was there. I couldn't see his face fully thanks to the sun at my back, which I could feel was powerful enough to start drying my clothes.

"I will go to the King," he told me.

"You mean 'We'." I corrected and Lucius stood up making me take a step back. He walked up to me and said,

"There is no 'we'," then he briefly looked down at me before walking past.

"Uh, I beg to differ on that one, as I am coming with you," I told him sternly, spinning around to face him. He was bent over the manmade pool that captured the water from the waterfall before it was then channelled back into an underground tunnel. It looked like some ancient version of an aqueduct. He was filling some sort of animal skin flask before dipping his head under the water and flipping it back out again. I sidestepped as the water splattered back at me, wiping the drops angrily off my face as I said,

"Did you hear me, I said I am coming with you," I told him again.

"No you're not," he told me turning to face me and pushing all of his wet hair from his eyes. It was the first time I finally got a good look at his face and he was utterly and annoyingly, breathtaking. His skin was a lush golden colour and his long hair was like the desert sand highlighted with almost white blonde streaks from obviously spending days riding in the sun. Which begged the question, why was Lucius, who I knew didn't like the sun, out in it in this ancient time?

I knew it wouldn't harm him as the legends would have you believe about Vampires, but he had made it clear a few times how he loathed it. So what had happened to him between now and my time to make him change? It obviously wasn't only his aversion to the sun that was different as the Lucius I knew certainly was a lot more vocal, that was for sure.

I had to wonder if by being a Vampire, the effects of it over the years hadn't changed him? Like a man without the light locked in a dark cell could slowly become blind, given enough time without it.

And speaking of eyes, the same intense mix of steel grey and ice blue eyes looked at me now as if seeing me for the first time also. His muscles flexed as though feeling something strange and not liking what it was, that or the sight of me was just making his skin crawl, I thought bitterly.

"Look you may not like it, but you can't do anything to stop me from coming with you," I told him and he raised an eyebrow at me, making me want to roll my eyes back at him. I was quickly getting sick of dealing with big macho alphas doing that at me.

"That would be a mistake to assume, little girl." Oh great, the little girl comment, like I hadn't heard that one before!

"I don't understand, why go to all the effort to rescue me if you are just going to leave me here stranded?"

"My only objective was to rescue the Princess, which I accomplished," he told me leaning back against the stone wall that surrounded the water deposit and folding his arms across his chest, making his biceps bulge in that mouth drooling way. Focus Keira, don't think about that kiss in the tower or the way his arms locked around you…don't do it…damn, I did it!

"Do you have any idea who I am?" I asked hating the spoiled way it sounded. He looked me up and down making me want to hide the way my outfit was now glued to me like a second skin, making me feel naked under his scrutinising gaze.

"The King's Concubine." I hated the way he said it but I hated even more the way he added,

"I hear he has many." This made it sound like I was no one but a well kept whore and was deluding myself into believing otherwise.

"I am his 'Chosen Concubine'." I told him hoping this would have a greater effect on him but he merely shrugged before saying,

"I met one of those once, she was also as spoilt as you are and born with a bag of silver in each hand." My mouth dropped open briefly before anger made it slam shut.

'You think I grew up with a silver spoon in my mouth! I grew up in a cul-de-sac in Liverpool, where our nearest bus stop had a window missing for three years! I had one neighbour who collected broken lawn mowers in the front of his house and another woman who used Christmas paper to cover her windows instead of curtains and named her cats after the days of the week… and she had three Tuesdays!" I shouted to Lucius who was looking at me as though I had lost my mind, but I didn't care.

"Look, I don't care what your personal issues with women are, I mean hell, for all I know you could have a fancy for other men in this time…" Oh now this got him moving. He stormed straight over to me and loomed into my personal space, quickly commanding it. I was just happy that I actually managed to provoke more than an icy response from him.

"I will happily show you what women like you are best meant for if that is your wish, for you are somewhat pretty enough for my taste…that taste having no cock in sight, is that understood?" he told me sternly and I swallowed hard before saying a small croaky,

"Understood."

"Good, then its settled," he said nodding once and moving away from me back to his weapons.

"Good, I'm glad. Now which way is it back to the city?" I asked turning back to the distance ahead and placing a hand over my eyes to shadow the sun.

"You will stay here." This yet again had me frowning.

"What!? No way, I am not being left here to die!" I protested as he started dressing back in what looked like his assassin gear.

"You have water and there are caves over there for cover. When I get back to the city I will let the King know you are here and *if* he still wants you, then he will send his people to get you." I hated the way he said 'if' like he doubted it and I swear at this point I think my eyes were twitching I was that mad! How was I going to get it through to this idiot version of Lucius how important this was?

"Oh right, so you are going to leave me next to a cave full of flesh eating Gorgon leeches and Pertinax's personal Hell army of demons whilst you go on your merry way…oh I don't think so!" I said stamping my foot. He raised himself up slowly and turned his head to look at me as if I had only just entered into this mess.

"And what do you know of Gorgons and Demons?" he asked me as though this should be impossible.

"Hello, I was in there too you know, what do you think I thought was chasing us, unicorns and pixies with sharp teeth?!" I snapped.

"You could see them?" he asked in a serious tone that told me Ooops, I had made a mistake, as it was obvious now that I shouldn't have been able to see them. Which had me wondering, had he tried to mask my memory of it the second we were out of danger? I couldn't see any other way, as it wasn't like I would have thought Roman soldiers could have scaled cave walls like that and on fire no less.

"That's what I have been trying to tell you! I am different and not just any Concubine." Oh yeah, now he was taking this seriously, especially when he quickly picked up a blade and had it pointed at my throat.

"Whoa! Easy there."

"Speak!" He ordered giving me a look as though he was only a breath away from killing me. I swallowed hard again and knew that this was it, I had to tell him everything.

"I am from the future, okay." Unfortunately, this sounded as ridiculous as I thought it would and his face said it all, so I quickly carried on.

"I came back in time with the others you rescued to save the world and stop the biggest war between Demons and Angels from breaking out on Earth." He looked at me a moment longer and pulled back his blade making me sigh with relief.

"I see…and the King, he knows of this?"

"Well, no, see I haven't been able to…" I started to try and make my point when he held up a hand to stop me.

"Say no more, for I understand now."

"Oh thank the…"

"Your mind has long been lost," he said interrupting me and basically telling me that he thought I was crazy before I could thank my lucky stars too soon.

"Look, ever heard of a prophecy? The words Apocalypse, Armageddon, end of days or even Judgement Day mean anything to you?! I am the King's Electus and I was sent here to…"

"Stop!" he commanded, silencing me for a second before I asked,

"What?"

"Say that again?" I thought back to what I had said and homed in on the word I knew he would respond to.

"I am his Electus," I told him, slower this time.

"How would you know of this?" he asked in a low, suspicious voice.

"That's what I am trying to tell you! I am his Electus and I was sent here to try and prevent the end of the world back in my time!"

"He would know if you were his Electus, for it is prophesied that once he sees her…"

"Yes, yes, I know all this, he would know instantly who I was, but we have been masking it from him." This had him frowning again.

"How?"

"My friend, the small one with the axe, she is an Imp and her gifts include being able to manipulate what people see, including Draven…I mean the King." I corrected shaking my head.

"Draven?"

"His name back in my time."

"And I am also in this time?" he asked obviously wanting to

know as most would. I took a deep breath knowing that finally he was listening to me and at least starting to think me slightly less crazy. This was proven shortly after I said,

"Yes, that's how I knew your name was Lucius."

"Call me Septimus, everyone else does."

CHAPTER THIRTY-ONE

WE HAD A THING ONCE

If I thought travelling across the desert was hard the first time, then doing so in a pair of flimsy slippers was next to being torturous! It quickly became obvious that this was Lucius' thing or at least what he lived for in this time. He was like some kind of Bear Grylls of the ancient world, knowing what we could eat and what would soon kill us or more importantly, what would kill *me,* considering I was the only mortal one in this situation.

When we had first started out he had unwrapped the sash from his waist and wrapped it around his head like a turban.

"Don't suppose you have another one of those hiding under there do you?" I asked nodding to the layers upon layers of hidden equipment he had on him. He just raised an eyebrow at me and walked on.

"I will take that as a no then," I muttered to myself and then ran a little to keep up with him.

"Then can I have yours…you know, considering you won't die of sunstroke or anything?" I asked trying my luck.

"No, but I can still burn," he said walking ahead of me again and I couldn't help but mutter,

"Pussy" in my anger.

"Fine, but just so you know that if I pass out then you're the one left carrying my ass!" This time he did stop and take notice of me. Then without a word he walked back to me, took me by the waist and I shrieked when he suddenly ripped a strip of fabric from my belly, quickly turning my tunic into a crop top.

"Oi!" I shouted at him after he just threw the long length of torn silk back at me.

"Now my belly is gonna burn!" I protested and he just calmly stated back,

"Yes, but you won't die from it." And then he continued walking, giving me no other choice but to follow, grumbling as I went. I wrapped the stupid length of silk around my head struggling the first few times to get it to stay and stop falling down.

And this was how our journey had begun.

At first I had been concerned that we weren't heading in the right direction as there was no city in sight. He begrudgingly informed me that we were following something called a qanāt which, from what I understood, was a Persian aqueduct, something the Persians were famous for building many years ago. It was mainly a gently sloping underground channel with a series of vertical access shafts, used to transport water from an aquifer under a hill. This way with the water travelling direct to the city below ground, it avoided any contamination and provided all year-round water supply. From what I also understood, they were channelled off to irrigate crops and the many surrounding gardens that the Persians were also famous for.

Of course most of this information I had to drag out of Lucius and it had been after hours of trying. At the beginning of our journey it had been mainly me trying to convince him further that what I was saying was true. Which not surprisingly, he still looked unconvinced for the most parts but so long as he was letting me tag along, then getting back to Draven in time was all I cared about.

"Back in your own time, you say I knew you?" he asked once I had caught back up to him yet again, as this seemed to be the theme of our journey…damn his long legs!

"Yeah, we knew each other." I told him dryly thinking back to how we first got acquainted.

"Because of the King?" Again this had me biting my tongue as I knew I had to be careful with what I told him, considering the feud between them didn't happen for some time yet and that was one can of worms I never wanted to be the one to open!

"Yes, although in my time you sort of went your separate ways for a time. But you have helped him save my life a few times," I said trying to skip past the complicated bit and emphasise more on the friendship we had, thinking if he knew we 'kinda had a thing' then he would cut me some slack in this time period.

"And the need for that happens a lot in your time?" he asked giving me a sideways glance. I laughed once and said,

"Unfortunately yes."

"Because you are this 'Electus' you spoke of?"

"I guess it comes with the territory," I said shrugging my shoulders.

"You are your own ruler of land?" he asked getting confused with the saying.

"What? Oh, no, that's not what I…never mind. It just means that the King's enemies usually want to use me either as bait or to kill me." Unbeknown to him of course, he was also in this unfortunate category.

"Is that what Pertinax wanted with you?" he asked.

"No, he just thought I meant something to the King but has no clue as to who I really am."

"And the King?" I gave him a confused look when he asked this.

"What about the King?"

"You said before that he also doesn't know who you really are, is this true?"

"Yes, that's right." I answered wondering where he was going with this.

"Then why would Pertinax believe the King would care what happens to one Concubine, when he has many?"

"Yes, yes, you keep saying that!" I snapped not wanting to be labelled like that with the rest of them.

"Because he loves me," I told him when he still looked at me for an answer. His short laugh had me close to growling at him.

"That is impossible."

"Oh jeez, thanks…don't hold back will you."

"He is only destined to love one human, as the Gods have permitted and what has been prophe…"

"Prophesied, yeah I know. 'Chosen One' remember. Besides what can I say, what is meant to be, is just meant to be." I told him.

"Like you travelling back in time?" he counteracted, which I had to admit, got me stumped.

"You still don't believe me?" I challenged.

"If what you told me is true, of what the King now faces alone thanks to time changing, then I fail to see how by making our time worse, you are therefore making yours better." Okay so he had a major point there and it didn't help that my only come back sounded as lame as it was in real life,

"We didn't plan for that to happen."

"Then tell me, what was your plan exactly, for I fail to see any gain in this?" At this point I was happy to go back to him just ignoring me.

"You know I think I liked you much better when you were always trying to get into my pants." I said forgetting myself. He stopped dead and I took a few steps ahead before stopping myself on a groan,

"Look don't make it an issue, it's not like we ever actually did it...well there was that one time with all the mud but that wasn't real and then in the tower but we stopped and..."

"Silence!" he hissed pulling me back roughly to him. I face planted his chest coming far too close to one of his many blades.

"Just so you know, I think having a nose suits me and I would like to keep it that way." I said trying to pull back but he just held me tighter and hissed down at me,

"I said quiet!" Then I followed his nod up ahead and saw what looked to have been left there from the Gods...*Horses.* Then of course I saw the Arabian looking bandits and that hope quickly deflated into a floppy mess and my body sagged against Lucius in what I hoped was only disappointment and not exhaustion like I suspected. Either way he held me up with his arm, curling me tighter against his side.

"I am going to sit you behind these rocks, don't come out until I say...understood?" I would have come back with a witty reply but my brain was too fatigued to even try. He slid me down where he said and pointed to the ground once more, telling me to stay there like a dog. Well just so long as this loyal pet was soon going to find themselves on the back of a horse, then I didn't give a shit what he called me.

I felt as though we had been walking for days or even weeks, not just the hours we had been. I had told Lucius of the importance of us getting there, knowing that without Sophia and Vincent to fight by his side, then all could be lost. He didn't seem too surprised about this, obviously knowing of the 'it takes three to take down the big bad Demon' thing. But when I asked him what he knew of Pertinax, this was when it was my turn to be surprised.

I found out during one of our brief stops for water and rest, that Lucius was actually an Assassin for Pertinax causing me to lose my temper and was close to losing my mind very quickly.

"Calm yourself, it is not what you think," he told me acting like he was simply dealing with an irrational human girl at the time and this was all very taxing on the poor killer for hire. Thankfully though he quickly explained that this was planned by the King and himself, for Lucius was not known to have an alliance with anyone at this time, let alone the King. Draven wanted to find a way of keeping a close watch on the Persian Devil who wanted him dead and thought that Lucius was just the man to do it.

But in order for him to play his part Lucius had to first become a supernatural weapon for hire before insinuating himself as Pertinax's right hand man and that meant recently killing the previous Emperor, Commodus only three months ago. This was how he knew about the successful attempt on kidnapping the Princess and quickly made plans to save her so that she couldn't be used against Draven in battle.

In fact, the original plan was for Lucius himself to go and kidnap Sophia with some of Pertinax's men, which he had planned on killing right alongside Draven when they reached the throne room.

Of course this was the version of events I had heard from Sophia, minus the small important detail of Lucius being involved. This might have been helpful but unfortunately still wouldn't have changed things because the major flaw in all of this was now...*me.*

Unknowingly, I had changed the course of history just by

being here, meaning that Sophia was not where she ought to be and also that Lucius wasn't there to intervene and convince Pertinax to let him take charge of the kidnapping.

I had asked him if he thought Sophia would get back in time and he assured me that his men were loyal to only him and that unlike us, they had horses waiting for them outside of the cave. All I could hope for was that I made it back in time to witness the fall of Pertinax the way Sophia had told me it would happen.

Now all we needed was a horse for ourselves and a chance for this miracle to happen. We didn't have long in the day left and I knew we would never make it there by sunset, not on foot anyway. Plagued with these thoughts I decided to peek over the rocks and see what was going on and how operation 'Horse steal' was going.

The second I saw the spray of blood coming from Lucius' blade as it sliced one of the bandits clean in half, I wished I hadn't. I realised very quickly that operation 'Horse steal' had quickly turned into operation 'let no man live'.

I couldn't help but start heaving, wondering where my hardy stomach had gone for these types of things? Maybe I was getting soft and needed to start watching more horror films when I got back. Okay, considering the majority of the time my life was one big horror story, given the number of attempts on my life was quickly racking up, I didn't think I needed to add any fake horror into this.

For starters I think that if an actual slasher baddie, serial killer came after me I would be like 'whatever asshole, get back to me after you have had a trip to Hell and then see if you can take me'. I knew this was big headed of me but the way I felt after dealing with Demons all these years, well then humans were gonna be a piece of cake…unless of course, you had a Roman army stood in your way, then… not so much.

"You can come out now." Lucius said wiping the blood off his blade with one of the men's turbans. Well from the looks of it, he certainly didn't need it now, I thought once again gagging from the sight. Six men all lay around dead but it could have been more, given how many pieces there were now spread across the sand.

"Were you trying to set a new record or something," I asked feeling myself turning green. He chose to ignore my comment and instead ordered me to,

"Get on." I gave him a wide eyed, 'Are you kidding' look as I looked up at the massive horse.

"Do you want to get there before nightfall?" he asked and I groaned knowing this was going to be a hard concept for him to grasp, but I felt I had little choice.

"I don't know how to ride a horse," I told him trying not to look embarrassed.

"There are no horses left in your time?" he asked and I inwardly groaned.

"There are but they are only ridden as a hobby, nobody depends on them for travel anymore," I told him knowing what question was coming next.

"Then how do you travel?"

"It's complicated but trust me when I say…you will love it," I said thinking back to the day I saw his own multi million-dollar collection of cars and knowing like Draven, what a speed freak he was. He raised an eyebrow at me and said,

"Fine, but it will slow our horse."

"Trust me when I say, so will I when I keep getting kicked off it." He rolled his eyes at me and then before he even gave me warning, I was being lifted next to the biggest horse of the lot and hoisted over its back. I was quickly starting to see another theme of the day and it included Lucius just doing what the hell he wanted with me. *Well, not everything,* I thought blushing.

The horse started acting skittish by bobbing its head up and down a few times, which quickly made me uneasy.

"Ahh...whoa, easy there," I said thinking these were the sorts of things you hear people saying to horses to get them to steady. Luckily for me Lucius wasn't far behind and pulled himself up, shifting closer to my back and fitting me snug in between his legs.

"Uh...we could swap places if that would be better." *Please be better, please be better*, I muttered in my head not knowing how long I could last with Lucius holding me this close.

"We wouldn't want you getting kicked off now, would we?" he whispered in my ear from behind and then reached around to grab the reins making me suck in a breath. The feeling of him being this close made me shut my eyes for a second trying to keep a cool head. What was it being around this guy that always had me all tied up in knots? Even like this where he was so different to how I was used to dealing with him. It was as if something in our own fates was also entwined as much as I was with Draven. Like some other forbidden side of me was meant to be with him as much as I was meant to be with Draven.

Whatever it was, it obviously affected him the same as it affected me, even in this time, even if he would never want to admit it. Loyalty on both our sides would forever forbid anything more than what we were, even if I had never been able to fully define what we were. Nor did I think I would ever be able to. In fact, the only certainty I had was that crossing that final line was not ever going to be in our cards, no matter how much I sometimes found myself weak and wanting to.

I would never be able to forgive myself, even though I had to admit it to myself that I loved Lucius, the brutal truth was always going to stand taller and that was...

I loved Draven more.

"So tell me more about this mud bath?" Lucius said bringing me out of my forbidden thoughts and I couldn't help but laugh, feeling more comforted by the side of the Lucius I knew and...

Loved.

CHAPTER THIRTY-TWO

RAINING ARROWS

During this time on horseback there wasn't much conversation between Lucius and I, for which I was more than thankful being this close to him. I couldn't help but wonder what he was thinking about all this? Did he believe that I was from the future now and was doing this to help me or was he just waiting for the point that he could dump me at Draven's feet and say, 'Hey I found this and thought you might want your crazy woman back.'

Whatever it was, as long as he got me to the battle then I didn't care. I kept watching the sun getting lower and lower in the sky, knowing that right now, time was against us. I thought back to Sophia's story, when she told me that when the sun touched the mountains in the distance, that was when the three of them could take him down and defeat him, once and for all.

I knew that Lucius had said that she would have a horse to ride back to the city, which gave Sophia a massive head start on us but I couldn't help fear that something might have happened.

It was a gut feeling that was gnawing at my insides the closer we got, telling me I was needed in this time. I don't know what it was but it was as though this moment in time played a bigger part in the reasons I was here. And no matter how I tried to rationalise it to being nothing but simple paranoia, the feeling wouldn't go away.

"We have to go faster," I told him over the sound of hooves racing across the sand. He didn't respond but as if feeling the unease for himself he kicked in his heels and shouted,

"OCIUS! YAA!" (Meaning 'Faster' in Latin)

We continued to ride like Jared's Hellhounds were yapping at our feet and if it hadn't been for the fear of Draven's life, I would have felt sorry for the horse. The only time we began to slow down was when we saw the smoke rising into the sky in the distance. We were approaching a nearby village that the Romans had obviously got to first as there was nothing left but utter carnage.

"Close your eyes," Lucius ordered me after I cried out in horror on seeing a dead man with his body speared to a tree in three places. When I didn't do so quickly enough and saw the four heads on pikes he obviously didn't want me to see, he placed a hand on my head and turned me into him so that my cheek was against his shoulder. I was thankful that I could no longer see it all, but the smell of the destruction and death lingered all around me. It acted as a brutal reminder of what I was trying to prevent back in my time only that would be on a much larger scale.

I wasn't naive to the sheer terror that humans themselves could cause and knew of the endless wars fought through greed and corruption. But on the face of it all, it was the unity of the human race that I had faith would one day rise above the pain and suffering that had been forced upon them, and they would unite to take a stand against any common enemy of peace.

SACRIFICE OF THE SEPTIMUS - PART 2

No matter the colour of skin or religious belief, whether you were gay or straight or battle scarred by life, we all had something in common. We all had a soul. We all had been given the chance to choose to walk the right path and not judge these differences but instead to embrace them. And not to allow something you don't understand grow into the destructive nature of hatred but instead to learn the power gained by simple acceptance.

This was what I was willing to give my life for. The hope that one day peace will be forever in our future and this…this life of innocent sacrifice will forever remain in our past, where it belongs. But this was my hope for my own kind and in order for that day to come, I needed to first battle against those who sought only for the destruction of a world they cared little for.

"We are past," Lucius said letting go of my head and I looked up to see he was right. The burning village was long gone and not just from view but from history as well, for no one would remember the sacrifices made by people with no names to pass on. Bodies buried in the ashes of their lives were forever gone and from the looks of things, with no one to even mourn them but the crops and livestock that would eventually perish alongside them.

This was all that war got you…*Death.*

The pointless death of others fighting for a power that would never be their own. And Pertinax wouldn't stop with Draven, just as he wouldn't stop at Persia. Men like him never stopped, so what of the Demons that lived behind their vessels like masks, hiding what they truly were from a world that would never have accepted them. Now stopping a Demon like Pertinax was a war worth fighting for and fighting for *that war* was a sacrifice worth dying for. But how many of the supernaturals living on earth can say that they would sacrifice themselves for the human race, for to give up that amount of power would be a powerful thing indeed.

"It should be just over this hillside now and we should see the battle, for I can hear that it has already begun," Lucius told me and I held my breath trying to ready myself for the sight. He pushed the horse even harder and soon Lucius was right, we could see for ourselves what had already begun.

The Roman army were stood in a square formation and looked to outnumber the Persians by unbeatable odds. Draven's city looked to be locked up tight and thankfully wasn't on fire as I would have most feared. The walls still stood and the palace was still a beacon of hope that there was time yet for this war to be won.

The Romans were all stood like one large structure, with their shields held in such a way that every side of the square looked to be protected by the massive metal rectangles. And this was all they had to fight with for the moment as Draven fought his wars very differently to the Romans. Instead of hiding away under cover Draven had ordered his men to circle the huge formation on horseback, riding around and around them at a distance.

"What is he doing?" I asked having never seen anything like it before.

"What the Persians do best. Rain down arrows from a far distance and wait for the Romans to fall," Lucius told me and he was right. Now that I knew what I was looking for I could see that even though the numbers looked in the Roman's favour, like this they were sitting ducks getting picked off one by one. It was incredible to witness and the skill involved at being able to fire arrows from the back of a horse in every direction was a sight to be seen.

"Pertinax!" I hissed pointing to the centre of the square,

where he was being protected until the last of his men fell, the coward. To him they were simply pawns and nothing more as he didn't care about his people being massacred around him and that was exactly what this was.

"Come on, I see riders approaching," Lucius said steering the horse away and further down the hill to where I could see for myself what Lucius could. You could tell straight away that it was a legion of Persian soldiers headed this way from the way they were dressed. But most of all I was surprised by who was leading them.

Suddenly I looked back at the battle and tried to spot Draven down there, almost frantic about his fate. Especially now that my worst fears had come true, for it was Vincent who was leading the small army of men this way.

Lucius pulled back on the reins bringing our tired horse to a stop. Lucius dismounted just as Vincent approached and then he reached up to grip me by the waist so he could do the same for me.

"Vardanis, my Prince, where is the King?" Lucius asked with an urgency that surprised me, letting me know now that he believed me when I spoke of the danger. Vincent dismounted his own horse and walked over to Lucius, who stood in front of me, his face looking grim.

"My friend, Lucius Septimus. I am afraid my brother is insane with rage and lost to grief of the likes I have never thought possible in our kind. Pertinax killed the woman he loved and therefore he will allow no one to aid him in seeking revenge. I tried to stop him but..." The rest of what Vincent said was lost on me for I ran past Lucius before he could stop me and grabbed Vincent by his chest piece.

"Where is he?! Where is he now?!" I shouted begging him to answer me.

"You're alive?!" he said as though I had struck him with my very own weapon named 'the truth' and now was my time to continue to do so because for the chance to save Draven, I would tell them everything!

"Yes, now tell me!" I screamed getting close to becoming hysterical. I felt Lucius' hand rest on my shoulder and drew in a deep breath knowing that his presence behind me was something I instantly found comfort in.

"He is down there waiting for the Romans to fall before riding into the centre to kill Pertinax alone," Vincent said looking grim.

"And Sophia, where is she?!" I asked hoping at least she was down there with him. He looked at me as if he had no clue who I was referring to so I shouted,

"Saphira! I mean Saphira!"

"My sister came back to us but she had been hit by a poisoned arrow." My hands flew to my mouth and I started shaking my head, taking a step back away from him and further into Lucius.

"Is she…?" I couldn't ask for it was too painful to say the actual words.

"No, she is unconscious but lives, although for how long, I have no clue," he said looking back at the battle, telling me what would eventually be the cause of all their deaths. I wanted to whisper up my thanks to the Gods that my friend still lived but all that came out was…

"No…no, it's all coming true…I am the cause." I started muttering to myself and Lucius pushed me to one side gently and spoke to Vincent himself.

"She fears he will not be able to take down Pertinax alone."

"And nor will he if I do not intercept the second army coming from the west and this army is not one fought by…

mortal men." Vincent told Lucius quietly, probably hoping I wouldn't understand. I looked up to the men who stood waiting at Vincent's back and now that he had said it, their helmets could no longer hide the truth...

Supernatural Warriors.

"They come from the mountains?" Lucius asked and Vincent nodded, telling him the same horde we faced were now coming for us. I had changed everything just by being here and now it was time for me to make it right.

"I must go and give him the time he needs, for if they reach the city then Pertinax will be unstoppable. We must have hope that he will defeat him or all is lost and all of us will fall." Lucius nodded understanding what was at stake.

"Your sister is safe but I don't know for how long," Vincent told me closing his eyes briefly as though seeing their last goodbye as a memory he could almost touch and then he added,

"She refused to leave the city so she hides in the Temple with my sister and your servant." I nodded instantly feeling better that at least they were safe...*for now*.

"Farewell my friend," Vincent said putting a hand on Lucius' shoulder before replacing his helmet and getting back on his horse.

"Wait! But you have to go down there! You have to help him fight!" I shouted up at him, grabbing onto the reins of his horse. He reached down and touched my face softly,

"Goodbye little sweet one, I wish my brother had known." Then he yanked on the reins freeing them from my hand and was off.

"NO! COME BACK!" I screamed as Lucius suddenly picked me up and moved me out of their way as his soldiers went off to battle the Demon side of Pertinax's army. I sobbed and screamed for them to come back but it was no use. Without

Sophia and Vincent by his side Draven would fall and this *time* would be forever changed. There was no way for the five of us to go back in time to prevent it happening and then maybe history would simply go back to how it was before we got here. It just wasn't a chance I could take, for the Janus gate might not let me return to put things right again.

No, if history was simply rewriting itself then it was time for me to give it one for the story books, one the world would never forget! For, it was now or never!

"We have to get down there, Lucius!" I shouted after he finally let me go once the danger of being trampled on by hundreds of hooves was long gone in the distance.

"I will go but you must stay here," he said looking back at the battle as if trying to weigh up how he would get down there in time. I followed his gaze and saw that the Roman army was now breaking away from formation. This was due to their great number of casualties that lay dead around what was once their only barricade against the onslaught of arrows. The sheer number of losses meant that they had eventually lost their advantage as the hollow square they had once formed around their ruler was now quickly closing in on him.

In sight of this Draven was now rallying his men forward for what looked like the final attack, breaking apart their defences once and for all. If this had been the only battle, then I would have been rejoicing early for it looked like the Persians had an easy victory. But I knew that unless you cut the head off the snake then it would simply keep coming at you and Pertinax was a big snake to fight alone. For he had a demonic army at the ready for when Draven fell, which would quickly swoop on in and destroy everything else in Pertinax's path.

"I can't stay here. Don't you understand, it takes the power of three!" I told him and when he gave me a look as if to say, 'what can you do?', I started shaking him.

"Look, you don't know what I am capable of! I am the Electus and I know that I am the only one who can help you do this! But we have to hurry!" I said pointing to the sight of Draven driving his men forward and he himself riding into the centre to meet Pertinax head on. Lucius looked back at me and then to Draven, looking torn between what he knew was right and what he thought he should do to save me.

"If I do this, then I will not be able to protect you," he told me and I knew he was wavering.

"Look at it this way, if we don't try then we are both dead anyway, because when Pertinax takes over this world there will be no one left to stop him!" I told him, knowing that this was the point he would cave.

"Well from the sounds of what Vardanis spoke of, I would say I am dead either way because if I take you into that battle and the King survives, then he will kill me for putting you at risk," he said dryly, not actually sounding as though he fully believed this.

"Don't worry, I will protect you," I said slapping him on the chest and then saying 'Oww' when one of his blades nicked my little finger. He just raised an eyebrow at me and shook head saying,

"And I am taking you into battle against a Persian Devil." I ignored this comment and looked back over the open sandy plain, which was quickly getting stained with blood.

"I don't think that horse is going to make it," he said looking over his shoulder at our horse that looked closer to passing out than ready to ride again.

"I don't think we have time for that…look!" I said pointing to where we could now see Draven fighting Pertinax and each of them were in their other forms.

"Can anyone else around them see their true forms?" I asked Lucius.

"No, why?" I looked him up and down and said,

"Because I think I know a quicker way." He gave me a questioning look and then asked in a weary tone,

"Why, what do you have in mind?" This was when I gave him a smile and said…

"You have wings, don't you?"

CHAPTER THIRTY-THREE

SACRIFICED

"You might want to stand back," Lucius warned as he took off his jacket and pulled his undershirt off over his head. I did as I was told knowing that he was getting ready to change into his Demon form.

"Don't be afraid," he said before bending over to place his hands on his knees. The first thing I saw was the black veins travelling along his body as though someone had just injected him with ink. They looked like lines on a map, pointing to one place... *his Demon side.*

Then taking another step back I watched as two massive horns burst free from the skin on his shoulder blades as if they themselves had ripped away from the rest of his skeleton and twisted back to allow his wings to come forth. Black charred skin stretched out between long bones that ended with razor sharp points and from what I remembered, these wings were unlike the ones I had seen on him before as they now looked brand new. They didn't look worn or broken in the places I remembered and even his claws looked as though they hadn't yet felt an enemy's flesh.

He stood up and stretched them out putting me in shadow for a moment as he blocked out the sun that was going down behind him. His skin looked paler, almost as though it had been dusted in chalk, with only the black lines of power pulsating through. His once grey blue eyes had disappeared completely, now being replaced with blood red pools of demonic hatred as he looked barely able to control this other side of himself.

It had been a long time since I had seen him like this, as after what happened in the Temple and the Triple Goddess ritual, he had forever changed. But now, in this time, this was the only form he knew and he looked like a newborn Demon, unlike the cocky, self-assured two-thousand-year old Vampire King I was used to.

"It's alright, don't be frightened," he told me again, obviously taking my startled look for fear. I gave him a grin, walked over to him and patted him on the back saying,

"Don't sweat it, I have seen you like this before. Besides, you're not that scary," I told him with a laugh, making him growl.

"Nope, still cute, now let's go," I said watching him bend down and pick up a sword.

"I hope you know what you are doing," he said pulling me to him and putting an arm around my waist.

"Me too," I muttered as I reached up and gripped onto his horns for something to anchor myself to as suddenly he turned and ran us towards the edge, throwing us both off. I couldn't help but scream as he let us fall for a moment before gaining the air flow beneath his wings. Then he quickly flew us up higher making my stomach turn.

"Did I mention I am afraid of heights?" I said in the arms of one of the most powerful Demons on earth, soon to be King of the Vampires and here I was scared of the height at which he could accidently drop me.

"I gathered," he said sarcastically, reminding me of my own Lucius. I buried my head in his shoulder as I saw him gaining more height so that we could fly directly over to where we needed to be.

"The King," he said and hearing this my fear of heights fled me and a new fear seeped in and overrode anything else.

"Draven!" I shouted knowing that we had to hurry. We were high above them both and Lucius had stopped, keeping us suspended in this position.

"There is only one way for me to do this," he told me looking into my eyes and trying to weigh up for himself if I was brave enough or not. I looked down just as Draven had been knocked to his knees ready for what looked like the killing blow. I knew what he was going to do so I looked back at him, held on tight and said,

"Do it!"

Then we fell.

Lucius had folded his wings in and suddenly we were free falling through the sky, ready to drop in at what I was praying was just the right moment. I felt the air fight against us and knew when we would land as Lucius tightened his grip on me. I opened my eyes to see Lucius drop us directly in front of Draven, who was still on his knees. Then Lucius pushed me towards Draven and spun around, opening his wings at just the right moment so that it deflected Pertinax's killing blow away from us all.

"YOU!" Pertinax snarled in his demonic voice as Lucius turned to face the enemy. I knelt down next to Draven and placed my hand on his bloody face to lift it up to look at me.

"Nāzanin?" he whispered in disbelief, as though being near death was deceiving his vision.

"It's me Arsaces, I am here now," I said before looking back to see Lucius circling around giving me a clear view for the first time of the beast we were up against.

Pertinax was a man no longer, and looked to have forgone his vessel altogether as the older man I saw in the hallway was now lay on the ground discarded like an old suit. In his place stood someone I would have said looked like the Devil himself, as he wasn't just huge but at least triple the size of a man. And with his reddish burst skin and giant horns, I would say he was stereotypically...*The Devil!*

All of his forehead, from his eyes upwards was two horns that reached up at least a metre above his head. They joined at the centre of his nose, making it look like a demonic helmet, one that was rippled down to the point and back up to the twisted horns that were tipped with gold, turning them into weapons. Eyes of black with tiny white dots at their centres stared down at Lucius with a hatred only found in such evil.

"HOW DARE YOU BETRAY ME SEPTIMUS!" The Demon roared extending his wings out and they looked big enough to scoop us all up in one go. They looked a very similar shape to Lucius' only on a larger scale and where his were black, Pertinax's looked like dragon's wings on fire. Lucius shrugged his shoulders and spun round his blade, telling him he was ready for the fight.

"What can I say...I like him better," he told him making the beast awaken in all his raging glory. He threw his arms back and roared out to the sky before swinging his colossal sword at him. Lucius had to use both hands to defend himself against the attack, or he would not have had enough strength to keep hold of his weapon.

"You're still alive?" Draven asked me and I looked back down at his injuries to see that he needed time to heal.

"I am. Lucius saved me and now it's time that *we* saved you."

"No! You need to run, get out of here!" he said grabbing on to me and then trying to push me away so that I would do as he asked.

"I am not leaving you!"

"GO!"

"NO! I know it takes the power of three to defeat him, now help me! What are his weaknesses…tell me?!" I shouted down at him before looking back to see that Lucius was still going strong.

"How do you know that?" he asked me and I wanted to roll my eyes.

"Now is not the time, just tell me!"

"He doesn't have any weaknesses. Every blow I make goes straight through leaving him untouched," he told me and I looked behind once more to see that he was right. Every time Lucius would make a killing blow against him, an area of his body would just turn into a black mist, surrounding the blade in smoke, making the thrust useless against him.

"You have to leave, please," Draven begged grabbing me to him once more but I wasn't listening. Instead I was trying to figure out what my gut had been trying to tell me. The first time they fought him they stabbed him in the heart but with his own weapon…was that it? Was that the only thing that could pierce his own heart?

"Can you stand?" I asked him and he nodded, lifting himself up now that part of his mangled leg had healed. He obviously didn't know that I could see him this way or the limp way his wings dangled behind him. It was so painful seeing him like this, for I was so used to seeing Draven as an unstoppable force. Which only served as a testament to what we faced now and the immense power we had to battle against.

I looked around where we stood to see that the battle against the Romans had almost been won, but the war against good and evil was far from it. Lucius was holding out against him, but I knew it wouldn't be like this for long. In fact, he had just knocked Lucius to the ground and was letting the huge sword swing down when suddenly arrows started flying in from all around us shooting straight through him, giving Lucius the few seconds pause he needed for him to roll away before the blade crashed into the hard sand.

The arrows continued flying thick and fast from all directions as Draven's men had started trying to defend their King. I had no clue what they thought they were firing into but when I looked at Draven's glazed eyes, I knew that he was the one controlling them all. Not one of the hundreds of arrows that flew at him made it through the black smoke but it was at least keeping him busy enough as he must have had to concentrate on not letting any get through.

This gave me the time I needed to run to Lucius and tell him my plan,

"I think it's the spear on his back, I think that is the only thing that will get through to his heart. We need to get it," he nodded and said,

"We don't have many options left. Do you think you can distract him without getting killed?" he asked over the bellowing din of Pertinax trying to fight against the rain of arrows.

"You mean can I annoy someone enough to get their attention? Yeah sure…but for them not to kill me, I guess we will soon find out," I told him but then Draven limped over and issued his new order,

"*I* will distract him, now go!" Lucius didn't need to be told twice as he picked up his sword after Pertinax had knocked it from his hand.

"Now you will run until you reach the city!" Draven told me and I was just about to argue with him when suddenly the earth beneath us started to shake.

"Ever had déjà vu?" I asked him, looking down at the ground to see the sand dancing two inches from the floor. This was how it started back in the hallway when we were first taken and any minute now I expected to see rock demons springing from the ground. However, this didn't happen...

Something else did.

"RUN!" he suddenly bellowed to me just as the earth seemed to open up next to us. Then it shot outwards like someone had just set off a bomb beneath the ground. Massive jagged rocks sprang up from nowhere and fired towards Draven's army around us, bursting from the sand like someone had set off a line of charges. The rocks beneath thundered along, traveling in lines like giant tentacles, attacking groups of his men causing chaos around us.

Then the rumbling seemed to centralise itself, focusing solely on where we stood. Draven grabbed my arm to steady me as the ground started to split off from the rocks, cracking down into the centre of the earth so that when it started to lift, we were left with a small diameter on which to fight.

"Great, even more heights." I grumbled as Pertinax continued to raise up his arms controlling the growing mountain on which we stood.

"You gonna stop asking me to run now?" I said looking down and Draven just growled back at me. At least, unbeknown to Pertinax, this was giving us the distraction we needed, as Lucius was already getting into position.

"He will need you to hold him back for it has to go directly into his heart!" I told Draven noticing that now, he was more steady on his feet.

"GO! I will distract him!" Draven looked torn but even he knew we only had one shot at this.

"Don't you dare die on me again!" he snarled, pulling me to him and giving me a quick kiss before running towards Lucius.

"Wouldn't dream of it," I muttered to myself before looking back at the Demon and seeing that he had finally stopped the platform from moving. I looked over my shoulder and gulped at the new height I found myself. It was like being on the top of a skyscraper about to fight King Kong.

"What I wouldn't give for Adam right about now," I grumbled knowing that the time had come. So I walked closer to him, opened my arms up and said,

"Hey Asshole! Yeah you! Do you have any idea who I am!?" I shouted up at him after picking up a rock and throwing it at him. He looked down at me and grinned.

"NOW I GET THE CHANCE TO PLAY WITH YOU!" he roared before lunging at me. I saw a quick glimpse of Lucius snag the spear from his back and I jumped to one side barely missing the swing of his sword as I watched it in slow motion travel over me, missing me by inches. The power of his thrust made his body spin with the action and there waiting for their chance was Draven and Lucius.

I sat up and shouted,

"NOW!" just as Draven grabbed the arm holding the sword back, so that Lucius was there ready to hammer the end of the glass spear into his heart. It hit its mark and the two of them jumped back to give it time to take effect but instead of the sound of defeat, it was only the sound of demonic laughter that met our ears.

"It didn't work, go, fly down and take her with you!" Draven shouted to Lucius who looked ready to do that.

"NO!" I shouted knowing that there was something we had missed…no, wait…it wasn't what *they* had missed, it was something that *I had missed*. Because they didn't know what I knew. They hadn't lived through this time like Sophia had.

"Think damn it!" I scolded myself.

"Look out!" Draven pushed me to one side just as I saw him sacrifice himself for me as he himself was pushed over the side of the platform.

"NO!" I screamed scrambling to my feet and racing to him as Lucius fought him back, slashing out at him over and over, no doubt praying to Lucifer that one blow would stick. That one hit would be enough of a…wait, was that it?

I ran over to the ledge to see that Draven was clung to the side climbing his way back up. I inhaled a thankful breath and looked back at Lucius knowing now what had to be done. It wasn't about where we hit him, it was about what we could hit him with.

What his weakness would be.

Because it was like I first thought…

'Stopping a demon like Pertinax was a war worth fighting for and fighting for that war was a sacrifice worth dying for. But how many of the supernatural lives living on earth can say that they would sacrifice themselves for the human race, for to give up that amount of power would be a powerful thing indeed.'

It was in that sacrifice where the power was held and it was also in the blood of both Heaven and Hell…*in Draven*. Those combined had been enough to pierce the heart of hatred. And now it was up to us to do the same. I was just moving back to allow Draven room to climb back over and I threw myself into his arms.

"I thought you were…!"

"I know," he said touching my cheek gently but our moment was short lived.

"I know a way to kill him. But you need to sacrifice your…"

"LOOKOUT!" Lucius roared but it was too late as we had no time to move. I fell forward into Draven as the weight of a body fell on top of me. I watched wide eyed as Draven too fell backwards and for long agonising moments I couldn't understand what had happened. I seemed to be sandwiched between the two men I loved and it was only when I saw the long wooden pole sticking from Draven's shoulder that I knew what had happened.

Lucius had thrown himself in front of us both as Pertinax had being trying to kill us with his spear. I turned around to see him laughing and celebrating by raising up his hands at his own victory of killing us all with one blow.

But this was when it happened…The rage.

My rage.

It was back.

CHAPTER THIRTY-FOUR

HELL HATH NO FURY LIKE A WOMAN SCORNED

It was strange feeling.

The feeling of becoming lost in a grief so great that nothing left in the world made sense to you. The only action left for you was as simple as taking death into your own hands and calling it revenge. And that was what loving someone to death really meant to you. It was the force to conquer within yourself and turn it into a power so great, that even you had to become something different just so that you knew how to handle it.

That was what I was.

I was a vessel for myself.

It was almost as though my body was being lifted and my limbs were being moved weightlessly through water. The tingling that usually came to me in my fingers was now all over my body, zinging around as though every single part of me was sparking back to life…a life that wasn't solely my own. I didn't feel fear or even really have an understanding about what I was about to do. All I allowed myself to feel was hate and mourning for those I thought I had lost. I let it fuel my blood as though changing it into something more.

I could see what I was doing as if watching from afar but yet not. I was lost somewhere between myself and what I needed to become. I saw my own hands snap down on the wooden pole that connected them, as though it was made from paper. I then lifted Lucius' lifeless body up as if he weighed nothing at all.

I lay him down and saw the damage that had been done far too close to a heart that I knew didn't belong to me, not in this lifetime or the one I should have been living. But nonetheless it was a heart that I cared for and would have given my life for if given the chance. I briefly heard him moan from pain so knew that at least he lived for now, my only hope was that when this was done, that I had my chance to say goodbye.

But it was far too late to think of this now, for the damage had been done, and this monster in front of me had already awakened the beast inside myself... one that I knew was more powerful than he.

So I stood looking down at Lucius' body one more time before turning back to face the Demon that had planned on taking everything from me. Thoughts of being with both Draven and Lucius flickered through my mind like a time capsule exploding. Hundreds of images flashing there over and over until I felt I would burst from the love I had. A love that with one look at Pertinax, and I knew he had tried to take it all away from me. I looked down at my hands to see the angry sparks of power lick out against the skin, like electrical charges desperate to be freed.

"No-one takes them from me," I snarled in a voice that didn't sound like my own. The Demon looked back at me and frowned for a moment before he smiled, happy he had one last obstacle to play with.

"OH GOOD, ONE MORE LEFT!" he snarled but this just managed to double the strength in my hands. I looked up feeling my eyes change along with the rest of my voice. Then I pushed out my hands and let the rage flow out of me and towards the cause of my pain.

"NO-ONE TAKES THEM FROM ME!" I roared and hit him with so much force it flung his body back, like Zeus himself had hit him with a lightning bolt forged from Mount Olympus. He flipped over and over until managing to stop himself just before going off the edge. He looked utterly stunned as he stared back at me from the sandy floor.

"BUT YOU'RE HUMAN!" he thundered back shaking his head, but hearing this only managed to cause this demonic side of me to build once more, taking it as such an insult that I released a scream so powerful that it could destroy the earth below.

"I AM THE ELECTUS!" The force of this started to shatter the mountain he had made and, with one section at a time, the tower started to burst, like each floor on a building being blown one after the other. We started to fall but I kept my hands facing down to the ground knowing that this would steady the top enough to take us down without it toppling over.

Pertinax looked all around him as if he couldn't believe that there was something facing him that was more powerful than he and worse still, it all came from a human girl.

The sound of the last part of the tower crashing to a stop was when I knew it was time to finish his life but something inside of me had waited because I wanted him to die closer to Hell than to Heaven. It was my gift to those waiting below and I smiled a sadistic smile thinking about what tortures awaited him there.

I walked back to Draven and knelt down on one knee, placing a hand to his cheek as he had done for me. I felt some part of my old self slipping back through so that I could look upon him with my own eyes and smile down at him with my own smile.

"You...you're...my..." He looked at me as if he couldn't believe I was real and then stammered out the sentence I knew exactly how to finish.

"Electus." I confirmed then suddenly yanked the spear free from his shoulder making him wince before snapping off the end to make it into a dagger.

"I have to finish this," I told him and he nodded to me, trusting me that I could. So I stood back up and turned to face the Demon for the last time.

"YOU CAN'T KILL ME, I AM A GOD!" he bellowed at me and before saying another word to him I started to run at him like Hell was powering me forward. He roared down at me just as he swung his sword but I knocked it back with the power that erupted from my hand causing the blade to shatter into thousands of pieces like glass. Then before he knew what to do, I leapt up at him and drove the bloody spear deep into his heart.

"Yes, but even Gods can die on Earth!" I told him as he looked down at the glass blade sticking from his chest as if this was the first time he saw that his body could bleed. The glass started to fill with his blood and the second it reached the top, something inside of me told me to take it as a trophy.

I pulled it out and jumped back from him just as he fell to his knees, exploding into a black cloud as he landed, one that was quickly sucked back down into Hell where I knew Lucifer would be waiting for him. Then I looked down at the black charred sand that I knew would be there for centuries to come. That type of evil doesn't leave the Earth without leaving its eternal scar.

The dust had barely settled when I heard Draven's call behind me.

SACRIFICE OF THE SEPTIMUS - PART 2

"Electus?" This acted like an off switch to the rage, cutting out my power in one single heartbeat. I dropped the blade into the black sand as I slammed back into myself, as if my vessel had been missing a soul. Then I turned and ran back over to him.

"I am here! I am here!" I told him, crying over his injured body.

"Ssshh, it's alright now. You're safe…you're finally safe," Draven said holding my head to him as I let my tears fall down his cheek and mine.

"I was so scared I had lost you," I told him and he hushed my crying again by telling me,

"You did it. You killed him."

"Not without your help and…Lucius, I have to save Lucius!" I suddenly shouted getting up and running to the other body, one that this time was silent. I skidded over next to him and lifted his head from the sand and into my arms.

"He is gone. There was nothing you could have done. He gave his life in sacrifice," Draven told me after getting up himself, holding a hand to his injured shoulder.

"No! I can save him!" I told him and Draven frowned down at me.

"It isn't…"

"I can, now bite me, for he needs my blood," I told him holding out my arm to him, making Draven frown before quickly trying to reason with me.

"No, it is impossible, there is no blood on Earth that can save him now." I looked back down at him and said,

"It's not the blood on Earth I am using, but the Venom of God!" I said and picked up his sword to slice into my own wrist before Draven could stop me. I cried out in utter agony and so that it wasn't all in vain, I quickly let it pour into his mouth as he had once done for me, gifting the power back that he had first given to me to restart his own heart.

"Come on! Drink damn it! DRINK!" I screamed down at him and the second I did I placed a hand over his heart, letting the small residue of power I had left spark from my fingers. His eyes suddenly opened and the blood red in his eyes started to turn black as he sucked back in the life I gave to him.

"ENOUGH!" Draven shouted ripping my arm away from Lucius' mouth as he could see my own life was being slowly drained away. I collapsed in his arms just as the last of my energy was fading away.

"Nāzanin! Nāzanin! Don't leave me!" Draven shouted down at me frantically and I just had enough strength to raise my head up to him and say…

"Call me Keira."

EPILOGUE

I opened my eyes to see I was being blinded by the sun and I blinked back the dark spots in my eyes a few times before things started to become clear.

"Wakey, wakey sunshine."

"Pip...is that you?" I asked in a groggy voice that grated on the back of my throat like I was trying to swallow sandpaper.

"The one and only," she said in her usual happy tone.

"Where am I?" I asked trying to sit up but finding it too difficult to accomplish.

"Well, you're not in Kansas anymore," she said and my eyes widened.

"We're home!? We finally made it back...back in time!?" I shouted no matter how painful it felt to the back of my throat.

"Uh, well about that..." she started to say as I lifted myself up to look for myself where we were. The first thing I saw was the desert sand outside of the stone arched window and my heart started to sink.

We were still in Persia.

But this wasn't the worst part I now faced. Not when I saw

the tall looming figure of Draven standing at the bottom of the bed with his arms folded.

Pip looked back over her shoulder and said,

"We have some explaining to do."

To be Continued

ABOUT THE AUTHOR

Stephanie Hudson has dreamed of being a writer ever since her obsession with reading books at an early age. What first became a quest to overcome the boundaries set against her in the form of dyslexia has turned into a life's dream. She first started writing in the form of poetry and soon found a taste for horror and romance. Afterlife is her first book in the series of twelve, with the story of Keira and Draven becoming ever more complicated in a world that sets them miles apart.

When not writing, Stephanie enjoys spending time with her loving family and friends, chatting for hours with her biggest fan, her sister Cathy who is utterly obsessed with one gorgeous Dominic Draven. And of course, spending as much time with her supportive partner and personal muse, Blake who is there for her no matter what.

Author's words.

My love and devotion is to all my wonderful fans that keep me going into the wee hours of the night but foremost to my wonderful daughter Ava...who yes, is named after a cool, kick-ass, Demonic bird and my sons, Jack, who is a little hero and Baby Halen, who yes, keeps me up at night but it's okay because he is named after a Guitar legend!

Keep updated with all new release news & more on my website

www.afterlifesaga.com
Never miss out, sign up to the
mailing list at the website.

Also, please feel free to join myself and other Dravenites on my Facebook group
Afterlife Saga Official Fan
Interact with me and other fans. Can't wait to see you there!

facebook.com/AfterlifeSaga
twitter.com/afterlifesaga
instagram.com/theafterlifesaga

ACKNOWLEDGEMENTS

Well first and foremost my love goes out to all the people who deserve the most thanks and are the wonderful people that keep me going day to day. But most importantly they are the ones that allow me to continue living out my dreams and keep writing my stories for the world to hopefully enjoy... These people are of course YOU! Words will never be able to express the full amount of love I have for you guys. Your support is never ending. Your trust in me and the story is never failing. But more than that, your love for me and all who you consider your 'Afterlife family' is to be commended, treasured and admired. Thank you just doesn't seem enough, so one day I hope to meet you all and buy you all a drink! ;)

To my family... To my amazing mother, who has believed in me from the very beginning and doesn't believe that something great should be hidden from the world. I would like to thank you for all the hard work you put into my books and the endless hours spent caring about my words and making sure it is the best it can be for everyone to enjoy. You make Afterlife shine. To my wonderful crazy father who is and always has been my hero in life. Your strength astonishes me, even to this day and the love and care you hold for your family is a gift you give to the Hudson name. And last but not least, to the man that I consider my soul mate. The man who taught me about real love and makes me not only want to be a better person but makes me feel I am too. The amount of support you have given me since we met has been incredible and the greatest feeling was finding out you wanted to spend the rest of your life with me when you asked me to marry you.

All my love to my dear husband and my own personal Draven... Mr Blake Hudson.

Another personal thank you goes to my dear friend Caroline Fairbairn and her wonderful family that have embraced my brand of crazy into their lives and given it a hug when most needed.

For their friendship I will forever be eternally grateful.

I would also like to mention Claire Boyle my wonderful PA, who without a doubt, keeps me sane and constantly smiling through all the chaos which is my life ;) And a loving mention goes to Lisa Jane for always giving me a giggle and scaring me to death with all her count down pictures lol ;)

Thank you for all your hard work and devotion to the saga and myself. And always going that extra mile, pushing Afterlife into the spotlight you think it deserves. Basically helping me achieve my secret goal of world domination one day...evil laugh time... Mwahaha! Joking of course ;)

As before, a big shout has to go to all my wonderful fans who make it their mission to spread the Afterlife word and always go the extra mile. I love you all x

ALSO BY STEPHANIE HUDSON

Afterlife Saga

A Brooding King, A Girl running from her past. What happens when the two collide?

Book 1 - Afterlife

Book 2 - The Two Kings

Book 3 - The Triple Goddess

Book 4 - The Quarter Moon

Book 5 - The Pentagram Child /Part 1

Book 6 - The Pentagram Child /Part 2

Book 7 - The Cult of the Hexad

Book 8 - Sacrifice of the Septimus /Part 1

Book 9 - Sacrifice of the Septimus /Part 2

Book 10 -Blood of the Infinity War

Book 11 -Happy Ever Afterlife /Part 1

Book 12 -Happy Ever Afterlife / Part 2

Transfusion Saga

What happens when an ordinary human girl comes face to face with the cruel Vampire King who dismissed her seven years ago?

Transfusion - Book 1

Venom of God - Book 2

Blood of Kings - Book 3

Rise of Ashes - Book 4

Map of Sorrows - Book 5

Tree of Souls - Book 6

Kingdoms of Hell – Book 7

Eyes of Crimson - Book 8

Roots of Rage - Book 9

Afterlife Chronicles: (Young Adult Series)

The Glass Dagger – Book 1

The Hells Ring – Book 2

Stephanie Hudson and Blake Hudson

The Devil in Me

OTHER WORKS FROM HUDSON INDIE INK

Paranormal Romance/Urban Fantasy

Sloane Murphy

Xen Randell

C. L. Monaghan

Sci-fi/Fantasy

Brandon Ellis

Devin Hanson

Crime/Action

Blake Hudson

Mike Gomes

Contemporary Romance

Gemma Weir

Elodie Colt

Ann B. Harrison

Lightning Source UK Ltd.
Milton Keynes UK
UKHW010628210122
397515UK00001B/144